JUSTICE FOR THE DAMNED

BEN CHEETHAM

First published in the UK in 2015 by Head of Zeus Ltd

9 7 5 3 1 2 4 6 8

A catalogue record for this book is available from
the British Library.

ISBN (PB): 9781784970420
ISBN (E): 9781784970413

Printed in the UK by Clays Ltd, St Ives Plc

Head of Zeus Ltd
Clerkenwell House
45-47 Clerkenwell Green
London EC1R 0HT

WWW.HEADOFZEUS.COM

JUSTICE FOR THE DAMNED

Ben Cheetham's first novel in the Steel City crime series, *Blood Guilt*, was a self-published bestseller. His short stories have been widely published in the UK, US and Australia. Ben lives in Sheffield.

THE STEEL CITY THRILLERS

BLOOD GUILT

ANGEL OF DEATH

JUSTICE FOR THE DAMNED

For Clare

Chapter One

Bryan Reynolds examined the tools of his trade – torch, plastic handcuffs, duct tape, Stanley knife, stun gun. He weighed the knife in his hand, extended the blade and thumbed its edge. He gave a little nod of satisfaction. The razor-sharp blade would easily slice through skin, muscle and cartilage all the way to the bone if necessary. And it would be necessary, although not right away. The first cuts would be shallow, designed more to inflict mental rather than physical pain. He was going to take his sweet time with Edward Forester. Kill him slower and harder than he'd ever killed anyone before. A barely visible tremor passed through Bryan's hands. Uncertainty wrinkled his scarred, wolfish face. In all the years he'd been in this game, he'd never known his hands to tremble before a job. But then again, this wasn't a job. This was personal.

Bryan's uncertainty deepened into a frown. Personal. He didn't like that word. Personal clouded your judgement, made you do things you wouldn't normally do. Personal got you caught and banged up for life.

He watched the burly skinhead in the passenger seat load bullets into an Olympic .380 BBM starter pistol, a real cheap and nasty piece of shit with no long-range accuracy, but enough close-range punch to put a man down. The pistols could be legally bought for a hundred quid, easily converted to fire live ammo, and sold on for five hundred quid. In recent years he'd made a nice little side profit trading them.

A thought came to Bryan: *You don't need to do this yourself. Why not have Les call a couple of the lads, let them dispose of Forester?* The question originated from the cool, calculating part of his brain that had served him so well throughout his criminal career, keeping him wealthy, healthy and free when most of his peers were dead or doing time. He knew he should listen to it, after all he'd been insulated from the hands-on side of the business for several years now. But another voice leapt up in opposition, a voice burning with irresistible rage. *You know why not! How can you even ask that question after what that piece of puke did?*

The trembling in Bryan's hands grew more pronounced.

He closed his eyes and sucked in the cool night air, trying to douse the fire in his head. Instantly, his mind conjured up images of his son Mark – not as the man he was now, but as the child he'd been fifteen years ago – and Edward Forester. The politician's hands were all over Mark, touching, groping, forcing. His own hand reached out unconsciously and his fingers dug into the dashboard until his knuckles were as white as his face.

'Let's do this.'

The words hissed through Bryan's teeth. He got out of the car, closing the door quietly, leaving it unlocked lest they needed to make a quick getaway. With Les following, he approached a red-brick, bay-windowed semi. The lights had been off in all the windows for an hour or so – more than enough time for the house's occupants to fall asleep. Les tapped Bryan's shoulder and pointed out an alarm box beneath the eaves. Bryan nodded without concern. He knew from experience that most people didn't bother to activate their burglar alarm before bed. And if the alarm did happen to be on, well, he had plenty of ways to convince Edward to deactivate it.

They made their way down the side of the house, stepping softly. A motion-activated security light clicked on, revealing a well-tended rose garden and a black Range Rover. They scuttled beyond the halogen glare and froze against the wall, alert for any sign that their presence had been noticed. The light went out. A minute passed. Nothing. They crept to the back door, pulling on balaclavas and latex gloves. The balaclavas weren't for Edward's benefit. Edward was soon to be dead, so it hardly mattered if he saw their faces. But Edward wasn't the only person in the house. There was also his wife. What had that crazy bastard Jim Monahan said her name was? Philippa something or other. It didn't matter. What mattered was that Bryan had promised Jim he wouldn't hurt her. And for once it was a promise he intended to keep – at least up to a point. Of course, if she gave them any trouble they'd have to slap her around a bit until she cooperated. But they'd take care not to do any permanent damage.

Bryan switched on his torch and directed it at the door's

lock. It was a simple Yale pin-and-tumbler of the kind he'd learned to pick long ago in his misspent youth. He inserted a slender torque wrench and a pick into the keyhole. He felt for the pins with the pick's upturned end, lifting each of them in turn. Once all the pins were raised, he gently turned the wrench and the lock clicked open. He gave Les a self-satisfied glance, which said, *Once you've got it you never lose it*. He taped the lock open – it always paid to have a guaranteed escape route.

As they stepped into a small utility room, a motion sensor in the corner of the ceiling blinked red, but the alarm didn't go off. Bryan gave an internal shake of his head. If the alarm had been on, Edward and his wife would at least have had a chance to defend themselves, however futilely. As it was, they'd be bound and gagged before they even knew what was happening. Bryan's own pad had a state-of-the-art alarm system that he never failed to activate before heading to bed. He also kept a machete and a samurai sword within easy reach. He would have kept a gun, too, if it wasn't for the fact that his criminal record prevented him from getting a licence. And he wasn't stupid enough to keep an unlicensed gun in his house, not with the coppers constantly trying to sniff out any old excuse to put him away.

Bryan padded upstairs, stun gun at the ready. A heady, almost intoxicating rush coursed through him. It'd been a long while since he'd felt the tingle of adrenalin, the heightened sense of being alive it gave. He realised suddenly how much he missed operating at the sharp end of the business. To look into the eyes of someone utterly at your mercy. To see them stripped bare of all their shallow pretensions of toughness. To know what was in their soul. Nothing could beat that feeling. In his time he'd gone to work on some of the so-called hardest criminals in South Yorkshire. Most of them hadn't lasted more than ten or fifteen minutes before they broke down. A few had held out for hours. But in the end all of them had blubbed and begged for their lives. A politician like Edward Forester probably wouldn't last five seconds. But Bryan hoped otherwise. It was so much more satisfying if they didn't fall to pieces too easily.

He eased open a door at the top of the stairs and frowned. An hour or so ago he'd watched the final light in the house go out. By his reckoning it had come from the window of this room. He'd expected to find Edward and his wife asleep in there, but the double bed opposite the doorway was unoccupied. A tiny shiver darted up his neck. Suddenly something didn't feel right. He motioned for Les to check a door on the opposite side of the landing. As Les twisted the handle, an electrical crackle came from behind Bryan. The instant he heard the familiar sound, he realised he'd made the biggest mistake of his life by setting foot inside the house. He just had time for a sharp intake of breath. Then it was as if he'd been grabbed and shaken by a gorilla. He collapsed to the carpet, twitching and spasming, knowing that this time he was the one on the wrong end of a stun-gun charge.

Through tear-blurred eyes Bryan saw Les jerk around, Olympic .380 in one hand, torch in the other, throwing ghostly shadows around. A baseball-bat-wielding figure emerged from darkness behind Les. The bat came down with bone-shattering force on his wrist, sending the gun thudding to the floor. He cried out. The next blow connected with the top of his skull, dropping him unconscious. But the figure wasn't finished. He rained down blow after blow on Les's head, producing a stomach-churning sound like a watermelon being pulped.

'Fuck's sake, that's enough.' The speaker was male with a thick local accent. Stun gun in hand, he stepped over Bryan and shone a torch at Les. Blood was seeping through the skinhead's balaclava. 'Look at the mess you've made. Mr Forester's not going to be best pleased when he sees that, is he? How's he supposed to explain that to his wife?'

'I'm sure he'll think of something. He lies for a living, doesn't he?' This came from a third man out of Bryan's line of sight. The voice was as hard and blank as a slab of stone, without any hint of an accent.

The landing light came on, giving Bryan his first good look at their assailants. The man with the baseball bat was thirtyish, well over six feet and built like a steroidal weightlifter. His neck had been all but swallowed up by ridges of shoulder muscle that made his shiny bullet head appear undersized. He was clean-shaven, with a petulant mouth, blunt nose and heavy-lidded eyes. Bryan recognised in those features the same brutish sensuality that ran through the veins of many of his own goons, men like Les who had a hard-on for inflicting pain. The man with the stun gun was much older, maybe fifty or fifty-five. He was a good foot shorter than his colleague and paunchy, but his shoulders were equally broad, making him appear almost as wide as he was tall. A greying goatee gave the illusion of a chin to his craggy, hard-drinking face. Watery eyes peered out from between red-rimmed pouches of flesh. The third man's age and height fell somewhere between that of his accomplices. His head was squarish, his face broad and flat, with a boxer's nose, blue-black stubbled cheeks and a monobrow. His eyes were equally dark – or rather his right eye was, the left was covered by a wad of bandages. There was something about him that reminded Bryan of someone else. In his dazed state it took him a moment to realise who that someone was. It was himself. Not himself now, but himself ten or so years ago. The man had a steely cold edge in his single eye. The same edge that Bryan had maybe, without even realising it until now, lost. And when you lost your edge in this business, you were well and truly fucked.

All three men were dressed in black bomber jackets that emphasised the whiteness of their latex-gloved hands. Their presence had, of course, taken Bryan by surprise. But another realisation had left him even more stunned than the hundreds of thousands of volts he'd been zapped with. He knew two of the men – the oldest was Stan Lockwood, the youngest was Liam Collins – and that knowledge made him wonder whether he'd been set up. Had Jim Monahan known these fuckers were lying in wait? He couldn't bring himself to believe it. The tale of betrayal and abuse Jim had told him had to be the truth. It was too convoluted to be a lie. Wasn't it? But then again, surely it was no coincidence that Stan and Liam, who were now zipping plastic cuffs onto his hands and feet, were ex-police.

Bryan tried to speak, but his brain didn't seem to be able to get the message through to his mouth, and all that came out was a garbled groan. An unpleasant warmth spread down the backs of his thighs. With a withering sense of shame, the most respected and feared gangster in South Yorkshire realised he'd shit himself.

Chapter Two

Jim Monahan felt tired right down to the core of his being, as if he'd been awake for days and days. Merely lifting the plastic cup of water to his lips and swallowing the rainbow of tablets lined up in front of him took an immense effort. There was aspirin to prevent blood-clotting, thrombolytics to clear the blockage in his artery, and other drugs to dilate his blood vessels, improve his heart's functioning, prevent life-threatening arrhythmias and numb the pain. He lay half listening to the doctor at his bedside, half thinking about the events that had led up to his heart attack. *Had Bryan Reynolds done it? Was Edward Forester dead?*

'The good news is, Mr Monahan, your heart attack was relatively minor,' said Doctor Advani, a softly spoken Indian woman with bobbed black hair and glasses. 'Only a small artery is blocked, so only a small area of muscle has been damaged. Provided you respond well to medication, you should make a full recovery in six to eight weeks. There's no need for surgery at this time.' The doctor put particular emphasis on the words 'at this time', making them sound like a warning. 'The bad news is, even with proper treatment you could suffer another heart attack.

However, there are steps you can take to lessen the risk of this happening. For the next couple of weeks you should avoid all heavy lifting, exercise that causes sweating or shortness of breath, and stressful situations. In the longer term you'll need to make some lifestyle changes. You'll have to quit smoking and drinking, change your diet, follow an exercise plan...'

The doctor's voice grew fainter, while Jim's thoughts grew more intrusive. *What if Forester isn't dead? What if Reynolds has bottled it? You should have hung around, made sure the bastard got the job done. Or better still you should have done it yourself. You were a coward not to. A fucking coward!*

Even through all the drugs, a needle of pain pricked Jim's chest. 'Are you in any discomfort?' enquired Doctor Advani, scrutinising the heart monitor.

'Just a little twinge.'

'I think we've gone through everything we need to for now. Tomorrow morning we'll discuss your rehabilitation programme in more detail. Try to get some rest.'

'How long do I have to stay in hospital, Doctor?'

'We'd like to keep you in for at least three or four days to monitor your condition.'

As the doctor turned to leave, a nurse entered the room. 'Mr Monahan's wife is here to see him,' she said.

Upon hearing the word 'wife', all thoughts of Reynolds and Forester were momentarily pushed from Jim's mind. Doctor Advani motioned for the nurse to take her to Jim's wife. *It has to be Margaret*, thought Jim. *Who else would call herself my wife?* The sound of the doctor in conversation with a familiar voice in the hallway confirmed his suspicion. A contradictory mixture of feelings swelled inside him. He wanted to see Margaret almost as much as he wanted to know whether Forester was alive or dead. And yet he didn't want her to see him. She could read him better than anybody. One look in his eyes and she would know. She would see what he wasn't and what he was. He wasn't the man she'd married. He wasn't even the man she'd divorced. He was someone who'd betrayed everything he'd once believed in. He was someone who'd tried to manipulate one man into murdering another. Irrespective of the intended victim's sickening crimes, that made him as good as a murderer, both in his own mind and in the eyes of the law.

Margaret appeared at the doorway. She approached Jim's bedside slowly, almost cautiously, as if she wasn't sure she should be there. She touched her hand to her mouth, lines spreading from the corners of her eyes as she took in the grey, haggard face of her ex-husband. Jim didn't want to look at her, but couldn't stop himself from doing so. Bare of makeup, her face showed its age, yet he couldn't imagine anything more beautiful as she said, 'Oh Jim, what have you done to yourself?'

Jim managed a faint smile. His voice came in a breathy whisper. 'Hello, wife.'

Margaret sat down at his bedside. 'I only called myself that because I was afraid they wouldn't let me in to see you.'

'I know, but it feels good to say it anyway.'

A different unease creased Margaret's forehead. 'I don't want there to be any misunderstandings about why I'm here. I care about you, Jim, but that doesn't mean I want us—'

'I know that too,' interjected Jim. 'Don't worry, Margaret, I realise there's no chance we could try again. I'm just happy you're here.' He turned his hand palm upwards, and somewhat hesitantly, Margaret rested the tips of her fingers on his. The warmth of her touch almost caused him to close his eyes.

A moment of silence passed, then Jim said, 'How did you know I was here?'

'I called your phone back. John Garrett answered. He told me what had happened.'

Jim's mind turned to the man Margaret had left him for. 'Does Ian know where you are?'

'No.'

'What did you tell him?'

A trace of awkwardness came into Margaret's voice. 'A friend of mine's going through a divorce. I told Ian I was going to see her.'

Jim's smile broadened. The fact that Margaret had lied suggested she felt guilty about seeing him. And why would she feel guilty unless she still had feelings for him? Almost in the same instant, like a blow to the solar plexus, it hit him that he was a selfish fool to hope a flicker of the love she'd once felt for him remained. It would be better for both of them if it didn't. That way it would hurt her less when the truth came out about what he'd done.

Margaret laughed softly through her nose. 'Always the copper. Even half dead, you can still get whatever you want to know out of me.'

Jim resisted an urge to shake his head. If he was still a copper, it was in name only. He reached for his water, not because he was thirsty, but because it gave him an excuse to look somewhere other than at Margaret.

'Now it's my turn to ask a question,' she continued. 'Earlier, on the phone, you said something had happened, that I'd find out what soon enough. What did you mean by that?'

'I'm not sure. That whole conversation's a blur. Like... like something from a dream.' Jim didn't want to lie, but he had to. He couldn't risk letting anyone in on the truth until he was certain Forester was dead.

'What about the other things you said, did you mean them?'

Fixing Margaret's hazel-green eyes with his dark brown ones, Jim answered without hesitation, 'Yes, I'm sorry and I do still love you.'

Now it was Margaret's turn to look away. The certainty of his words exposed his lie. He remembered their phone conversation perfectly well. He was simply being selective about what he did and what he didn't tell her. The same as he'd been most of their married life. When they'd first got together, he used to talk about his job. But over the years he'd grown more and more silent about the things he saw every day – the murder victims whose lives had been snuffed out by fists, knives, bullets and countless other causes; the junkies dead with needles hanging out of their arms; the abused and neglected children. At first she'd thought his silence was to protect her. Later she'd come to realise that wasn't the case. He'd shut her out not to protect her, but because he needed to hold on to his anger, his frustration, even his fear. Those were the things that fuelled him, that kept him sharp. They'd also eaten away at him, gradually shaping him into a man she barely recognised, a man she could no longer love. When she'd heard his voice on the phone, the barriers he'd built around himself were down. She'd felt his love and pain, and it had awoken something within her she'd thought no longer existed. It had made her wonder – even hope – that maybe the man she loved had returned. She saw now that he hadn't.

Jim entwined his fingers with Margaret's but she drew her hand away. 'I should get going. The doctor says you need to rest, and Ian will be getting worried.'

To hell with Ian. Stay with me, please! Jim thought the words but didn't say them. 'Thanks for coming to see me.'

Margaret smiled thinly. 'I'm just glad you're alright, Jim. Your phone call nearly gave me a heart attack too.'

'Sorry about that.'

Margaret shook her head in a way that said, *Don't apologise*. 'Just promise me you'll listen to the doctors and do what they say.'

'I'll try, but you know me.'

'Yeah. Stubborn as they make them.' Margaret hesitated as if unsure whether to say anything else, but then she continued, 'Have you got your phone? I'll give you my mobile number in case... well, in case you need it. It would be best if you didn't call my home phone again.'

Jim opened his bedside cabinet and took his phone out of his jacket. Margaret told him her number and he entered it into his phone's memory. He looked at Margaret with a hesitancy that matched hers. He knew he shouldn't ask the question in his mind, but he couldn't hold it back. 'Will you come see me again?'

Margaret gazed at him uncertainly. Then, with a quick nod, she stood and left.

For the first time since regaining consciousness, Jim allowed himself to close his eyes. With Margaret's face fresh in his memory, he felt able to confront the void of sleep. But as he drifted off, another face rose up to blot hers out. Edward Forester's features paraded across the screen of his mind like suspects in a line-up. Brown eyes set in deep sockets. Straight, sharp nose. Pearly white smiling teeth. Ruddy, clean-shaven cheeks. Bald crown fringed by a natural tonsure of neatly cut grey-flecked brown hair. And like an echo in a cave, three words kept reverberating through his thoughts. *Alive or dead, alive or dead...*

Chapter Three

From his driver's seat, Reece Geary watched the woman get out of a car on the opposite side of the road. She was somewhere in her late twenties, almost painfully slim with shoulder length strawberry-blond hair. She was dressed in a white vest that provided scant protection against the chill night air, a barely there denim skirt and white stilettos that bumped her height up from five foot nothing to five foot seven. Her face was caked with makeup – already full lips made even fuller by glossy pink lipstick; matching blusher concealing the paleness of her high cheekbones; eyebrows pencilled in arching lines over intense green eyes. To her customers, the woman's name was Ginger. To Reece, she was Staci.

Reece's eyes flicked to the man in the car. Balding, glasses, scruffy beard. Just some middle-aged nobody. But some middle-aged nobody who minutes earlier had fucked the woman Reece loved. It tore him up to think about another man being inside Staci. To imagine hands other than his own groping her breasts, lips other than his own touching hers. He shook his head. The picture in his mind wasn't true to life. Staci didn't allow any of her punters to kiss her. Not even her regulars. That was one of her rules. Kissing was an act of love, of passion. Fucking, fellatio, hand jobs, for her these were mechanical acts, acts of necessity. But even so, the image remained in his brain, stuck there like some sharp-clawed animal trying to escape its cage. The car pulled away. Reece fought down the urge to pursue it, pull it over and pound his heavy-knuckled fists into the middle-aged nobody's face.

Lighting a cigarette, Staci approached a man slouching in the shadows of a factory building locked up for the night. The man was dressed in black tracksuit bottoms and an oversized black leather jacket. His face was gaunt and skull-like. He had bad teeth, bad skin, tattoos of tears falling from the side of his right eye and a dark blue snake on his shaved scalp. His name, Reece knew, was Wayne Carson. He was a small-time pimp and drug dealer with maybe ten girls working for him. All of them were addicts whose need to work the streets was born out of a desperate craving for the next needleful of heroin. All of them, that is, except Staci. Reece had seen to that. He'd got her into a recovery programme. She'd been clean for nearly three months now. But the debt she'd worked up during the years of her addiction still needed to be paid off, and she'd never be free of Wayne until it was.

As Staci handed Wayne a thin wad of banknotes, Reece's expression leapt from anger to hate. He wanted to hurt Wayne more than he'd ever wanted to hurt anyone before. Every time he saw the scag-faced bastard he found it harder and harder to resist the urges that clawed within him for release.

Staci teetered towards a nearby corner, where a couple of similarly dressed girls were leaning against railings that ran alongside Burton Weir. Behind them, palely illuminated by streetlights, the River Don cascaded in foamy brown torrents down the weir's slope.

Reece got out of his car and approached Staci. He could feel Wayne's gaze following him. He didn't return the stare, fearing that if he looked into the pimp's poisonous little eyes he might lose control. He knew the feeling between them was mutual. Staci was one of Wayne's best earners. She supplied him with a steady flow of cash and he supplied her with scag. That was, or had been, the basis of their relationship. The balance of power had lain firmly with Wayne. Reece had come along and shifted that balance. The equation was simple – the longer Staci remained clean, the more she regained control of her life. Every penny she repaid Wayne brought her closer to her goal – to get out from under her debt and get on with starting a new life. *A new life*. Those weren't Staci's words, they were Reece's. He wanted them to be together, to have everything other couples had – a house of their own, children. All the things he'd never given a shit about until he met her.

Staci frowned at the sight of Reece. 'What are you doing here?'

Reece shrugged. 'I just wanted to see you. Can't I come see my girl?'

'Yeah sure, but...' Staci cast an uneasy glance at Wayne. 'I'm working. You know how Wayne feels about you seeing me when I'm working.'

'I know how he feels about me seeing you anytime. He'd have opened my head up like a tin can if I wasn't who I am.'

'And you'd have done the same to him if you weren't who you are.'

Reece's voice came in a low growl. 'I'd have done much worse than that.'

Staci's frown intensified. Catching hold of Reece's arm, she drew him to a spot where the gushing of the weir allowed them to speak without being overheard. 'You shouldn't talk like that in front of the other girls. What you say might get back to Wayne.'

'I hope it does. I hope it makes the prick do something – something that'll give me a reason to tear his ugly head off.'

Staci dug her long fingernails into the hard-packed muscle beneath Reece's grey suit. 'For starters, Wayne wouldn't do anything to you. He's not that stupid. He'd do it to me. And you know how good he is at hurting girls who piss him off.'

Reece knew alright. Always quick to brag about the control he had over his girls, Wayne had once told him how he kept an old-style police truncheon wrapped in foam to punish any of them who stepped out of line. He'd boasted that he knew how to hit them in ways that were excruciatingly painful, yet barely left a mark. He'd even offered to show Reece how to do it. *Once I've given the bitches a couple of love taps with my truncheon, they never fuck with me again.* Those had been Wayne's exact words. A tremor passed through Reece's arms as he recalled them. Ridges of muscle tautened against Staci's fingers.

'And for seconds,' continued Staci, her grip and voice

softening, 'when I said you'd have done the same to Wayne if you weren't who you are, I wasn't only talking about what you do for a living, I was talking about what's inside there.' She pressed her palm against Reece's chest, looking up into his dark brown eyes. 'You couldn't kill anyone. I know that.'

'How?'

'Because you've got gentle eyes.' Staci brought her hand up to stroke the skin around Reece's eyes. Even in her seven-inch heels, she had to draw him down towards her to kiss his lips. He responded hesitantly, his gaze flicking towards Wayne. She trailed her hands down his square-cut cheeks, angling his gaze away from the pimp. Her tongue teased his lips apart. Reece's hesitation dissolved like mist in the sun. The lines of anger fading from his face, he circled his arms around her back, crushing her thin but full-breasted figure against the slab of his torso. She smelled of strong, sharp perfume, cigarettes and something else, something faint yet muskily sweet that set his heart pounding.

Staci pulled away with a ripple of laughter. 'That's what I like about you, Reece. You kiss like a hungry man at an all-you-can-eat buffet.'

His voice came in a husky murmur. 'Let's go somewhere where we can be alone.'

'I've got to get back to work.'

'No, you don't.' Reece pulled a handful of banknotes out of his pocket. 'There's five hundred quid there.' He jerked his chin at Wayne. 'Give it to that prick. Tell him I'm buying you for the rest of the night.'

Staci looked at Reece as if she wasn't sure she liked what he was saying, but she accepted the cash and tottered across to Wayne. The pimp's eyes alternated between it and Reece, narrowed with a mixture of suspicion and barely concealed hostility. Staci thrust the banknotes into his hand. As she turned away, he quickly stashed them somewhere on himself. Eyes fixed on Reece, he jetted saliva through his brown-stained teeth.

Reece's long powerful fingers slowly curled and uncurled at his sides.

Staci took Reece's hand and drew him towards his car. 'We can go to the house,' she said. 'The other girls will all be out working.'

Chapter Four

Stan tugged Bryan's balaclava up over his mouth and gagged him with duct tape, whilst Liam jerked plastic handcuffs tight around his wrists and ankles. When they were done with Bryan, they turned their attention to Les.

'Is he alive?' asked the man with the bandaged eye.

Stan felt for a pulse in Les's wrist. 'Just about. I don't reckon he will be for much longer, though. Big boy here's done a proper job on him.'

'What else was I supposed to do?' protested Liam, his voice surprisingly thin and squeaky for such a hulk of a man. 'He had a gun.'

'We needed him alive.'

'He is alive.'

'Yeah, but he's unconscious. He can't talk if he's unconscious, can he now, big boy? It kind of restricts the whole talking thing.'

An angry flush rose up Liam's cheeks. He opened his mouth to make a retort but before he could the one-eyed man intervened. 'Enough bickering.'

'Sorry, Tyler,' said Liam.

Sorry, Tyler, Stan mouthed mockingly at Liam as Tyler

rifled through their captives' pockets until he found Bryan's car keys. Looking at Liam, Tyler motioned at Les. 'Carry him to the car. We'll take the other one.'

'Aren't we going to have a look and see who they are?'

'Later. For now we just need to get them out of here.'

With a grunt, Liam heaved Les's limp body over his shoulder.

'And try not to get any more blood on the carpets,' added Tyler as Liam started downstairs. Motioning for Stan to get hold of Bryan's feet, he reached for the gangster's hands. They carried Bryan to the Range Rover and dumped him in the boot alongside Les.

'Wait here,' Tyler told his companions. He hurried back upstairs, tripping to his knees halfway up. A spasm of irritation twisted his face. He quickly smoothed it away. The loss of his eye had fucked up his depth perception, especially when it came to determining distances closer than a metre or so. But there was no point getting pissed off about it. As his training had taught him, he was simply going to have to adapt, and fast.

He flipped open a knife and cut away the bloodstained carpet. Tucking it under his arm, he returned more slowly to the Range Rover. He tossed the carpet into the boot, before climbing into the driver's seat. The air inside the vehicle was suffused with the warm, heavy smell of faeces.

'I think one of the dirty buggers has shit himself,' Liam said from the back seat, his words muffled by the hand covering his nose and mouth.

'Either that or your nappy needs changing,' said Stan.

'Fuck you, Stan.'

Tyler sharply shushed his companions, cocking an ear towards a portable police scanner on the dashboard as a constable called for assistance with a suspected burglary in Attercliffe. Without turning the headlights on, Tyler reversed out of the drive. He proffered Bryan's car keys to Stan. 'You follow us.'

'I'll do it,' said Liam, eagerly reaching for the keys.

Stan snatched them up. 'The fuck you will.'

'Don't be a prick, Stan. You know I've got a weak stomach. The stink in here's making me want to puke.' Liam turned to Tyler. 'Come on, Tyler, let me drive—' He broke off at the stony, silencing look Tyler gave him.

'Stay close, but not too close,' Tyler said to Stan. 'If anything goes wrong, we'll split up and meet back at the farm.'

A smirk curling the corners of his mouth, Stan flicked Liam a wave and got out of the Range Rover. In reply, the big man gave him the finger.

'Keep your eyes on our friends back there,' said Tyler. 'And you'd better not puke or I might be tempted to feed you to Kong along with them.'

A slight shudder running through his muscular frame, Liam twisted around to watch the captives. Bryan was straining against his bonds and struggling to speak through his gag. Liam jabbed him with the baseball bat. 'Lie still, unless you want a real taste of this.'

Tyler waited for Stan to start the engine of their captives' red Subaru before turning on the Range Rover's headlights and accelerating away. He constantly moved his head from side to side to compensate for the reduction of his peripheral field of vision as they headed south through a sprawling suburb of Victorian terraces, inter-war semi-detached houses and boxy, homogenous new estates. When they hit open countryside, they turned west, skirting along the edge of the city, climbing steadily across a hump of moorland. To the road's left a dark expanse of valley dotted with pockets of lights opened up. The road began to drop down, winding around a rocky escarpment. At the bottom of the valley, it passed through a picture-postcard village of stone cottages. A few miles further on, they came to another village, beyond which a bridge crossed a reservoir glimmering beneath the moon. The road began to climb again, snaking its way through a thickly wooded river valley. The landscape took on a more isolated, inhospitable look. Hills loomed up on either side, crowned by bleak, barren moors. Except for an occasional farm, there were no more houses.

Tyler turned onto a dirt track, its edges overgrown with brambles and bracken. Trees leaned towards each other across it, interlocking boughs like embracing lovers. He pulled up at a farm gate, to either side of which a wire fence extended into the trees. 'PRIVATE STAY OUT' was written in white paint on a piece of wood nailed to the gate. Next to it was another sign that read 'BEWARE! GUARD DOGS RUNNING FREE'. Tyler allowed himself the faintest of smiles at the warning. There were no dogs on the farm. But there was something else. Something much more effective.

Liam unlocked a padlock, uncoiled a chain from the

gatepost, and opened the gate. As he waited for Tyler and Stan to drive through it, he eyed his surroundings with quick glances. In many places, there were holes in the earth beneath the dark canopy of trees as if someone was searching for buried treasure, but there was no sign of whatever had dug them. He clicked the padlock back into place and climbed somewhat hurriedly into the Range Rover.

After half a mile or so, they emerged into a grassy field. A drystone wall caked with moss ran alongside the track. At the far side of the field, a ramshackle collection of barns surrounding a two-storey stone farmhouse was pressed against a steep hill. They drove under the cover of a barn roofed with corrugated iron sheets that rattled and squeaked in the wind gusting down from the hilltop.

Liam stepped warily out of the Range Rover, directing a torch beam into the barn's cobwebby corners.

'They won't be hanging around here at this time of night,' Tyler reassured him. 'They'll be in the woods.'

'Just making sure.'

'Don't worry, Liam, even if they were here they wouldn't take a bite out of you,' said Stan. 'They're not cannibals.' His pot belly quivered as he laughed at his own joke.

'You wouldn't laugh if you'd seen what they can do.'

'Shut up and help me carry our guests into the house,' said Tyler.

Once again, Liam hoisted Les over his shoulder like a sack of grain. Les let out a gurgling groan. Liam slapped him on the backside. 'That's it, pal, come on wake up. There's someone here who wants to talk to you.'

'This is the dirty sod who's shit himself,' said Stan, hauling Bryan out of the boot. A dark stain stretched from Bryan's groin down to his ankles. Stan jerked his hands away. 'Oh Christ, it's coming out of the bottoms of his trousers.'

'Stop fucking around and get hold of him,' ordered Tyler.

Liam chuckled. 'Go on, Stan. Do as the man says.'

They carried their captives to the farmhouse. To a casual observer the house would have looked almost derelict – its walls were studded with mould and moss; several windows were boarded up; rainwater dripped from guttering sagging over the porch. But a closer inspection would have revealed that its front door was newish, some of the slate roof tiles had recently been replaced, and all the unbroken windows were fitted with iron bars. Tyler lowered his end of Bryan to the ground, unlocked the door and switched on a light, illuminating a filthy, threadbare hall carpet and peeling wallpaper. A mildewy scent wafted out the door.

Stan dragged Bryan inside. A muffled groan came from the gangster as his head bumped up several steps. Tyler locked the door and they made their way to a room that was empty except for an old chest of drawers against one of the walls and a chair in the centre of the floor. The chair was metal and bolted to floorboards mottled with dark stains.

'Put that one in the chair first,' said Tyler, indicating Les. 'We might as well see if we can get anything out of him before he gives up the ghost.'

Liam dumped Les on to the chair. He secured Les's wrists to the armrests with steel handcuffs, and lashed his upper body to the back of the chair with a leather strap, cranking it so taut that he couldn't slump to one side no matter how hard he was hit. Stan propped Bryan up against a wall in front of the chair. 'There you go, matey, we don't want you to miss the show, do we now?'

'Right, let's have a look-see who we've snagged,' said Tyler.

Liam and Stan peeled away their captives' balaclavas. For a long moment, they stared at the unveiled faces. Then they exchanged troubled glances, before giving Tyler a *What the hell do we do now* look.

In response, Tyler slowly shook his head and murmured through his teeth, 'Oh fuck.'

Chapter Five

Reece parked outside a two-up two-down terraced house perched at the top of a steep cobbled street overlooking the bright lights of the city centre. Staci led him along a hallway, its woodchip-papered walls yellowed with damp, up some narrow stairs to a room just big enough for a single bed and a wardrobe. An assortment of perfumes, lipsticks, eyeliners and other cosmetics cluttered the carpet in front of a rectangle of mirrored glass propped against the wall. On the window ledge there was an ashtray overflowing with cigarette butts – since going cold turkey Staci had taken to smoking two or three times her usual daily number of cigarettes. She drew some thin curtains that barely kept out the draught from the rotten, rattling window frame, and flopped on to the bed. She patted the duvet, indicating for Reece to lie down next to her.

With a slight hesitancy, he did so. He didn't reach to touch Staci. It wasn't only the meanness of the room that dampened his desire, it was the photos pinned to the corkboard on the wall above the head of the bed. They were all of the same young girl. In some of them she was only two or three years old, in others she was maybe six or seven. She had strawberry-blond hair with a slight curl, sparkling blue eyes, chubby cheeks and an ever-present mischievous gap-toothed grin. In most of the photos she was alone, but in several a woman was squatted next to her, arms wrapped around her shoulders. The woman was unmistakably Staci, but her face was fuller, her eyes brighter, her figure more curvaceous. And she was smiling, a wide smile that showed her gums. Reece had seen her smile, but never like that.

'Beautiful, isn't she?' said Staci, following Reece's line of sight.

'Yes. Like her mother. How long has it been since you saw her?'

'One month and nine days,' Staci answered without needing to think. 'They placed her with a new foster family last week.'

'That's good. I mean, at least it's better than her being in a home.'

Creases of pain spread from the corners of Staci's eyes. 'I'm going to get her back. Once I've paid off Wayne and got on my feet again, I'm going to get my Amelia back and start being the mum she deserves.'

Reece rested one of his hands across both of Staci's. 'I know you are. All you've got to do is stay clean.'

Staci glanced at Reece, hope and doubt churning in her eyes. He squeezed her hands. 'You can do it, Staci. I know you've done it before and relapsed. But that's not going to happen this time, because I won't let it. I promise.'

Staci's eyes searched Reece's face as though she desperately wanted to believe him, to trust in him, but the life she'd led made it almost impossible to do so. And yet she had to trust someone. Bitter experience had taught her that she couldn't do what needed to be done alone. The thought knotted her stomach. She lowered her eyes momentarily. And when she raised them it was as if a shutter had opened, only slightly, but it was open. Tentatively, almost cautiously, she leaned in to kiss Reece. Heat rose again in his heart and groin. But it was tempered by the feeling that the girl in the photos was watching him. He reached past Staci and turned the corkboard to face the wall. In an instant, the shutter clicked back shut.

'Why did you do that?' Staci snapped.

'I'm sorry, Staci. I can't do this with her looking at us. It doesn't feel right somehow.'

'It's never bothered you before.'

'Maybe that's because I didn't feel like I do now.'

Staci's eyes narrowed. 'And how exactly do you feel?'

'I'm not sure. It's hard to put into words.'

Staci made a contemptuous little noise in the back of her throat. 'Don't bullshit me, Reece. You're scared. Scared I'll actually pull this off and get Amelia back. You don't want some kid getting in the way of your fun.'

'That's not it at all.'

'Then what is it?'

'I...' Reece trailed off awkwardly. He'd never been particularly good at expressing his feelings. In the past, he hadn't had much reason to do so. Sure, there'd been other women – casual flings, even one or two serious relationships. But nothing had prepared him for anything approaching what he felt for Staci.

A sharp light came into her eyes. 'Tell you what, Reece, just forget it. Fucking forget I've even got a daughter.' With a practised, mechanical movement, she peeled off her vest top. 'So what's it going to be? A wank, a blowjob, the full monty?'

Reece's thick black eyebrows bunched together. 'Don't talk to me like that. I'm not a punter.'

'Aren't you? You've paid for me.'

'I didn't pay to fuck you, I paid so you wouldn't have to fuck any other men tonight.'

'Well you shouldn't have bothered. I'd rather be turning tricks. At least the punters are only fucking with my body, not my head.'

Reece heaved a sigh. Generally he was good at reading people, but he was confused by the mixed messages he got from Staci. It wasn't simply that she blew hot and cold. There seemed to be an almost schizophrenic split to her character. Sometimes she was as hard as the gritstone edges that delineated the southern border of Yorkshire, impervious to insults. Other times she would blow up or collapse into tears at the slightest thing. It was difficult to say which version of her he found more attractive. Or why he found her attractive in more than a passing-fancy kind of way at all. He'd been around prostitutes long enough to know they were nothing but trouble. She should have made him want to run away as fast as he could. But instead she made him want to risk everything for the chance to be with her. The power she had over him already was frightening.

He was afraid that if he told her how it hurt like a physical ache to be apart from her, how he wanted to keep her and everything she loved safe from and uncorrupted by this squalid world they inhabited, then he would lose what little control he had left of his emotions. And he wasn't sure he was ready for that to happen, not while she was still under Wayne's thumb.

'I want to be with you and everything that comes with you, Staci,' said Reece. 'You believe that, don't you?'

Staci looked at him with that searching gaze again. There was something almost pathetic about the puppyish roundness of his eyes. The harshness faded from her features but the shutters behind her eyes remained closed. With a slight nod, she slid his suit jacket off his bearish shoulders, loosened his tie and lifted it over his head. He caught hold of one of her small hands and tried to kiss it, but she slipped free of his grasp and expertly unbuttoned his shirt and trousers. He shuddered as her fingers, then her lips, traced the outline of the taut muscles of his chest. He lifted her head and kissed her. She allowed him to do so for a moment, before gently but firmly pushing him onto his back and straddling him.

As always with Reece, Staci was the one in control. That was how he liked it. He hadn't said so. She just knew. Years of screwing for a living had made her finely attuned to reading a man's desires. They'd also left her unsure of what she wanted from a man. Physically, he was the kind of man she'd always been attracted to – dark, roughly handsome, powerfully built. The attraction was psychological too – at least partly so. In public, he gave off an air of brooding strength that made her feel safe. In private, there was a vulnerability, a neediness about him that she was less comfortable with. Amelia's father had been the same. His love and need had been all-consuming until the birth of their daughter. No longer able to get the attention he desired from Staci, he'd sought what he needed elsewhere. The memory made her wonder whether what Reece felt for her was real and lasting or just a passing infatuation.

They made love slowly, both forgetting – if only for the briefest of moments – the things that prevented them from giving themselves to each other completely. Then they lay with her head in the crook of his shoulder, sharing a cigarette.

Staci reached under the bed and took out a little black notebook and biro. Inside the book was a list of numbers that gradually decreased as she turned the pages. She subtracted her own takings for the night plus the five hundred quid Reece had given her from the previous number on the list and wrote down the new tally.

'So how much do you owe him now?' asked Reece.

'Fourteen thousand, three hundred and fifty quid.'

Reece's voice took on an edge of bitterness. 'How many more men do you need to fuck to come up with that?'

Staci shot him a sharp look. 'I've told you before, Reece, if we're going to be together you can't be asking questions like that.'

'I'm sorry, Staci. It's just that it kills me to think of you with other men.'

'I'm not with them.' She touched her temple. 'Not in there. I'm with you.'

'I know, but—'

'But nothing. I don't have a choice. This is what I have to do. Either you get your head around it or this isn't going to work.'

'It's not simply that I'm jealous. I worry about you.'

'Well you don't need to, I can take care of myself.' Staci snuggled into Reece's chest, pushing her fingers through its darkly curling hair. 'Although I have to admit, it's kind of nice to have someone worry about me.' She jerked her head up suddenly, as if their conversation had reminded her of something she'd been meaning to say. Her mouth opened, but before she could speak Reece's phone rang.

He retrieved it from his jacket. The name 'Doug Brody' flashed up on its screen. He put it to his ear. 'What's up?'

A deep, gravelly voice responded. 'Where are you?'

'With Staci.'

Doug made a little snorting noise, as if to say, *I should have known*. 'You need to go see Wayne. He's dragging his feet about paying up.'

The muscles of Reece's forehead twitched. 'I'm not sure I'm the best bloke for that job. You know how I feel about that arsehole. If he gives me any shit I might not be able to keep my hands off his throat.'

'I don't give a fuck how you feel about him. It's because of you he's pissing us about. So you're going to sort this out and make things right. Knock him around a little if you really need to, but nothing too serious. OK?'

'OK.'

'And Reece, remember what I said, you've been doing a good job. Keep it that way and you might get in on the real money.'

'I'll call you as soon as I've spoken to him.' A slight tightness in Reece's voice hinted at some inner tension other than his dislike for Wayne.

'Good lad.'

Reece hung up. He stared at the phone for a few seconds as if he couldn't make up his mind whether to pocket it or hurl it against the wall. He returned it to his pocket and started to pull on his trousers. 'I've got to go. Work to do.'

'Stay a bit longer,' said Staci. 'There's something I need to talk to you about.'

'It'll have to wait.'

'It can't wait. It's important.'

There was a troubled note in Staci's voice that caused Reece to pause and look at her as she went on, 'You remember I said my friend Melinda had gone AWOL? Well, she's still not turned up.'

'Refresh my memory. When did you last see this Melinda?'

'Nine days ago. I was the last person to talk to her before she went missing.'

'We don't know that she's missing.' Reece's tone was soft, reassuring. 'She could be anywhere. Is she a local girl?'

'I don't think so. I think she came from further north. Leeds or Bradford or somewhere around there.'

'What about friends?'

'She didn't have any besides me. Not that I know of anyway.'

'What's her surname?'

'I don't know.'

Reece spread his hands as if to illustrate a point. 'You see, that's the problem. Your friend lives off the radar. For all you know Melinda might not even be her real name. Whor—' He stopped himself from saying the word. 'Women in your line of work change their names and addresses like they change their lipstick. So when one goes AWOL, it's almost impossible to say whether there's something sinister behind it or they've simply moved on to some other place.'

Staci waved away Reece's words with an impatient flick of her wrist. 'I know all that. Why do you think I haven't reported her missing?'

'So what do you want from me?'

'I want you to do what you do fucking best! Sniff around. See what you can find out. Look, I know you think Melinda's just upped and left. But you're wrong. Something bad's happened to her, the same as it's happened to all those other girls.'

Reece's heavy brows angled down into an intrigued, if slightly bemused, frown. 'What other girls?'

'I don't know their names or how many of them there are. I just know other girls have gone missing.'

'Are you suggesting there's someone out there abducting prostitutes?'

'I'm not suggesting anything. I'm stating a fact. It's been going on for years. Everyone who works the streets around here knows it.'

Reece pursed his mouth doubtfully. 'Nothing's reached my ears.'

'Maybe that's because you're not listening,' Staci retorted with an accusatory ring in her voice. 'You're not even hearing what I'm saying. Melinda hasn't moved on. Some sick fuck who gets his kicks out of hurting prostitutes has taken her. Am I getting through to you? Are you understanding me?'

'Alright, Staci, take it easy. I'll look into it.' Reece took a notepad and pen out of his jacket. 'So tell me what you know about Melinda.'

'She's a lovely girl, really down to earth. The kind of person who'd do anything for you if—'

Reece held up a hand to cut her off. 'Let's start with the simple stuff. What does she look like?'

'I've got a photo of her on my phone.' Staci scrolled past numerous photos of Amelia until she found what she was looking for. In the photo a girl in her late teens or early twenties was sitting on a stool at a bar, bottle of alcopop in hand. Melinda was a skinny bottle-blonde with a pretty face marred by acne scars visible even through heavy makeup. She had smiling blue eyes and smiling lips. She was wearing an off-the-shoulder black lacy top, a tight black miniskirt and calf-high wet-look PVC boots. A silver stud in the right-hand side of her nose caught the camera's flash.

'I'm going to need a copy of this.'

'I'll text it to you.'

'How tall is Melinda?'

'Maybe a couple of inches taller than me.'

Reece jotted down '5′2″, 7½ stone'. He tapped the phone's screen with his pen. 'When was this taken?'

'A couple of weeks ago. We were celebrating because she'd had an HIV scare that turned out negative.'

'Is it possible this scare made her decide to stop prostituting herself?'

'No way. It wasn't the first time it'd happened. It's an occupational hazard.'

Reece couldn't help but wince a little.

'Don't worry,' said Staci, reading his expression. 'I'm clean. I get tested every month.'

'Have you got a phone number for Melinda?'

Staci nodded. 'But her phone's been switched off ever since she disappeared.'

Staci scrolled through her contacts to Melinda's number. Reece punched it into his own phone. The call went straight through to an answering service. 'Hi, Melinda, my name's Reece Geary. I'm a friend of Staci's. She asked me to contact you because she's concerned for your safety. If you're in trouble, whatever it is, I may be able to help you. Please don't hesitate to contact me on this number, anytime, night or day.' Reece left his number and hung up.

'You're wasting your time,' said Staci. 'I've already left her dozens of messages.'

'Not necessarily. People in trouble are often more willing to talk to a stranger than a friend.' Reece picked up his pen and notepad again. 'Where did Melinda live?'

'In Wayne's flat on Wicker. She was his flavour of the month.'

'And how was their relationship?'

'Stormy. You've seen how Wayne is. But Melinda knew how to handle him.' Staci darted a glance at the door. Her voice dropped. 'If you're thinking Wayne might have something to do with her disappearance, you're barking up the wrong tree. The guy's a nasty prick, but he's not a killer.'

'How do you know? Wait, don't tell me. He's got gentle eyes.' There was a thick vein of sarcasm in Reece's tone.

Irritation flashed in Staci's gaze, but she suppressed it and said evenly, 'No he hasn't got gentle eyes. He's got the eyes of a man who gets off on hurting people. I should know, I've seen the look in them as he's beat the crap out of other girls. But I've never seen him lose control and go too far. After all, we're not much use to him if we're too badly hurt to work.'

Reece's voice came tight and hard. 'And what about you? Have you looked into his eyes as he's beat the crap out of you?'

Staci knew better than to answer such a question. 'Take it from me, Wayne's the last person to be involved in Melinda's disappearance. She was a good worker. And besides, he had a real thing for her. He treated her differently to the rest of us. He was always buying her clothes, shoes and other stuff. And he gave her as much free dope as she wanted. That's why I know she hasn't run off. She had it good with Wayne. Or at least as good as this kind of life gets.'

'You say you were the last person to talk to Melinda. What did you talk about?'

Staci shrugged. 'Nothing much, just the usual stuff. She was pissed at Wayne because he was making her work when she had a cold. It was raining, so business was a bit slow. But she was hoping one of her regulars would show up.'

'Who?'

'She didn't say.'

'And did this regular show up?'

'I dunno. A punter picked me up and when I got back she was gone.'

Again, Reece couldn't stop a slight wince from tugging at his face. An image of Staci in the front seat of a car, legs splayed, some faceless stranger grinding against her, rose out of a dark hole in his mind. He thrust it back down. 'Do you know the names of any of Melinda's punters?'

'I know some of their first names. But they're probably not their real names.'

'You'd recognise their faces, though.'

'Yes. Well, only the regulars.'

'OK, so what I need you to do is if you see one of them take a photo on your phone. And if they're in a car, get a photo of their reg too.'

Staci frowned uneasily. It went against every instinct she had to secretly photograph punters. There was Wayne to consider too. If he saw her doing it she'd be in big-time trouble. She gave a sudden determined nod. 'I'll do it. For Melinda I'll do it.'

'Earlier on you said,' Reece read aloud from his notepad,

'"some sick fuck who gets his kicks out of hurting prostitutes has taken her". Assuming you're right, what makes you think Melinda's abductor was a man?'

Staci's mouth twisted into a caustic smile. 'Aren't they always?'

There was little arguing with that rhetorical statement. Reece felt an illogical little stab of guilt, as if he was somehow partly to blame for the actions of his gender as a whole. 'I think that's enough to go on for now.' He pocketed his notepad and finished dressing. Staci followed him downstairs to the front door.

'Promise me you'll call as soon as you find anything out.' All the edge was gone from her voice. She simply sounded desperately concerned.

'I will, but don't get your hopes up. I probably won't have much to tell you. And just in case – God forbid – you're right, promise me you'll take extra care out there.'

'I always do, babe.'

Reece stooped and kissed Staci lingeringly. When he drew away, he licked his lips and wiped his hand across them as if he'd tasted something delicious yet toxic. He quickly turned and left.

Chapter Six

Melinda jerked awake from a cold and sweaty nightmare to an even worse reality. Her gaze dazedly travelled the tomb-like room's concrete ceiling and windowless walls, which were faintly illuminated by a red light glowing from a head-height horizontal slit in a metal door. There was a spray of rusty-red stains on the adjacent walls. She knew it was blood because her captor had taken great relish in telling her it was. There were stains on the mattress she was lying on too. Blood, sweat and semen. Her blood, her sweat, her captor's semen. She scratched at the sores that had developed under the steel collar locked around her neck. Initially she'd tried to ignore the itching, but as time had passed there seemed less and less point in enduring it. She'd come to accept that she was never getting out of this place, so what did it matter if her scratching left scars? A chain ran from the collar to a pulley in the ceiling, then to a bolt in the wall. She had just enough slack to walk to the end of the mattress, where there was a bucket for pissing and shitting in. Not that she had much desire or strength left for walking. In the hours after she'd been abducted, almost all she'd thought about was escaping. But as hours had turned into what seemed like days and weeks – she'd quickly lost track of time – her thoughts had turned from escaping to dying.

Sooner or later she was going to be killed. That much was obvious from the films she'd been forced to watch of other women being tortured. In them, her captor pushed grotesquely large dildos into the sexual orifices of his victims. He attached crocodile clips wired up to some electrical source outside the room to their nipples. He sliced off ragged flaps of their skin with surgical instruments. And the more they sobbed, screamed and pleaded for mercy, the more aroused he became. *This is what's going to happen to you, bitch.* That was what he'd told her, and he'd been as good as his words.

Melinda drew her legs up to her chest, hugging her arms around her knees. The movement sent blades of pain shooting from her bruised and torn genitals, through her stomach into her chest. A whimper rose up her throat. She forced it back down with a swallow. She was done whimpering. She was done sobbing, screaming and pleading. Her captor gorged on fear like a leech does blood. Well, she would give him no more of it. Not even if it provoked the twisted fuck into killing her. If this was the only life she had left, she was better off dead. She'd considered suicide. She was pretty sure she could rig some way to hang herself with the chain and collar. But she wasn't desperate enough to attempt it. Not yet.

Melinda's heart lurched with sickening force at the sound of multiple bolts being drawn back. Her head jerked up as the metal door scraped open. Her captor entered the room. As usual, he was wearing a black leather gimp suit with peepholes for his eyes and nipples, and a zip at his mouth and groin. Only the zip at his mouth was currently open. Like a great red slug, his tongue emerged through it, running slowly back and forth. The skintight suit hugged the contours of his broad shoulders, thick arms, slightly paunchy belly, and spindly legs that seemed to be attached to the wrong torso. Almost femininely large brown nipples jutted through the peepholes. In another context, Melinda might have found the sight comical, even pathetic. But here in this airless dungeon it made her bladder spasm with fear.

Melinda assumed her captor wore the mask because he got a kick out of it. She'd seen his face on the night she was abducted, so there wasn't any point in concealing it – that is, unless he and the man who'd brought her here were two different people. The thought had crossed her mind, especially as her captor switched between several accents and voices. Sometimes his accent was broad Yorkshire, other times it was as posh as Prince Charles. Sometimes his voice was slow and almost gutturally deep, other times it was fast and almost childishly high-pitched. She would have become convinced that more than one man was involved in her abduction, if it hadn't been for two things. Firstly, the tone of the voice didn't always match up with the same accent. Secondly, the eyes behind the mask never changed. They were always the same, like cold little piss holes in the snow. She'd come to the conclusion that the point of the mask and the different voices was simply to fuck with her head, to keep her in a state of confusion. It was all part of the game. And the name of the game was control. Layer by layer, he was stripping away her identity, her dignity, her sanity. Already she could barely remember who she'd been before she was abducted. Soon all that would be left of her was an empty husk with no will of its own.

'Hello, my sweet little whore.' Today his voice was excited, high-pitched, well-spoken. 'How are we feeling?'

Melinda stared at the gimp. Her gaze wasn't confrontational, it wasn't scared. It was simply blank. But inside she was shaking so badly it took all of her willpower to keep her teeth from chattering. *No more*, she kept mentally repeating to herself. *No fucking more!*

The gimp held up a long yellow rod with two black prongs at its end. He pressed a button and electricity crackled between the prongs. 'You know the drill. On your face. Hands behind your back. Move or even flinch and I'll give you a taste of my rod.' The gimp gave a strange little chuckle, as if he'd made a joke.

Melinda rolled obediently onto her front, biting back a wince as the collar chafed her sores. She held herself perfectly still as her captor pulled away the thin, rough blanket that covered her scrawny naked form and clicked metal cuffs on her wrists and ankles, squeezing them painfully tight against her bruised skin. 'Good girl,' he breathed in her ear, rolling her back over. 'I've brought some new toys for us to play with.' He opened a holdall and withdrew an object that was familiar to Melinda from S&M sessions with punters. It was a stainless steel device about seven inches long with a small wheel at one end. A series of evenly spaced short, sharp spikes radiated from the wheel. 'Have you seen one of these before? Answer with a nod or a shake of your head.'

Melinda nodded.

The gimp gave a click in his throat, annoyed his toy was nothing new to her. 'Do you know what it's called?'

She shook her head.

'It's a neurological wheel. Originally it was used to test nerve reactions as it was rolled across the skin, like so.' The gimp pushed the pinwheel lightly over Melinda's stomach, producing a sharp, prickling sensation.

Again, she held herself as motionless as a dead thing, allowing no flicker of expression to cross her features.

'Nowadays it's more commonly used as a sex toy,' continued the gimp. 'Of course, most people only use it to stimulate the flesh. They don't press down hard enough to puncture it. But where's the fun in that?' He ran the wheel across Melinda's stomach again, this time with enough force to leave a trail of bloody full stops.

She gave no sign of having felt anything. The gimp raked the wheel across her breasts and nipples several times, pushing the pins in deeper with every pass he made. Still nothing. Not even the faintest of moans. He scrutinised her face for any sign of pain. There was none. She stared at the ceiling as if seeing through it to some other place – a place where no pain could reach her. He flipped her onto her front again, and attacked the backs of her thighs and her buttocks, going at it so viciously that soon clumps of ploughed up flesh and skin clogged the pinwheel. He stopped suddenly and hurled the device aside as if it disgusted him.

'Fucking bitch. Fucking whore.' His slightly breathless voice quivered not with pleasure but with anger. He grabbed the chain close to the wall and, grunting with effort, hauled down on it until Melinda's toes dangled a couple of inches above the mattress.

The pain of the pins piercing and tearing Melinda's flesh had been agonising. But it was nothing compared to the pain of being hanged. She felt as if her neck was stretching like a rubber band, and as if her head was expanding like a balloon. Her tongue protruded. Her eyes bulged. Bloated veins wormed their way across her forehead and temples. But even worse than the pain was the fear. The room was swimming before her eyes. Blackness was seeping in from the edges of her vision. Soon, she knew, she would lose consciousness, maybe never to regain it. Every instinct, every thought screamed at her to beg her captor to stop. But somehow, calling up some reserve of strength she never knew she possessed, she resisted and resisted, until darkness came crashing down on her. And suddenly she was no longer scared, and an overwhelming feeling that everything was going to be fine spread warmly through her.

As rapidly as it had come down, the darkness receded. Air swelled Melinda's lungs in a huge gulping gasp. She woke up to the realisation that she was lying in an awkward heap on the mattress. Her eyes roamed the room like those of a lost little child. *Where am I?* she wondered. *How did*

I get here? Then the gimp mask loomed into view and she remembered and all the fear came rushing back.

'That's it,' said her captor, his voice tauntingly soft. 'Breathe, breathe.'

Melinda sucked in another lungful of the fetid air. She barely had a chance to exhale before the chain jerked taut again. This time unconsciousness was almost instantaneous. She had a strange feeling that time was moving past her blurringly fast. A jolt hit her like a hammer. Streams of blood-red light split the darkness as her pupils rolled back into view. It seemed to her that she was waking from a long sleep. Again came the thought, *Where am I? What's going on?* A figure was straddling her, hands clasped one on top of the other, compressing her chest.

'Welcome back,' said the gimp. 'I thought I'd lost you for a moment there.'

He gave Melinda a few seconds to get some oxygen back into her body, which was trembling now no matter how hard she tried to control it. Then he reached for the chain again. She quickly lost count of how many times he choked her out and revived her over the next few minutes or hours or whatever it was. All she knew was that at the end of it she was still alive. And she was in pain beyond bearing. Despite her best efforts, tears streamed silently down her cheeks.

'Well, well,' said her captor. He didn't sound angry any more. He sounded amused and pleased. 'You've got more about you than I thought.' He rubbed his leather-encased hands together, like someone eagerly anticipating a challenge. He left the room, returning after a moment with a bottle of water, a towel and some other items. He tilted the bottle against Melinda's lips. She drank, but coughed most of the water back up her raw, swollen throat.

'Slowly, or it won't stay down,' cautioned her captor as she drank again. He dampened the towel and began dabbing away the blood trickling from the dozens of tiny puncture wounds on her body. When he was done, he unlocked the padlock that secured the collar to her neck, unscrewed the top from a tube of antiseptic cream and gently rubbed it into her sores. 'There now, doesn't that feel better, hmm?'

Shudders of fear and confusion racked Melinda's body. In some strange way her captor's apparent concern was more terrifying than his anger. She at least had some slender grasp of why he tortured her. But this... this was beyond her comprehension. Didn't he intend to kill her after all? Or was he simply keeping her alive to play with later? Like a cat toying with a little bird. He reached into the holdall. She went rigid, expecting him to reveal some new implement of torture. But instead he took out a pre-packaged cheese and ham sandwich. 'Are you hungry?'

Melinda nodded.

Her captor pressed the sandwich into her hand. 'Don't try to eat it right away. Your throat's too swollen.'

He locked the collar back on to Melinda, then unlocked the cuffs from her wrists and ankles. She stared at him, her eyes shot through with burst blood vessels and tormented uncertainty, as he gathered up his bag and stood to leave. He closed the door without a backward glance. The bolts grated into place.

Melinda's gaze dropped to the sandwich. For a long moment she stared at it as though expecting it to disappear in a puff of smoke. Then, clutching it to her chest like a prize, she did what she'd promised herself she wouldn't do again – she began to sob loudly and uncontrollably.

The deep-set little eyes that were pressed to the other side of the slit in the door grew heavy-lidded with satisfaction.

Chapter Seven

As Reece drove back to Burton Road, he fought down rising anger. He wasn't angry at Wayne for not coughing up his dues – that merely pissed him off a bit. It was the thought of Wayne beating Staci, or for that matter, any other woman. In his book there was nothing lower, nothing more despicable, than a man who liked to use his fists on a woman. Wayne badly needed teaching a lesson that would make him think twice about hurting the girls who worked for him. And Reece couldn't think of any better man for the job than himself. But as with every lesson, there would be a time and a place for it, and now wasn't that time. Right now all he needed to focus on was keeping Doug happy. That was how he would get into the real money, the money that would give Staci and Amelia the chance to start a new life. A life with him.

His thoughts turned to Staci's theory about Melinda's disappearance. Was it possible she was right? It wasn't hard for him to believe there was some kind of psychopath prowling the streets for prostitutes to abduct. Prostitutes were the perfect victims. The majority of them were runaways and drug addicts, leading transient existences. If they disappeared, it was often months or even years before they were reported missing, by which time the investigative trail was stone cold. What he found harder to swallow was the idea that there was a killer at large in the area who'd been getting away with it for years, maybe even decades. Surely even the most cautious killer couldn't go unnoticed over such a long period of time.

Reece's line of thought was disrupted by the sight of Wayne Carson. The pimp was slouched in the same spot as earlier, puffing on a cigarette. Reece pulled over, took an extendable steel baton from the glove compartment and got out of the car. Spotting him, Wayne flicked away his cigarette and shoved his hand inside his jacket.

With a jerk of his wrist, Reece extended the baton. 'Get your fucking hand where I can see it or I'll break it off.'

Wayne drew his hand back into view, fingers spread to show that it was empty. 'I was just gonna get what I owe you, that's all.'

Reece stopped a pace from Wayne, the baton raised, ready to split his nose open like an overripe tomato. *Go on*, said Reece's eyes, *just give me a fucking excuse*. 'So get it. Slowly.'

The pimp delved into his jacket again and removed a wad of crumpled cash. Reece snatched it away from him. Just the feel of the banknotes in his hand told him there weren't nearly enough of them. He eyeballed the money, then Wayne. 'Where the fuck's the rest of it?'

Wayne hawked and spat a jet of phlegm through his teeth close to Reece's shoes, glaring at him defiantly. 'That's all you're getting. After the way you've fucked me over, you're lucky to be getting anything.'

'What do you mean, the way I've fucked you over?'

'Staci's one of my top earners and you're trying to steal her from me.'

'How can I steal her from you? You don't own her. No one does.'

'Fuck you. You know what I mean. If it wasn't for you, there's no way she'd have got it together enough to even think about leaving me.'

Reece stepped closer to the pimp, lowering his head so that their brows were almost touching. His voice came heavy with the threat of violence. 'You mean she'd still be pumping her veins full of your shit.'

Wayne didn't flinch from Reece's words, but as he spoke a tremor in his voice betrayed his nerviness. 'I've totted up what I reckon you owe me for her. I'll be deducting five hundred quid from my payments each month until you've paid off your debt.'

'And what am I supposed to tell Doug?'

'Not my problem.'

A slow smile spread across Reece's face. 'Oh, you're wrong about that. Because if you don't give me the rest of what's due, there'll be no more tip-offs, no more looking the other way. But best of all, you'll get no more protection from me. And if that happens, I won't just take Staci from you, I'll take everything you've got. I'll fucking destroy you.' He jabbed a finger at Wayne's ear, and this time the pimp flinched. 'Are you hearing me, you rat-faced fuck?'

'You can't do that,' retorted Wayne, just barely managing to keep up his defiant air.

Reece took out an ID card with his name, photo and detective inspector's rank on it. 'You see that? That means I can do what the fuck I want. You've already got a couple of convictions behind you. Fuck up again and I guarantee you you'll be eating prison food for the next few years. Is that what you want? Maybe you like to eat shit.' He put his forehead against Wayne's and pressed hard. 'Is that what you like?'

The pimp shook his head. Reece thrust the cash back into his hand. 'I'll be coming to see you again tomorrow, and you'd better have the money.'

Reece drew away from Wayne, still eyeballing him. The pimp avoided his gaze, pale with impotent anger. 'There's something else I want to talk to you about,' said Reece. 'One of your girls went AWOL last week.'

Wayne's lips drew into a gap-toothed scowl. 'Someone's got a big gob. It's going to get them into trouble one of these days.'

Reece's hand shot out and grabbed the pimp's throat. 'Don't you even fucking think about it. Do you hear?'

'Get off!'

Wayne vainly tried to squirm free. Reece's hand tightened, choking off his air. 'Do you fucking hear?'

Eyes bulging, Wayne nodded. Reece released him. 'Now tell me about Melinda. Start with her surname.'

'Why the fuck would I know her surname?' muttered Wayne, rubbing gingerly at his throat.

'I hear you had a special thing for her.'

'Look, policeman, all I need to know about a girl is

whether they're a good fuck. And believe me, Melinda is.'

Reece gave the pimp a glare of undisguised revulsion. 'Any idea where she might be?'

'If I knew where she was, she wouldn't be there. She'd be here working her patch.'

'There's a rumour that she might have been abducted.'

'Bollocks,' Wayne retorted in an offended tone. 'No one round here would dare mess with one of my girls. She's buggered off, that's all. Probably gone back to whatever shithole she came from.'

'So she's taken all her belongings with her, has she?'

'What belongings? She didn't have much more than the clothes on her back.'

Reece recalled what Staci had said about Wayne always buying Melinda stuff. 'Would you mind me coming round to your flat and checking that out for myself?'

'Yeah, I would fucking mind. Unless you've got a search warrant.' The corner of Wayne's mouth lifted into a crooked smile. 'But I'm guessing this isn't an official investigation.'

Reece resisted the urge to smack the cocky grin off the pimp's face. 'If you've got nothing to hide, why not just let me take a look around?'

'Cos I don't like you, that's why.'

Reece could have forced Wayne to take him to his flat, but he saw little worth in doing so. He got no sense that Wayne was hiding anything. Like Staci had said, Melinda was – or rather, had been – a valuable asset to him. Sure, he might have slapped her around a little to keep her in line. But kill her, no way. At least not intentionally. 'I'll see you tomorrow,' he said, turning to head back to his car. 'Don't disappoint me.'

As Reece ducked into the driver's seat, Wayne called after him, 'Staci doesn't want your dick, policeman, she wants your wallet.'

Reece's fingers twitched on the baton's grip at the pimp's words, which echoed his own doubts. He found himself almost hoping that when he returned to collect what was owed Wayne failed to produce the goods. As he drove, he phoned Doug.

'Have you got it?' asked Doug.

'No.'

Doug's voice rose in irritation. 'Why the fuck not?'

'He's got cash-flow problems. I've given him another day to come up with it.'

There was a second or two's silence, then, 'I think we'd better meet up.'

'I thought you were on duty.'

'I just clocked off. I'll see you at the usual place.'

'On my way.'

Heaving a sigh, Reece headed into the city centre. He parked close to the grim, grey-stone façade of the cathedral and made his way to a nearby bar. The place was almost empty. A barman was cleaning tables in preparation for closing up. Reece ordered a beer, and taking a slug of it, approached a man sipping whisky at a table. With his lean, tanned cheeks and baby-blue eyes, at a glance Doug passed for the same age as Reece. Upon closer inspection, a network of crow's feet and the slight bagginess of his jawline betrayed his age as being more like forty-five than thirty-one. As did his hair, which was dyed several shades darker than its natural colour and carefully styled in an attempt to conceal a bald patch on the crown. A sharp blue suit, a white shirt with the top couple of buttons undone and a thick gold chain around his neck completed the impression of someone who fancied himself as a ladies' man.

Reece sank onto a chair opposite Doug. 'Anything interesting go down tonight?'

'Bryan Reynolds went for a drive with one of his sidekicks. They gave us the slip in Darnall. The DCI's not a happy chappy,' said Doug. 'What happened with Wayne?'

'I told you, he's got cash-flow problems.'

Doug responded with a noise in his throat that made it clear what he thought of Wayne's excuse. 'You can't give these scumbags a millimetre. If they think they can play you—'

'No one's playing me,' cut in Reece.

'You sure about that?'

Looking into Doug's cynically knowing eyes, Reece got the feeling his colleague wasn't simply referring to the 'scumbags' who paid for their protection. 'Positive,' he replied with a certainty he didn't feel. 'Wayne will pay up tomorrow, and if he doesn't—'

Now it was Doug's turn to cut in. 'If he doesn't, you come down on him hard. Make sure he understands that the only reason he's in business is because we allow him to be.'

'Oh, I'll make the little prick understand alright. Don't worry, Doug, I won't let you down.'

Doug smiled with an easy confidence. 'I know you won't, Reece. I knew that the moment I realised you were Frank Geary's boy.'

A line twitched between Reece's eyes at the mention of his father's name. He took a swallow of beer to hide it.

'By the way,' went on Doug. 'How's your dad doing?'

Reece thought about the last time he'd seen his dad, a couple of days ago. He thought about the brackish brown blood his dad had coughed up. He gave a small shrug of his big shoulders. 'He has good days and bad days.'

'Have the doctors given a prognosis?'

'If they have, Dad isn't saying.'

'Sounds like him. He always was a closed-mouthed bastard.' Doug reached across the table and patted Reece's arm. 'Don't worry, your old man's as tough as they come. I reckon he's got a good few years left in him yet.'

Years. Reece shook his head at the word. He wasn't convinced his dad had months, let alone years, left in him. It wasn't only the bleak articles he'd read online about survival rates for people whose lung cancer returned after a period of remission, it was the way the weight was dropping off. The speed of it was terrifying. He could almost see him wasting away in front of his eyes. 'No one's tougher than cancer.'

'I don't know about that, but I'll tell you this, I'd sooner put a bullet in my head than go through chemo,' said Doug.

A crooked smile flickered on Reece's face as he reflected that Doug was probably more frightened by the thought of what chemo would do to his looks than the disease it treated.

Doug emptied his glass and indicated Reece's bottle. 'Want another?'

Reece shook his head. 'I'm driving.'

'Since when did that matter?'

He approached the bar and returned with their drinks. 'I'll tell you something else, there's no way I'm going to be doing this job forever. Five years from now I'm going to be lying on a beach all year round in Thailand with some big-titted bird feeding me margaritas. No fucking way am I going to end up like Jim Monahan.'

'What do you mean? What's up with Jim?'

'Haven't you heard? He's had a heart attack.'

'Christ almighty. Is he dead?'

'I don't know.'

Reece puffed his cheeks. 'I saw him just the other day. He seemed fine.'

Doug snorted. 'That bloke's been a heart attack waiting to happen for years. Do you know why? He let the job get on top of him.'

'Jim's a hell of a copper.' Reece swallowed a mouthful of beer in salute. 'Real old school.'

Doug gave another, louder snort. 'He's not old school. Your dad was old school. And he was a far better copper than Jim Monahan too, not because he was the greatest detective in the world, but because he knew it was us against,' he pointed at the street, 'them. You can trust a copper like your dad no matter what happens. You can't trust coppers like Jim, idealists who've always got to do what they think's right.' He leant forward, eyes sharp with intensity. 'It's not doing the right thing, or even upholding the law, that matters most in this job. It's the people you work with. It's having their backs and knowing they've got yours at all times. That's what matters most. Guys like Jim don't understand that. They come into the job thinking they can make a difference. When they realise they can't, they start to hate it. But by that time they've given up so much for it they can't bring themselves to just walk away. They want to go out with a bang. And that's when the coppers around them get hurt, maybe even end up dead.'

'You mean Amy Sheridan. That wasn't Jim's fault.'

'Bollocks it wasn't. She wouldn't have been outside the hospital with the Baxley lad if it wasn't for Jim. He got himself barred from ICU by stepping on that psychiatrist's toes.'

'That psychiatrist was a child molester.'

'Yeah, but Jim didn't know that at the time. And anyway, that's beside the point. The point is crusaders like him seem to think they answer to a higher power than the rest of us normal cops.'

'Are we normal cops?'

Doug scowled as if the question was an insult. 'Course we fucking are. We're no different to anyone else, we're just smarter.' He sipped his whisky, studying Reece over the rim of his glass, a glimmer of a frown in his shrewd eyes. He swallowed his frown with the whisky. 'Listen, I understand why you look up to Jim. I used to look up to him myself.

But think on this: if you'd been his partner it'd be you, not Amy, lying in the mortuary.' His voice was friendly, almost fatherly. 'Luckily for you, you're not his partner, you're mine, and I look after my own. Always remember, Reece, the only person in the world a cop can trust is another cop.'

The muscles of Reece's jaw tightened. Was that a sideways dig at Staci? 'What about when we're not cops any more? Who do we trust then?'

Doug grinned. 'Once a cop always a cop. I thought you'd have learned that from your dad.'

The line twitched between Reece's eyes again. His dad had taught him a lot of things, but that saying wasn't one of them. As an image of his dad sitting alone coughing up the lining of his lungs filled his mind, the words sounded more like a warning than a recommendation. He washed the image away with a swig of beer. 'There's something I want to ask you. Have you ever heard any rumours about someone abducting prostitutes in the city?'

Doug raised an eyebrow. 'When you say "someone", you mean a serial killer. Right?'

'Possibly, I don't really know.'

'And let me guess where you heard this rumour. One of your whore's workmates has gone missing and she's convinced they've been abducted. Right?'

Reece's fingers tightened on the beer bottle at the word 'whore', but he kept his voice carefully emotionless. 'Right.'

'So now your whore wants you to look into the other whore's disappearance.'

Stop fucking calling Staci a whore! The words pushed at Reece's lips. He nodded, afraid that if he opened his mouth they'd come bellowing out.

'But you're not going to waste your time on this bullshit,' went on Doug. 'Because you know your whore's friend isn't really missing, she's just found somewhere else to turn tricks.'

'Don't—' Reece started to snap, but checked himself.

'Don't what? Don't call your girlfriend a whore. Why not? That's what she is, isn't it?'

Reece turned away from Doug's all too perceptive eyes. The bottle trembled under his vice-like grip.

Jabbing a finger against the table for emphasis, Doug said, 'Always call people what they are. That way there's no confusion.'

'I'm not confused.'

'Then you must know that just as you'll always be a cop, your girlfriend will always be a junkie whore.'

That was too much for Reece. He jerked his face towards Doug, eyes blazing. 'The fuck she will be!'

Doug spread his hands. 'Easy, big man. I know it's hard to hear the truth, but I'm just trying to save you a lot of heartache later on.'

'You don't know Staci. All she wants is to get out of that life and get her daughter back. And I'm going to do whatever I can to help her. Do you hear me?'

'I hear you. And who knows, maybe I'm wrong, maybe she can change.' *And maybe pigs can fly*, Doug's eyes seemed to add.

Reece shoved his chair back and stood. 'I'm going home. I'll see you tomorrow.'

'No you won't. Remember, you're taking your dad for his chemo.'

Reece rolled his eyes towards the ceiling, reflecting sardonically that the evening's events had at least driven that particular unpleasant thought out of his head, even if it had only been replaced with other almost equally unpleasant thoughts.

'Tell him good luck from me,' continued Doug.

The thought of what tomorrow held weighing in his stomach like a heavy stone, Reece returned to his car. As he started the engine, Doug tapped the window. Reece lowered it and Doug proffered him a scrap of beermat. There was a name written on it. Vernon Tisdale. 'He's a journalist at the South Yorkshire *Chronicle*,' explained Doug. 'At least he used to be. I don't know what he's up to nowadays. I wouldn't be surprised if he's six feet under. He was a real porker. Must have weighed well over twenty stone last time I saw him. Anyway, a few years before your time, he came to us with a list of missing prostitutes he believed had been murdered.'

Reece's eyebrows lifted. 'So it's more than just a rumour then.'

'Only in the overactive imagination of Tisdale and the whores he'd been speaking to. It didn't take us long to realise his list was a load of bollocks.'

'Bollocks in what way?'

'Well, for starters, several of the so-called victims had

died from natural causes and drug overdoses. And for seconds, others on the list had simply moved out of the area. So you see, that's why I know your whor— your girlfriend's little theory is nonsense. But hey, if you want to waste your time on nonsense, that's up to you. Just so long as you don't let it get in the way of your real work.'

'I won't. Thanks, Doug.' Reece pocketed the scrap of beermat, and flicking Doug a wave, accelerated away.

Chapter Eight

So what the fuck do I do now? wondered Tyler. He scratched at his bandaged eye socket. The painkillers were wearing off. Soon, he knew, the itching sensation would build to a throbbing pain deep enough to make even him grimace. It still hadn't really sunk in that his left eye was gone. When he glanced from side to side, he could feel his eye muscles moving as though it was still there. The surgeon who'd operated on him in a makeshift backstreet surgery had explained that his eyeball was too badly damaged to be saved, and what's more, considering that the wound stopped just millimetres short of his brain, he was lucky to be alive. Tyler had accepted the news with his usual inscrutable air. He felt no anger towards Mark Baxley for stabbing him. He would have done the same himself in Mark's position, only he'd have made sure to push the broken plastic handle all the way through the eyeball into the brain.

Bryan bellowed through his gag, goggling his eyes in a way that said far more clearly than his muffled words, *Take this fucking thing off me!*

Tyler headed into the hallway, motioning for Liam and Stan to follow. Liam slammed the door and looked wide-eyed at his colleagues. 'This is fucked. This is so fucked. Why would Bryan Reynolds want to kill Edward Forester?'

'That's not our concern,' said Stan, his dour Yorkshire voice as steady as ever. 'We've been contracted to do a job, and we have an obligation to complete that contract.'

'Are you off your rocker? If we kill Reynolds we'll have every psycho with a gun in Sheffield after our arses.'

'Well we can't let him go. He's seen our faces. And anyway, who's to know it was us that killed him?'

'Forester knows,' said Tyler. 'And if Reynolds's goons know about Forester, they'll go after him and try to make him talk.'

'Fuck, you're right,' said Liam. 'And there's no way that prick will keep his gob shut. Well, that's it then. We've got no choice. We have to kill them both.'

'Make your mind up,' said Stan. 'A moment ago you were all for letting Reynolds go.'

'No I wasn't. I just wasn't sure what we should do.'

'You sounded sure enough to me.'

Liam turned to Tyler. 'So are we going to kill them or what?'

'As far as Reynolds goes, the question isn't are we going to do it,' said Tyler. 'It's how do we compensate for what we're going to lose? We make as much from Reynolds in five or six months as what we're being paid for this job.'

'Simple,' said Stan. 'Forester's going to have to pay more.'

Tyler nodded. 'A lot more.'

'And when he's paid us, we do him in too. Right?' said Liam.

Tyler scratched his bandage again. Christ, the itching was enough to drive you crazy. 'I'm not sure about that. Killing a gangster is one thing. No one is going to miss a scumbag like Bryan Reynolds. Killing a politician is another thing entirely. We'll have every copper in South Yorkshire looking for us.'

'We already have after what you did to that policewoman,' pointed out Stan.

'Yeah, well, that wouldn't have happened if the bitch had backed down.' The briefest flash of irritation – not at Stan, but at himself – showed in Tyler's tone. He motioned at the door to what they half-jokingly referred to as the interrogation room. 'You two get back in there and keep an eye on our guests.' With a glance at Liam, he added, 'That's all. Don't lay a finger on them, don't even talk to them. Is that clear?'

Nodding, Liam and Stan headed back into the room. Tyler pulled out a mobile phone and dialled. The call was answered on the first ring. 'Is it done?' enquired a gravelly voice.

'We've got a problem. The target turned out to be Bryan Reynolds.'

'Oh it did, did it?'

'You don't sound too surprised.'

'Maybe that's because earlier tonight I learnt that Reynolds is Mark Baxley's dad.'

A momentary silence from Tyler was the only outward sign that the news had needled him. 'You might have warned me.'

'By the time I found out, you were already on the job. Besides, how was I supposed to know Reynolds knew about Forester?'

'That's the big question, isn't it? Who told Reynolds?'

'Well, it was Jim Monahan who figured out the Baxley lad is Reynolds's son.'

'Monahan.' Tyler's eye narrowed fractionally. 'Wasn't he the partner of that bitch I had to put down?'

'Uh-huh. But even if he's somehow managed to connect Forester to Mark Baxley, I can't believe he'd leak the information. He hates Reynolds worse than every other copper in South Yorkshire put together.'

A shadow of a wince darkened Tyler's features as pain spiked through his empty eye socket. 'This is getting messy. I don't like messy.'

'Perhaps it's a mess we can turn to our advantage. With Reynolds gone–'

'Reynolds isn't gone yet,' corrected Tyler.

'Yeah, but he will be once you've finished questioning him. And with him out of the picture, there's going to be a huge power vacuum for someone to fill.' A thrill of excitement rippled through the voice on the other end of the line. 'Maybe that someone is us.'

'We're not ready to make a move like that.'

'I disagree. This is our big chance. Come on, Tyler, we've been talking about doing this for years.'

Tyler was silent for some moments. Then he said, 'I'm going to arrange a meet with Forester and try to squeeze more cash out of him.'

'Well don't squeeze too hard. He's a handy man to have in our pocket.'

'That depends on who knows about the connection between him and Mark Baxley. If Jim Monahan knows, Forester's got to go.'

'I really can't see how Jim could have made that connection. Not unless Grace Kirby told Mark Baxley before she died. But if that were the case, the whole department would know about it.'

'Well someone knows.'

'Point taken, but I still say we don't do anything to Forester until we're sure who that someone is. Agreed?'

'Agreed.'

Tyler hung up and dialled another number. Edward Forester's voice came on the line, calm but tinged with an undercurrent of anxiety. 'Have you got the bastard?'

'We need to meet.'

'What for? If it's money you want, I'm not paying you a penny unless you've got him. We agreed, payment in full when—'

'I know what we agreed,' interrupted Tyler, 'but the situation's changed.'

'How so?'

'It's difficult to explain. You really need to see for yourself.'

Edward huffed an angry breath down the line. 'A contract is a contract. I don't see why it makes any difference if the situation's changed.'

'Look, either you meet me where I say, or I'll come to

your house. It's up to you.' Tyler's voice was as cold as a dead fish.

'Are you threatening me?'

'I don't make threats.'

The politician's breathing grew hesitant as anger turned to uncertainty. 'Alright. Where?'

Tyler described the location of a layby not far from Ladybower Reservoir, adding, 'I'll be there in twenty-five minutes. You be there too.'

Tyler returned to the Range Rover. He drove to the meeting place as fast as he dared with his vision the way it was, careering around the dark bends of the Snake Pass. Events were moving fast. He knew he had to move faster if he didn't want them to swallow him up and shit him out. When he reached the layby, Edward Forester's Jag was already there. He wasn't surprised. The politician's country pad was only three or four miles away. He pulled in facing the Jag and flashed his lights, signalling Edward to come to him. As Edward got out of his car, Tyler pressed a button and a concealed electronic compartment in the dashboard whirred open. He removed a Glock 9mm and a small black cloth bag from it. Resting the gun on his thigh, he twisted in his seat so that his remaining eye faced the passenger door.

Edward strode through the headlights like a man well aware of his place in the world – and that was a place which didn't include being intimidated by employees, no matter what the nature of their job was. He yanked the passenger door open. 'You'd better have a bloody good reason to—' His voice caught in his throat at the sight of the Glock.

'Get in and close the door.'

'What is this?' There was a tremor in the politician's voice. His eyes darted between the gun and Tyler's poker-faced gaze.

'Get in and close the door.' Tyler's voice was as blank as his expression, yet there was a force behind it that caused Edward to do as he said. Tyler proffered the bag to his passenger. 'Put it on your head.'

'Now just hang on a bloody minute,' said Edward, rediscovering some of his indignant courage. 'I pay you, and pay you well. I know you've had a rough time these past few days, but that doesn't mean I'm going to sit here and let you treat me like this.'

A rough time? I've lost a fucking eye! Tyler shoved the thought away. To think like that was not only unprofessional – after all, as Edward had said, he was paid well to risk his skin – it was weak. And if there was one thing he hated it was weakness. 'Please, sir, just do it,' he said, realising he had to give the politician a token that his authority was, at least in some degree, still acknowledged. 'It's for your protection. It'll be safer for you if you don't see where we're going.'

Edward stared at Tyler, an uneasy, calculating glimmer in his deep-set brown eyes. 'How long will this take?'

'The sooner you do as I ask, the sooner you can get home to your bed.'

'I wasn't in bed.' Edward took the bag and pulled it over his head. 'OK, let's bloody well get this over with.'

Tyler slid the Glock into his jacket and reversed onto

the road. Neither man spoke during the drive back to the farmhouse. As Tyler pulled up, the front door opened and Liam emerged, dragging Bryan Reynolds's skinhead sidekick along the ground by his hands. 'Wait here, and keep the bag on,' Tyler said, jumping out of the car. A glance at the skinhead's battered, blue-tinged face told him the man was dead.

'I didn't touch him,' said Liam, his high-pitched voice sounding like a child pleading innocence. 'He just died.'

'Put him in the barn.'

'That's what I was doing.'

Tyler took hold of Edward's arm. The politician flinched as if he'd been prodded awake. 'Can I take this thing off my head now?'

'In a moment.'

The moon had disappeared behind a cloud, shrouding the encircling hills and woods in impenetrable darkness. There was no way Edward would be able to identify his surroundings. But Tyler saw no reason to risk that he might get a glimpse of some stray detail that could help the police, or whoever, locate the farmhouse. He knew from experience that it was often the tiny details that were the difference between being caught or not. He drew Edward out of the vehicle and guided him towards the farmhouse. Once they were inside and the door was closed, he removed the bag.

Edward's eyes darted around, curious and nervous. Tyler headed towards the rear of the hallway. His tongue sliding dryly across his lips, Edward followed him to the interrogation room. Stan was in the process of securing

Bryan to the chair. Bryan's wrists had been cuffed to the chair's arms, but the leather strap hadn't yet been cranked tight around his chest. The instant he saw Edward, Bryan jerked halfway to his feet, his teeth gnashing against his gag, his eyes swelling out of his head, gleaming pure hate.

Stan punched Bryan in the solar plexus, dropping him back onto the chair. Winded, Bryan continued to strain wildly against his bonds. Wrapping one arm around the gangster's neck, Stan grabbed the bicep of his other arm. He pushed down on the back of Bryan's head, cutting off the blood supply to his carotid artery. As Edward watched Bryan go limp, he ran his tongue over his lips again, only now it left a trail of glistening saliva, as if he'd smelled something that made him hungry. Stan pulled the strap taut. The gangster's eyelids flickered open. His head rolled from side to side, a confused, lost look on his face.

'Do you know him?' Tyler asked Edward.

Edward shook his head. 'I've never seen him before in my life.'

'His name's Bryan Reynolds.'

'Bryan Reynolds.' Edward's forehead creased, as if the name was familiar but he couldn't quite place it. 'Who is he?'

'He's a drug dealer, amongst other things.'

Edward nodded as his memory was jogged. 'Ah yes, I knew I'd heard his name before. But isn't he some kind of major organised crime guy?'

'He controls the trade of narcotics and prostitution in Sheffield.'

Edward's forehead bunched into a deep frown. 'And this man came to my house. Why?'

'To kill you.'

'Yes, yes, I know that,' Edward shot back impatiently. 'But why? Why does this man want to kill me?'

'He's Mark Baxley's father.'

Edward's mouth dropped open. 'Yes, now you've said it I see the resemblance,' he murmured, lifting a finger to his lips, touching them softly, almost caressing them. 'Stephen told me he wasn't Mark's father. I always wondered who the real father was.' His frown returned suddenly, deeper still. 'But how the hell did he find out about me?'

'That's what we're here to try and find out.' At a signal from Tyler, Stan tore the duct tape off Bryan's mouth.

'You're fucking dead!' The words exploded from Bryan like pent-up steam. He jutted his head towards Edward, veins and tendons standing out in his thick neck. 'I'm gonna tear your cock out by the roots!' He twisted towards Stan. 'And you. I thought you were a stand-up bloke. How much is he paying you? It must be a shit lot if you're willing to work for filth like him. Or maybe you're the same as him. Maybe you get your kicks out of sticking your dick in kids too.'

Stan made no reply, but he shifted on his feet as if he was uncomfortable.

Grabbing Bryan's head between his hands, Tyler wrenched it around to face him. 'Who put you on to Mr Forester?'

Bryan bared his teeth in a savage grin. 'I'm going to give

you a chance. Let me go and give me him,' he jerked his eyes at Edward, 'and I'll let you live.'

For a moment, Tyler seemed to consider the offer. Then he shook his head. 'I made a contract with this man.'

'He's not a man,' spat Bryan. 'He's an animal!'

'Regardless of what he is, I...' Motioning to Stan, Tyler corrected himself. '*We* have a duty to carry the contract out.'

'And what about your duty to me? Don't I pay you to protect me?'

Tyler scratched his bandage thoughtfully. 'He's got a point there. I think this is, what do you call it, a conflict of interest.'

'There's no conflict of interest here,' Edward piped up, the tremor back in his voice. 'I've paid you to do a job, so bloody well do it!'

'You haven't paid us yet.'

'That's merely semantics! As soon as the job's done, you'll get your money. And...' Edward cleared his throat as if what he was about to say pained him. 'And seeing as it's turned out to be such a difficult one, I'll chuck in a completion bonus of, let's say, twenty thousand pounds.'

Tyler fixed the politician with his unreadable gaze. 'Each.'

Edward's tongue flickered between his lips, dry once again. He stared at Tyler for a second, then nodded.

'Whatever he's paying you, I'll double it,' said Bryan.

'This isn't a sodding auction,' snapped Edward.

'Isn't it?' Tyler rested back against the drawers, folding his arms, looking expectantly from one man to the other.

Edward stood silent, his expression wavering between anger and nervousness. Liam's hulking form filled the doorway behind him. Edward's gaze flinched over his shoulder as Liam enquired, 'What's going on?'

'Mr Forester was just expressing his willingness to compensate us for unforeseen difficulties. Weren't you?'

With a hiss through his teeth, Edward said, 'Alright, alright, I'll match Mr Reynolds's offer, plus sixty thousand.'

'That makes it four hundred thousand.'

'No, only three hundred and—' Edward broke off. He heaved a breath. 'Yes, you're right. Four hundred thousand it is.'

'Six hundred,' said Bryan. 'Six hundred thousand quid if you let me carve this cunt up here and now. All you need to do is dispose of his body.'

Liam gave a little whistle. 'I'd say that's a pretty damn good offer.'

Edward's gaze danced around the room as if searching for an escape route. 'This is absurd! How do you know this man even has that kind of money?'

Bryan's eyes glittered with brutal amusement. 'Oh, they know I'm good for it, alright.'

'I won't have you holding me to ransom like this.' Edward pulled out his phone. 'We'll bloody well see what Charles has to say about this.'

'What makes you think he's got any influence out here?'

asked Tyler. But as the phone started to ring, quick as a striking snake, he snatched it away from the politician and cut off the call.

Red blotches stained Edward's cheeks. His lower lip protruded like a child about to have a tantrum. Deep laughter suddenly boomed around the room. All eyes turned towards Bryan. 'Anyone got a dummy?' he asked, his broad chest heaving against the leather strap. 'I think boo-boo needs one.'

The colour in Edward's cheeks drained to a white mask of rage. 'Seven hundred thousand!'

'Eight,' shot back Bryan.

'Nine.'

'A million and a half.'

'Tw—' Edward stumbled over the word, his breath coming short between his quivering lips. 'Two million!'

Like an auctioneer bringing down his hammer, Tyler smacked his fist in his palm. 'Sold.'

'Fuck that!' shouted Bryan. 'Three—'

Tyler silenced him with a short hard elbow to the cheek. 'No more bids. Congratulations, Mr Forester.'

'You're dog meat!' Bryan exploded. 'All of you. Fucking dog meat! I'm going to cut you up and feed you to my bitches.'

Tyler motioned for Edward to leave the room. They stepped into the hallway and he closed the door, only barely muffling the enraged gangster's roars.

'You understand it's going to take a few days to come up with the money,' said Edward. He had his voice firmly back under control now, but an oily sheen on his upper lip betrayed the strained state of his nerves.

'And you understand that, considering the change in the terms of our deal, I'm going to need to see the money up front.'

'You'll get your money, don't worry about that. You just concentrate on fulfilling your side of the bargain.' Edward stabbed a finger at the door. 'I want to know everything that bastard knows. And when he's finished talking, I want him to die in the most agonising way possible.'

Tyler regarded the politician coldly. The idea of torturing someone simply for the hell of it held no appeal for him. He hurt people as part of his job, nothing more. But that didn't mean he was uncomfortable with sadism. If Forester wanted Reynolds to suffer beyond what was absolutely necessary, Tyler would be happy to make sure he got his full money's worth. 'I strongly suggest you don't return to Sheffield until this is over.'

Edward gave Tyler a look: *Do you take me for a fool?* 'I have no intention of doing so.'

Tyler returned to the interrogation room and said to Stan, 'Take Mr Forester back to his car. See that he gets home safely.' He handed his colleague the cloth bag, adding meaningfully, 'And make sure he stays safe.'

Stan nodded. He approached Edward, holding out the bag. 'Put that on your—'

'Yes, yes, I know,' Edward broke in, snatching it off him.

'One more thing, Mr Forester,' said Tyler. 'Have you ever heard the name Jim Monahan?' As he asked the question, his gaze moved quickly to Bryan. The gangster's face showed no trace of recognising the name.

'No. Why? Who is he?'

'You needn't concern yourself with that. I'll expect to be hearing from you.'

Edward lifted the bag towards his head, but hesitated, his eyes lingering almost ruefully on Bryan. 'What are you going to do to him?'

'We're going to have a nice little chat,' said Tyler, motioning Liam to close the door again.

Chapter Nine

Jim stared at his bedside television. It was tuned into a twenty-four-hour news channel, and had been since a nurse woke him with breakfast. So far there'd been no mention of any incident concerning Edward Forester. That bothered him, although not quite enough to have him reaching for the phone. Not yet. It was only half past eight. If Reynolds had done as promised, Edward Forester would be dead and his wife, Philippa Horne, would most likely be tied up, terrified but unharmed. When neither of them turned up for work, their colleagues would phone to find out where they were. And when their calls went unanswered, sooner or later – most likely sooner considering Edward Forester's status – some poor sod would be sent to look for them. At which point it would only be a matter of hours before the story broke. If that. A story like this was too big to be contained.

Jim's gaze fell to the handheld tape recorder he'd retrieved from his jacket. Soon it would be time to turn it over to Garrett. A queasy feeling rose from the pit of his stomach. Not at the thought of what would happen to him. But at the thought of what he'd done. He squeezed his eyes shut as if trying to block out the memory. Had he really sought to provoke Reynolds into murdering Forester? He could hardly believe it. It was as if the heart attack had jolted back into focus something he'd lost sight of, some glimpse of the values that had driven him to join the police. How could he have ever thought murder was the answer? He thrust the question from his mind. It was too late for such thoughts now. The person he'd once been was gone, buried under too many years of frustration and relentless struggle to ever be exhumed.

Doctor Advani and a nurse entered the room. 'How are you feeling this morning, Mr Monahan?' asked the doctor.

'A lot better, thanks. I've got no pain in my chest.'

The doctor checked Jim's heart monitor readouts, before taking his notes from the end of the bed and jotting down her observations. 'You appear to be responding well to the medication. Your blood pressure is still high, but within an acceptable range. There's no sign of arrhythmia. Have you had any further shortness of breath or dizziness?'

'No.'

Doctor Advani gave an approving nod. 'I've scheduled another echocardiogram for this morning to determine the extent to which the blocked artery has opened up. I'll be in to see you again after lunch. In the meantime, I've brought you some literature on heart attacks and recovery.' She placed several booklets on Jim's bedside table. 'If you read through them, I'll answer any questions you have next time we talk.'

She continued on her rounds, leaving the nurse to dole out Jim's meds. As he swilled them down, DCI Garrett and DCS Knight appeared at the door. Jim almost choked on a tablet at the sight of them. *You've got some serious explaining to do, Detective Monahan.* Those were the last words he remembered Garrett saying to him. But he wasn't ready to do any explaining. First, he had to be sure about Forester. He quickly laid the booklets over the tape recorder. It wasn't necessary, but he felt a guilty urge to do so anyway.

When the nurse left, the two men approached Jim's bedside. Garrett wore the look of someone who hadn't been sleeping well. There was a heaviness about his movements that was made all the more apparent by the Chief Superintendent's energetic stride. With his clear, sharp blue eyes peering out from under a high-domed forehead, DCS Knight gave off his usual air of purpose and authority. 'How are you feeling, Jim?' he asked.

'Not too bad.'

'You gave us all a real fright yesterday,' said Garrett. 'It's lucky for you I was at your house when I was.'

'I suppose so.'

All three men were silent a moment. A question hung unspoken between them. *Why were you at my house?* That's what Garrett and Knight were waiting for Jim to ask. But he wasn't about to open that can of worms unless he had to. Garrett looked uncertainly at him as if debating whether to open it himself. The only reason he hadn't already done so, guessed Jim, was that he'd been warned off talking about anything that might stress the patient.

'I spoke to Ruth Magill yesterday,' Garrett said at last.

'She told me the identity of Mark Baxley's biological father.'

So he wasn't at the house because he'd found out I contacted Grace Kirby after all, thought Jim. Her mobile phone clearly hadn't been found. That was another piece of luck. It gave him a little breathing space. A trace of a sardonic smile tugged at his mouth as he reflected that a doctor's warning was no match for Garrett's ambition. With the connection of Mark to Bryan Reynolds, this had become a career case for the DCI, one that could make or break him.

'Why did you withhold that information from me?' went on Garrett.

'I wasn't withholding it from you. I just wasn't sure it had any real bearing on the case.' Jim's answer was a half-truth at best. Reynolds might not have been directly involved in the events surrounding Mark's abduction and Grace Kirby's death, but he'd played a major role in creating the circumstances that led to them.

'Whether or not—' Garrett started to say, his voice rising. At a cautioning glance from DCS Knight, he caught himself, then continued in a quieter, if no less admonitory tone, 'Whether or not it has any bearing is irrelevant. I'm your commanding officer, and as such I expect to be kept fully informed of all developments. This is a very serious matter. I could have disciplinary charges brought against you.'

'No, you couldn't, because you're not my superior. I quit, remember.' The words felt good to Jim. Not that they changed anything. Cop or not, disciplinary charges would be the least of his worries when the full facts came out.

'Ah, so that's what you meant when you said you weren't a detective any more. I had wondered.'

'You've just gone through a heart attack, Jim,' said DCS Knight. 'This isn't the time for you to be making major life decisions. This is the time for you to be concentrating on making a full recovery.' His gaze moved between Jim and Garrett. 'So, for now, let's put aside any talk of disciplinary charges and quitting. OK?'

'OK,' said Jim.

Garrett nodded his agreement, giving Jim a thin-lipped smile that seemed more like a forced reflex than a genuine expression of emotion.

'Have you told Mark about Bryan Reynolds yet?' asked Jim.

'No,' said Garrett.

'Then I think it would be best to keep it that way.'

'Possibly, but that decision isn't yours to make.'

Jim turned appealingly to DCS Knight. 'Mark's been through so much already. He knows nothing about his father, so telling him would gain us nothing.'

'Don't you think he's got a right to know?' asked DCS Knight.

'Yes, of course. But does he really *need* to?'

DCS Knight frowned in thought for a moment. Then he said, 'I agree that telling Mark at this time would almost certainly do more harm than good. But I'm not ruling out telling him at some point in the future.'

A ripple of relief went through Jim. Garrett's lips tightened in irritation, but he had no choice other than to swallow his superior's words. 'Before we let you get back to resting, is there anything else you haven't told us about this case?' asked the DCI.

The bastard just can't help himself, thought Jim. *Perhaps he's more of a copper than I've given him credit for.* 'I don't think so.'

'You don't think so; does that mean you're not sure?'

'It means there's nothing I can think of right now. But then I'm not exactly feeling altogether with it. They've got me on more drugs than a lab rat.'

Garrett stood chewing on his thoughts momentarily. Then, with the air of a man reluctantly capitulating, he said, 'Well if anything comes to mind, be sure to let us know.'

'I will. Before you go, sir,' Jim said the word 'sir' as if it tasted sour, 'can I ask how the investigation's going?'

'I don't think it'd be wise for us to go into all that right now. The doctor warned us to avoid talking about anything that might stress you out.'

That didn't seem to concern you when you were asking me the questions, Jim reflected wryly. He didn't feel the need to point this out to Garrett. But then, the DCI didn't need to say anything to answer his question. His reticence, his very presence, told Jim everything he needed to know, both about the investigation and about Edward Forester. The investigation was going nowhere fast and Forester hadn't yet come onto the radar in any shape or form, otherwise Garrett wouldn't be here prodding him for information, he'd be out there chasing down leads, and perhaps, even more importantly as far as he was concerned, formulating his media strategy.

'I'll bring you up to speed when you're out of hospital,' went on Garrett. 'Take care, Jim. Get well. We need you back.'

Jim detected no note of insincerity in Garrett's voice. The DCI didn't have much liking for him, that much was obvious. But there was respect, grudging though it may have been. The queasy feeling rose in him again, and again he forced it back down with a hard swallow. It was too late for regrets. It was too late for everything, except seeing his plan through.

'Too bloody right we do,' said DCS Knight, patting Jim's arm. 'You're one of our best. We're not going to let you get away so easily.'

'Oh, one more thing,' said Garrett, as the two men turned to leave. 'Pathology's backed up because of everything that's been happening, so it looks like Amy Sheridan's funeral is going to be delayed. We're not sure for how long, but it shouldn't be by more than a week or two.'

By then, thought Jim, *if everything goes to plan, I'll be suspended from duty or maybe even locked up*. It was almost a relief to know he wouldn't be at Amy's funeral. Just the thought of having to look into the eyes of her children, knowing he may have inadvertently contributed to their mother's death, was enough to make guilt claw his insides.

'You should also know that I'm nominating Amy for a posthumous bravery award,' added Garrett. 'I'm sure you'll agree she's more than deserving of one.'

Suddenly Jim's breathing felt tight in his throat, so that all he could do was nod. He turned his head away from Garrett and the Chief Superintendent, closing his eyes. Tears pushed at his eyelids. *Don't you dare cry for her*, said a bitterly recriminating internal voice. *You don't have the fucking right*.

Chapter Ten

Edward Forester paced back and forth beneath the oak beams of the living-room ceiling, his footsteps echoing on the polished floorboards. The eyes of a shaggy grey wolfhound lazily followed him from where it lay curled up on a silk rug. Behind the dog, smoke curled up a chimney in a grand stone fireplace. In one hand Edward held a cigarette, in the other a cordless telephone. Twenty paces took him from leaded arched windows at the front of the room, to French doors overlooking a patio and landscaped gardens at its rear. 'This is totally unacceptable,' he was saying into the phone, his voice angry, but not loud.

'I'd say it's a pretty fair price considering what they stand to lose,' came the reply, its tone uncompromising.

Edward gave an incredulous little laugh. 'You call two million quid a fair price? I call it extortion, pure and simple.'

'I'm sorry you feel that way, Edward, but I'm not sure what you expect me to do.'

'Talk to them.'

'What makes you think they'd listen?'

'Don't play games with me, Charles. You bloody well know you could make them listen.'

'I think I've done enough to help you already, Edward.'

Edward's voice got lower, more intense. 'Need I remind you that your name was in Herbert's little black book too? Along with a whole lot of others.'

'Yes but you've destroyed the book, haven't you?' The question was asked calmly, but there was a note of warning in it.

'Of course I have. I'm merely pointing out that this isn't only about me.'

There was a brief silence, then, 'I've got to go, Edward. I don't think we should talk again for the time being, not unless it concerns official business.'

The line went dead. Edward scowled at the phone. 'Well bloody bugger you too!'

He continued pacing, the cigarette burning down in his fingers. As he passed the fireplace, his eyes flicked towards a clock set in a mahogany case on the mantelpiece. He let out a hiss. It was only a quarter to nine! Fifteen minutes. He still had fifteen more minutes to wait before his next phone call. Time seemed to be stretching out interminably.

Catching the faint sound of an engine, Edward peered out the windows towards a tall yew hedge that had been cut into battlements. At the centre of the hedge stood wrought iron gates topped with spikes. A gold-lettered inscription on the ironwork read 'Southview Manor'. A long gravel driveway led to the imposing grey-stone house where Edward lived on the all too rare occasions when he wasn't down in London or obliged to show his face in his constituency. He'd fallen in love with Southview the moment he saw it back in the early eighties, long before Philippa came into his life. It had needed to be extensively renovated. But that hadn't concerned him – money was no object. What had concerned him was isolation and privacy. And Southview had those qualities in spades. Beyond the encircling gardens and hedges, there was a deep wooded valley to the south, drystone-walled fields to the east, and a high moorland topped with dark gritstone crags to the north-west. The nearest neighbour was a farmhouse half a mile away. He'd never spoken to its occupants. He only spoke to people like them when it was necessary. And since they weren't his voters, it wasn't necessary.

There was no sign of passing traffic in the quiet lane that ran parallel to the garden. Edward squinted skyward, thinking maybe he'd heard a plane. But there was nothing to be seen in the cloud-dotted sky either. His forehead twitched. Was it Bryan Reynolds's goons come to kill him? He dismissed the idea. Few people knew about Southview. It was his sanctuary, his refuge where he went to escape from everything, including Philippa. The same things that had first attracted him to the house, put her off living there on a full-time basis. And that suited him fine. More likely the loathsome fat man who'd returned him to his car was out there keeping tabs on him. It was in that one-eyed bastard Tyler and his goons' interest to ensure he was safe. After all, he was worth a lot of money to them.

Two million quid! The number rang out in Edward's head like a funeral bell. Even for him, that kind of money wasn't easy to come by. But come by it he must, otherwise he'd soon be joining that crazy bitch Grace Kirby in the mortuary. Of that much he *was* certain. He'd walked out of the farmhouse with the feeling that he'd come closer to his own death than ever before. All the way home he'd trembled as if he was coming down with a chill. He glanced at his hands. Even now, hours later, they were still shaky. He clenched his fingers to steady them, anger surging through him. What would his colleagues, never mind the opposition MPs, think if they saw him like this? They'd think he was coming apart at the seams, that's what. And maybe they'd be right. *Two million bloody quid!* How had things got so out of hand so quickly?

'Stephen Baxley,' Edward muttered, the name lingering on his tongue like the taste of vomit. If Stephen hadn't been so weak when it came to dealing with Grace Kirby, none of this would be happening. No, that wasn't quite fair. The blame didn't just lie with Stephen. It lay with himself, too. He should never have allowed himself to be convinced to let that little slut live. It was the one mistake he'd ever made. And now, fifteen years later, it was coming back to bite him with a vengeance.

Edward ground his knuckles against the glass. *One mistake. Two million quid.* It was a painful lesson, but as his mother used to say, he would learn it, and learn it well. The worst part wasn't even the money. Money, like the desires that had moulded him, was simply something that was there. The worst part was the phone call he would soon be making. The thought of that brought fat, glistening tears to his eyes.

He wiped them away with a harsh swipe. 'Get a grip,

man,' he scolded himself. 'Remember who you are. You're better than them. Better than all of—'

Edward fell silent at the sound of footsteps on the stairs. A woman of about fifty entered the room. Bobbed russet-brown hair framed dark eyes, a straight nose and full lips. A tailored beige business suit outlined her slim, well-proportioned body. Philippa regarded her husband with more curiosity than concern. 'Have you been up all night?'

'What are you doing dressed like that?' Edward asked, ignoring her question.

'What do you think I'm doing? I'm going to work.'

'Oh no you're not. We discussed this, Philippa. Neither of us is going to work today.'

'I've not got time for this, Edward. I've got a meeting with the Licensing Sub-Committee at ten.'

'You'll just have to rearrange it, like I've had to rearrange all my meetings.'

'And what about the speech I'm giving this afternoon at the opening of Sheaf Steel's new hydraulic press? I can't very well rearrange that, can I?'

'Oh, to hell with the sodding hydraulic press.'

'The national media's going to be there, Edward.'

'To hell with them too!'

Philippa exhaled a sigh that suggested infinite patience. 'Perhaps if you told me what this is all about...' She trailed off and took a step closer to her husband, eyes narrowing. 'Have you been crying?'

Edward's eyes filled with indignation. 'Of course I bloody well haven't.'

'Yes, you have. I can see it.' Philippa indicated the phone. 'Who have you been talking to?'

'No one. I was about to make a call.'

'To who?'

Edward hesitated. Only for a second, but it was enough to suggest some reluctance to answer his wife's question. 'My mother.'

Philippa shook her head. 'I should have guessed this had something to do with her.' The word 'her' was spoken with a disdain approaching hatred.

'This isn't her fault, it's mine. The fact is, I made a bad judgement. I invested a lot of money in someone and they let me down.'

'What someone?'

'Stephen Baxley.' Edward didn't like to admit to a connection with the disgraced dead businessman. But if politics had taught him anything, it was to sprinkle his lies with just enough grains of truth to make them believable. He knew, too, that the lie needed to be as alarming as it was credible if he wanted Philippa to swallow it.

Her perfectly plucked eyebrows bunched together. 'How much have you lost?'

'A couple of million.'

'Two million! Christ, Edward. How could you have kept this from me?'

He spread his hands in a kind of helpless gesture. 'I didn't want to worry you. I had everything under control, but then Stephen went and... and did what he did. If the press get a sniff of this, my political career will be all but over.'

'Then don't give the buggers a reason to start sniffing around by hiding away.' Philippa took her husband's hands between hers, her voice earnest and firm. 'Get out there and carry on as if everything's fine.'

'I would do if it was just the press I was worried about. But as we both know there are a lot of people who'd like to see me fall from grace. Jealous, vindictive people. Old Labour buffoons, socialist and communist sympathisers who pretend to believe the love of money is the root of all evil, but who turn out to be the greediest bastards of all as soon as they get a taste—' Edward stopped as his wife pulled a face that suggested she'd heard the same rant many times before. 'The point I'm making is, there are people who would gladly hurt you to hurt me. That's why I need you here with me until I've put my finances in order.'

'You mean until your mother has put your finances in order.'

A ripple disturbed Edward's face, like the surface of a pond breaking. 'All I'm asking you for is two or three days.'

'And what am I supposed to tell everyone in the meantime?'

'I don't know. Tell them we've both come down with the flu or something.'

'I don't like lying, Edward.'

'I know.' Philippa's reputation for honesty and integrity was one of the things that had first attracted – if attracted was the right word – Edward to her. It gave an added sheen to his own reputation as a plain-speaking Yorkshireman. But he would never have married her if he hadn't detected a certain flexibility beneath her seemingly unbending attitude. He was good at sensing things like that, things that appealed to his self-interest. 'I also know how good you are at it when the need arises.'

Philippa sighed deeply again, this time in defeat. 'I tell you what, Edward. I'll take the rest of the week off. But I'm going to have to make that speech.'

Edward thought over his wife's words momentarily, then said, 'OK, but you don't leave this house until an hour before the opening. And when you're done there, you make your excuses and come straight home. Agreed?'

'Agreed, just so long as you get on that phone right now and call your mother.'

'I will do,' Edward glanced at the clock, 'in five minutes. You know how much she hates being disturbed before nine these days.'

Sucking her teeth with irritation, her footsteps heavier than before, Philippa headed back upstairs to change out of her work clothes.

'Love you, darling,' Edward called after her.

'Do you?' she shot back. 'Sometimes I wonder.'

Edward wondered, too, as he had done many times over the course of their eighteen-year marriage. Did he really love his wife? If love meant needing someone, then yes, he loved her. If it meant wanting to hold and be held by them through the darkness of the night, then no, he didn't love her. There was only one person in his life he'd ever felt like that about. His gaze dropped to the phone. He stared at it a long moment, before hesitantly dialling.

After a single ring, almost as if his call had been expected, his mother picked up. 'Who is this?' Mabel Forester's voice was a touch hoarse, but strident as ever.

'It's me.'

'Who's me?'

A prickle that was part irritation, part anxiety travelled down Edward's arms. His mother knew exactly who 'me' was. The caller display would have told her that before she even answered the phone. She was just playing funny buggers, the same as she always did when he'd done something to incur her displeasure. 'It's Edward.'

'I didn't recognise your voice. It's been that long since I last heard it.'

'It's only been three weeks.'

'More like four. And at my age a month's a lifetime.'

'Oh, Mother, don't be so dramatic. You're as healthy as a horse and will probably outlive the lot of us.'

'That's where you're bloody well wrong, Edward.' As always when she was angry, a Yorkshire twang peeked out of Mabel's self-consciously well-spoken accent. 'I've been on antibiotics for the past fortnight.'

'What for?'

'I've had a chest infection.'

'When you say "had", does that mean you're better now?' For once, the concern in Edward's voice was genuine to the point of fear. All through his childhood and for most of his adult life, his mother had worked twelve or fifteen hours a day, seven days a week, relentlessly building her cake-making enterprise into the multimillion-pound business it was today. In recent years, she'd cut herself some slack. But at seventy-eight, she still put in more hours than most of the executives she'd employed to take over her workload. He couldn't remember the last time she'd taken a day off for illness. He'd always thought she would go on forever. The sudden realisation that she wouldn't, that one day she would die, brought with it a clutching sense of panic, and something else too, something he wasn't yet ready to acknowledge.

'What do you care if I'm better?' Mabel retorted. 'If you cared you'd call.'

'I've been meaning to, but I've just been so busy.'

A tremor of hurt shook Mabel's voice. 'How long does it take to pick up the phone and say "Hello, Mummy. How are you?" One or two minutes, that's all. Am I not worth even worth one or two minutes of your precious time?'

'Of course you—'

'To think of everything I've done for you,' Mabel continued as if she hadn't heard her son, 'of everything I've sacrificed, and this is the way you treat me. It almost makes me wish I hadn't got better.'

'Please don't say that.' Edward's voice was trembling too now.

'Why not? Sometimes I think it would be easier for both of us if I just died.'

'No, Mummy, you can't die.' Edward screwed his face up like a child, tears suddenly spilling down his cheeks. 'I'm sorry I didn't call. It won't happen again.'

'Do you promise?'

'Yes, I promise. Just don't leave me alone, please don't leave me—' Edward choked off into deep, wrenching sobs.

'Shh. Hush, my darling.' Mabel's tone was suddenly gentle and reassuring. 'Mummy's always here for her little man. You know that, don't you?'

Edward mumbled through his tears, 'Yes, Mummy, I know.'

'Good boy. Now take a deep breath, dry your eyes and tell Mummy all about it.'

How do you know I've got anything to tell you? Edward knew better than to ask the question. If there was one thing his mother despised above anything else, it was people trying to play her for a fool. Early in her career, many of her competitors – mostly men – had made the mistake of underestimating her. As she took great pleasure in pointing out, all of them had long since gone – or, more accurately, been driven – out of business. Edward never usually rang her at this time of day. She knew well enough that he wasn't phoning simply to say hello. He managed to bring his tears under control sufficiently to speak clearly. 'I'm in serious trouble. I've lost some money. A lot of money.'

'How much?' There was no surprise in Mabel's voice. When her son told her the amount, the line was ominously silent a moment. Then she asked, 'So who do you need me to buy off this time?'

'It's not like that. I made a bad investment.'

Edward started to feed his mother the same lie he'd fed Philippa, but she cut him off with a humourless, biting laugh. 'Who am I, Edward?'

He ran his tongue across his quivering bottom lip. 'You're Mummy.'

'And what does Mummy know?'

'Everything. Mummy knows everything.'

'That's right. Now start again from the beginning, and this time tell me the truth.'

'I... I can't. Not on the phone.'

'Then I'll just have to come up there.'

'No! It's not safe for you to come here.'

'All the more reason for me to do so. If you're in some kind of danger, Edward, my place is there with you.'

'Please—'

'No more arguments. I've got one or two work things to take care of, but I should be with you by this evening. And for God's sake, pull yourself together, Edward. No more crying. Remember who you are. You're better than them. They have no right to judge you.'

'Yes, Mummy. Sorry. Thank you, Mummy.'

The line went dead. Edward glanced at the mahogany clock, a familiar mixture of dread and delight vying with each other in his heart as he calculated the hours until his mother's arrival. Sniffing back his tears, he flung the phone onto a sofa and strode from the room. With the wolfhound padding after him, he climbed two flights of stairs to a cavernous attic, cluttered with boxes and antique furniture. At the rear of the attic, sunlight slanted through a round window, illuminating a galaxy of dust particles. He took a nail out of a chest of drawers by the window. Dropping to his haunches, he pushed it into a hole in a floorboard. He pulled the floorboard loose, reached into the cavity beneath and withdrew a little black book. He flicked through it until he found the page he was looking for. It was discoloured by a brownish-red stain, but not sufficiently to obscure the writing thereon. The dog peered over his shoulder, sniffing at the book.

'Smells good, doesn't it, Conall? There's no other smell quite like it.' Edward ran his finger down the page. 'You see those names? They think they're safe. But if I go down, I'm taking them with me. Every last fucking one of them.'

Chapter Eleven

Reece sat in his car, staring at the semi-detached house he'd grown up in. It was looking a little the worse for wear these days – the garden was overgrown; the window frames needed a new coat of paint; bricks showed through in places where the pebbledash cladding had flaked off. Sighing deeply, he got out of the car and approached the front door. He tried the handle. The door wasn't locked. As he stepped into the hallway, a musty smell of old cigarette smoke, fried food and body odour assaulted his nostrils. Unopened mail was strewn on the doormat. Through an open door at the end of the hallway, a pile of pots was visible in the kitchen sink. Since finding out about his illness, his dad had all but given up on household chores. It wasn't that he didn't have the energy for them, he'd simply ceased to care about the upkeep of the house. Not that he'd ever had much interest in it. That had been his wife's domain.

'Dad,' called Reece, gathering up the mail and making his way to a living room that showed signs of a woman's touch in its matching floral wallpaper, carpet and three-piece suite – signs that were being steadily blotted out by food, drink and cigarette stains. The room was stiflingly warm. Heat pumped from a gas fire. The dusty mantelpiece above it was cluttered with photos, some of them in frames, others merely propped against the wall, all of the same woman. She was well-built, verging on stocky, with the same good-looking angular features, moody brown eyes and dark hair as Reece. There were more photos of her balanced on top of a television. As always, it struck Reece as ironic that his dad surrounded himself with pictures of his late wife, considering that he seemingly couldn't stand the sight of her when she was alive.

Pale sunlight slanted through half-drawn curtains onto a figure slumped in an armchair near the window. Frank Geary's chin rested against his chest. A string of saliva stretched from his lips to the slight bulge of his belly. His nostrils trembled as he snored. The low morning sun picked out every wrinkle, crease and broken vein in his unshaven face, making him look even older than usual. His pyjamas hung loosely on his frame, which although still big, was rapidly being consumed by the malignant tumours in his lungs. A mug rested in his lap, tilted halfway over so that some of its contents had spilled out.

Reece picked up the mug and sniffed the dregs of milky tea. They gave off a strong tang of whisky. 'For Christ's sake, Dad.'

Frank stirred, opening one bloodshot eye. 'What are you doing here?' he growled in a voice sanded down by a lifetime of heavy smoking.

'Have you forgotten you're going for chemo today?'

'Course I haven't bloody forgotten. I wish I could forget it.'

'Then why aren't you dressed?' Reece tapped his watch. 'We're supposed to be at the hospital by ten.'

'What are you talking about? My chemo doesn't start until one.'

'Yes, but remember Doctor Meadows wants to run some tests beforehand.'

'Tests,' Frank snorted. 'I'm sick of tests. What's the point of them?'

'Doctor Meadows wants to find out how you're—'

'I know what the bastard wants to find out,' Frank interrupted, his voice rising. 'I just don't see why he needs to do more tests to tell him what's bleeding obvious. I mean, look at me. Just about the only thing I'm not losing is my hair.'

'Come on, Dad. You've just got time for a quick shower and shave.'

Reece stooped to help his dad to his feet. Frank slapped his hand away. 'I don't need your help. Not yet.' Arms trembling, he pushed himself upright.

'I'll make you some breakfast,' said Reece.

'Don't bother. You know I can't keep anything down after chemo.'

'Even so, you should eat something.'

While his dad was showering, Reece made tea and toast and took it up to him. Frank emerged from the bathroom, shaved and smelling of the same strong aftershave he'd been using for as long as Reece could remember. Hot water and razor burn had brought some colour into his face. Scowling, he lashed out, knocking the plate from his son's hand. 'I told you I don't want any fucking breakfast! Christ, you're just like your mother. You never bloody listen.' He pushed past Reece into a bedroom, slamming the door behind himself.

Sighing, Reece retrieved the plate and returned to the kitchen. The sound of coughing came from upstairs. It continued for a minute or two, rising to a hacking, choking pitch, then subsided. A moment later, Frank slowly descended the stairs. He waited by the front door, breath grating in his throat, lips compressed into a pained line. Knowing that any show of concern would only draw more of his dad's anger, Reece headed outside to the car.

Neither man spoke as they threaded their way through the dregs of rush-hour traffic. Oppressed by the silence, Reece turned on the radio. The news was on, and as always over the past few days, the newsreader was talking about the spate of murders that had rocked the city. 'Police are still searching for the man who shot and killed Detective Inspector Amy Sheridan,' the newsreader announced. 'He's described as thirty to forty years old, five feet eleven to six feet two, well-built, with dark brown eyes and hair. He was last seen wearing a black bomber jacket, and is thought to be driving a black Range Rover. He's also known to have suffered a serious injury to his left eye. He's armed and extremely dangerous. If you see the suspect, under no circumstances approach him. Call the police on the number provided at the end of this piece. Meanwhile, police have confirmed that the gun used in the killings of well-known local accountant Herbert Winstanley and his wife Marisa at their Grenoside house, was also used to shoot dead the prominent psychiatrist Doctor Henry Reeve. Speculation continues as to whether known prostitute, Grace Kirby, was responsible for all three deaths, and if so what motivated her to commit such brutal—'

The newsreader was silenced by Frank switching to another channel. 'I'm so sick and tired of hearing about these murders.'

'What do you make of it all?'

'I'm buggered if I know or give a shit. Anyway, what you asking me for? You're the copper, not me.'

'I thought it was once a cop always a cop.'

Frank barked out a hoarse laugh. 'Who told you that?'

'Doug Brody.'

'Yeah, well, Doug's always had a talent for talking out of his arse.' Frank pressed his hand to his mouth as another spasm of coughing racked him. When he drew it away, an oyster of blood-speckled phlegm glistened in his palm. Quickly wiping it on a handkerchief, he said croakily, 'You want to know what I really think? Scumbags will always be killing each other. And so what if they do? Why should we care?'

'What are you saying? That we should just sit back and let them wipe each other out?'

'Why not? What's a few less perverts and whores in this world?'

Reece shot his dad a sidelong glance. Had he detected

a slight stress on the word 'whore'? Had his dad been talking to Doug about Staci? He'd obviously been talking to someone working the Grace Kirby case as he knew it involved sexual perversion – a detail which had so far been kept from the media. 'And what if these scumbags start hurting innocent people?'

'That's when we should crack down on the bastards with everything we've got. And I don't just mean throw them in jail.' Frank clenched his fist, displaying white lines of scars on his knuckles. 'I mean we should hurt them like they hurt us. Fear, that's the only thing their world respects. Remember that.'

The muscles in Reece's jaw stood out as his teeth clenched. He didn't need to be told to remember that. He still had the scars to remind him of how his dad had applied that philosophy not just to criminals, but to everyone in his life.

The boxy, grey outline of Weston Park Hospital loomed into view. Reece parked up and started to get out of the car. 'You don't need to come in with me,' said Frank.

'Are you sure?'

'There you go again. Just like your mother. Course I'm bloody sure. I wouldn't have said so if I wasn't.'

Look, I'm just trying to do my best here. The words flashed through Reece's brain, but he knew saying them would be a waste of breath. When the diagnosis had first been made, the oncologist had warned Reece that his father might undergo some personality changes during his course of treatment. *Some people accept their illness*, he'd said.

Others become angry and resentful. Reece hadn't been able to detect any such changes. But then his dad had always been an angry bastard. 'Call me when it's over and I'll come pick you up.'

Frank hauled himself out of the car. As Reece watched him head into the hospital, he thought, *I hope you're right. I hope I am more like Mum.*

Reece pulled out his iPhone, navigated to the BT phone book and searched for 'Tisdale, Sheffield'. There was no H. Tisdale listed. He scrolled through his contacts until he found the number of Alan Dobson, a crime reporter at the South Yorkshire *Chronicle*. He'd already spent a fruitless hour earlier in the day on the phone to various morgues and hospitals, trying to find out if anyone fitting Melinda's description had been brought in. Now it was time to try a different tack. When Alan picked up, Reece said, 'Hi, Alan, this is Reece Geary. I was wondering if you could help me out. I'm trying to track down Vernon Tisdale.'

'Old Vernon. He retired some seven or eight years ago. Health issues.'

'Have you got an address for him?'

'Can I ask what this is in regards to?'

'I'm afraid I can't go into that.'

'Oh come on, Reece, you can give me a hint. You know, you scratch my back and I'll scratch yours sort of thing.' When Reece made no reply, the journalist added, 'Tell you what, I'll ask a question or two and you just give me yes or no answers. Has this got anything to do with the recent murders?'

'No.'

'Are you certain of that?'

Reece hesitated again. It would have been simpler to get Tisdale's details from the PNC Vehicle File database, but he was reluctant to do anything that might draw the attention of his superiors. The last thing he wanted was to have to come up with some bullshit to explain to DCI Garrett how he knew Staci and why she'd come to him with the information about her missing friend. He wondered, not for the first time, whether there could possibly be any connection to the events surrounding Grace Kirby. The only connection he could see – and it was a tenuous one at that, considering Grace had never been arrested for streetwalking in Sheffield – was that both cases involved prostitutes. Of course, that didn't mean there weren't other as yet unseen connections. 'Yes, I'm certain. And no more questions.'

'Fair enough. Give me a minute and I'll dig out Vernon's details for you.'

The line was silent a moment, then Alan came back on it and gave Reece a landline number and an address in Crookes, only five or so minutes' drive away. 'Have you got a mobile number for him?' asked Reece.

Alan chuckled as if he'd heard something funny. 'Vernon was a real old-school kind of journalist. He thought mobiles were the devil's work.'

Reece thanked him, hung up and accelerated out of the car park.

Vernon Tisdale's house was halfway along a street of

terraced houses. Like Reece's father's house, it showed signs of neglect: rotting window frames; a green streak of damp down the wall where the guttering was leaking. Reece knocked on the front door. Half a minute passed. No answer. He tried again. Still no response. He was about to head back to his car when the door opened just wide enough for a face to peer out. The face was as fat and round as a full moon. A scruffy greying beard fringed its purplish lips. Jaundiced-looking eyes stared uninterestedly at Reece from above cheeks that wheezed in and out as if their owner had been exerting himself.

'Vernon Tisdale?'

'Who wants to know?'

Reece explained who he was, adding, 'I'm making inquiries into a missing prostitute that may, or may not, be connected to other similar disappearances in this area. I'm told you're the man to speak to about such things.'

'Is this an official investigation?'

'No. I'm making inquiries on behalf of...' hesitation touched Reece's voice, 'a friend.'

A flicker of interest disturbed the man's expression. 'In that case, I'm Vernon and you'd better come in.'

Vernon dragged the door halfway open before it seemed to jam against something. He was wearing grubby grey tracksuit bottoms and an equally grubby Hawaiian shirt. His stomach, which bulged like a sack of grain over his waistband, brushed against the wall as he turned away from Reece. As Reece entered the house, he saw what was preventing the door from fully opening. Piles of tattered yellowing newspapers and magazines were stacked floor-to-ceiling all along one side of the hallway, leaving barely enough room for Vernon to squeeze past. No wonder it had taken him so long to answer the door, reflected Reece. The air smelt bad, only it wasn't simply stale like at his dad's house, it was rotten enough to almost knock you over.

Reece followed Vernon into what might once have been a dining room. There was a table against the outside wall, almost buried by the newspapers and cardboard boxes piled on and around it. Many of the boxes had a date scrawled on them, although they didn't appear to be arranged in any particular order. The earliest date Reece picked out at a glance was 1980. A cat as fat and scruffy as its owner lay curled up on a battered leather armchair. Opposite the chair was a sofa with an old television close enough to it to switch channels without a remote. Vernon shooed the cat away and motioned for Reece to sit. As he did so, a faint scrabbling sound from somewhere amongst the clutter drew his attention.

'I've got mice,' explained Vernon. 'They're incontinent, you know. Never stop pissing and shitting.' He jerked his thumb at the cat. 'That's why I got her. Not that the lazy bugger's much cop at catching them. You want a cup of tea?'

'No thanks.' Reece wasn't normally squeamish, but he couldn't have swallowed a mouthful in that house of mouldering, mice-eaten newspapers.

'What about something stronger?' Vernon retrieved a bottle of Scotch from the carpet.

'I'm driving.'

'That never seemed to bother most of the coppers I used to know.' Vernon poured a generous measure of whisky into a chipped mug. With a grunt, he lowered his bulky frame onto the sofa. 'So tell me about this missing prostitute.'

'I don't know for sure that she's actually missing. She may just have left town.'

Vernon raised an eyebrow. 'Do you know how many prostitutes have *just left* this city never to be heard of again over the last thirty or so years?'

'No.'

'Neither do I. Not exactly. But I'm willing to bet it's a lot more than have *just left* most other comparably sized cities in this country, if you get my meaning.'

As Reece filled Vernon in on the details of Melinda's disappearance, the ex-journalist scribbled down some brief notes. 'Have you got a photo of her?' asked Vernon.

Reece showed him the photo of Melinda drinking in a bar. Vernon nodded as if he'd seen something familiar. 'She's certainly his type.'

'Whose type?'

'Freddie Harding. He likes them young and skinny.'

Lines of surprise creased Reece's forehead. 'Are you saying you know who the perp is?'

'Let me show you something, Detective Inspector.' Vernon heaved himself to his feet and waddled towards the wall of cardboard boxes. He rifled through several of them, before finding what he wanted. He unfolded a map of Yorkshire and laid it on the sofa. It was dotted with red marker. Most of the dots were concentrated around Sheffield, Barnsley and Doncaster. A triangle had been drawn in black marker linking the three built-up areas. Roughly at the centre of the triangle there was a black dot. 'Back in 1998 I drew up a list of prostitutes I believed to have been abducted and murdered between 1980 and that year. When I mapped out their disappearances, I found there was an unusual concentration in three areas. Seven in Barnsley, nine in Doncaster, and thirteen in Sheffield.'

'How many of those are still classified as missing?'

'All of them. I mapped this out in 2001, after your pals had scratched off several of the names on my list. And this only represents disappearances up until that time. More girls have gone missing since then.'

'How many more?'

Vernon shrugged. 'Who knows? Who even cares? You're the first person I've spoken to about this stuff in years.'

Reece pointed at the black dot. 'What's that?'

Vernon traced the outline of the triangle with a chubby finger. 'As you can see, the map of disappearances forms a triangle. I believed the killer might live within this triangle.' He poked his finger at the black dot. 'That's Mexborough, where Freddie Harding lived back in 2001.'

'So who's Freddie Harding?'

Vernon returned to the boxes and dug out a cardboard folder. He withdrew a mugshot-style photo of a man's face and handed it to Reece. 'That's Freddie.' The man was somewhere in his late thirties or early forties. He had thinning brown hair, sideburns, small brown eyes and a small mouth with a receding jaw. A thick scar drew a diagonal furrow across his face from left to right. There was something weasel-like about his long, thin face and shifty little eyes. 'I took that photo in 2001 after he was arrested.'

'What was he arrested for?'

'In March of that year, he beat and raped a prostitute on wasteland off Pitsmoor Road. During the attack, he boasted that he'd done the same thing to other girls. Luckily for her, a passer-by heard her screams and ran to help her. Freddie got away, but turned himself in four days later. At the trial he admitted to fantasising about kidnapping and raping prostitutes, but claimed the assault had been the one and only time he'd crossed the line into real life. He was sentenced to nine years, but received a three-year discount for an early guilty plea. He had another two years knocked off for good behaviour and was paroled in 2005.'

No surprise showed in Reece's eyes, only a kind of knowing fatalism. 'What makes you think Freddie wasn't telling the truth about the assault?'

'One of the prostitutes on my list was last seen getting into a white van. At the time of Freddie's arrest he drove a white van.'

'Lots of people drive white vans.'

'Still, it's a pretty big coincidence, don't you think?'

Reece nodded. 'But you need a lot more than coincidence to convict someone. You need witnesses and forensic evidence. And I'm assuming none of those things were forthcoming.'

Vernon gave a dismissive grunt. 'Let me tell you a bit more about Freddie Harding. And when I'm done, maybe you'll realise just how dangerous he is. Shortly after Freddie was born, his father abandoned his wife and son. Freddie's mother turned to drugs and prostitution. And Freddie ended up in and out of children's homes throughout his childhood. I've seen his records from his time in care. He's described as a quiet child, prone to violent outbursts and acts of petty revenge. He was also a compulsive liar. The only thing he was consistent about was his feelings for his mother, Brenda. He hated her with a passion that grew stronger each time he was taken into care.'

Reece's eyebrows drew together as his thoughts turned to Staci and her daughter Amelia. Did Amelia harbour similar feelings? And if not, how long would it be before her love curdled into hate? Vernon's voice dragged him back into the moment.

'At sixteen, Freddie got a council flat and a job as a brickie. A couple of years later he married Emma Shaw, a girl he'd gone to school with. The marriage only lasted a couple of years before Emma filed for divorce. I tracked her down and asked her why she'd left him. She told me he was a pervert who got his kicks out of slapping her around in the bedroom. Here's where it gets really interesting. While in prison, Freddie went to a psychiatrist for help. He told the psychiatrist that when his wife left him it brought back all the feelings of betrayal and abandonment he associated with his childhood. That's when he says he started to have fantasies about killing his mother. The only problem was she'd died of AIDs several years earlier. So he transferred his fantasies on to all women in her line of business.'

Vernon withdrew a sheet of paper from the folder and handed it to Reece. On the page was a photocopy of some handwritten notes. Fragments of sentences had been highlighted with fluorescent marker. Fragments such as 'diagnosis of antisocial sociopathic personality disorder', 'poses a significant danger to women', 'struggles to control impulses' and 'displays symptoms of sexual psychopathy'. 'That's a sample of the psychiatrist's notes,' said Vernon. 'Don't ask me how I got hold of them. There are pages and pages more. They describe how Freddie can only get real pleasure from hurting and humiliating women. And how his ultimate fantasy is to kill prostitutes and film himself having sex with their corpses.'

Reece held up a hand to signal that he'd heard enough. 'I get the picture. This guy's one sick puppy, and he's certainly not lacking for motive. The question is, has he got it in him to follow through on his fantasies?'

'He beat an eighteen-year-old girl half to death,' said Vernon, with an incredulous twitch of his unhealthily purple lips.

'Yes, but would he have killed her if he hadn't been scared off?'

'I guess we'll never know for sure. I'll tell you something I do know. In the first three years of Freddie Harding's imprisonment, reported disappearances of prostitutes in this area dropped significantly.'

'How significantly?'

'Enough for your people to take a long hard look at Freddie and see if they could connect him to the girls on my list.'

'Obviously they couldn't.'

'Not true. Freddie was a well-known kerb-crawler. He'd been arrested numerous times over the years. He was also a regular of several workmates of the missing girls. But none of them reported that he'd ever been violent against them. What's more, he was never seen to pick up any of the missing girls.'

'Except possibly the one who was seen getting into the white van.'

'Yes, but as you pointed out white vans aren't exactly uncommon.'

Reece's eyebrows knitted in thought. 'So what was Freddie's game? If his MO is violence against prostitutes, why did so many of them come away from him unhurt? Was he simply working himself up to the attack?'

'I think there's more to it than that. Here, take a look at these.' Vernon dug out two more photos and passed them to Reece. One was a grainy mugshot of a peroxide blonde woman in her late twenties or early thirties. She had a thin, hard-bitten face and glazed, drugged-looking brown eyes. The other was of teenage girl with dyed blond hair showing black at the roots, large brown eyes and hollow cheeks. Vernon pointed first at the older woman, then at the girl. 'That's Brenda Harding and that's Ellen Peterson, the girl Freddie raped. They could be mother and daughter, don't you think?'

'Almost.'

'I think when Freddie saw Ellen he lost control and just had to have his way with her right there and then.'

'So the Pitsmoor attack was opportunistic.'

Vernon nodded. 'And that was Freddie's downfall. When Ellen survived, he realised the game was up. So he spent a few days erasing any physical evidence connecting him to the missing girls, before handing himself in and pleading guilty in return for a reduced sentence.'

Reece's gaze returned to the photo of Freddie Harding. 'Let me get this straight, you're suggesting this guy used to drive around red-light districts posing as a customer so he could scout out his victims.'

'Exactly.'

'But why pick up other prostitutes and risk coming onto the police radar?'

'Sometimes the best place to hide is in plain view.'

Reece looked at Vernon doubtfully. 'Someone would have to be either very stupid or very clever to try that.'

'Oh, take it from me, Freddie's very clever. Not that you'd know it when you first meet him. In fact, he can come across as a little slow. But underneath there's a kind of cunning intelligence.' Vernon gestured towards his boxes. 'Like my mice. You know what the little buggers are up to, but it's almost impossible to catch them at it.'

'So what happened after Freddie's release, did disappearances rise again?'

Vernon shrugged. 'In 2004 I had a heart attack – well, several heart attacks actually. I ended up having a triple bypass. In 2006 I retired. That was me off the story.' He gave Reece an intent look. 'So, DI Geary—'

'Call me Reece.'

'So, Reece, have I convinced you that Freddie's someone you should be looking at?'

'He's clearly a very dangerous individual. Still, it's a stretch to see how he could have murdered twenty-nine prostitutes over a period of thirty plus years and avoided discovery.'

'At least twenty-nine, and that's just from 1980 to 2001,' corrected Vernon.

'So where's he taking them? That's a hell of a lot of bodies to get rid of.'

'There's only one way to find out.' Vernon took a scrap of paper out of his shirt's breast pocket and handed it to Reece. There was an address in Wath upon Dearne written on it. 'That's where Freddie's living now.'

'I thought you said you'd been off the story since 2006.'

'That doesn't mean I haven't kept tabs on where Freddie's at. I've often thought about staking him out, seeing where he leads me, but... well, as you can see, I'm just not up to it.' Vernon turned back to the boxes, fished out another folder and handed it to Reece. 'If you still need more convincing, you should have a read through these.'

Reece read aloud what was written on the folder. 'The Damned.'

'That's what I call them, because that's what they are,' Vernon said, matter-of-factly.

The folder contained a wad of typewritten pages, each

with a photo of a young woman stapled to its upper right corner.

'You can have that and Freddie's file. I've got plenty more copies,' continued Vernon. 'Well, I think I've told you just about everything. So unless I can change your mind about having a drink...'

Taking the hint, Reece tucked the folders under his arm and stood to leave. 'Thanks for your help, Vernon.' He paused by the front door to hand the ex-journalist a card with his name and telephone number. 'If you think of anything else, give me a call.'

'Will do. Oh, by the way, you never told me the name of the prostitute who came to you for help.'

'I didn't say it was a prostitute, and I'd rather not mention their name.'

A sly smile played on Vernon's lips. 'Sorry, I was just digging for information. I was a journalist for forty-odd years. Old habits die hard. You do right to keep your friend's name to yourself.' He pointed at the folders. 'You'd do right to be careful about who you show those to as well. The powers that be buried those names a long time ago. They won't thank you for resurrecting them, not unless you can come up with some hard evidence.'

And what are the chances of that, wondered Reece, *if a full investigation failed to implicate Freddie Harding in the prostitutes' disappearances?*

'You never know, you might get lucky,' said Vernon as if reading Reece's mind. 'As far as I'm aware, Freddie's managed to stay off the police radar since his release. If he thinks no one's interested in him, he might have let his guard down.'

'Or maybe he's a reformed man.'

Vernon wheezed out a doubtful laugh. 'Freddie Harding, a reformed man. Somehow I don't think so. Like I said, old habits die hard.'

Reece turned to leave, but hesitated, his expression growing somewhat sheepish. 'One more thing, would you mind not telling anyone about my coming here?'

Vernon laughed again. 'Who would I tell?'

As Reece returned to his car, he drew in a deep breath of fresh air. He'd come away from the newspaper-swamped house with a lot more than he'd expected, perhaps more than he could handle. Going it alone, there was only one likely way he could come up with anything new on Freddie Harding – staking him out, tailing him everywhere he went. But that could take weeks, months, even years. Time he didn't have, what with the demands of his dad's illness, Doug Brody, and his job. He sighed. It would almost have been preferable if his inquiries had hit a dead end. That way he could have at least told Staci he'd tried. As it was, instead of focusing on working towards their new life, all his spare energy would be sucked into what would almost certainly turn out to be a futile undertaking. And what if he did turn something up? What then? How the hell would he explain his unofficial investigation to DCI Garret?

Reece cut his thoughts off sharply. His gaze dropped to the folder of 'The Damned'. There were twenty-nine names in there. Thirty if you added Melinda to the list. If

Vernon was right, they'd died terrible deaths at the hands of a depraved killer. Surely they deserved a few days of his time. Otherwise how could he dare call himself a copper or, for that matter, a man fit to take care of a woman and her child?

He brought up DCI Garrett's number on his phone and hit dial. Garrett picked up and said, 'DI Geary. How's your dad doing?'

'Actually, sir, that's what I'm phoning about. He's not doing too well. Sorry, I realise this is a bad time, but I need the rest of the week off.'

The DCI's voice took on an unfamiliar sympathetic tone. 'No need to apologise, Reece. Your dad has to come first. I understand that. You take as long as you need. And give your dad my best wishes.'

'I will. Thank you, sir.'

Reece hung up. Once more, a sense of futility rose in him. *Take as long as you need*, the DCI had said. But how long did he need? Vernon had spent years trying to nail Freddie Harding. How, in a matter of days, was he supposed to succeed where the ex-journalist had failed? Vernon's words came back to him. *You never know, you might get lucky.* Sometimes luck was enough. But a cop who depended on it didn't deserve to be in the job. He shook himself free of his thoughts. It had been a while now since he'd felt like he deserved to be in the job. He ducked into his car and plotted Freddie's address into the satnav.

Chapter Twelve

When Jim returned from his echocardiogram, he found Margaret waiting in his room. She was dressed for work in a black trouser suit. Traces of tiredness showed through her makeup. He felt a mingling of happiness and sadness at the sight of her. He wanted her to be there. And more than anything, he wanted her to want him. But he knew that even if she did, he couldn't allow himself to give in to that want. Margaret smiled. 'It's good to see you on your feet.'

Jim resisted the urge to smile back. He kept his voice carefully emotionless. 'Shouldn't you be at work?'

'I'm on my way there. I just thought I'd stop by and see how you're going on.'

'Well, I'm feeling much better.' Jim approached his bed, avoiding Margaret's gaze.

'I've brought you something.' Margaret placed a Tupperware container on the bedside table. 'It's steamed salmon, rice and vegetables. I know it's not what you like to eat, but you're going to have to get used to that kind of food from now on.'

'I'll bet you told Ian it was for your lunch, didn't you?'

A slight frown formed on Margaret's forehead. 'I can't

stay long. I've got some free time this afternoon. I could come back then, if you like.'

'I'm seeing Doctor Advani after lunch.'

'Yes, but that won't take all afternoon, will it?'

'I don't know.' Jim's voice was brusque. 'You'd have to ask her.'

A moment of silence passed. Then Margaret spoke, and the hurt in her voice hurt Jim. 'I'm a little confused, Jim. I thought you wanted me to come see you.'

'I do.' The words were out before Jim could remind himself of all the reasons he shouldn't say them. He looked at Margaret. Any remaining pretence of being emotionless was stripped away, as he'd known it would be, by the sight of her gentle face. 'It's just that there are things going on...' He tailed off.

'You mean the things you mentioned on the phone?'

'Yes.'

Margaret's hurt turned to concern. 'Are you in some kind of trouble?'

'I really can't talk about it.' Guilt flickered in Jim's eyes. 'I'm sorry, Margaret. I know I shut you out during our marriage. And I know I'm doing the same thing now. Believe me, I don't want to, but—' He fell silent again. He'd already said more than he meant to. If Margaret went to John Garrett with her concerns, he could find himself having to answer all sorts of awkward questions.

Margaret smiled thinly. 'At least you're acknowledging that you shut me out. I suppose that's something.' She stood up. 'I'm glad you're feeling a little better. If you ever want to talk, you know where I am. Bye, Jim.'

Jim watched her leave, clenching his teeth to stop himself from calling her back. He knew that if he did, it would all come spilling out, the whole incriminating truth. His gaze fell to the Tupperware container. He placed a hand on its warm lid, telling himself it had to be this way, hating himself for not having swallowed his pride and pleaded with Margaret to come back to him years ago, before things had gone beyond the point of no return. He turned his attention to the television. There was still nothing on the news channels about Edward Forester. An uneasy frown creased his features, but he resisted the impulse to reach for the phone and try to find out what was going on. *Give it a couple more hours*, he told himself. He rested back against the pillows, letting out a long breath. He tried to focus on what needed to be done, but his mind kept drifting back to Margaret, her hair, her eyes. He found himself fantasising about being with her in some sunny place. It didn't matter exactly where, just so long as it was far away from his job.

At midday, Jim was woken from a sleep he hadn't realised he'd fallen into by a nurse with his medication. As he swallowed the tablets, he scanned through the news channels. Still nothing. That decided him. He picked up the phone, dialled Directory Enquiries and asked for the number of the Sheffield constituency office of Edward Forester. When the operator came back with it, Jim asked to be connected. He knew that if Forester was dead there was a good chance the police would be monitoring his office telephone. In which case, the call would quickly be traced back to him. But he figured that didn't matter. After all, if Forester was dead the truth would have to come out anyway. A woman picked up and said, 'This is the office of Edward Forester, Labour MP for Sheffield South-East, how can I help you?' The woman sounded calm and businesslike. There was nothing in her voice to suggest anything was amiss.

'Can I speak to Mr Forester please?'

'Mr Forester isn't here. I'm his PA. Can I help you?'

'I was told he was going to be in the office today.'

'I'm sorry about that, but he's suffering from the flu. If you'd like to leave your name and contact number, I'd be glad to pass them on to him.'

'That's OK. It's not an urgent matter. I'll phone again in a few days' time.'

Jim called Directory Enquiries again and asked to be put through to the Town Hall office of Councillor Philippa Horne. This time a man answered. Jim asked him the same question and was told that Philippa wasn't working in the office today. Jim hung up, his forehead lined with thought. He'd detected no hint of a lie in either the woman or the man's voice. But that didn't mean much. Both of them could have been coppers. If they were, he'd soon know about it when their colleagues turned up at the hospital wanting to talk to him. And if they weren't, well, Bryan Reynolds had either backed out of or failed in his attempt to kill Edward

Forester. Whichever the case, it was only a matter of time now before he knew what the score was. Of that he was certain. What he wasn't so sure about was which way he wanted it to go. On the one hand, he might be facing a life sentence. On the other, Forester would remain free to continue his depravity.

Jim's line of thought was broken by the approach of a porter with the lunch trolley. Jim shook his head when the porter made to place a tray on his bedside table. 'I just need a knife and fork.'

The salmon, rice and vegetables tasted bland to Jim, but he savoured every mouthful. It was a long time since he'd eaten food cooked with real care. After lunch, the hours seemed to drag by interminably. Every passing minute lay heavy on him. Every sound in the corridor brought with it the expectation that some of his colleagues had arrived to question him. Towards late afternoon, Doctor Advani came to see him. 'Good news, Mr Monahan,' she said. 'The echocardiogram shows your artery has opened up. Given proper medication, rest and diet, I see no reason why you shouldn't soon be back to your normal self.'

The blood rushed from Jim's face. Not at the doctor's words, but at what he was seeing on the television screen over her shoulder. The local news was on. It showed a live image of Philippa Horne. For an instant, Jim thought she was at a police press conference, appealing for information. But then he realised her face wasn't that of a grief-stricken wife, it was that of a politician playing to the cameras. She looked confident and relaxed as, gesturing at a huge piece of machinery behind her, she said, 'This hydraulic press, the largest of its kind, will create up to eighty new jobs, as well as having a knock-on effect for—'

'Are you feeling alright, Mr Monahan?' Doctor Advani's voice drew Jim's attention away from the screen. 'Your colour has suddenly dropped.'

'I'm fine.' As Jim said it he realised it was true. He *was* fine. A sense of relief hit him, a sense that he'd been pulled back from a precipice. He'd thought his life was over, but now he had a second chance – a chance to try and make things right with Margaret. He found himself caught up again in his fantasy of them together in some place of sunshine and happiness. But this time he didn't resist it, he allowed it to wash over him like a summer breeze. The breeze turned cold as Edward Forester's face intruded on his daydream. A shudder of revulsion ran through Jim. He could leave behind his job, but he could never leave behind the knowledge of what Forester had done and what he would do to others. No matter how far away he went, there was no escaping that. It would always be there, like a shadow blocking the sun. There was only one way to break free of it. He had to bring Forester to justice. *But this time*, he told himself, clenching his fist, *I'll do it right. This time it will be real justice, not vigilante justice. You owe that much at least not just to yourself, but to Mark, to Grace, to Amy, to everyone that filthy bastard's ever hurt.*

Doctor Advani took Jim's wrist and began to count his pulse beats.

'I told you, I'm fine,' said Jim, swinging his legs out of bed.

'What are you doing?'

'Checking myself out of hospital.'

The doctor's eyebrows drew together. 'No, no, Mr Monahan, you need to remain here for another two or three days.'

'But you said my artery has opened up.'

'Yes, but there's no guarantee it'll stay that way. You need to rest. Too much physical activity could bring on another heart attack.'

Jim took his clothes out of his bedside cabinet and started to change into them. 'Look, Doctor, I'm not about to start running around. All I want to do is get a proper night's sleep in my own bed.'

'Physical activity isn't the only factor to consider. We need to monitor your condition to be sure your medication is—'

'I'm sorry,' interrupted Jim. 'I know you mean well, but I'm going and that's all there is to it. Now if you could just sort out whatever tablets I need.'

Doctor Advani looked at Jim for a moment, her eyes troubled. 'Please wait here.' She made her way to the nurses' station. After a conversation with the head nurse and another doctor, she returned to Jim. 'Is there nothing I can say to change your mind?'

'No.'

Doctor Advani proffered a pen and a clipboard with a sheet of paper on it. 'You need to sign this. It's a disclaimer that exonerates the hospital in the event of serious complications or death directly related to your early release.'

Jim signed and passed it back. The doctor handed him another sheet of paper. 'This is a prescription. You can pick it up at the pharmacy on the ground floor. Then you must go straight home to bed and stay there for at least forty-eight hours. And at the first sign of pain or breathlessness, you must phone an ambulance.'

'I will. And thanks.'

As Jim gathered together his belongings, Doctor Advani spoke about how he'd need to return to the hospital for a check-up in a few weeks, and how he'd have the opportunity to take part in a cardiac rehabilitation programme. Jim nodded as if he was listening, but his mind was focused on one thing and one thing alone – nailing Edward Forester. He caught the lift downstairs, picked up his prescription and made his way outside. It was a cold, clear day. As he breathed in the sharply fresh air, a clean feeling spread through him. As though the pain of his heart attack had somehow washed away all the mistakes he'd made, all the bad things he'd done. The illusion was broken by the feel of the tape recorder in his pocket. People were dead who might not have been if he'd done things by the book. Nothing could wash that away.

Jim ducked into a taxi and gave the driver his home address. As they navigated through the early afternoon traffic, his thoughts turned to Bryan Reynolds. It was hard to believe the gangster had changed his mind about killing

Forester. Reynolds wasn't the type to back out of anything. So what had happened? That was the first thing he needed to find out.

Jim was relieved to see his car still parked outside his house. He paid the fare and approached it. The keys weren't in the ignition where he'd left them. He went into the house and rifled through drawers until he found the spare set. He turned to leave, but hesitated. He stared uncertainly at the phone, before reaching for the handset and dialling Margaret. She picked up and said, with a note of surprise, 'Jim, is that you?'

'Yes.'

'But this call's from our home—' Margaret pulled up and quickly corrected herself, 'from your home number.'

A faint smile curled Jim's lips at his ex-wife's Freudian slip. 'I discharged myself from hospital.'

'What? Why?'

'There's something important I need to do.'

'What's more important than your health?'

'I'm calling because I wanted to apologise for the way I was earlier. And to tell you not to worry about me. I thought I was in trouble, but... well, the situation's changed.'

'That's great, Jim, but you didn't answer my question.'

'I will do when there's time. I'll answer anything you want.'

'Anything?'

Jim caught the doubtful note in Margaret's tone. 'Anything at all. I promise. I'm not the same man you were married to, Margaret. Some things have happened recently that have changed me. I'm not just talking about my heart attack. So much...' He paused a beat, then continued, 'Like I said, there's no time to go into it right now. There's something I need to do. I'll call you as soon as I'm done and we can get together and talk. If you want to talk, that is.'

When her reply came, Jim let out a low breath of relief. 'Sure, Jim, I'd like that. Just promise me you'll take care of yourself. Whatever you're up to, it's not worth dying over.'

'Believe me, I've no intention of dying. In fact, quite the opposite. I want to make a fresh start.' More accurately, Jim might have said, *I want to make a fresh start with you.* But the time wasn't right. Not yet. 'Bye, Margaret. I'll speak to you soon.'

Jim drove into the city centre and parked up opposite a takeaway in a terraced row of shops. Above the door a sign in oriental-style lettering read 'Xinchun Chinese Takeaway'. The takeaway hadn't yet opened for business. Jim resisted the temptation to knock on the door and find out if it its owner, Li Xinchun, was in. Li was a known criminal who'd been seen by surveilling officers entering Bryan Reynolds's strip club the previous night. There was a chance that he, too, had subsequently been put under surveillance. The chance was small – after all, the majority of Reynolds's associates were criminals, and it simply wasn't possible to keep tabs on them all – but it was there.

As Jim watched the takeaway, he popped pills out of blister strips and washed them down with bottled water. When he was done, he released a long, weary breath. He'd been buoyed up by the early autumn air, but now an almost irresistible heaviness was seeping into his body, tugging at his eyelids. He needed something to stave off the sensation. With a habitual movement, he took a cigarette packet out of his glove compartment. The cigarette was almost between his lips before he realised what he was doing. He looked at it with a momentary frown of longing, then returned it to the packet. A movement inside the takeaway attracted his attention. The short, stocky figure of Li Xinchun emerged from the front door and got into a white Transit van. As Li pulled away, Jim scanned the street for any vehicles that showed signs of following him. There were none. He accelerated after the van.

Li headed out of the city centre towards the industrial sprawl of Attercliffe. After a couple of miles, he turned into the car park of a cash-and-carry warehouse. Jim pulled up behind him, boxing the van in. Li got out, frowning in his direction and saying, 'Hey, you can't park—' He broke off, rolling his eyes as he recognised Jim.

Jim lowered his window. 'Get in.'

Li shook his head. 'I don't want anything more to do with you. You've caused me enough trouble already.'

'And I'll cause you a shit lot more if you don't get in.'

Li stared undecidedly at Jim for a moment, then with a sigh he ducked into the passenger seat. He sat shaking his head, waiting for Jim to speak.

'Tell me about this trouble I've caused you.'

'Some of your colleagues came to see me yesterday. They kept me up half the night asking questions about Bryan Reynolds.'

'And what did you tell them?'

Li pulled an offended face. 'The same as I always tell them – fuck all.' His tone became accusatory. 'The Minx was being watched. That's why you sent me in there, isn't it?'

'Yes.'

'*Yes*, is that all you've got to say? Don't I even get an apology? You've dropped me in it big-time. They're saying I've broken my parole conditions. They're threatening to return me to prison unless I give them something on Bryan.'

'So give them a little something.'

Scowling, Li made a dismissive gesture. 'Fuck that. I wouldn't give them the shit off my arse. I'd rather serve out the remainder of my sentence. Actually, the way things are going maybe it'd be better if they do take me into custody.'

'What do you mean by that?'

Li squinted searchingly at Jim. 'Where's Bryan?'

'Funny you should ask that, because I was about to ask you the same thing.'

The squint turned into a look of dismay. 'I knew it, I knew the moment I saw you that you were trouble. Why couldn't you have just left me alone? I'm not dealing any more. I run a clean business. I don't deserve this. Do you hear me, copper? I don't fucking deserve to end up at the bottom of the Don because of you.'

Jim held up a hand to calm Li. 'You're not going to end up at the bottom of the Don.'

Li shot him a look saying, *The fuck I'm not*. 'Bryan's people have been calling me all day. He left The Minx last night without saying why or where he was going. No one's heard from him since. His people are starting to get worried. They want answers from me. I told them I don't have any. That I was just delivering a message.'

'Did you tell them who you were delivering it for?'

'No.' Li paused a breath, before adding meaningfully, 'I don't know what your game is, copper, and I don't want to know. But I hope for both our sakes that nothing bad has happened to Bryan.'

Jim was surprised to find himself thinking, *I hope so too*. Li was right, he didn't deserve this. The last thing he needed was another death on his conscience. 'Have you got any relatives outside the city?'

'I have a cousin down in London.'

'Then you should go stay with him.'

'I can't do that without permission from my parole officer.'

'Forget permission. Just do it and don't tell anyone where you're going. What's your mobile number?' Jim scribbled it down on a scrap of paper as Li told him. 'I'll contact you as soon as I manage to track down Bryan. Do you need any money?' Li shook his head. As he reached for the door handle, Jim added, 'I'm sorry.'

'No, you're fucking not,' muttered Li, getting out of the car.

Jim pulled his car forward so that Li could reverse out of the parking space. As he watched the van accelerate away, his mind turned over the possibilities of what might have happened to Reynolds. When men like him suddenly disappeared it usually meant one of two things – they'd either gone into hiding or they'd been killed. And Reynolds had no reason to go into hiding. Jim puffed his cheeks. He hated Reynolds and everything he stood for. If a rival dealer had murdered him, he would have bought the whole station a round of drinks in celebration. But he'd never meant for him to die like this. If dead he really was. Jim struggled to see how Forester could have got the better of Reynolds without help. Not that Forester was lacking for that kind of help.

Another possibility occurred to Jim. Maybe Reynolds was alive but being held captive. Forester wasn't the type to have someone killed without first finding out everything they had to say. He'd proven that by abducting Mark. Perhaps right now Reynolds was being tortured for information about what or who had led him to Forester. Shoving the car into gear, Jim accelerated fast out of the car park. If he was right, time was in short supply. Reynolds was as tough as granite. He wouldn't give up a name easily. But even the hardest rocks break when put under enough pressure. Jim's heart squeezed at the realisation that he might soon find himself the subject of unwanted attention from both Reynolds and Forester's goons.

Reflecting that he'd been more than a bit premature in telling Margaret he was out of trouble, Jim made his way to Woodhouse, a former pit village on the city's south-eastern outskirts. He eased up on the accelerator as he passed Forester's red-brick semi. The place appeared unoccupied – Forester's Jag wasn't in the driveway; the curtains were drawn although it was still light. Maybe he had decided to take up residence elsewhere for the time being. That would have been a smart move, and Forester was clearly a smart man. Jim did a U-turn and drove back past the house, his shadow-ringed eyes scouring its windows. Just because the place appeared to be empty didn't mean it was. If Forester had brought in some heavies for protection, they might be lying in wait for anyone searching for Reynolds. Jim saw nothing to suggest such was the case, and there were no vehicles parked on the street near the house.

He parked up out of sight of the house, but within view of its driveway. He forced himself to let the tension out of his body. All he could do now was watch and wait and hope that someone or something led him to Reynolds. Traffic built as rush-hour started, then slowed as the afternoon wore into evening. No one pulled into the driveway. The sun dipped behind the chimney pots of Woodhouse. Jim drove along the street again and pulled over outside Forester's house. Its windows were as dark as the night sky. He stared at them a long moment, then retrieved some latex gloves, a torch and an extendable baton from the glove compartment. The time for watching and waiting was over.

As Jim made his way up the garden path, he noted the alarm box blinking beneath the eaves. If he was going to risk breaking into the house, there wouldn't be much time to look around. He would have to move quickly. His heart gave a heavy beat, as if unhappy at the thought of being forced to work hard. Glancing about to make sure no one was watching, he headed around the back and chanced the door handle. His eyebrows pinched together as the door slid open a crack. Silence. Obviously the alarm wasn't on. Had the door been left unlocked by accident or design? He squinted at the doorframe. The tape holding back the lock indicated the latter possibility. Most likely, he reasoned, Reynolds had wanted to ensure he could make a quick escape. His straining ears caught no sound of movement from inside.

Extending the baton, Jim nudged the door further open with its tip. Cautious as a stalking cat, he entered the house. His torch's beam revealed no signs of a struggle in the kitchen, dining room or lounge. He padded upstairs. Frown intensifying, he dropped to his haunches beside the missing square of landing carpet. It appeared to have been roughly cut away. There was a tiny smear of something on the skirting board to his left. He peered closely at it. Blood! He ran a finger over it. Dry blood. Surely it had to belong to Reynolds or his skinhead sidekick. No doubt, the carpet had been removed because it too was bloodstained.

Jim quickly checked out the bedrooms, bathroom and study. There were no further signs of a struggle. The house was as empty as it appeared from outside. So where the hell was Forester? Was he down in Westminster? Jim doubted it. If he wanted to stay off the radar, London was hardly the place for him to do it. More likely he was somewhere few people knew about. Perhaps a second home in the countryside. Or perhaps he was with his mother in Totteridge – assuming of course that she was still alive. The first possibility struck Jim as more probable. Surely Forester wouldn't want to risk getting his mother mixed up in this mess.

Jim returned to the study. There was a PC on a desk. He switched it on, but it was password protected. He rifled through the desk's drawers, searching for a utility bill or letter that might point him in the direction of Forester. Apart from the usual array of stationery, the drawers contained nothing of interest. He turned his attention to a filing cabinet. Its top two drawers contained more of the same. The bottom one was so full of papers it was difficult to open. They mostly consisted of copies of old speeches and newspaper cuttings dating back three decades. All the articles involved Forester acting in some capacity as a politician, except one. At the bottom of the drawer, nestling like a pressed flower between the pages of a speech, there was a cutting from the South Yorkshire *Chronicle* dated 12 January 1996, with the headline 'Man dies in Huddersfield House Fire'. Beneath it, a brief article continued, 'A man in his late sixties has died following a house fire in Huddersfield. The fire happened at around 1 a.m. at a house in the suburb of Deighton. The man has been identified as local resident Norman Harding. Investigators are still trying to confirm the cause of the fire.'

Jim pocketed the article and returned the rest of the papers to the drawer. He rifled through the master-bedroom's bedside tables. They only contained female underwear. In a bedroom across the hall, there was only male clothing. *I've been happily married for nearly twenty years to Philippa*

Horne. The quote from Forester's website popped into Jim's head. Being 'happily married' obviously didn't extend to sharing the same bed.

Reluctantly, Jim made his way downstairs. He would have liked to conduct a more thorough search, but he'd already spent far too long in the house. In the hallway, he plucked a cordless phone from its base unit and tried 1471. A toneless voice informed him that the phone had last been called at eight o'clock the previous day – roughly an hour after he'd phoned Forester. The number had an 01433 area code, which he knew belonged to the Hope Valley area of the Peak District, a few miles south of Sheffield. He made a note of it, then scrolled through the numbers stored in the phone's contact list. One caught his eye. It was the same number he'd just written down, listed below the word 'Southview'.

'Southview,' he murmured. What was Southview? A place? A house name? Whatever it was, it was worth checking out.

Jim returned to his car. He dropped heavily into the driver's seat, utterly drained of what little energy he'd had. He desperately wanted to continue the search, but his body was screaming for rest, and he knew he couldn't afford to ignore it.

Chapter Thirteen

When the cleaning lady came out of the bedroom, Edward went in and inspected her work. Everything had to be just so. Every surface had to be spotlessly clean. The bedsheets had to be tucked in so tightly that not a single crease remained. And most importantly of all, there had to be a vase of fresh lilies on the dressing table. Mabel Forester adored the scent of lilies. Edward hated it. To him they smelt sickly sweet, like cheap perfume. He frowned at a tiny smudge on the window. He pointed it out to the cleaner, who quickly polished it away. Nodding approval, Edward headed down to the kitchen where Philippa and a woman in chef's whites were bustling about. The chef was cutting a filet mignon into individual steaks. Edward's nose wrinkled. Steak. Something else his mother loved which he loathed. When he was a child, she'd fed him steak several times a week. And she'd always made sure to remind him how lucky he was to be eating it. He could still hear her saying, *When I was a little girl we couldn't afford to eat meat more than once a week, and even then it was just liver and onions.* She refused to have liver in her kitchen. To her mind, it was a food of poverty. When he left home for university, Edward had made a point of eating the stuff on a regular basis. He didn't particularly like its grainy texture, but it had given him a small measure of satisfaction to know how much his mother would have disapproved.

Edward flinched at a knock on the front door. 'She's here,' he hissed at Philippa.

Philippa pulled off her apron and checked her reflection in a mirror. After smoothing down a few strands of hair and fixing a smile in place, she reached for her husband's hand and gave it a reassuring squeeze. He took a breath and they made their way to the door. As he opened it, he tugged his hand free of Philippa's.

Mabel Forester was being helped out of the back seat of a sleek black Mercedes by a chauffeur. She was a small woman, slim as a blade, and barely five feet tall. But what she lacked in size, she more than made up for in personality. Even at seventy-eight, her hollow-eyed, high-cheekboned face had a kind of severe beauty. Lipstick and blusher disguised the smallness of her mouth and the paleness of her complexion. A glossy black shoulder-length wig concealed her thinning grey hair. Her cheeks had the unnatural tightness of plastic surgery. She was wearing a pink Chanel suit that gave her a look of old-time sophistication. But it was her eyes that really showed her personality. Unlike her son's dullish brown eyes, hers were so vividly blue that they almost seemed to be illuminated from within. They sparkled with an indomitable vitality and energy that made a mockery of her apparent need to be helped from the car. Edward and Philippa exchanged a knowing glance as Mabel made a great show of slowly climbing the steps to the door.

She ran her gaze over her son and daughter-in-law with a look that somehow managed to convey both affection and disapproval at once.

'Hello, Mother,' said Edward, leaning in to kiss the cheek she offered him. The faintest of shudders ran through him as his lips brushed her ever so slightly furry skin.

Philippa kissed Mabel too. 'You're looking well.'

'Am I?' Mabel shot back.

'Yes. I must say, Mabel, you seem to look younger every time I see you.'

'You're looking well, too, dear. Have you done something different with your makeup?'

Philippa's nostrils flared a fraction at the backhanded compliment, but her smile didn't slip. 'No.'

'Well something's different. Maybe it's your hair.'

Philippa opened her mouth to reply that she hadn't changed her hair either. But Mabel was already transferring her gaze to the real object of her interest. 'You look tired, Edward.'

'I'm fine, Mother.'

Mabel raised her eyebrows to indicate she didn't believe that for a second. 'Have you lost weight?'

Edward gave a nervous little laugh. 'I wish.'

A smile softened Mabel's face as a shaggy grey wolfhound came loping out of the living room. The dog nuzzled her, his head almost level with her shoulders. 'Hello, old boy,' she said, ruffling his fur. 'I've got something for you.' She took a bone-shaped chew out of her handbag and put it in the dog's mouth. Tail wagging, Conall retreated to the lounge with his prize. At a gesture from Philippa, they followed the dog. Mabel seated herself in an armchair by the fireplace. Philippa settled onto a sofa opposite her. They sat stiffly, while Edward poured them each a glass of sherry. 'How was your journey, Mother?' he asked, settling onto the sofa, keeping a little distance between Philippa and himself.

'Fine,' she replied with a small yawn.

'Are you tired? Would you like a lie down before dinner?' asked Philippa.

'I'm not tired in the slightest, dear.' The implication was obvious – Mabel wasn't interested in small talk.

They sipped their drinks in silence, Mabel studying her son like a doctor searching for signs of illness, Edward staring at his lap, Philippa's gaze hovering between the two of them as if unsure where to land. The reason behind Mabel's visit hung in the air between them like a bomb waiting to be detonated. Mabel finished her sherry and held out her glass for a refill. As Edward obliged, she said to Philippa, 'Why don't you go and check on how dinner's coming along, dear.' It wasn't quite a command, but neither was it a question. This time Philippa's smile faltered, not much, but enough to be noticeable. She glanced uncertainly at her husband. At a slight nod from him, she stood and left the room.

'Close the door, will you?' Mabel called after her. 'There's a terrible draught coming through it.'

Philippa closed the door just loudly enough to make her displeasure known. Mabel's gaze returned to Edward. He sank back down onto the sofa, hanging his head like a guilty child. Mabel moved to sit next to him, so close their thighs touched. In a conspiratorially low voice, she said, 'You can have the money—'

Edward jerked his head up, relief flooding his face. 'Oh, thank you, Mummy! Thank you. Thank you.'

'Hold on, Edward, you didn't let me finish. I was going to say, you can have the money on two conditions. Firstly, when I ask you a question, I want the truth. Is that understood?'

Edward nodded.

'Secondly, and more importantly, I want us to be close again.' Mabel laid a bony hand speckled with liver spots over her son's hands. 'Like we used to be.'

Edward looked at his mother a moment. Then his eyes dropped away from hers, and swallowing as if he had something in his throat, he nodded again.

'You've got no children,' continued Mabel. 'So you can't know how much it's hurt to feel you drifting away from me.'

'I'm sorry. I've just been so busy.'

'Well from now on you're going to make time for me. And nothing and...' Mabel shot a meaningful glance towards the door, 'no one is going to get between us.' She gently touched Edward's cheek. 'I'm going to take care of you, as only a mother can.'

He squeezed his mother's hand, then kissed it. 'No, Mother, this time I'm going to take care of you. We're going to be a proper family again. I promise.'

'Oh, Edward, it makes me so happy to hear you say

that.' Mabel drew her son's head onto her shoulder, stroked his hair and murmured in his ear, 'Now tell Mummy all about it.'

'There's a man. He knows about something I did. If it comes out I'll be ruined.'

'What did you do?'

'I made an... error of judgement. It happened a long time ago. I always worried that one day it might come back to haunt me, and now it has.'

A knowing glint shone in Mabel's bright blue eyes. 'What's her name?'

'Grace Kirby.'

'That name seems familiar.'

'She killed... murdered some friends of mine.'

Mabel pushed her son's head away, disgust curling her upper lip. Like a nail scratching on a blackboard, she hissed, 'You mean the whore who's been all over the news.'

Edward put a finger to his lips, glancing anxiously towards the door. 'Please, Mother, keep your voice down.'

Mabel ignored his plea, continuing angrily, 'Just like your father. He could never keep his hands off whores either.'

Now it was Edward's turn to raise his voice. Another thing his mother never missed a chance to tell him was how much he put her in mind of his father, both in the way he acted and looked. From an early age he'd come to realise he was a constant bitter reminder of the man she more often than not referred to as simply 'the bastard'. 'I'm nothing like my father.'

'How would you know? You were too young to remember when the bastard walked out on us for that slut.'

'I know I'd never do anything like that. I know blood is the only thing you can trust. I know it because you taught me so. You made me what I am. Not him.' Edward looked at his mother with an almost pathetic need in his eyes. 'I love you, Mummy. I love you more than I'll ever love anyone else.'

Edward's words smoothed the lines of anger from Mabel's face. Once more, she pulled him onto her shoulder. 'I know you do, darling,' she soothed. 'Now tell me more about this man. Is he blackmailing you?'

'It's worse than that. He doesn't want money, he wants to hurt me.'

'Well you know what we do to people who want to hurt us, don't you?'

'Yes, Mummy. We hurt them first.'

'We don't just hurt them.' Mabel's voice dripped with vicious intent. 'We destroy them and wipe out any trace that they ever existed.'

'It might not only be him. There may be others.'

'If there are, we'll deal with them too.'

Edward pressed his face into his mother's shoulder. His voice came muffled. 'Oh God, I've made such a terrible mess of things.'

Mabel drew him down further, so that he was nestling against her bosom. 'Shh, hush now. Mummy's here, and Mummy will make everything better. Just like she always does.'

Chapter Fourteen

Freddie Harding's house was a dour pebble-dashed little semi on an estate of such houses. The windows and door of the adjoining house were boarded up with metal grilles. The gardens of both houses were overgrown and strewn with litter. There were muddy wheel ruts where Freddie's front lawn had been used as a driveway. Although it was dark, the curtains of his house weren't drawn. A light glowed in the upstairs window. But Reece felt sure no one was in. He'd watched the house for most of the day now without seeing any sign of movement. The light had probably been left on to ward off burglars while Freddie was out. Not that a light would be much of a deterrent to some of the characters prowling the estate. Reece had already been checked out by several gangs of glowering, tracksuit-clad teenagers. They knew better than to do anything more than eyeball him, though. They'd been trained from birth to spot a copper from a mile away.

Reece glanced at the dashboard clock. Eight p.m. A crease appeared between his eyebrows. Why hadn't his dad phoned from the hospital yet? Had something gone wrong with the chemo? Another thought quickly followed. *What the hell are you doing here when there are people elsewhere who need you? People you love.* His gaze dropped to the folders on the passenger seat. He picked up one and opened it. A grainy black and white mugshot of a chubby-faced young woman stared at him from the first page. Underneath it a brief bio read, 'Roxanne Cole, 21 years old. Worked as a prostitute in the Wheatly area of Doncaster. Last seen alive on 20 February 1980. Reported missing on 26 February.' He flipped the page and was greeted by a smiling girl with big eyes and boyishly short hair. His gaze skimmed over her bio. 'Jennifer Barns, 19 years old. Doncaster prostitute. Last seen on Thorne Road on 12 July 1983.' Another page. Another photo. A woman with sad, expectant eyes that seemed to suggest she knew what was coming to her. 'Angela Riley, 22, Sheffield prostitute. Disappeared from Neepsend Lane, 18 November 1984...' And so it continued. Page after page. Face after face. Name after name. The unloved, the damaged, the forgotten, the damned. *They* were why he was here.

Reece's phone rang. A number he didn't recognise flashed up. He answered it. 'Am I speaking to Mr Reece Geary?' enquired a man's voice.

'Yes.'

'This is Doctor Meadows of Weston Park Hospital. I'm calling on behalf of your father—'

'Is he OK?' Reece cut in anxiously.

'He had a strong reaction to the chemotherapy. We're keeping him in overnight as a precaution. He should be fit to go home tomorrow morning.'

'Can I see him?'

'Visiting hours are over for today. Besides, it's best if you just let him rest.'

Reece's attention was attracted by a white Transit van pulling onto Freddie's garden. 'Thanks for letting me know, Doctor.' Reece hung up as the man himself got out of the van. Freddie was wearing heavy-duty black shoes, navy blue trousers and a light blue short-sleeved shirt. He'd lost almost all of his hair since 2001. All that remained were some scruffy tufts at the sides of his head. He'd put on some weight too. His belly had grown paunchy and there was a puffiness to his face that hinted at a heavy drinking habit. But his small, closely spaced eyes had lost none of their weasel-like shiftiness. He lifted a bundle of parcels out of the back of the van and carried them into his house. *Maybe he's a delivery driver*, reasoned Reece. Whatever, it made sense not to leave the parcels in the van, especially in an area like that. A downstairs light came on. Freddie appeared at the window and drew the curtains.

According to the plates, the van was four years old. So it couldn't be the same vehicle one of the missing prostitutes had been seen getting into before Freddie's 2001 arrest. Reece photographed the van with his phone, then leaned back against the headrest. His thoughts returned to his father. He released a heavy breath. It promised to be a long night.

As the hours crawled by, tiredness nibbled at the edges of Reece's concentration. He kept himself alert by knocking back energy drinks. They tasted like shit, but did the trick. Shortly before midnight the downstairs light went off. Minutes later, Freddie emerged from the house. He'd changed into trainers, blue jeans and a black sweatshirt, so presumably he wasn't working. *Where are you going at this time of night?* wondered Reece, as Freddie got into his van and reversed out of the makeshift driveway.

With Reece following at a discreet distance, Freddie headed west through the silent night-time streets and pulled onto the M1's southbound carriageway just north of Sheffield. Reece fully expected him to turn off the motorway at Sheffield and head into the red-light district. But the van continued on past the city towards north Derbyshire.

Reece's phone rang again. This time he recognised the caller's number. Doug Brody. 'Shit.' The word whistled through his teeth as he remembered that he'd promised Doug he'd have Wayne Carson's money for him by tonight. He put the phone to his ear. 'Sorry, Doug, I haven't got it yet,' he said, getting straight down to business.

Doug's voice came back at him gruffly. 'Why the fuck not?'

'You remember what we spoke about last night, well I'm following up on a lead I got—'

'I don't give a toss what you're doing. Get your arse over to Burton Road right this second and collect what we're owed.'

'But I'm tailing—'

'Are you deaf?' Doug shut him down again. 'I said right now. Fuck your lead. You know, Reece, I'm starting to suspect your heart's not in this little business enterprise of ours.'

'That's not true.'

'Then prove it.'

'OK. I'll call you as soon as I've got it.'

Reece stared at Freddie's van with a conflicted expression. The van passed a junction. With a reluctant twist of the steering wheel, Reece pulled onto the slip road. As he headed back towards Sheffield, something pricked at him, like a thorn working its way deeper into his flesh with every mile he put between himself and Freddie. It took him a while to work out what it was. Shame. He felt ashamed. *You're doing this for Staci and Amelia. So that they can be a family again*, he told himself. But the feeling didn't go away.

When he reached Burton Road, he found Wayne in his usual spot idly watching his girls work the street. As Reece jammed on the brakes in front of him, Wayne jerked away from the factory wall as if snapping to attention. Reece jumped out of his car and strode towards him. 'Have you got it?' he growled.

Wayne raised his hands with a shrug as if to say, *Got what?*

'Right, that's fucking it.' Reece grabbed Wayne's arm and spun him around. 'Hands against the wall.' Kicking Wayne's legs apart, he patted him down.

'Go ahead. Search me,' sneered the pimp. 'I'm clean.'

Reece reached into Wayne's jacket pocket and pulled out several foil wraps. 'Oh really. So what's this then?' He opened one of the wraps, revealing a small, sticky black lump. 'Looks like Mexican Mud to me.'

Wayne twisted around, the blue snake tattoo on his scalp rippling as if alive as his face contorted in outrage. 'That's not mine! You planted that shit.'

Reece seized Wayne's arm and bent it up behind his back. He snapped a pair of handcuffs around his wrists. 'You're under arrest for dealing drugs. You don't have to say anything, but it may harm your defence if you do not mention—'

'This is bullshit! You can't do this. I'll tell everyone what you did.'

Reece gave a sharp laugh. 'Try it. I'm a policeman with seven years' service. You're a scumbag pimp and dealer with a string of convictions. Who do you think they're going to believe?'

Wayne writhed against Reece's grip. 'You motherfucker.'

'Calm down, Wayne. I'd say there's less than five grams of heroin here. Which means you're only looking at two to five years. That should be just long enough for you to figure out whether it was worth your while not coughing up your dues.'

Wayne stopped struggling. His head dropped. 'Alright.'

'Alright what?'

'Alright, Detective Geary, uncuff me and I'll get it for you.'

'Where is it?'

'Close by.'

'Show me.'

Wayne motioned with his chin towards a rusty grating at the foot of the wall. Stooping, Reece pulled it loose and reached inside the aperture. He withdrew a plastic bag with a roll of cash inside it. 'It's all there,' said Wayne, his mean little mouth spreading into a smile of false bravado. 'I meant to pay up all along. I was just fucking with you for fucking with me and what's mine.'

Reece pocketed the cash, then released Wayne. The pimp rubbed his wrists. There were red marks where the cuffs had bitten into them. Reece gave him a steady, hard look. 'If you fuck with me again, money or no money, you're going down. Do I make myself clear?'

'Crystal.' As Reece turned towards his car, Wayne muttered sarcastically, 'You're a real credit to your job, Mr Policeman. With you around, the people of this city can sleep soundly.'

The pimp's words pushed the thorn of shame deeper. Wincing, Reece ducked into the car. As he drove, he dialled Doug and said, 'I've got it.'

'Good work, Reece. I knew you wouldn't disappoint me.'

Good work! What's good about it? Reece felt like spitting back. 'Where do you want to meet?' His monotone voice gave away nothing of what he was feeling.

'Nowhere tonight. There's no rush. I'll drop by your place in the morning.'

Reece's mouth compressed into a thin line. *If there's no rush, why the fuck couldn't this have waited?* He kept the thought to himself. He knew Doug was just needling him for failing to collect on time. 'See you then.'

He tossed his phone aside as if it disgusted him. Not for the first time recently, he found himself thinking, *How the fuck did it ever come to this?* He slowed down alongside a prostitute, lowered his window and asked, 'Have you seen Staci?'

'She's not working tonight. I don't think she's feeling very well.'

Reece thanked the girl and, face creased with concern, headed for the tiny terraced house where Staci rented a room from Wayne. Her bedroom light was on. He knocked on the front door. One of the girls who lived with Staci opened it. 'Is Staci in?' he asked.

'She's ill.'

'What's up with her?'

'Not sure. Stomach bug, I think.'

Reece looked intently at the girl. She stared back at him, po-faced. His cop's nose smelled a lie. It occurred to him with a growing sense of unease that seeing as Wayne had decided to teach him a lesson, maybe he'd taught Staci one too. 'Can I go up and see her?'

'She's sleeping.'

'So why is her bedroom light on?'

Without waiting for the girl's response, Reece pushed past her and headed upstairs. Staci was lying in bed with the duvet pulled up to her chin. Her eyes were closed as if she was sleeping. But when Reece padded forwards and tried to peel the duvet off her, she clutched it to herself and said, 'Don't.'

Reece gently but unyieldingly continued to pull the duvet down. His face contorted with rage at the sight that greeted him. Staci's arms and legs were a welter of faint truncheon-shaped marks. He stared at them a moment. Then, like an irresistible tide, his anger turned him around and swept him downstairs. Staci's shrill voice followed him. 'Please don't, Reece. You'll only make things worse.'

Staci's appeal didn't stop Reece. Nothing short of being cuffed and locked up could have stopped him. Tyres squealing, he accelerated away from the house. As he raced back towards Burton Road, his powerful hands flexed on the steering wheel with convulsive intent. He mounted the kerb, screeching to a halt in front of the startled pimp. The instant Wayne saw the look in Reece's eyes, he knew what was coming. He turned to flee as Reece leapt out of his car. But his junkie's lungs were no match for the policeman's muscular athleticism. Reece caught up with him by Burton Weir. Wayne was by no means a small man, but Reece picked him up and slammed him into the railings as easily as if he were a rag doll. As the weir roared dully beneath them, he drove his fists over and over again into the pimp. At first, Wayne attempted to defend himself with little success. After a while, though, his hands dropped limply to his sides. Wayne's lips split like rotten fruit, blood gushed from his nose, his ribs cracked audibly, but still Reece kept on pummelling him.

'Stop!' The word was screamed so loudly that it pierced Reece's rage. Glancing around, he saw Staci dashing towards him. 'For Christ's sake, Reece, you'll kill him!'

'So what if I do?' Reece retorted, breathing hard. 'At least then you'd be free.'

'But you wouldn't be. Please, Reece, this isn't you. This

isn't you,' Staci repeated, as if trying to convince herself her words were true. Reece saw fear in her eyes. Not of Wayne, but of him. Horrified, he released the pimp. Wayne slumped down against the railings, eyelids flickering, breath wheezing through his mashed lips.

Reece turned away from Staci and started to head for his car, but she caught hold of his arm. 'Come back to the house,' she said.

Reece stared at the pavement, his expression dazed, like someone who'd been shaken out of a deep sleep.

'You'd better get him out of here,' said the girl who'd answered the door to Reece. 'I'll call an ambulance.'

Staci led Reece to his car. She started to get behind the wheel, but he said, 'I'll drive.'

'Are you sure?'

He nodded. They drove to the house in silence. Reece dropped heavily onto the bed. His chin dropped heavily onto his chest. 'Let me see your knuckles,' said Staci. He turned his hands over. His knuckles were smeared with blood – mostly Wayne's, but his own too from where his skin had split. Staci pulled a tin with a red cross on top from under the bed. 'In my line of work it pays to keep a first-aid box handy,' she explained, tearing open an antiseptic wipe.

'How did things get so twisted around?' Reece said, more wondering out loud than really asking. 'I joined the police to protect people.' He held up his bloody hands. 'Now look at me. How did I get like this? Did something make me this way, or have I always been this way and just didn't know it? Doug knew it. He knew the first time he looked in my eyes that I was someone he could use to do his dirty work.'

'You know what I see when I look in your eyes,' Staci said gently. 'Someone who's willing to do anything for the people he loves.'

'You don't understand: I swore an oath.'

'And I let social services take away my Amelia.' Staci's voice was suddenly angry. 'So don't tell me I don't fucking understand.' Sighing, she went on more quietly, 'We all have things we wish we could take back in our lives, Reece. No one's perfect. So your hands are a bit dirty. So what? Whose aren't, these days?'

'Jim Monahan's.'

'Who's he?'

'Someone I used to work with.'

'What do you mean used to?'

'If Wayne reports this my career will be over.'

'Don't talk daft, Reece. Wayne won't breathe a word.'

Reece knew Staci was right, but he half wished otherwise. At least that way he wouldn't have to walk around feeling like a fraud any more. He met Staci's gaze for the first time since they'd been in the house. Her battered face made him think about his mother, about the way she used to look after his father had worked her over. Why had she stayed with him? It was a question Reece had asked himself countless times without ever coming up with an answer. 'I'm no good for you,' he said.

'Yes you are.'

Reece shook his head. 'What if... what if I do the same to you one day?'

'You won't.'

'How do you know?'

'Because I just do.'

Reece opened his mouth to say something else, but Staci softly shushed him. She cleaned his knuckles and applied plasters to the cuts. Then she drew him into her arms, holding him tight. He closed his eyes and gradually drifted off with the dull, meaty sound of his fists thudding into Wayne still seeming to echo in his ears.

Chapter Fifteen

Someday I'll have a place like that, thought Stan Lockwood, as his eyes greedily surveyed Edward Forester's moonlit house. He particularly liked the way it stood alone, miles from anywhere. A man would really be able to be himself in a house like that, without fear of interference. It would be like having your own little kingdom. He sipped warming brandy from a hipflask – a habit he'd acquired during long, tedious stints of surveillance back when he was on the force – as he daydreamed about how he'd rule his kingdom.

He stopped drinking as a white van passed his car. He'd been careful to pull off the lane behind some bushes, so the driver didn't see him. The van slowed almost to a halt outside the politician's house, then accelerated for two hundred metres or so, before turning into the trees on the opposite side of the road.

Uncertainty wrinkled Stan's jowly florid face. Should he call Tyler for back-up? He decided against it. Tyler wouldn't be best pleased if he dragged him away from the farm for no good reason. It was probably just a poacher. It was hunting season, after all, and the woods around here were full of pheasants. Still, it needed checking out. Stan opened a compartment in the dashboard and took out a torch and a Glock pistol.

Shivering at the touch of the night air, Stan got out of the Range Rover and cautiously made his way towards where the van had turned off. A few metres from the edge of the trees there was a wire gate about two and a half metres high. A sign with bold red lettering read 'PRIVATE LAND. TRESPASSERS WILL BE PROSECUTED'. A fence stretched out to either side of the gate. Beyond it a dirt track descended gently into the woods. Stan squinted into the deeper darkness beneath the trees. There was no sign of the van. His gaze returned to the gate. It was bolted and padlocked. That probably meant the van was there on legitimate business. Probably, but not definitely. Padlocks could be picked easily enough. Besides, he'd learned the hard way that it was always the suspect you didn't check out or the lead you didn't follow up that came back to bite you on the arse.

Pocketing the torch and gun, Stan took hold of the wire fence. With surprising agility for a big man, he heaved himself upwards and threw a leg over the top of the fence. There was a sound of ripping material as his body followed. He swore softly to himself, fingering a tear in the crotch of his trousers. Gun in hand, he advanced along the track. Barely enough moonlight penetrated the trees for him to see where he was going, but he was reluctant to use the torch for fear of giving himself away. It had rained recently, and his feet squelched on the muddy ground. Cold water seeped through his trainers. He scowled at the darkness, thinking: *Whoever's driving that fucking van better have an innocent reason to be here, otherwise I'm going to take great pleasure in putting a bullet in them.*

After maybe four or five hundred metres, the track terminated at a roughly circular clearing. The van was parked at the centre of the clearing in front of a flat-roofed, one-storeyed, rectangular building. From behind a tree, Stan watched for several minutes. There was no sign of movement. He circled around to the back of the building, then crept towards it. He tripped and fell into a shallow trench hidden by long, crackly dead grass. A harsh caustic smell stung his nostrils. Lye. His grandmother used to make soap out of the stuff to clean clothes. But there was, he knew, another use for lye – bury a body in it and that body would dissolve into a brownish jelly, not overnight but in a surprisingly short time. Tears burning his eyes, he clambered out of the trench. It was about half a metre wide and maybe a couple of metres long. His brow furrowed. Could this be an open grave waiting to be filled? Or was someone simply using it to dispose of hazardous waste?

Gun raised and ready, Stan continued towards the building. As he drew closer, he saw that it had windowless concrete walls and, at the side facing the clearing's entrance, an iron door that no light or sound penetrated. What the hell was this place? An old bomb shelter? Whatever it was, someone had obviously found a use for it. Whether that use was legal or not, he couldn't have cared less. Just so long as it didn't put Edward Forester in danger.

Stan peered into the van. Empty. He risked briefly

switching on the torch, figuring that if he couldn't see into the building, whoever – if anyone – was inside it, likewise couldn't see out. He jotted down the reg, then retreated to the cover of the encircling trees. His mobile phone palely illuminated his face as he dialled a number. A man's voice groggy with sleep answered, 'Christ, Stan, what the hell are you doing calling me at this time?'

'I need you to run a reg for me.'

'Has someone turned up at Forester's place?'

'Not exactly.' Stan quickly explained the situation. 'It's probably nothing, but it'll put my mind at rest to know who the van belongs to.'

'OK. Call me back in five.'

The required minutes ticked by. Stan redialled. This time his call was answered on the first ring. 'Are you sure about that reg, Stan?' The voice on the other end of the line no longer sounded sleepy, it sounded apprehensive.

'Positive. Why? Does it belong to one of Reynolds's goons?'

'No.'

'So why do you sound so worried?'

'Does the name Freddie Harding mean anything to you?'

'Freddie Harding,' repeated Stan, searching his memory. 'I don't think so.'

'Well it should do. You were working in CID when he was arrested back in 2001.'

Stan's eyebrows lifted. 'Now you say it, I do remember. He raped a prostitute, didn't he?'

'Yeah, but there was something else too. A local journo

claimed he had evidence Harding might be responsible for abducting and killing whores.'

'That's right. He came to us with some crazy theory about Harding being a serial...' Stan's words died away as his thoughts returned to the trench and the lye. 'Jesus fucking Christ,' he continued in a harsh whisper. 'You don't think—'

'It doesn't matter what I think. If Harding has some sort of connection to Edward Forester, whatever they're up to is none of our business. Have you got that?'

Stan's blotchy drinker's nose twitched with irritation, but he said, 'Yes, Doug, I've got it.'

'Good. Remember who you are now, Stan. Leave the police work to me.'

Chapter Sixteen

It was still dark when Jim awoke from a fitful night's sleep to a throbbing nicotine withdrawal headache. Upon arriving home he'd all but collapsed into bed, only to wake every hour or so, agonising over Bryan Reynolds. One question kept turning in his mind: why should he care whether Reynolds was alive or dead? The man was a parasite, feeding off the weakest in society. He deserved to be crushed out of existence. So why not simply leave him to his fate and concentrate on bringing down Edward Forester? He struggled to come up with a satisfactory answer. Maybe it had something to do with his own brush with death. He didn't know. All he knew was his conscience wouldn't allow him to abandon the gangster. He was also acutely aware that the best intentions in the world wouldn't mean a thing unless he could come up with some sort of lead fast. The first thing was to find out where Forester was lying low. Not that there was much chance the politician would be careless enough to lead him to Reynolds, even if by some miracle the gangster was still alive. But whoever had dealt with Reynolds might well be keeping an eye on Forester in case any of the gangster's goons came looking for their boss. And if he could identify Forester's accomplices or associates, or whatever they were, that would surely bring him closer to both finding the gangster and nailing the politician.

Jim retrieved his notepad and the newspaper cutting from his jacket. A telephone number for somewhere called 'Southview' and a sixteen-year-old newspaper article about a house fire. It wasn't much, but it was all he had to go on. Massaging his pounding temples, he went to his study. He swallowed his pills as he waited for the PC to boot up. He Googled 'Southview Peak District'. Top of the search list was a map of South View Street in the village of Bamford. He clicked on a link to images of the street. It consisted of modest cottages. Not exactly the sort of places Forester would go for. He scanned further down the list. There was another South View Street in the neighbouring village of Bradwell. Again, Jim couldn't picture Forester staying in its terraced cottages or bungalows. On the next page a listing for somewhere called 'Southview Manor' caught his eye. The link took him to the website of a local historical society. There was a photo of a large grey-stone house with tall, arched windows and cod-medieval battlements, overlooking expansive gardens. Moorlands and gritstone crags loomed over the house, creating an air of gloomy isolation. Underneath the photo a paragraph described how the house had been built in 1822 by a wealthy London industrialist as a holiday retreat for his family. *Now that is Forester's sort of place*, thought Jim. Further down the page there was a historical map of the High Peak with the manor house marked on it. He printed the page off.

The next thing was to call the number, but it was still far

too early for that. Jim turned his attention to the newspaper cutting. He navigated to the website of the South Yorkshire *Chronicle* and searched their archives for the article. There were several links to related articles. The first read 'Police question dead man's son over Huddersfield house fire'. Jim clicked on the article, which began, 'Police say a fire at a residential address in Huddersfield in which a 67-year-old man perished is being treated as suspicious. A forensic examination of the property confirmed an accelerant was used to ignite the fire. Detectives are appealing for anyone who saw anything suspicious in the area on the night in question to come forward. It has also been revealed that detectives are interviewing Freddie Harding, the 34-year-old son of the dead man.'

Jim's brow creased. Freddie Harding. There was something familiar about that name. He navigated to the next article, whose headline ran, 'Police puzzled by mystery blaze'. Beneath it the article continued: 'Detectives are still trying to solve the mystery of a suspicious house fire that killed a Huddersfield man. The dead man's son was questioned but released without charge after it was confirmed he was working as a delivery driver in Mexborough on the night of the fatal blaze. Detectives have renewed their appeal for anyone with information to...'

Jim's gaze drifted away from the text. He typed 'Freddie Harding' into the search box. Several pages' worth of articles came up. The oldest related to the house fire. The final article about the fire was dated 15 April 1997, and shed no light on who the culprit might be. There was a gap of just under four years before the next article, whose 3 March headline ran 'Sheffield prostitute brutally raped'. A flicker of memory passed over Jim's face. An eighteen-year-old prostitute had been raped and beaten on wasteland off Pitsmoor Road. A passer-by had frightened her attacker away. Jim knew what happened next. A few days later a man walked into a police station and confessed to the attack. That man was Freddie Harding. Jim hadn't worked the case, but it had stuck in his mind because it was so rare for rapists to give themselves up. The following article, which was dated 7 March, confirmed Jim's memory was accurate. Its headline ran 'Mexborough man hands himself in to police for rape of prostitute'.

The name of the article's author – Vernon Tisdale – triggered another jolt of memory. Vernon had disappeared off the scene a few years ago, but with his colourful dress sense and poor personal hygiene he wasn't someone you forgot easily. Even harder to forget was the crime reporter's theory about a serial killer operating in the area. Vernon had gained a certain notoriety after presenting DCS Knight – who at that time was a DCI – with his infamous list of 'The Damned'. It had quickly become apparent that the list was flawed. Prostitutes had a way of disappearing for all sorts of reasons. Even so, a couple of things had kept Jim from completely dismissing the journalist's theory. Firstly, some of the women genuinely did seem to have vanished off the face of the planet. And secondly, Vernon had been so utterly convinced he was right it was hard not to listen to him. The overweight, shambling journalist may have been a somewhat off-the-wall character, but he was as shrewd as they came. If he believed there was a killer out there targeting prostitutes, then there was good reason for it. Vernon had even had a favourite suspect for the killer – Freddie Harding. His suspicion had never been proven, of course. But still, all this didn't explain why the hell Edward Forester was interested in the murder of Freddie Harding's father.

At the foot of the article there was a photo of Freddie Harding. Jim's eyes jolted wide as if at a revelation. Harding looked like a nasty piece of work – mean slit of a mouth, sunken stubbly cheeks, scar like a sword cut running from above his left eyebrow to the right side of his mouth. But it was his eyes that caught Jim's attention. Jim had seen those eyes before, only they'd been in another man's face. How had Grace Kirby described them to Mark? *Nasty pissy little brown eyes.* Yes, that was it. Only she'd been talking about the Chief Bastard, aka Edward Forester. Jim opened an extra tab and brought up a photo of the politician. Harding and Forester's eyes were the same colour, the same shape, even their bushy arched brows were the same. There were other similarities between the men. Both were balding. Harding's teeth were crooked and overlapping, as Forester's had been before he had them straightened. Their noses were sharp and straight. There were differences too. Forester's lips were fuller. There was more flesh on his face. His complexion was ruddier. But what really set the men apart was the same thing that connected them – their eyes. Harding seemed to be reluctantly facing the camera, almost as if afraid of what it might expose. Forester, on the other hand, stared directly into it with a confidence that was probably intended to suggest openness and trustworthiness, but which came over as arrogance to Jim.

'They're related,' Jim murmured. They had to be. How else to explain not just the similarities in their appearance, but the fact that Forester had kept the cutting? Jim navigated to an ancestry search site he'd used before to track people down. He searched the birth records index for Edward Forester. No hit. He changed the surname to Harding. The result came up – 'Born: 1955; Birthplace: Sheffield; Parents: Norman Harding, Mabel'. Mabel had obviously changed her and her son's surname back to her maiden name after divorcing her husband. He searched for Freddie – 'Born: 1962; Birthplace: Mexborough; Parents: Norman Harding, Brenda'. So Norman had remarried and had another kid, but this time he seemingly hadn't completely abandoned it. How would that have made Edward feel? Angry, certainly. Angry enough to kill, quite possibly. *Maybe that's the way to nail Forester*, thought Jim. *If I could somehow connect him to Norman Harding's murder—*

He pushed the idea aside. That case was almost as cold as the Mark Baxley abuse case. If a team of detectives hadn't been able to crack it back in 1996, how the hell was he going to do so now? Better to concentrate on Edward and Freddie. Was there any connection, beyond blood, between the brothers? One instantly sprang to mind – both were predatory sexual deviants. Whether that was a product of nature, or nurture, or both, didn't concern him right then.

What concerned him was finding out if the brothers had ever met. If they had, maybe they'd exchanged more than simply family stories. Maybe they'd shared, even indulged together in their warped fantasies. His thoughts returned to the Huddersfield house fire. Freddie had been questioned. Why? Clearly something had led the police to suspect he might have had it in for his dad. Considering Norman's track record, it was entirely possible he'd given his youngest son as much reason to hate him as his eldest. A crooked smile pulled at Jim's mouth as he imagined the brothers bonding over their father's murder. Secrets like that had a way of bringing people together more closely even than love.

Jim did a quick internet search for Vernon Tisdale's phone number. If the journalist was still alive, it would be worth talking to him. Knowing Vernon, he would have a lot of info on Freddie Harding that not even the police were aware of. He wasn't surprised when the search came up negative. Vernon had always hated phones, preferring to do his talking face to face. Jim glanced at the clock. It was still too early to start phoning around for a contact number. He printed off a photo of Freddie Harding, then showered and shaved. There was nothing in the kitchen suitable for him to eat, except some stale bread. He toasted it and, ignoring his body's cravings for caffeine and nicotine, ate it dry with orange juice. Watery sunlight dribbled through the windows. As its faint warmth washed over him, he closed his eyes and drew in a slow breath. A telephone number and a newspaper cutting. It wasn't much to go on. But then again, sometimes not much was enough.

Chapter Seventeen

The ringtone drilled its way into Reece's sleeping brain. Lifting one eyelid, he groped in semi-darkness at his clothes piled on the floor. His phone rang off as he pulled it from his jacket – '5 Missed Calls' flashed up on its screen. All of them from Doug. He frowned. It must be something important for Doug to be so keen to contact him at this time of the morning, especially when they were going to be meeting up soon enough anyway. His thoughts returned to Wayne Carson. An image of the pimp's pulped face flashed across the screen of his mind. With a heavy sigh, he started to get up, intending to return Doug's call in the bathroom where he wouldn't disturb Staci. He paused upon realising she wasn't in the bed. Was she in the bathroom? He touched her side of the bed. The sheets were cold. Wherever she was, she'd been gone a while.

Pulling on his trousers and shirt, Reece left the bedroom. Staci and another woman's voice drifted up the stairs. He made his way down to find them both cradling mugs of tea at the small, tatty table in the equally small, tatty kitchen. The woman appeared to have just finished a hard night working the streets. She was wearing high-heeled calf-length black boots, a tiny black skirt and matching vest top. A Celtic band tattoo encircled her left bicep. Thick makeup couldn't disguise the wrinkles and shadows around her eyes. Or the scars on her lips, nose and forehead. Whatever beauty she'd once possessed had long since been stripped away by the street. Reece found himself grimacing internally. Her old whore's face was a warning as to what lay ahead for Staci if he failed to get her out of this life.

'This is Amber,' said Staci, glancing at Reece. 'She's just told me something you should hear.'

'It's probably nothing,' said Amber, her voice hard and weary at the same time. 'But when I heard about Melinda's disappearance, it reminded me of something that happened to me back in the early nineties.'

'How early?' asked Reece.

Amber's brow creased. 'Ninety-one, I think,' she said unconvincingly.

'You think?'

A defensive edge came into Amber's voice. 'Yeah, I think. It were a long time ago. So pardon me if I can't remember the exact year, but that doesn't stop me from remembering what those bastards the Winstanleys and their pals did to me.'

The mention of the Winstanleys banished any last vestiges of sleepiness from Reece's eyes. 'You mean Herbert and Marisa Winstanley?'

Amber gave Staci a caustic look. 'Gaw, he's a sharp one, this bloke of yours.'

In turn, Staci shot Reece a glance that warned him to shut up. Taking the hint, Reece folded his arms and waited for Amber to tell her tale. Lighting a cigarette, she began, 'I was working on Rutland Street one night when this van pulled over—'

'What colour was it?' interjected Reece.

The creases reappeared on Amber's forehead. 'Red... no, white. Oh, I don't know. Anyway, what does it matter what fucking colour it was? Do you want to hear what I've got to say or not?'

'Sorry, I won't interrupt again.'

Amber took a long drag to collect her thoughts. 'The bloke driving the van was about the same age as you. He looked harmless enough, so I got in. He drove out towards Grenoside. He was drinking whisky and he asked if I wanted some. I hadn't been on the job long, so I was stupid enough to say yes. I only took a sip, but it must've been spiked cos the next thing I knew my head was spinning and I could barely see straight. The bloke pulled over. He tied my hands and blindfolded me. I was scared shitless. I thought I was as good as dead. But he didn't kill me. He drove me to a house. When he took the blindfold off, I was in this huge room. It was like something off the telly, all posh furniture and paintings on the walls. There were other people there – men and women, but mostly men. I don't know exactly how many. I was so out of it, it was hard to tell. Some of them were naked. Others were dressed in, y'know, bondage gear.'

Amber paused for another drag, before continuing in a voice deadened by years of exposure to the seedy side of life. 'Herbert – I didn't know that was his name until I saw him on the telly the other day – he was the first to rape me. His bitch wife held me down while he did it. Then his pals took their turns with me. They didn't just rape me. They whipped me until I was bleeding. They tied rope around my neck and strangled me until I passed out. They tore me up with huge dildos. One of the bastards bit my right nipple so hard it almost came off. I've still got the scar. I dunno how long it went on for. It seemed like hours. I thought I was gonna die. But I didn't. When they were done with me, the bloke from the van blindfolded me again and took me back to Rutland Street. He gave me a couple of hundred quid and threatened that if I went to the police, me and my family would be hurt. He knew my parents' names and where they lived. He said the people at the house were very important people and that if I wasn't afraid of being beaten up, they could easily arrange for me to go to prison for a long time instead.'

'And did you go to the police?' asked Reece.

Amber gave him that special look of contempt that people who'd been operating on the wrong side of the law for as many years as her reserved for coppers. 'Course I fucking didn't. This is the first time I've told anyone what happened to me.'

'So why are you telling me now?'

Amber gave a shrug as if the reasons didn't matter. 'There's nothing those bastards could do to me any more that hasn't already been done a hundred times over. And, well...' Her voice faltered for a second. A glimmer of something that might have been guilt came into her bloodshot eyes. 'It's been bothering me, y'know, thinking about what they did to me and what they might be doing to other girls. I've been wanting to speak to someone for a long time, but I never knew who to go to. No offence, but I wouldn't trust most coppers as far as I could piss. Staci tells me you're not like most coppers, though.'

No I'm not, thought Reece. *Most coppers would be ashamed to be like me.* 'The Winstanleys are dead. I don't think they're going to be holding any more parties.'

'This isn't just about the Winstanleys. There are others out there like them, other parties at other big houses.'

'How do you know this?'

'Not much around here gets by me. I've heard things about what goes on at these parties. Things that make me realise how lucky I am to even be here to talk about this stuff. Things like how for the right money you can buy girls or boys of any age – and I mean any age – for sex or worse.'

Reece frowned, thinking about the vile DVD Jim Monahan had recovered from the Baxleys' house, and asking himself, *What could be worse than that?* There was only one thing he could think of. 'By worse, you mean murder.'

Amber lit another cigarette with the end of her old one. 'Murder, torture, whatever. Y'know, for years there's been rumours of a serial killer popping off girls around here. But it's all bullshit. There's no serial killer out there. That's just what *they* want us to believe.'

'Who's they?'

'Who do you think? The Winstanleys and all their very important pals.'

'Do you know any of their names?'

Amber shook her head. 'I was so out of it that night I

176

couldn't even tell you what any of them look like. It only came back to me about the Winstanleys when I saw them on the telly. I do remember the van driver. I'll never forget that prick's ugly little face.'

'So what does he look like?'

'He's white, with brown eyes and hair. He was thinning on top back then, so he's probably bald by now. He had a thin face and bad teeth. But what I remember most about him is he's got this scar,' Amber traced a diagonal line with her finger from her left eye to the right side of her mouth, 'across his face.'

Reece's heart was suddenly thumping. 'Wait here.' He hurried out to his car and fetched Freddie Harding's photo. He showed Amber it. 'Is that him?'

'Yeah, that's Freddie Harding.'

Reece looked at her in amazement. 'You know his name.'

'I saw his face on the telly a few years ago after he raped some poor girl.' That same flicker came into Amber's eyes. 'I know I should've gone to the police. Believe me, I wanted to, but... well, I was too scared. Not just for myself. My parents are dead now, but they were still alive back then.' She looked at Reece as if seeking understanding. He offered her none, but neither was there judgement in his eyes. He'd seen all too often how fear could erode trust, until a kind of apathetic paralysis set in. 'To be honest, I'm still scared shitless,' continued Amber. 'But when I saw what that Kirby girl did, I thought to myself, if she's willing to die to take those bastards down, then I should be too. Don't get me wrong, I don't want to die. But I don't want these sickos to keep on getting away with it either. Enough is enough, y'know.'

Reece closed his eyes, rubbing his forehead. His skull was pounding as if he was hung-over. The recent spate of murders, the Winstanleys' parties, Freddie Harding, they were all connected to each other, and possibly to the disappearance of thirty prostitutes. There was no way he could hold onto this information. He had to take it to the DCI. But how the hell was he going to explain coming by it without risking being brought up on charges himself? He could cook up some story for Staci to feed to his colleagues. But the last thing he wanted to do was put her in a position where she was forced to lie to protect him. If anyone found out they were in a relationship, not only would the case be severely compromised, but so would any chance she had of regaining custody of Amelia.

'What are you going to do, Reece?' asked Staci as if reading the uncertainty in his mind.

'I'm not sure. I need to speak to Doug Brody.'

'Who's Doug Brody?' asked Amber, looking worried at the idea of Reece repeating what she'd told him to anyone.

'He's my partner. Look, Amber, if what you've said is true—'

'It is,' she broke in sharply, angered by the slight challenge in Reece's words.

'Then I need to talk to my colleagues. This is too big for me to handle alone. Have you spoken to anyone else about this?'

'No.'

'Keep it that way. And try to stay off the streets for today at least.'

Amber pulled a face that suggested that would be problematic. 'I need to earn, y'know.'

Reece knew – he'd clocked the needle track-marks on Amber's arms. Such a habit was a ravenous beast that constantly needed feeding. 'How much do you need?'

'A couple of hundred should do it.'

Reece went upstairs and counted out the required amount from Wayne's protection money. He returned to the kitchen and gave it to Amber. She looked at him uncertainly, as if unsure whether to be grateful or worried. 'What do I have to do for this?' she asked.

'Just keep your head down while I work out what's the best thing to do. Have you got a number I can contact you on?' Amber gave Reece a number, which he entered into his phone. 'And where do you live?'

Amber jerked her thumb towards the front of the house. 'Just across the street. At number forty-eight.'

'OK, here's what's going to happen. You're going to go buy whatever you need to tide you over for the day. Then you're going to go home and stay there until I, or one of my colleagues, get in touch.' Reece tried to smile reassuringly, but it came out twisted, more like a grimace. Smiling had never come naturally to his square-jawed face. 'And don't worry. You did the right thing coming to me.'

Reece's phone rang. He glanced at the screen. It was Doug again. 'I've got to take this.' He headed upstairs, putting the phone to his ear.

'At fucking last!' barked Doug. 'I've been phoning you for hours.'

'I know.'

'So how come you haven't returned my calls?'

'I was just about to.'

'Where are you?'

'At Staci's.'

Doug huffed as if to say, *I should have known*. 'I got a call from Wayne last night. He'd just got out of A&E with a broken nose and a couple of cracked ribs. As I'm sure you can imagine, you're not his favourite person right now.'

Reece had guessed this was coming. 'The bastard asked for it, Doug. You should see what he's done to Staci.'

'She's one of his best whores. And you're trying to steal her away from him. What did you expect him to do?'

A knot of anger rose into Reece's throat. 'I'm not stealing anyone. Just because she owes that bastard money, doesn't mean he owns her.'

'Yes it fucking does. And you're her only way out. Jesus, Reece, you're a copper. Can't you see she's using you?'

Fuck you, Doug! The words pushed at Reece's lips, but he didn't let them out. Maybe Doug was right. Maybe Staci was using him. But he didn't care. He loved her, and there was nothing he could do to change that. He thought about saying as much, but he knew Doug would probably just laugh and call him a sentimental fool.

Some of the harshness left Doug's voice. 'I'm only trying to look out for you, Reece. I don't want to see you fuck up your career over this.'

I'm a copper on the take, thought Reece. *My career's already about as fucked up as it can get.* 'I have to go to Weston Park Hospital to pick up my dad.' His tone was no longer angry, but there was a cold, distant edge to it. 'I'll meet you in the car park at eight o'clock.'

Doug sighed. 'OK, Reece, if that's how you want to play it.'

Reece closed his eyes, thinking about everything he'd learnt over the past couple of days. He knew he'd stumbled onto something huge. The kind of case that could have made his career – if he'd done it right. But when had he done anything right in his whole miserable life? He clenched his fists with frustration. His eyes snapped open at the sound of Staci's voice. 'Amber's gone. Who was that on the phone?'

'Doug. I've got to go meet him.'

'Do you trust him?'

'He's my partner,' Reece stated simply. He looked searchingly into Staci's eyes. 'Besides, sooner or later everyone's got to trust someone. Right?'

Staci blinked. Her gaze dropped away from Reece's momentarily. When she looked back up, there was concern, even fear in her eyes. 'Be careful, Reece. This whole thing gives me a bad feeling. The people Amber was talking about, they'd kill anyone to keep their secrets, even a copper. Look at what happened to that woman detective. What was her name?'

'Amy Sheridan. And that's not going to happen to me.' Reece smiled, and this time it came naturally. He wished Doug was here to see the look in Staci's eyes. *Maybe then he'd understand why I've fallen for her so hard*, he thought, taking her hand, drawing her towards him and kissing her tenderly.

'Do you have to go right away?' she murmured, lifting his hands to her mouth and kissing his scabbed knuckles.

Reece nodded. As much as he wanted to crawl back into bed with Staci, there was no time. They headed downstairs. 'I'll see you.'

'When?'

'Soon.'

Staci held his hand as if reluctant to let it go. 'Thanks for what you did last night. No one's ever done anything like that for me before.'

Reece kissed her again, then left. As he drove to the hospital, he held on to Staci's parting words. Perhaps beating up Wayne hadn't been the right thing to do. But he'd had to do something. And sometimes maybe something was enough.

Reece pulled over at a cash machine and withdrew two hundred quid to replace what he'd given to Amber. When he got to the hospital car park, he found Doug waiting for him. He parked alongside his partner's souped-up silver Subaru. The first time he'd seen the car, Reece had said it looked like the sort of thing a drug dealer would drive. To which Doug had replied, 'If it's good enough for a dealer, it's good enough for me.' Reece had laughed at the time. He wouldn't have found the comment so funny now.

Reece got into the Subaru and handed over the protection money. Doug began to count it. 'It's all there,' said Reece.

Doug nodded an *I believe you*, but he continued to count.

'What's the matter?' asked Reece. 'Don't you trust me?'

'Course I do. It's Wayne I don't trust. I wouldn't put it past him to try and pass us counterfeit notes.' Doug took out the cash-machine-fresh banknotes and inspected them closely. 'For instance, look at these twenties. When have you ever seen a junkie with money as clean as this?'

'I put those in there.'

'Why?'

'I gave some money to a woman who's helping with my inquiries into the disappearance of Staci's friend.'

'Ah yes, Melinda the missing whore. I was just about to ask you how your search is going.'

'There have been some...' Reece searched for words that would adequately convey the significance of the information he'd obtained, 'interesting developments.'

'So let's hear it.'

'I went to see Vernon Tisdale. You already know about his theory. Well, he put me on to this guy—'

'Yeah, Freddie Harding,' interrupted Doug. 'I know about him too.'

'But did you know he's connected to the Winstanleys?'

Doug's brows lifted with interest. 'Connected how?'

Reece told Doug about Amber. When he was finished, Doug gave him a weighing-up look, as if reassessing what he thought he knew about his partner. 'This Amber doesn't exactly sound like the most reliable of witnesses,' he observed.

'I know, but if even half of what she said is true, this

might be the break we need to blow this case wide open. Amber remembered the Winstanleys when she saw them on the news. Maybe with the right prodding, she'll remember other names and faces. Or maybe we can get Freddie to talk.'

'Why would he talk? We've got nothing on him, except the words of a junkie whore.'

'Fair point, but if nothing else, we've got to put people on him twenty-four hours a day. We've got a whole series of murders on our hands, we've got God knows how many people involved in abduction, abuse, maybe even murder at the Winstanley house, and this scummy little bastard,' Reece jabbed his finger at Freddie Harding's photo, 'is in it right up to his neck. I was tailing him last night when you called. He was heading south on the M1.' A look of frustration came into his brooding brown eyes. 'I only wish I'd kept on tailing him. Who knows, he might have led me straight to Melinda or some other poor girl.'

'And what if he had? How would you have explained that to the DCI?' Doug tapped his temple. 'Think, Reece. If Garrett gets even a sniff that there's something going on between you and Staci, you're finished. The most important thing is to keep your name out of this.'

'How do we do that?'

'Don't worry about that. I'll handle it. You just leave everything to me from now on and concentrate on looking after your dad. And for Christ's sake, stay away from Staci until this is over.'

Reece's face creased. The thought of staying away from

Staci, even for a few days, left him with a sinking, empty feeling, but he gave a reluctant nod of agreement.

'Don't look so miserable,' said Doug, laying his hand on Reece's shoulder. 'You've done good work here, both with Wayne and this Freddie Harding business.'

'What if Wayne had died? I could've fucked everything up.'

'You've got a temper on you, that's for sure,' Doug chuckled. 'But that's not such a bad thing. Sometimes in this line of business violence is the only thing that gets results. You've just got to learn to channel your anger. Use it, don't let it use you. Do you understand?'

Reece nodded, although he wasn't sure he could control his anger. When the red mist descended, it was like some other force took over. He'd been that way his entire life. The only thing that had ever been able to get through to him at such times was his mother's voice. No, that wasn't true, he realised. Staci's voice had punctured his rage. And now he had to stay away from her for who knows how long. He heaved a sigh.

'Listen, things might be changing around here soon,' went on Doug. 'Something's happening. Something big. If it comes off, you and me could both be in the money.' He held up a fistful of Wayne's cash. 'And I'm not talking about this kind of money, I'm talking about real money. Enough to pay off Staci's debt and have plenty left over. You've just got to keep your head down and do as I say. OK?'

'OK.'

'Good lad. Now I'd better get to work.' Doug pointed at

the hospital. 'And you'd better get in there and see how your dad's going on. But before you do, give me this Amber's contact details.'

Reece wrote down Amber's number and address. 'Go easy with her. She's scared.'

'I wouldn't worry about her. These old whores are as hard as nails.' Doug peeled off a couple of hundred quid from the protection money and proffered it to Reece. 'Buy your dad something nice.'

With a hesitation so slight as to be barely perceptible, Reece took the money. 'Call me if there are any more developments.'

'Will do.'

Reece got out of the car. He watched Doug accelerate away, then headed into the hospital and asked a receptionist which ward his dad was on. His dad was sitting up in bed, eating breakfast. There was a jaundiced tint to his sucked-in face. Compared to the powerful man who'd used to effortlessly carry Reece for miles on his shoulders, he looked achingly frail. Reece could hardly bear to see him like that. But neither could he bear to turn away. 'Hello, Dad. How are you feeling?'

'How do you think I'm bloody feeling?' Frank Geary's voice was as strong and gruff as ever. Reece felt a small measure of relief to hear it. Frank jerked his thumb at a doctor. 'If the cancer doesn't kill me, those buggers will with their tests and so-called treatments.'

'Have they said when you can go home?'

'Doctor Meadows wants to speak to me before I leave.

They tell me he'll be round at about nine, but you never know in these places. So you might as well sit your arse down.'

With a defeated air, Reece dropped into a chair. He stared at the floor, not seeing it, thinking about Doug – the expensive suits, the flash jewellery, the perma-tan. Was that how he wanted to end up?

'Did you win?'

Frank's voice brought Reece back to the moment. 'Win what?'

Frank indicated Reece's scabbed knuckles. 'The fight.'

A tiny smile pulled at Reece's mouth. Whatever else his dad had lost, he still had a policeman's eye for details. 'There was no fight, Dad.'

Frank made a doubtful face. 'I'd ask if you were in some kind of trouble, but I know you wouldn't tell me if you were.'

Reece said nothing. Frank inclined his head slightly, as if his son's silence confirmed what he'd said. He proffered a bowl of cereal to Reece. 'Here, you look as if you need this more than me.'

Reece cast a searching, almost suspicious look at his dad. It was the first time in as long as he could remember that the old bastard had shown an interest – albeit in a sidelong manner – in his well-being. The thought came to him, *Why now?* As far as he could see, there was only one answer. And it was an answer that caused panic to bubble up in his chest.

Chapter Eighteen

Edward Forester flinched when his bedside phone rang, but he made no move to pick it up. He licked his lips rapidly, eyes anxious and uncertain. The ringing stopped. He heard Philippa's muffled voice. She must have answered the call downstairs. Jumping out of bed, he hurried onto the landing. 'Who?' Philippa was saying. 'Sorry, no one by that name lives here... No problem. Bye.'

'Who was that?' Edward asked, descending the broad, curving staircase.

'Wrong number.' Philippa headed into the kitchen, cup of tea in hand.

Edward dialled 1471 and was informed that the caller's number was unavailable. Frowning, he followed his wife. 'Was it a man or a woman?'

'A man.'

'Who did he ask for?'

'Linda someone-or-other. Why? What does it matter?'

'It matters because...' Edward hesitated, glancing uneasily at the housekeeper who was frying eggs. The eggs, he knew, were for his mother. She always ate two for breakfast. And she was very particular about how she liked them done – they had to be sunny side up, the yolk liquid and unbroken, the white retaining a slight translucence. The housekeeper plated up the eggs on a tray along with a pot of tea, a jug of warm milk and a bone china cup and saucer. Edward waited for her to leave the kitchen, before continuing, 'Because there are people out there looking for me, people who'd like nothing better than to see me dead and buried. And I'm not just talking about my political career.'

Philippa arched a well-shaped, ever so slightly contemptuous eyebrow. 'Oh, don't be so melodramatic.'

Edward bent close to his wife. His words came in a low hiss. 'You just don't get it, do you? I owe millions. There's no knowing what people are capable of when there's that much money at stake.'

'You know what, darling, you're starting to sound a little paranoid.'

Edward slammed his palm against the table. 'Don't you dare call me paranoid! Just look at what happened with Stephen.'

'Calm down, Edward. You'll give yourself a heart attack. The fact is, you're not facing bankruptcy. Your mother will pay off your debts and this whole thing will blow—'

Philippa was interrupted by the sound of a loud crash from upstairs. 'What the hell's that now?' said Edward, hurrying back into the hallway. As he started up the stairs, the housekeeper ran out of his mother's room. Her eyes were wide with shock and there was a red mark on her cheek.

'She hit me,' exclaimed the housekeeper, swaying between tears and anger.

Edward rolled his eyes with exasperation, but not surprise. He'd guessed the moment he saw the housekeeper's face what had happened. 'Why?'

'She said her eggs weren't done right. I told her there was nothing wrong with them, and the nasty old cow slapped me.' The housekeeper headed past Edward towards the front door.

'Please don't leave, Mrs Adams,' said Philippa.

'I'm sorry, Mrs Horne, but I won't stay in this house a second longer whilst she's here.' The housekeeper pulled on her coat and stormed out of the door.

Philippa spun towards her husband, her eyes livid. 'She's gone too far this time, Edward,' she said, loudly enough for her voice to carry upstairs. 'What in God's name makes your mother think she—'

'I know, I know,' interjected Edward, spreading his hands in a shushing motion. 'I'll speak to her. You go after Mrs Adams. Calm her down, make sure she hasn't got it into her head to go to the police. The last thing we need right now is them poking their noses in around here.'

Expelling a sharp breath, Philippa hurried after the housekeeper. Somewhat more slowly, Edward made his way upstairs. He drew in a deep breath, before entering his mother's bedroom. The breakfast tray lay upturned on the rug beside her bed, a puddle of milky tea spreading outwards from it. Conall was tentatively lapping at the steaming liquid. Mabel Forester was propped against pillows, arms folded across her breasts, which sagged heavily beneath a white satin nightgown. A hairnet was stretched over her raven-black wig. Shorn of makeup, her wrinkles stood out like lines on white paper. 'Has that dreadful woman gone?' she asked sharply.

Edward shooed the wolfhound out of the room. 'Yes.'

'Good.'

'No, it's not good, Mother. It's not bloody good at all! You can't hit someone just because they do or say something you don't like.'

'Why not? How else will they learn?'

'What if she goes to the police?'

Mabel gave a dismissive flick of a blue-veined hand. 'I only gave her a little tap. You seem to forget, Edward, I worked as a housemaid before you were born. I know how these people's minds work. She'll sulk for a day or two, then she'll be back. And next time she'll cook my eggs exactly as I like them.'

'Times have changed, Mother.'

'Maybe, but people haven't.'

Edward shook his head, unconvinced. 'This is the last thing we need—' He broke off as his mother's lips formed an injured pout.

'I heard what that woman called me. A nasty old cow. Is that what you think of me too?'

'Of course not.'

'Are you sure? You don't sound sure.'

A sigh slipped past Edward's lips. He knew what his mother wanted. He'd played this game a thousand times.

He approached the bed, sat at her side and rested his hands on hers. His voice took on a childish tone. 'I think you're the best mummy in the whole world.'

Mabel drew Edward towards her, pillowing his head against her breasts. He allowed her to do so with an expression of bland resignation, like someone performing an unpleasant but necessary duty. 'I used to hold you like this when I was breastfeeding you,' she said, smiling at the memory. 'You'd only ever feed off my right breast. You used to kick and scream if I tried to put you on my left one. Ever since then my right nipple has been bigger than my left. Here, feel the difference.'

Edward struggled to contain a shudder as his mother guided his hand to her nipples. The right one was far larger, and smooth and hard as a bullet. 'You see, Edward,' she continued, 'we all have our particular likings. Who can say where they come from? They simply exist inside us all. There's no point fighting them. Accepting who you are, not fighting or apologising for it, that's the mark of a true leader.'

Edward closed his eyes, nestling more deeply into his mother's bosom. He'd heard these words, or ones like them, many times before from her. They always gave him a strange soothing tingle at the back of his head. 'You're right, Mummy. I'm sorry for shouting at you. I'm just so damned worried about this money issue.'

'There's no need to be. The money will be here before midday.'

'In cash?'

'Well, from what you told me, I assumed the people you're dealing with wouldn't want a banker's draft.' Mabel stroked her son's bald head. 'And once this person who wants to hurt you has been...' she searched briefly for the right words, 'taken out of the picture, we can get on with being a family again. Can't we?'

This time, Edward couldn't quite contain the tremor in his voice as he said, 'Yes, Mother.'

Chapter Nineteen

After making sure his number was withheld, Jim called Southview. A woman picked up and said, 'Hello.'

'Can I speak to Linda, please?' said Jim, keeping his voice carefully accentless.

'Who?'

'Linda Jones.'

'Sorry, no one by that name lives here.'

'I must have the wrong number. Sorry.'

'No problem. Bye.'

Jim hung up. He hadn't needed to ask who he was speaking to. He recognised Philippa Horne's voice from the television. So Councillor Horne and, presumably, her husband too were lying low at Southview Manor. The next thing was to put eyes on them, see what they were up to. But first he needed to make another call. He punched in the number for Bob Stone, a crime reporter at the South Yorkshire *Chronicle*. 'Hi, Bob, this is Jim Monahan,' he said, when the journalist picked up. 'I need a favour. I'm trying to track down Vernon Tisdale. Have you got his contact details?'

'Vernon, what do you want with that old hack?' enquired Bob.

'I need to ask him a couple of questions about a case he reported on.'

'What case?'

'Ah, that'd be telling.'

'Hang on a moment, Jim. I'll see if anyone around here knows where you can find him.'

The line was silent for a minute or two. Then a different voice came on it. 'Hi, Jim, this is Alan Dobson. Bob tells me you're looking for Vernon.'

'That's right.'

'Seems he's a popular man these days. Reece Geary phoned me yesterday asking for his address.'

Jim frowned. He knew Reece, although not very well. The young DI had only been on the Major Inquiry team a few months, and Doug Brody had quickly taken him under his wing. Jim didn't have much liking for Doug, either as a cop or a person. Not that Doug wasn't good at his job. He had sharp instincts and a nose for tracking down criminals. He also had a well-earned reputation for having a quick temper and an arrogant streak as wide as the M1. He struck Jim as the kind of man who wanted everything his own way or no way at all. And that was a dangerous quality in a cop.

What was Reece doing contacting Vernon? Had Freddie Harding somehow come onto Garrett's radar? Jim couldn't see any other reason for Reece's interest in the retired journalist. But how the hell had Garrett made the connection – if connection there was – between Harding and the recent murders? Had a new witness come forward? And if so, was Garrett onto Edward Forester as well? The possibility provoked mixed feelings. On the one hand, Jim wanted nothing more than to see Forester brought down. On the other, if the DCI moved on Forester, the first thing his accomplices would surely do would be to destroy anything that might incriminate them. And if Bryan Reynolds was still alive that would include him.

Picking up on Jim's brooding silence, Alan said sarcastically, 'I'm glad to know communication between you guys is as good as ever. I don't suppose you'd be willing to give me any hints as to what—'

'The contact details, please,' cut in Jim, his tone flat but urgent. Before he went anywhere near Forester, he had to find out what the deal was with Reece. If Forester was under some kind of suspicion, his house might be being watched. In which case, if a copper supposedly on sick leave was seen in its vicinity, there would be a lot of difficult explaining to be done.

'No, I thought not,' said Alan. He gave Jim Vernon's number and address. Jim thanked him and headed for his car. It would be a bad idea, he knew, to phone Vernon. The ex-journalist was the kind of guy who liked to do his talking face to face. He drove fast to Vernon's house, running red lights. He hammered on the front door, his face twitching with impatience. Eventually, the door creaked open and a pudgy face peered out, blinking like a mole at the morning sun.

Vernon's eyes widened a little with recognition. 'Well, well, Jim Monahan.'

'I need to speak to you.'

Vernon's lips flicked into a smile. 'Yeah, well, I assumed you weren't here to fix my guttering.' Opening the door as wide as it would go – which wasn't all that wide – Vernon motioned for Jim to enter. Jim followed him along the newspaper-cramped hallway into the equally cramped back room. 'So, Jim, what can I do for you?'

'One of my colleagues came to see you yesterday. I need to know why.'

Vernon slowly lowered his bulk on to a sofa. He stroked a fat tabby that was curled up next to him. Both the cat and its owner treated Jim to a searching look. 'The last time I saw you, I seem to remember you were busy trashing my reputation.'

'That's not true. I was one of the few people who gave some credit to your theory. The fact is, Vernon, your list was flawed. I knew it, DCS Knight knew it, and I think even you knew it.'

Vernon's lips vibrated as he expelled a sharp breath. 'How many prostitutes have to go missing before you people sit up and take notice? Fifty? A hundred?'

Jim's face tightened into a little grimace. Vernon's words stung him. He wanted to retort that the number of missing women or the fact that they were prostitutes was irrelevant; every life was worth the same in the eyes of the law. But he knew that wasn't true.

'You're quick enough to take notice when so-called upstanding citizens like the Winstanleys get popped off, though. Aren't you?' continued Vernon, his voice bitterly accusatory.

'The Winstanleys were shot to death. There was no evidence that a single one of the women on your list died as a result of foul play,' Jim reminded him.

Vernon snatched up a wad of papers and stabbed his finger at a photo of a young woman paperclipped to the uppermost sheet. 'Twenty-nine women still missing to this day. If that doesn't constitute evidence of foul play, perhaps you can tell me what does.'

Jim heaved a sigh. 'Look, maybe you were right and we were wrong. I don't know. All I know is our investigation didn't turn anything up to substantiate your theory.' Vernon opened his mouth to say something, but Jim held up a hand. 'Just hear me out. I didn't like the way the investigation was shelved, but there was nothing I could do about it. Not back then. Things are different now. I'm going after someone. I can't say for sure whether he's connected to your missing prostitutes, but I do know that he's a rapist and a child abuser. And I know he's been involved in several murders and that other people will die if you don't help me.'

'Is this someone Freddie Harding?'

Jim shook his head. 'Although he may be involved in this. I can't give you a name. Not because I don't trust you. But because I don't want to make you an accessory to what's happening. You see, the truth is, I'm acting on my own here. If you were to pick up the phone and tell my DCI what I'm doing, I'd find myself up on disciplinary, possibly even criminal charges.'

Jim fell silent with an expectant look. He'd left himself dangerously exposed, but he could see no other way of piercing Vernon's armour of resentment about the way his list of 'The Damned' had been dismissed. He just hoped he'd read Vernon right. The ex-journalist had always struck him as someone with no liking for officialdom. Vernon's scraggly beard split into a smile. 'It's funny, Reece Geary said something very similar.'

The implication of Vernon's words was obvious – Reece hadn't come here in an official capacity either. So Garrett wasn't on to Forester. The realisation brought a familiar mixture of feelings with it: disappointment that no new evidence had come to light; and a sort of tentative relief that he might yet have the opportunity to rescue Bryan Reynolds. 'So why did Reece want to speak to you?'

'He's searching for a friend of a friend. A missing prostitute called Melinda.'

'What about the friend he's helping out, did he give you their name?'

'No.'

Jim's brows drew together. It was one thing not telling Vernon the friend's name, but why would Reece keep it from Garrett? Unless he was protecting someone who stood to get in trouble if he investigated through official channels. Echoing his thoughts, Vernon said, 'I'd say it's a fair bet they're someone Reece is keen his superiors don't find out he's involved with.'

'So what did he tell you?'

'Not much. Just that he's not sure Melinda's actually missing. That she might have simply left town. He showed me a photo of her. She's a young girl, maybe nineteen or twenty, junkie-skinny, dyed blond hair, blue eyes.'

'And what did you tell him?'

'That she's Freddie Harding's type. You remember Freddie, don't you? Violent rapist and all round nice guy.'

'Yes, I remember him.'

'Chances are your colleague's tailing him right this moment.' Vernon rubbed his chubby hands together in anticipation. 'I can hardly wait to find out where Freddie leads him.'

The lines between Jim's eyes deepened. If by some chance Freddie Harding led Reece to Edward Forester, the rookie DI could find himself in serious danger. He had to talk to Reece, find out what he knew, warn him. The question was, how much could he risk telling Reece in return? To some extent, at least, perhaps the two of them could work together on this thing. After all, it seemed they were both operating well outside their job description. He would have to tread carefully, though. The last thing he wanted to do was embroil Reece in a mess that could finish his career before it had barely started. 'Did Reece give you his number?'

Vernon took a business card out of his shirt pocket. 'Don't you guys even exchange numbers these days?'

'My phone was stolen.' Jim entered Reece's number into his phone's memory, and handed the card back along with his own card. 'Do me a favour, call me if anyone else contacts you about Reece or Freddie Harding or anything connected to what we've been talking about.'

As Jim turned to head for the front door, Vernon heaved himself to his feet. 'Before you leave, Jim, tell me one thing. How is the guy you're after connected to Freddie?'

'You always were one of the sharpest journalists around, Vernon. I'm sure you can work that one out for yourself.' Jim gave Vernon a look that was part concern, part warning. 'A piece of advice, though: if you do work it out, keep it to yourself. There are people out there who'd kill you without blinking to protect that information.'

Vernon raised his eyebrows as if amused by the idea. 'Sounds like this thing is a lot bigger than one or two people.'

'Just remember what I said, Vernon. And thanks for your help.'

Jim shook Vernon's hand, stepped outside and dialled Reece.

Chapter Twenty

Lulled by the warmth of the ward, Reece was half dozing when Doctor Meadows showed up. 'Morning, Mr Geary,' he said to Reece's father. 'How are you feeling today?'

'Not great, Doctor,' said Frank. 'But a lot better than yesterday.'

'Good. How's the nausea?'

'Well, I've kept my breakfast down.' Frank grinned, exposing tobacco-stained teeth. 'And that's no mean feat considering what the food's like around here.'

The doctor tapped a folder he was holding. 'The results of your X-rays and blood tests have come back. I'd like to discuss—'

'Hang on a moment please, Doctor.' Frank turned to Reece. 'Go wait in the corridor.'

Reece frowned. 'I think I should hear what Doctor Meadows has to say.'

'I don't give a damn what you think.' The familiar abrasive edge was back in Frank's voice. 'Just do as I bloody well tell you.'

Reece looked askance at Doctor Meadows, who gave a slight apologetic shrug. Reluctantly, Reece rose and headed for the corridor. Once again, a constricted feeling took hold of his chest. Why didn't his father want him to hear what the doctor had to say? Had the cancer spread? Was the old bastard going to die? His phone rang. A number he didn't recognise showed on its screen. 'No mobile phones on the ward,' said a nurse. 'Switch it off or go outside.'

Reece was about to cut the call off, but he hesitated. What if it had something to do with Staci or his unofficial investigation? Putting the phone to his ear, he went through a pair of double doors. 'Hello?'

'Hello, Reece.'

Reece recognised the voice, but was so surprised to hear it that his own was doubtful. 'Jim?'

'Uh-huh. Where are you?'

'I...' Reece stumbled a little over his words. What the hell was Jim Monahan doing phoning him? And why did he want to know where he was? 'I'm at Weston Park Hospital with my dad. Why?'

'We need to meet up and talk.'

The furrows on Reece's forehead intensified. Was that a note of relief he'd caught in Jim's voice? 'I thought you were in hospital.'

'I was, but I'm not any more. Listen, Reece, can you get away from the hospital for a while?'

'My dad's with the doctor now. It shouldn't take long, but then I've got to take him home and—'

'That's fine,' cut in Jim, his voice quick with urgency. 'I know where Frank lives. I'll see you at his house.'

'What's this about, Jim? Have you been talking to Doug?'

'No. Look, I'll explain everything when I see you. And do me a favour, Reece. Don't go mentioning this to Doug or anyone else until I've had chance to speak to you.'

'Erm... OK.'

Reece slowly removed the phone from his ear, his thoughts whirring. *What possible reason*, he wondered, *could Jim have for wanting to talk to me? Maybe it's got nothing to do with Freddie Harding or the Winstanleys*, part of his mind tried to reassure him. Another part dismissed the possibility. Jim had never contacted him outside work before. In fact, they'd barely exchanged more than half a dozen words on any subject. What's more, everyone knew the Grace Kirby case had got under Jim's skin. *But if he hasn't been speaking to Doug, what makes him think I know anything worth knowing? Has he got some sort of line on Amber, or maybe even Staci?* Reece clenched his teeth at the idea. His jaw relaxed as it occurred to him that maybe Vernon Tisdale had contacted Jim. The two of them must have known each other from way back. The possibility was preferable – just – to Jim having talked to Amber or Staci. But it would still leave some uncomfortable explaining to be done.

Reece started to dial Doug, but hesitated as Jim's parting words echoed back to him. Why didn't Jim want him to talk to anyone? Was it perhaps because he too was operating beyond the bounds of his job? Jim and DCI Garrett hadn't exactly seen eye to eye on the Grace Kirby case. There were even whispers of disciplinary proceedings being initiated against Jim. The more Reece thought about it, the more likely it seemed to him that he was right. After all, Jim had suffered a heart attack. He wasn't even on active duty.

Reece returned the phone to his pocket. Doug didn't have much liking for Jim. As far as he was concerned, Jim wasn't to be trusted. 'He's got no dirt on his hands,' Doug had once said. 'You can't trust a bloke with no dirt on his hands.' He would flip out if he thought there was a possibility Jim knew about Reece's off-the-record investigation. And Reece couldn't deal with that now. Not on top of everything else.

As if he was dragging something heavy behind him, Reece re-entered the ward. The curtain had been drawn around his father's bed. An image suddenly came into his mind of himself being dismissed from the force in disgrace. He grimaced. If the cancer didn't finish his dad off, finding out his son was a bent copper almost certainly would. *Stop panicking*, he told himself sharply. *You don't know what Jim wants. And even if he does know about Staci, it's not necessarily the end of your career. Remember what Doug said, you can't trust a man with no dirt on his hands. But maybe that's not the case any more. Maybe Jim's got some dirt on him now – dirt you can use.*

When Doctor Meadows emerged from behind the curtains, Reece accosted him. 'What's the story, Doctor?'

'I'm sorry, Mr Geary, you'll have to speak to your father.'

Reece felt a flash of irritation, but didn't push the issue. Doctor Meadows had sworn an oath that bound him to the duties of his job, just as Reece had. Only, unlike Reece, the doctor was obviously intent on keeping his oath. 'Can you at least tell me whether he's fit to go home?'

'He can go as soon as his discharge forms have been sorted out.'

Thanking the doctor, Reece stepped through the curtains. His dad was getting dressed. Reece waited silently, knowing there was no point attempting to convince him to tell him what the prognosis was. Once his dad had made up his mind, there was no changing it. He studied his dad's face for any indication of whether the news was good or bad. But he could read nothing in his dark eyes. A nurse brought the discharge forms. After signing them, they headed to Reece's car. The journey passed in silence, until Frank said gruffly, 'Stop sulking, Reece.'

'I'm your son,' Reece shot back. 'Don't you think I have a right to know if you're going to live or die?'

'No, I don't.' Frank stabbed a finger at his chest. 'This cancer is mine. And I'll deal with it. It doesn't concern you.'

'How can you say that?'

'Easy. I just open my mouth and the words come out.'

Reece shook his head at the facetious remark. 'How the fuck Mum put up with your bullshit for so many years, I'll never know.' The words took Reece by surprise as much as they did his dad. He'd thought them a thousand times before, but never dared voice them.

Frank's mouth drew into a scowl. 'Unlike most people these days, your mother understood the meaning of love and loyalty.'

Reece gave a short, harsh laugh. 'If love and loyalty mean letting someone beat the shit out of you for forty years, you can fucking keep them.'

Frank's right hand shot out and grasped his son's jacket collar. His other hand curled into a fist. Reece hit the brakes, forcing the car behind to swerve sharply. He twisted towards his dad, but made no attempt to break free of his hold. 'Go on then.' His voice was bland and taunting. 'Hit me. That's what you're best at, isn't it? Hitting people you know won't hit back.'

Frank's eyes burned. His fist twitched as if he was about to prove his son right. But instead he released his grip and, as a fit of coughing took hold of him, pressed his hands to his mouth. The coughing continued for a minute or so. When he drew his hands away, their palms glistened with blood-threaded saliva. 'Take me home,' he croaked, wiping his hands and mouth on a tissue.

Reece accelerated back into the flow of traffic. To his surprise, he felt as calm as a windless lake. In the past, whenever he'd thought about standing up to his dad it had always brought on waves of anxiety. Frank stared out the window, lips pressed into a tight line. *Who's sulking now?* thought Reece.

When they arrived at the house, Reece's calm was disturbed by the sight of Jim's car.

'Is that Jim Monahan?' Frank wondered aloud, a note of unease in his voice.

'Yes,' said Reece, pulling into the driveway.

'What the hell does he want?'

Reece made no reply. Before getting out of the car, Frank cleared his throat and drew his broad, thin shoulders back. A kernel of sympathy opened inside Reece. His dad was plainly embarrassed for his old colleague to see him in such a state. His voice a little too loud and cheery, Frank called to the approaching detective, 'Hello, Jim, it's been a long time.'

Smiling, Jim extended his hand. 'Too long.'

A frown wrinkled Frank's face as he accepted the handshake. 'Christ, you look bloody awful.'

'You don't look so great yourself.'

'Yeah, well I've got cancer. What's your excuse?'

'Heart attack.'

Reece frowned too as he took in Jim's haggard features. It had only been a few days since he'd last seen him, but everything that had happened between then and now had clearly taken a toll on his health. 'Are you sure you shouldn't be resting?'

'Thanks for your concern, Reece, but I'm fine.' Even as he spoke, Jim swayed on his feet. He put out a hand and steadied himself against Reece.

'No, you're bloody not,' said Frank. He jerked his thumb at the house. 'Let's get him inside.'

Wrapping a muscular arm around Jim's back, Reece helped him into the house. Jim dropped heavily onto the sofa. With an unsteady hand, he pulled out a blister strip of tablets. 'Get him some water,' Frank said to Reece.

Frank lowered himself into his armchair, looking at Jim with concern and curiosity. 'You should be in hospital.'

'Bugger that.'

'I know how you feel. I can't stand those places either.' Frank chuckled. 'Christ, look at us. Some of the nastiest bastards in South Yorkshire used to fill their pants at the sight of us. They'd laugh in our faces if they saw us now.'

Reece returned with the water. Jim thanked him and knocked back a handful of tablets. They sat in silence for a moment, while a little colour seeped back into Jim's face. 'Do you want a cup of tea?' asked Frank.

Jim shook his head. 'I'm not supposed to have caffeine.'

'And I'm not supposed to have cigs. But that doesn't stop me.'

'Dad, you really should listen to the doctors,' Reece said, in the tone of weary rebuke he'd come to use whenever discussing his dad's cavalier attitude to his illness.

Frank scowled. 'Bollocks. No doctor's going to tell me what I can and can't do.'

'Do you mind if I talk to Reece alone?' asked Jim.

'You mean you didn't come here to see me?' Frank said, with an expression of mock hurt. Grinning, he stood and left the room.

'Big Frank Geary,' said Jim. 'He's not changed a bit.'

'Except he's not so big any more.' Reece's tone wasn't unfriendly, but neither was it particularly friendly. 'So what do you want to talk about?'

'A missing prostitute.'

Reece's stomach dropped like a stone in water. He kept his expression carefully blank. 'What—'

'Before you say anything else,' cut in Jim, 'you should know that I've spoken to Vernon Tisdale.'

Fucking Vernon, thought Reece. *So much for not telling anyone.* He waited for Jim to continue.

'You should also know that it was Alan Dobson who told me you'd been to see Vernon. So you've got no reason to feel pissed off at Vernon. He was reluctant to say anything until he found out that, like you, I'm acting on my own.'

'The DCI doesn't know about you speaking to Vernon?'

Jim shook his head. 'As far as he's concerned, I'm still in hospital.'

Relieved but still cautious, Reece said, 'So Alan Dobson contacted you.'

'No. I contacted him for the same reason you did. Here's the thing, Reece – and I'm putting myself on the line telling you this – I'm going after someone I believe to be connected to the recent murders. I don't have any hard evidence against this person. All the same, I know he's guilty and I'm going to bring him down no matter what it takes.'

No matter what it takes. The words were uttered with a peculiar, almost unnerving intensity. They seemed to Reece like a warning and a challenge. This case had obviously become a personal obsession for Jim. And that made Reece uneasy. It also filled him with a kind of awe. He wished he had the same passion for the job. But he didn't. The only thing he'd ever really felt like that about was Staci. 'Is that someone Freddie Harding?'

Jim shook his head again. 'It'd be a hell of a lot easier if this was just about Freddie Harding. But I'm afraid it's much more complicated than that.' He narrowed his eyes speculatively. 'You don't seem all that surprised by what I've said.'

'That's because I'm not.' Uncertainty flickered in Reece's

eyes, then faded. There was little point in not telling Jim about Amber. It was all going to come out soon enough anyway. 'A witness has come forward. A prostitute who was abducted by Freddie Harding in the early nineties and taken to the Winstanley House.'

So I was right about there being a new witness, thought Jim. The realisation brought both excitement and apprehension. It was obvious now that Forester and Harding had met and exchanged a lot more than simply tales of their upbringing. But was Reece aware of Forester's involvement? As Reece recounted Amber's story, it became clear he wasn't. Jim's mind raced through the implications of what he'd learned. Freddie Harding might be the key to breaking the entire case. That much was obvious. What wasn't so obvious was how to get enough leverage to make him spill about who else was involved in what went on at the Winstanley house. No court was going to convict Harding on the testimony of a prostitute who'd kept her ordeal to herself for over twenty years. Not without hard evidence to back it up.

'Why did this Amber come to you?' asked Jim. He waited for an answer, until it became obvious Reece wasn't going to give one. 'I take it from your silence that you're worried your answer could get you into trouble. And I'm not going to lie to you, it could. I'm guessing that this Amber is the one who asked you to look into the missing prostitute. And that you didn't go to Garrett because you're involved with her in some way.'

Reece struggled to keep his expression from betraying

the turmoil inside him. Jim's guess was too close to the mark for comfort. 'The DCI knows about Amber.'

Jim's eyebrows lifted. 'He does?'

'That's why I thought you might have spoken to Doug. I told him about Amber earlier today and he's going to the DCI.' Reece paused as if to consider carefully what he was about to say. 'He's going to keep my name out of it.'

'What about this missing girl Melinda? Does Doug know about her?'

'Yes.'

'So I assume he's going to tell Garrett about her as well.'

'No.'

Jim frowned. 'Why not?'

Because that would mean involving Staci, and I can't allow that to happen, thought Reece. But he said nothing.

Jim's probing brown eyes studied Reece. His gaze fell briefly to Reece's grazed knuckles. He gave a little nod as if something had occurred to him. 'I think I understand what's going on here. This isn't just about protecting your career. There's someone else you haven't told me about, isn't there? Someone you want to keep out of this.'

A steely glimmer came into Reece's eyes. 'I think I've said all I want to say to you, Inspector Monahan.'

'Fine. But think on this, Reece. By not telling Garrett about Melinda, you might be condemning her to death.'

'I don't think so. If Freddie Harding's involved in her disappearance, I think he'll lead us to her. I followed him from his house in Mexborough yesterday. He was heading down the M1 into Derbyshire.'

'Derbyshire,' said Jim, as if to confirm he'd heard right. But he was speaking to himself not Reece. And he was thinking, *Southview is in Derbyshire.*

'It was the middle of the night. My gut told me he was up to no good, but...' Reece trailed off abruptly.

'But what?'

'Something important came up. I had to break off from tailing him.'

Jim wondered whether the 'important' thing had something to do with whoever Reece was protecting. The steeliness was gone from his eyes. In its place, there was an awkward, almost guilty glimmer that made Jim ask himself, *Is it simply that he's involved with a prostitute, or is there more to it than that?* Whatever the case, Reece was clearly deeply conflicted. Jim decided not to press the matter, knowing Reece would simply clam up on him again. 'Is there anything else I should know?'

'I don't think so.'

'You showed Vernon a photo of Melinda. Can I see it?'

Reece's forehead creased with indecision. 'It wouldn't do you any good. Besides, I've done everything that can be done to find her.'

'You've not done everything. I guarantee you that.'

Jim's statement carried the authority of over three decades in the job. There was no denying the truth of it. Reece took out his phone and brought up Melinda's photo. 'She went missing eleven days ago. Apparently, there have been rumours on the street for years that someone's been abducting and killing girls. The word is Melinda's fallen victim to the same killer. When I told Doug, he directed me to Vernon.'

'Can you text me that photo?'

'Sure.'

'Where did Melinda live?'

'I... I'm not sure.' Reece stumbled slightly over the lie. Melinda had lived with Wayne Carson. And Reece didn't want Jim going anywhere near Wayne. 'But I can find out.'

'Then do so. There might be some form of ID there with Melinda's surname. Of course, the easiest thing to do would be to get hold of something with her fingerprints on it. If she's been working the streets for a few years, there's a good chance her details are in the system.'

'How am I supposed to do that without giving the DCI the heads up?'

'With great difficulty. I'd do it for you myself if I wasn't on sick leave.'

Reece pressed a finger to his forehead. A throbbing ache was growing behind his eyes. 'I'm sorry but, like I said, I've done what I can. This is someone else's problem now.'

'Bollocks it is.' Jim's voice was hard with reprimand. 'You're a copper. That means Melinda's your problem. And if you don't see that, you're in the wrong line of work.'

'Maybe I am.'

'I'd like to disagree with you, but from what I've seen I'm inclined to think you're right. You care, that much is obvious. But your head's all over the place. And in this job that can end up costing lives.' Jim's eyes faded away from Reece as his mind returned to Amy lying on the pavement, blood bubbling from her throat. Shaking his head as if to throw off the memory, he refocused his gaze. 'Do you realise you haven't even asked me who I'm going after?'

'I didn't think you'd tell me if I did.'

'You're right about that. You may have told me what I wanted to know, but you've been far from straight with me. I don't know what you're mixed up in, Reece, but it seems to me you've got a lot of thinking to do about who and what you want to be.'

Reece's face clouded. Jim was right. He felt as if the job, Staci and Doug had hold of him and were all pulling in different directions. The strain was growing too much for him to bear. Sooner or later, he knew, something would have to give. Still, Jim's preachy tone irritated him. 'It seems to me I could say the same thing to you.'

'And you'd be right to. My heart's not been fully in the job for a long time now. So when I'm done with this case, I'm done with the job too.'

'You're retiring?' There was doubt in Reece's voice.

Jim smiled thinly. 'Why's that so hard to believe?'

Reece glanced towards the door as if trying to gauge whether anyone was listening at it. 'Dad talked about retiring for years. But he never did, until his health left him with no choice. What do old cops do when they retire? Go on a cruise? Sit at home watching the telly?'

I hope I get the chance to do even that, thought Jim. 'To be honest, I don't really know what I'm going to do. All I know is I've given just about all I've got to give.'

Jim glanced at his watch. Time was ticking on. The

revelations about the new witness and the missing prostitute had only served to reinforce the sense that he needed to get out to Southview and put eyes on Edward Forester. He would have liked even more to put eyes on Freddie Harding. Freddie didn't have the same need to be cautious as his brother, so surveilling him may well have proven to be a more fruitful line of inquiry. But Jim knew there was no way he could risk going near him if Garrett was on the ex-con's case.

As Jim stood to leave, Reece said, 'So you've got my back.' It wasn't quite a question, but neither was it a statement.

'As best I can, but like I said, it might not be enough. Call me if there are any new developments. Oh, and there's no need for Doug to know we've talked. The more people in on this thing, the more chance there is of word getting back to Garrett.' Jim gave Reece a meaningful look, adding, 'Don't you agree?'

Reece nodded.

'I'll see myself out.' Jim looked at Reece a moment longer, as if trying to make his mind up about something, then said, 'I hope you work out what you want in life. I never really did until it was too late.'

He headed for the door. He paused at the foot of the stairway and shouted, 'I'm off now, Frank.'

Frank emerged from his bedroom and slowly descended the stairs. 'I'll walk you to your car.'

'I won't say see you,' said Jim, as they made their way along the drive. 'Because let's face it, who knows where either of us will be in the future.'

Frank smiled grimly. 'I know where I'll be a few months from now.'

Jim looked at him, his face creased with sadness. 'Is it that bad?'

Frank nodded.

'Does Reece know?'

'I haven't said anything, but he's got a good idea of how it is.'

'I'm sorry, Frank.'

'Don't be. I'm not. I've had a good life. I'm not proud of everything I've done, but then who is?' There was no bravado in Frank's voice, just acceptance. 'It's funny, I never thought I'd hear myself talking like this. But since my Shirley died, well...' He tailed off, as if unsure how to put his feelings into words.

Jim extended his hand, and Frank took it. 'Take care.'

'You too.' A troubled light came into Frank's eyes. 'There's only one thing about kicking the bucket that really bothers me.' He glanced towards the house. 'Reece isn't like me. He lets things get to him. He's a good lad, but he needs someone to keep him on the right track.'

'Doug Brody's taken a shine to him.'

Frank scowled. 'The only person that flash prick gives a toss about is himself.'

'Maybe, but he knows his way around the job as well as anyone.'

'This is about more than the job. It's about not letting Reece get himself into something he can't get out of.'

Jim's thoughts turned to the murderous undertaking he'd

entered into with Bryan Reynolds. Reading the silent appeal in Frank's eyes, he said, 'I really don't think I'm the person to be giving Reece that kind of guidance.'

'I'm not asking you to. Just keep an eye on him. That's all.'

Jim's brow creased in uncertainty for a moment. Then he said, 'I'll do what I can, Frank, but one way or another I'm not going to be around for much longer myself.'

'Thanks, Jim. This, well, it means...' Frank hesitated once again with the awkwardness of someone not used to expressing their feelings.

With a nod, Jim indicated that he knew what it meant. He removed his hand from Frank's and ducked into the car. As he accelerated away, he watched his ex-colleague fade from view like a ghost in the wing mirror. He felt time pressing in on him from every side. A storm of questions swirled in his mind. *Is Reynolds still alive? Has he given my name up? Am I both hunter and hunted? How do I expose Forester for what he really is? Will I even have to or will his brother inadvertently do it for me?* His thoughts started to turn towards Margaret, but he slammed a mental door on her image. He couldn't allow himself to think about her. Not until he had the answers.

Chapter Twenty-One

It was late morning when the gate intercom buzzed. 'That'll be Rupert,' said Mabel, setting aside the newspaper she'd been reading. The front cover headline read 'Hunt For Policewoman's Killer Continues'. She motioned to Edward. He obediently rose from his armchair and, with Conall loping along by his side, went into the hallway.

'Rupert who?' asked Philippa.

'Rupert Hartwell. My financial manager. He's here with the money.'

'That was quick.'

'Yes, well I arranged for the money to be made available as soon as I got off the phone to Edward yesterday.'

'But Edward didn't tell you how much he owed until you got here last night.'

'He didn't have to.' Mabel's bright red lips curled into an icily confident smile. 'Nobody knows Edward as well as I do. I see his mind as clearly as you see your own. If you were a mother, you'd understand. But, of course, there was that problem with your ovaries.'

The two women stared at each other from opposing

sofas, with barely even a superficial sheen of civility in their eyes. Fine lines quivered at the corners of Philippa's lips, as if she was fighting to hold in a furious retort. She looked out of the window at the sound of tyres crunching gravel. A Mercedes pulled up. A balding, late-middle-aged man in a pinstripe suit got out of it. He was carrying a large aluminium briefcase. Edward met him at the door and, casting a nervous glance at the gates, ushered him quickly into the house.

'Welcome to Southview, Rupert,' said Mabel, standing to greet the man. 'How was your journey?'

Rupert patted the briefcase. 'Let's just say that carrying around this sort of money doesn't make for a particularly relaxing experience.'

'Would you like a cup of tea? Or perhaps a nip of something stronger to calm your nerves?'

'Tea would be fine, thanks.'

'Mrs Adams!' called Mabel.

'She's gone home,' Philippa reminded her pointedly.

'Oh yes. Well then, would you do the honours, dear?' Mabel spoke without bothering to look at Philippa.

Philippa gazed rigidly at her mother-in-law, her lips tight with suppressed anger. At a nudge from Edward, she shot him a sharp glance. Seeing the silent plea in his eyes, she released a loud breath through her nose and left the room.

Mabel motioned for Rupert to open the briefcase. He laid it on the coffee table, turned the rollers of the combination lock and clicked it open. Mabel and Edward stared at the neatly packed wads of fifty-pound notes. 'I don't think I've ever seen so much cash before,' said Edward, with a trace of reverence in his voice. He wrenched his eyes away. 'I need a drink. What about you, Mother?'

'Just a small one.' Mabel's face was impassive, but there was a trace of strain in her voice. For years, she'd worked her guts out for every penny. Money came to her easily now, but it didn't leave her any less easily than it had when she was fighting tooth and nail to establish her business.

As Edward poured them each a sherry from a crystal decanter, Rupert said to Mabel, 'There are some forms you need to sign.'

She shut the briefcase and turned her back on it. Rupert produced a sheaf of forms. 'I know it's none of my business, Mabel,' he said, as she signed them, 'but what do you need all this cash—'

'You're right, Rupert,' she cut him off, 'it's none of your damn business.'

Philippa reappeared with a tray of tea. She passed a cup to Rupert and poured one for herself. They sat sipping their drinks, the atmosphere as silent and heavy as the briefcase. Edward's eyes kept darting towards the mantelpiece clock. Philippa frowned into her cup, as if trying to find the answer to some troubling question therein. Mabel sat upright like a queen, her gaze moving slowly between the two of them.

'I'd better be going,' said Rupert. He rose, leaving his cup half full.

Mabel rose too, reaching to shake his hand. 'Thank you,

Rupert.' She flicked Edward a meaningful look. 'It's good to know there's one person in my life who I can always rely on to do what needs to be done.'

With a deferential bow of his head, Rupert turned to leave. Edward showed him out of the front door. Then he withdrew a phone that Tyler had given him the first time they met. There was only one number programmed into it. Edward let the dial tone ring five times, then hung up. He waited half a minute, before redialling. Tyler picked up on the third ring and asked in his usual flat voice, 'Have you got it?'

'Yes.'

'Bring it to the same place as last time ASAP.'

The line went dead. Edward raised a hand to touch the hollow above his upper lip. An oily dampness had formed there, as it always did when he had to do something that made him nervous. He wiped it away and returned to the living room. 'Where are you going?' asked Philippa as he picked up the briefcase.

'Where do you think? The sooner this matter is resolved, the sooner we can get back to normal.'

Mabel stood and headed into the hallway to fetch her long cashmere coat.

'What are you doing, Mother?' asked Edward, frowning after her.

'What do you think I'm doing? I'm coming with you.'

Edward shook his head vehemently. 'No, Mother. You can't do that.'

Mabel's eyes flashed. 'Don't you tell me what I can do!'

She stabbed a bony finger at the briefcase. 'If you think I'm trusting you with that, you can bloody well think again.'

'What are you saying? That you think I'm going to run off with it?'

'You haven't got the balls to run off,' snorted Mabel. 'Money or no money, you'd last about ten seconds alone out there in the big wide world.'

Edward's face trembled around the edges where fat blurred his features. Hurt shone in his meanly spaced eyes. 'Please, Mother, these people I'm dealing with—'

'Are businessmen,' cut in Mabel. 'And if there's one thing I understand even better than I understand you, it's business.'

'You should give Edward more credit,' said Philippa, her voice vibrating with indignation. 'He's not got where he is today without having struggled to get there.'

Mabel laughed, a full-throated laugh of withering contempt. 'Struggle! What do either of you know about struggle? When my ex-husband ran off and left me with a baby, I had nothing. And I mean nothing. No job, no money, no education, no prospects. So when I started up my business, it was sink or swim, live—'

'Or die.' Philippa finished her mother-in-law's oh so familiar words, rolling her eyes as if to say, *Christ, do we really have to hear this again?*

Edward winced. If there was one thing his mother hated even more intensely than eggs done the wrong way, it was being mocked. The light in Mabel's eyes burst into flame. With surprising speed for a woman of her age, she stepped forward and whipped her hand across Philippa's face. For a moment, Philippa stood in mute shock, a hand pressed to her stinging cheek. Then, her voice a whisper of fury, she said to Edward, 'I want this hateful bitch out of our house right this instant.'

Mabel laughed again. 'Your house? Who do you think pays the mortgage on this place?'

Philippa kept her gaze fixed on her husband. 'Tell her to leave, Edward, or—'

'Or what?' butted in Mabel. 'You'll leave? Well go on then. Get out. Because I'm not going anywhere.' She turned to Edward. 'Am I?'

Like iron filings caught between two magnets, Edward's eyes danced back and forth. They finally came to rest on Mabel. 'No, Mother, you're not going anywhere.'

Directing a smug smile at Philippa, Mabel hooked her arm possessively through Edward's. Her face pale except for the red-hot slap mark, Philippa glared at mother and son as if unsure who she despised more.

'I'm sorry, Philippa,' said Edward.

'No, you're fucking not! You've never been sorry for anything in your entire life. You look out for yourself, and to hell with everyone else. You've never loved me. Not really.'

'That's not true.'

'Isn't it?' With a kind of gleeful venom in her eyes, Philippa turned to Mabel. 'You want to know why you don't have grandchildren. It's not because of my ovaries. It's because your precious son is impotent. He hasn't been able to get it up for years. At least, not for me. Who knows? Maybe if I looked a bit more like you, things would have been different.'

'How can you say such a—' Edward began to exclaim, but Mabel silenced him with a hiss.

The older woman's nose wrinkled, but her smile remained, giving her the look of a malevolent gnome. 'Don't dignify her filthy remarks with a reply, Edward. She's not worthy of your attentions.'

'No one ever has been, have they?' countered Philippa. 'Except you.'

Mabel tugged on Edward's arm. He gave his wife a wounded, pathetically helpless look. Then his head dropped and he allowed himself to be drawn towards the front door. Turning her back on Philippa, her head as high as Edward's was low, Mabel said, 'I expect you to be gone when we get back.'

'Oh, don't worry. I will be.' Philippa's voice was still hot with anger. But there was also a thickness in it, as if she was fighting back tears.

Mabel led Edward to a garage around the side of the house. Wearing a dazed, sulky expression, he patted his pockets. 'Are these what you're looking for?' Mabel handed him his car keys, exhaling sharply. 'For God's sake, Edward, stop pouting and stand up straight. Remember, people are dangerous animals. And what must you do when dealing with dangerous animals? You must project confidence and authority or you'll be attacked.'

Taking a deep breath, Edward drew himself up to his

full height. His mother was right, he knew. Dealing with Tyler and his goons was really no different to dealing with his fellow politicians. If they sensed weakness, they would tear him apart like a pack of hungry jackals. He opened the Jag's passenger door for his mother, then headed around to the driver's side. He laid the briefcase on the back seat, and got behind the steering wheel. He checked his reflection in the mirror, smoothing out any creases of anxiety, replacing them with a well-practised look of self-assurance.

'That's better,' said Mabel, reaching out to stroke Edward's jawline with her forefinger. 'There's the man I brought you up to be. There's the politician who one day will go on to become a great leader of this country.'

'A great leader,' Edward repeated tentatively, as if trying the words on for size.

'Say it again and know it.'

As Edward pulled away from the house, he said the words over and over with growing force. Mabel leaned her head back and made a small sound of appreciation deep in her throat.

When they arrived at the layby, a Range Rover was waiting for them. 'Please let me do the talking, Mother,' said Edward.

Mabel raised an eyebrow as if to say, *We'll see*. 'Don't let me down, Edward. Remember who you are.'

They got out of the car and approached the Range Rover. Edward helped his mother into the back seat, before climbing in after her. The bull-necked fat man with the goatee beard was sitting behind the steering wheel. What was his name again? Shaun or Stan or something like that. The man twisted around, his broken-veined face knitting into a frown. 'What the fuck? You were supposed to come alone.'

'This is my mother.'

'I don't give a toss who she is. You're bang out of order bringing her here.'

Mabel pointed to the briefcase. 'There's two million pounds of my money in there. Until I know for certain that I'm getting what I'm paying for, I go where it goes.'

Stan looked at them undecidedly, fidgeting with something in the pocket of his jacket. A touch of nervousness came back into Edward's face. He blinked when Stan pulled out a phone, dialled and put the phone to his ear. 'He's here. And he's got his mother with him... I know, I know, but what else can we do? It's her money. She wants to make sure she's not being ripped off... OK, see you soon.'

Stan returned the phone to his pocket. He took a cloth bag and a roll of duct tape out of the glove compartment. He handed the bag to Mabel. 'Put that on your head.'

Mabel hesitated to do so, holding the bag distastefully between her thumb and forefinger.

'Look, lady,' continued Stan, 'either you put that on or this situation isn't going to turn out well.'

'Is that a threat?'

'It's a promise.'

'Just do as he says, Mother,' put in Edward.

Mabel stared at Stan for a moment with not the slightest trace of fear in her eyes. Then, almost tauntingly slowly, she pulled the bag down over her face. Stan tore off a strip of duct tape. 'There's only one bag,' he said to Edward. 'So this will have to do for you.' He slapped the strip over the politician's eyes a little harder than was necessary.

As the Range Rover pulled out of the layby, Edward clutched the briefcase to his chest. His other hand sought out his mother's. She pushed him away with fingers as dry as old parchment, hissing under her breath, 'Remember who you are.'

Remember who you are. Edward's face twisted into something between a scowl and a sneer. She'd been saying those words to him his whole life. The irony was he'd never felt as if he really knew who he was. There'd always been a hollowness inside him, a sense of emptiness and disconnect. Only one thing had ever made him feel truly whole – pain. Pain was the wire that connected him to the world. Not his own pain, but the pain of others. To look into the eyes of someone in agony, there was nothing more real than that. He'd spent a lot of years wondering why he was like he was. For a long time he'd blamed his father. He knew differently now.

Edward felt the Range Rover brake and turn onto the farm track. As the vehicle juddered along the rutted lane, he licked his lips in anticipation. He suddenly realised he was looking forward to seeing the farm again. So much pain had been inflicted in that place. You could feel it hanging around like an invisible miasma. The Range Rover braked again. There was the sound of a door opening, followed by the scrape of a gate swinging open.

A short time later, the vehicle pulled to a halt again. 'Leave that on,' said Stan as Mabel started to remove the bag. When she ignored him, his voice rose angrily. 'I said—'

'I heard what you said,' Mabel interrupted, returning Stan's stare unflinchingly. 'But I've had enough of this nonsense.'

With an angry shake of his head, Stan reached back to yank the duct tape off Edward's eyes. 'Bloody hell!' yelped Edward as the tape took half his eyebrows with it.

Mabel eyed the rundown farmhouse and collection of equally dilapidated outbuildings with distaste. She climbed out of the Range Rover, her nose wrinkling. 'What's that godawful stink?' Her high heels sank into several inches of mud as she stepped away from the vehicle. She stretched out her arms, swaying. 'Edward!' she called shrilly. 'I'm falling.'

Edward dashed to her side. Hooking his free hand under her arm, he guided her towards the house. One of her feet came out of its shoe. She threw her arms around Edward to keep from stepping in the mud. 'Mother!' he shouted, fighting to keep his balance.

Stan watched with amusement playing around his mouth. Tyler emerged from the house and took in the scene impassively. Stan's smile disappeared at the sight of him. 'She took the bag off when we got here. I told her not to but she wouldn't listen.'

Tyler scratched disinterestedly at his bandaged eye.

'How's it feeling?'

Tyler gave a what-does-it-matter shrug, and thumbed over his shoulder. 'Go and open up the cellar.'

'Where's Liam?' asked Stan, heading into the house.

'He's dealing with that other thing.'

Arms crossed, Tyler watched the Foresters struggle towards him. Edward was flushed and a touch breathless by the time they reached the doorstep. Mabel glared up at Tyler. 'Thanks for all your help,' she said, her voice venomous with sarcasm. 'What a gentleman you are.'

Mabel's words didn't dent Tyler's inscrutable expression. He motioned her to enter the house. Once they were all inside, he locked the door. Mabel's sharp gaze travelled around the hallway's damp-stained walls and grubby carpet. 'Delightful place you've got here, Mr... What did you say your name was?'

'What do you want to know my name for?'

'I like to know who I'm doing business with. I'm Mabel Forester.'

'CEO of Forester Cakes. A company you built up from nothing, and which now accounts for a quarter of the UK cake market. You made a profit of 8.9 million last year.'

'Well, well, I'm impressed. You're obviously not as ignorant as you look.'

Something approaching amusement glimmered in Tyler's eye at the backhanded compliment. 'I like to know who I'm dealing with too. You can call me Tyler.'

'It's a pleasure to meet you, Tyler.'

Tyler nodded as if in reciprocation, although his expression suggested he had no feelings on the matter. 'If you'll please follow me, we'll get down to business.'

As he led them towards the back of the house, Mabel

gave Edward a look as if to say, *See, that's how it's done.* They entered a kitchen of sorts. There was a grimy ceramic sink underneath a barred window. Empty and mostly doorless cupboards lined the walls. On a scratched old table in the centre of the room there was a camping stove, a kettle, several mugs and a jar of instant coffee. To the right of the table, a door led to a flight of basement stairs illuminated by a bare bulb. The stairway exhaled a fetid odour suggestive of some animal living in its own filth. Edward put his hand to his mouth. But his eyes shone as though the sight of the stairs, or maybe the smell, brought back some cherished memory.

Tyler cleared the table and gestured for the briefcase to be laid on it. Edward glanced at his mother. She gave a nod, and he set down the case and opened it. Tyler looked at the money. If he was pleased or otherwise, there was nothing in his demeanour to show it. He picked up a wad of banknotes, flipped through it, returned it to its place and closed the case.

'Is everything to your satisfaction?' asked Edward.

In answer, Tyler approached the basement door and called down the stairs, 'Bring him up.'

There came the sound of scuffling, dragging footsteps. Stan pushed Bryan Reynolds into the room. The gangster's hands were cuffed behind his back and his mouth was gagged with duct tape. His pastel blue suit was torn and streaked with filth. Excrement stains stretched down the inside of his trouser legs. His long blond hair was dishevelled, revealing a pink bald spot. His left eye was swollen shut.

Apart from that, his granite-hard face was uninjured. The last time Edward had seen him, Bryan's eyes had blazed with hate and menace. All that was left of that flame was an exhausted glimmer. He had the look of a defeated man, a man who'd accepted his fate.

Mabel eyed Bryan as if he was a species of insect she'd never seen before. 'Is this the man?'

'Yes,' said Edward.

'Who is he?'

'He's a criminal. A drug dealer. One of the biggest in South Yorkshire.'

'So I suppose you could say we're doing society a favour by getting rid of him,' observed Mabel. She turned to Tyler. 'What happens now? How will you,' she paused for the right words, 'do him in?'

'We need to ask him some questions first.'

'Let's get on with it then. I don't want to spend a moment longer than I have to in this place.'

'I suggest you and your son wait here, Mrs Forester.'

Mabel shook her head. 'I want to hear for myself what this...' she pointed at Bryan, 'thing has to say.'

'As you wish, but I warn you, there will be blood. Lots of it.'

Mabel smiled – not a pleasant smile. 'Don't worry about me, Tyler. I'm not squeamish.' She motioned for him to lead the way. At a glance from Tyler, Stan shoved Bryan into the hallway.

'Where are we taking him?' Edward asked as they passed the interrogation room.

'To meet some friends of mine,' said Tyler.

Edward frowned. 'I don't know if I like the idea of yet more people knowing about my involvement in this matter.'

This time Tyler did smile, though it was only a pale ghost of the real thing. 'You needn't worry about that.'

At the foot of the steps, Tyler turned to Mabel. 'Would you like me to help you?'

'I'd like that very much.'

Mabel extended her hand, but Tyler stooped and lifted her like a husband about to carry a bride over the threshold. She gave a girlish giggle of delight as he effortlessly whisked her across the muddy yard. Edward hurried after them, brow furrowed as if unsure whether he approved of his mother being manhandled in such a fashion. They entered a barn whose walls were lined with rusty iron troughs. The floor was even more awash with mud than the yard. 'Bloody buggering hell!' swore Edward as the stinking green-brown slime sucked at his shoes.

Towards the rear of the barn a ladder led up to a hayloft. Tyler set Mabel down at the foot of it. She theatrically touched her hands to her cheeks. 'I think I'm blushing.'

'Go up and lower the harness,' Tyler said to Stan.

Stan climbed the ladder. He slung down a rope with a crude leather harness attached to its end. With a practised movement, Tyler kicked Bryan's legs out from beneath him. The gangster went down hard and lay winded, gasping for breath. Tyler removed Bryan's shoes and socks. Then he undid Bryan's trousers and yanked them off, along with the black G-string he was wearing underneath. He held up the G-string, and Stan guffawed at the sight. Tyler stared down at the prostrate gangster, whose penis was shrivelled with cold and fear. It always struck him how even the toughest of men could be instantly made to look pathetic and vulnerable by the simple act of removing the lower half of their clothing. He fastened the harness around Bryan's legs and waist, then signalled Stan to take in the slack. As Stan did so, Tyler turned to Mabel. 'I'm afraid you're going to have to climb up there too, Mrs Forester.'

'I think I can manage that,' she replied, taking hold of the ladder. 'I'm a lot stronger than I look.'

'I don't doubt it.'

'Careful, Mother,' said Edward, anxiously watching Mabel climb the ladder. At its top, Stan took her hand and helped her into the hayloft.

Edward went up next. Before following him, Tyler bound Bryan's legs with duct tape. A strange, hungry kind of gleam came into Edward's eyes as they took in the hayloft. There was no hay in it. But there were other things. The rope was attached to a winch, which in former days must have been used for hoisting bales of hay. Bags of pig feed were stacked against one wall. Against another there was a wooden workbench. An array of tools hung on the wall above the bench – hacksaws, pliers, hammers, knives, a chainsaw – along with several plastic raincoats and pairs of goggles. Beneath the bench there was a portable tin bath. Slowly running his tongue over his lips, Edward approached the bench. There were deep scores and dark stains on its surface. He peered into the bath. A thin layer of some viscous red-black substance was congealed in its base. A shudder tingled through him as he inhaled the sour metallic smell it gave off. He glanced around at the sound of the winch being cranked. Stan was operating its handle. Tyler was peering over the edge of the loft. Edward joined him.

Bryan was dangling a metre or so above the floor. He writhed and gave off muffled screams as each turn of the handle jerked him upwards a few centimetres, causing the harness to bite deeper into his testicles. Edward gazed down at him almost wistfully. He hadn't seen a man in that kind of pain before. He'd expected to enjoy the spectacle, but he would never have thought he'd find anything arousing in it. The sight of fully developed genitalia had always faintly revolted him. And yet there was a throbbing in his groin that made him wish he could be alone with Bryan.

When Bryan came within reach, Tyler hauled him onto the floorboards and tore away the duct tape. Bryan's breath came out in a gasp of saliva. His eyes bulged at Edward. The pain seemed to have rekindled the light in them. Edward smiled inside at the sight. He liked to see a bit of fight in people. Not too much, mind, but enough to keep things interesting.

Tyler waited for Bryan's breathing to settle down. Then he pulled out a handgun and pressed its muzzle against the gangster's head. 'This doesn't have to be hard. It can be quick and easy. We know you weren't acting alone. Just tell us who put you on to Mr Forester, and it'll all be over in a second.'

Bryan's bloodshot eyes moved to Mabel. His voice

came in a hoarse whisper. 'You must be so proud to have a child-raping piece of filth for a son.'

Mabel gave no sign of having heard Bryan. Tyler slapped the gag back on him. He turned towards the barn's entrance, cupping his hands to his mouth. 'Sooee!' he called in a high pitched voice, rising to a near shriek. He repeated the call several times in thirty-second bursts.

'I hear them,' said Stan.

From outside there came the sound of rapidly approaching grunts and snorts. A drove of twelve pigs ran scuffling into the barn. Some were pink like human flesh, others were mottled with black patches. They ranged in size from a couple of curly-tailed piglets to a boar as big as a bullock. Led by the monstrous boar, they thrust their snouts into troughs in search of food. Finding none, they set up an eardrum-piercing squealing.

Tyler jerked Bryan into a sitting position so he could see the pigs. 'I imagine a man in your line of business already knows this, but for the benefit of these people,' he indicated Edward and Mabel, 'I'm going to tell you anyway. There's no better way to get rid of a body than feeding it to pigs. A pig can and will eat just about anything – flesh, ligaments, bones. But best of all, when that meal comes out the other end, there's no trace left of what it used to be. There's only one part of the body a pig can't digest.' Tyler tapped the gun against his teeth. 'Teeth are harder than bones. They pass through the digestive system too fast for the stomach acids to break them down. So there's only one thing to do. You have to pull them all out first.'

Without having to be told, Stan fetched Tyler a pair of pliers and a long butcher's knife. Edward had the feeling he was watching a well-rehearsed routine as Tyler continued, 'Before we get to that, I think you should get more closely acquainted with my friends down there. Especially him.' He pointed to the huge boar. 'His name's Kong. You and him should get on well. Last week there would have been four piglets down there, but he's eaten two of them since then. And when their mother tried to stop him, he killed and ate her as well. He did it right out there in the yard. Like he wanted us to see. I know he's only a pig, but sometimes when I look in his eyes I think I see this glimmer of something. This little twinkle of malice.'

'He's an evil old bastard, that's what he is,' said Stan.

'Or perhaps he was just hungry.' Tyler briefly seemed to muse this over. Then with a sudden movement of the knife, he made two deep slashes in Bryan's thighs. Bryan squirmed and moaned. 'What was that?' asked Tyler. 'Did you say something?'

Bryan gave a spasmodic shake of his head.

At a glance from Tyler, Stan took hold of the winch's handle again. Tyler pushed Bryan over the edge of the loft. Blood coursed down Bryan's legs and dripped from his feet. The pigs milled about underneath, snouts raised, sniffing the air eagerly. As Bryan came within reach, Kong barged his way through the scrum and got the gangster's whole foot in his powerful jaw. Bryan was jerked around like a bundle of cloth as Kong swung his muscular neck from side to side. Even through the gag, Bryan's screams were loud enough to be heard above the cacophony of grunts and squeals.

'Bring him up,' said Tyler.

Stan worked the winch, rocking back on his heels like a fisherman reeling in a big catch. Bryan's screams grew louder as his body was stretched taut between Kong and the rope. Tyler added his weight to the winch, and with a wet tearing sound Bryan jolted free of the boar's jaw. The screams stopped with equal suddenness, and Bryan hung limp as a fresh corpse as he was hoisted back into the loft.

'My God,' breathed Edward, staring wide-eyed at the mangled remains of Bryan's foot. 'That thing's taken almost his entire foot off.'

'Is he still alive?' asked Mabel.

Tyler stooped over Bryan and checked his pulse. 'Yes.' He removed the gag and slapped Bryan's face. 'Wakey wakey.'

Bryan's eyelids flickered. The whites of his eyes, then his pupils came into view. Like someone surfacing after a long time under water, he sucked in a gasping breath. His eyes bulged vacantly as if he didn't know where he was. 'Look at me, Bryan,' said Tyler.

Bryan focused on Tyler's face. A light of horrified realisation lit up his eyes.

'Give me a name.' Tyler's voice was low, almost a whisper. 'Just one name and all this will stop.'

Bryan was trembling uncontrollably. His pupils kept trying to roll back. But somehow, from somewhere, he managed to summon up the strength to shake his head. Tyler glanced at Stan, who nodded as if to say, *Fair play. He's one tough bastard.* They carried Bryan to the workbench and chained him down.

As Stan gripped either side of Bryan's head, Tyler pushed the pliers savagely into the gangster's mouth. Bryan let out a muffled, gagging scream as Tyler clamped down and began to yank and twist. Neck veins bulging with the effort, he tore out a couple of teeth whose roots glistened like grisly pearls. Bryan choked on the blood gushing from the deep sockets they'd occupied. Stan turned Bryan's head to the side so that the blood ran out of his mouth.

Tyler squatted level with Bryan's face. 'That's two. Only another thirty to go.'

Bryan's mouth opened and closed. A whistling, gurgling sound that might have been words came out. Careful not to get within biting range, Tyler bent closer. 'What was that?'

Bryan's lips formed another slur of agonised sound, this time just barely identifiable as words. Tyler's brow wrinkled uncharacteristically.

'What did he say?' Edward asked.

'Jim Monahan.'

'You mentioned that name once before. Who is he?'

'Are you sure that's what he said?' Stan asked, his face screwing into a doubtful frown.

'Yes.'

'But how the hell could Jim Monahan have found out about Mr Forester?'

Irritation stirred beneath the surface of Tyler's dark,

unreadable eye. The question was immaterial. What mattered was that he had, and what they were going to do about it. 'Could he be on the take?'

'No way. I used to work with him. He never took dirty money in his life.'

'Oh my God,' said Edward, his face paling with realisation. 'He's a policeman.'

'He's one of the lead detectives on the Baxley case,' said Tyler.

Edward raised his hands halfway to his head in panic. 'Christ, I'm finished.'

'Don't talk foolish, Edward,' snapped Mabel. 'Use your head. If this Detective Monahan is in cahoots with a gangster, he'd hardly want his superiors to know about it.'

'She's right,' said Tyler. 'The situation might not be as bad as it seems. If Monahan's dirty, I don't see why we – or more accurately, you – shouldn't be able to pay for his silence.'

Stan shook his head. 'Jim Monahan, dirty? I just can't see it. The guy would have had to have a complete personality transplant.'

'Well let's hope he has, because if he's on some sort of personal crusade, we could be in trouble.'

Edward pointed to Bryan. 'Could he be lying?'

Tyler looked searchingly into Bryan's bloodshot, bleary eyes. He saw no defiance there, only pain and resignation. 'No. He's done.'

'So what do we do?'

'We make some inquiries, find out a bit more about DI Monahan.'

'And what if we find he's not interested in money?' Edward asked with a flickering smile, as if doubting such a thing could be possible.

'Then our options would be very limited.' As if to illustrate his words, Tyler gestured at the metal tub. Stan dragged it halfway out from under the bench, positioning it beneath Bryan's head. 'You should stand well back,' Tyler said to Edward and Mabel.

As mother and son retreated to the far side of the hayloft, Tyler and Stan each put on a raincoat and goggles. Stan took hold of Bryan's head again. With a swift, precise movement of the butcher's knife, Tyler cut Bryan's throat. Arterial spray fanned into the air. Bryan made a noise like a drain emptying. His eyes bulged. Tyler turned his back on the gangster, leaving him to bleed out like a pig. He hoisted a bag of feed onto his shoulder and emptied it over the edge of the loft. As the pigs stormed the food, Tyler descended the ladder. Stan threw several more bags of feed down to him. He split them open and filled the troughs.

'You can climb down,' Stan said to Edward and Mabel. Seeing them peer uneasily at the pigs, he added, 'Don't worry, they won't bother you now they've been fed.'

Edward glanced at Bryan. 'What about him?'

'We need to cut him up into small enough bits for the pigs to swallow. You don't want to be around for that.'

Edward's expression seemed to suggest otherwise, but he climbed down the ladder. Shooting nervous glances at the pigs, he waited for his mother to follow him. Tyler made to pick Mabel up, but Edward palmed him away. 'I can manage, thank you,' he said, with a note of jealousy in his voice that brought a delighted gleam to Mabel's eyes.

Tyler shrugged and headed out the barn. His knees buckling slightly, Edward picked his mother up and followed him to the Range Rover. After lowering her onto the back seat, he breathlessly asked Tyler, 'So what happens now?'

'Like I said, we'll make some inquiries. I'll be in touch as soon as there's anything to say.'

'It's always a pleasure dealing with a professional,' said Mabel, extending her hand.

Tyler shook it just long enough to note how dry it was. Then he shut the door and turned to Stan. 'Same drill as last time.'

Stan nodded and climbed into the driver's seat.

As the Range Rover pulled away, Tyler took out a mobile phone. He swapped the SIM, scanned through the contacts to 'Doug' and pressed dial. A brusque voice came on the line. 'What's up?'

'He came through with the money,' said Tyler.

Doug barked a short, triumphant laugh. 'Two million quid. Fuck me. We're rich.'

'Yeah, well, we may not get the chance to enjoy it. We have a serious problem. Reynolds gave up a name. Jim Monahan.'

'Jim Monahan,' repeated Doug, sounding even more dubious than Stan had. 'No way. Reynolds was just fucking with your head.'

'No he wasn't.'

'Believe me, Tyler, Jim Monahan is the last person in the world to have had dealings with Bryan Reynolds.'

'And you believe me when I tell you, I looked in Reynolds's eyes and there was nothing but the truth left.'

'Well, if you're right, we're in deep shit.'

'Sounds like you don't think we'll be able to pay Monahan off.'

Doug laughed again, only this time there was no amusement to it. 'You'd have a better chance trying to pay off the pope. The guy's a fucking crusader. If he's involved in this, it's got nothing to do with money.'

'In that case, there's only one thing we can do. And we'd better do it fast. Monahan's got to be wondering what's happened to Reynolds by now.' Doug scanned the dark line of trees to the east of the farm contemplatively. 'He may already be searching for him.'

'That's not very likely. Jim's in hospital. He had a heart attack a couple of days ago.'

'How serious?'

'I'm not sure, but from what I've heard he's not going to be doing much detecting for a while.'

'So that buys us some time. But he's not going to be in hospital forever. And when he gets out, it's safe to assume he's going to go after Edward Forester.'

'If by that you mean he's going to try to kill him...' Doug blew a doubtful breath. 'Look, I can just about buy the idea of Jim using Reynolds to do his dirty work. In a fucked up kind of way it even makes sense. He was probably hoping the pair of them would do each other in. But Jim kill Forester himself? No way would he do that. No way in the world.'

'How do you know? Seems to me you don't know this guy very well at all.'

'I know him well enough. I'm telling you, Tyler, I've worked with the guy for years and he's not a killer.'

'Well let's hope you're wrong, because if he tries to bring Forester down legitimately he might very well achieve his aim.'

'Jim's got nothing on Forester. If he did, he wouldn't have needed Reynolds.'

'Maybe, but I don't think it'll take him long to find some skeletons in his closet.'

'Freddie fucking Harding.' Doug hissed the name into the receiver. 'Do you think Jim knows about him?'

Tyler gave a mental shrug, seeing no point in replying to a question he couldn't possibly know the answer to. 'I think Edward Forester is the kind of man who'll try to take the whole world with him if he goes down.'

'So what are you saying? That we should do him before he does us?'

'I'm saying this situation is starting to get out of hand. There are too many people involved, too many people who might talk. Forester, his mother—'

'His mother!' Doug broke in.

'He brought her with him. And before you give me an earful, I didn't have any choice in the matter. It was her money. She wasn't going to hand it over without checking us out. Besides, she's as sharp as they come. I don't think we need to worry about her opening her mouth. Not unless any harm comes to her son. Right now I'm more concerned about your boy Reece.'

A defensive edge came in to Doug's voice. Reece was his protégé, someone he was trying to mould into his own image. He felt a certain fatherly protectiveness towards him. But even more than that, he was acutely aware that if Tyler's doubts proved to be well founded, the fallout would land on his shoulders. 'Reece doesn't even know you exist.'

'That's as maybe, but he's on to Freddie Harding. And it doesn't take a genius to work out where Harding might lead him.'

'Yeah, but Reece is off Harding's case.'

'Are you sure of that?'

'Course I fucking am. He thinks I went to Garrett with what he told me. He wouldn't dare go near Harding, especially not when it might put his little whore at risk. And anyway, I trust Reece. I realise that doesn't mean much to you, Tyler. But I'm a copper. And if a cop can't trust another cop, then he's in the wrong line of business.'

Now it was Tyler's turn to laugh – a laugh as silent and empty as the dilapidated farmhouse. *Do you know how fucking absurd that is coming from a bent copper?* The words passed through his mind, but he knew saying them would achieve nothing other than to trip Doug's hair-trigger temper. Doug might have been as bent as a six-pound note, but he retained a perverse pride in his job. That much was obvious from the way he spoke about the cases he was working. He'd been a copper for nearly twenty years. His sense of identity and honour was bound up in the job. Tyler had long ago given up ideas such as honour. They served no purpose for him. He lived by one simple rule: deceive everyone else but never yourself. If Doug wanted to indulge in self-deception that was up to him, just so long as he didn't put his co-conspirators in danger. 'In this line of business, trust alone doesn't always cut it,' said Tyler. 'I want you to take Reece with you on that thing we were going to do today.'

There was a slight uncertain pause before Doug spoke. 'I'm not sure he's ready.'

'It doesn't matter whether he's ready or not. What matters is that he gets some dirt on him. I mean real dirt, the kind that could cost him ten or twenty years if he ever opens his mouth.'

'What about you? Are you still coming?'

'No. Let's just see how your boy gets on before we expose ourselves any further.'

'Don't you worry about Reece. He'll come through with flying colours.'

Doug spoke with his usual gruff confidence, but Tyler caught a forced note. Doug may have been guilty of self-deception, but he was no fool. He knew exactly what was at stake. 'So what's the plan?' asked Doug, shifting the focus away from himself. 'How do we deal with Jim Monahan?'

'Well there's no way we can get at him in hospital. Not after everything that's happened recently.'

'We could put someone on his house.'

'I can't see him going back there. He's probably guessed

by now that we've got Reynolds. So he's got to assume Reynolds has spilled about his involvement. Which means we've got to assume he's going to be ready for us.'

'Then we sit on Forester's house. If you're right, Jim will come to us sooner or later.'

'*If* I'm right. And even if I am, it's asking for trouble just sitting around waiting for him to come to us. I prefer to be the hunter, not the hunted.' Tyler's voice grew thoughtful. 'What we could do with is some kind of bait, something that would bring the good detective to us at a place and time of our choosing.'

Doug made a low noise in his throat as if he might have an idea. But he hesitated to speak his thoughts.

'You've got something on your mind,' stated Tyler. 'Let's hear it.'

'A possibility occurred to me, but it would be risky. Jim has an ex-wife. Everyone in the department knows he's still in love with her. If we snatched her, heart attack or no heart attack, Jim would come running.'

Tyler considered the idea, the faintest of creases between his dark brows. 'It could work, but I'm not sure I want to complicate matters further by bringing yet someone else into this. Let me think on it a while.'

'And what about Forester? How do we deal with him?'

'The way things stand there's a lot more money to be squeezed out of Mr Forester. Once Monahan's out of the picture, we take a long hard look at the lie of the land and make a decision. Bear in mind, though, that if Forester goes, his mother has to go, and maybe even Freddie Harding too.'

Doug was silent a moment, as if weighing up whether it was worth having all that death on his conscience. He gave a little laugh. 'Well at least the pigs wouldn't go hungry for a while.'

There was a hollow ring of bravado in Doug's tone. And well he should be worried, thought Tyler. Taking out a cop was bad enough. But getting rid of people with the Foresters' wealth and influence could bring down a shit-storm too great for any of them to survive. 'Let's just try and make sure it doesn't come to that. From now on we need to keep things tight. Do I make myself understood?' The silence on the other end of the line told him that he did, but he wanted to hear Doug say it. A note of warning cold enough to freeze a man to death came into his voice. 'Do I make myself understood?'

'Yes,' Doug responded, his voice sharp with stung pride. 'Look, I know I fucked up putting Reece on to Vernon Tisdale. But let's get one thing straight, Tyler, I'm not some goon for you to talk to like shit. We're equals in this, remember?'

'Just don't let me down again.'

'Or what, eh?' Doug crossed over from anger into rage. 'Or fucking what?'

Now it was Tyler's turn to hold his silence. He let its meaning sink in a few seconds, before hanging up. Doug's rage didn't concern him. He'd been dealing with men like Doug Brody – arrogant pricks who thrived on confrontation – his whole life. He knew how and when to push their buttons. Sometimes the best way to do that was by lying, other times it was by making sure everyone knew exactly where they stood. Now was the time for the latter. And if it made Doug hate and fear him, all the better. In his experience, when the shit came down, hate and fear were as strong a bond as love.

Tyler swapped SIM cards again and phoned Edward Forester. 'We're not going to be able to buy Jim Monahan off,' he told the politician.

'Oh, come now, everyone's got their price.'

'Not Monahan.'

Edward made an unconvinced sound. 'So how much is it going to cost me to *deal* with him?'

'Five hundred thousand.'

Edward let out a huff of wry laughter. 'My, my, a relative bargain compared to the last little problem we had to deal with. Hang on a moment.' The muffled sound of Edward speaking to his mother filtered down the line.

Mabel Forester came on the phone. 'Do it and the money's yours.'

That was all Tyler needed to hear. He hung up and headed back into the barn. The pigs had almost emptied their troughs. Kong squinted at him with that little gleam in his ever-hungry ruby red eyes. Careful not to let the boar move into his blind spot, Tyler picked his way through the milling mass to the ladder. He knew that if he slipped over in the ankle-deep mud Kong would be on in him a heartbeat. The thought of being eaten alive by that big bastard was almost enough to make him shudder.

In the hayloft, Tyler took down the chainsaw and yanked

it to life. The pigs squealed in chorus as the deafening roar filled the barn. Slowly, precisely, he lowered the rotating blade. As it chewed into the dead gangster's ankle, Tyler dispassionately wondered how many more times he was going to have to do this to keep Edward Forester's skeletons hidden.

Chapter Twenty-Two

All the way back to Southview, all Edward could think about was how he'd felt as he watched Tyler torture Reynolds. Even when Tyler phoned to tell him Detective Inspector Monahan needed to be got rid of, it only briefly distracted him from the memory of *that* feeling. To look in someone's eyes, to see them seeing their life and death in your eyes. Nothing came close to that. Not money. Not politics. Not sex. And certainly not love. *Love!* The word made him want to spit. What was love anyway, if it wasn't about power and control?

Several times during the drive, Edward caught his mother glancing disapprovingly at him. He knew what she was thinking – she was thinking the tremors running through him were a nervous after-effect of what he'd seen at the farm. But that wasn't it at all. *The hunger* – that was what he called his need to indulge his appetites – always came on like the beginnings of a fever. At first everything would buzz and tremble hotly inside him. Then the hunger would hit him, cold and hard. He knew how to control it nowadays. Most of the time. When he was younger, it had been different. A name came into his mind. *Wendy Atkins*. He blinked and her plain, freckled, eleven-year-old face passed like a ghost before him. Christ, he hadn't thought about her in years. Her mother had worked as a cleaner at his house. One summer's day, she'd brought Wendy with her. He was thirteen at the time, just over the cusp of puberty. The instant he'd seen her, the hunger had hit him with overwhelming force. It wasn't simply that he'd been sexually attracted to her. It was that he'd scented her weakness. In the timidity of her movements and the shy glances she'd given him, he'd read a neediness, a yearning to be liked.

Edward licked his lips at the memory. He'd always had a talent for identifying weakness in others and manipulating them into doing what he wanted. It hadn't been difficult to entice Wendy to the old lumber shed in the woods at the bottom of the garden. It had been more difficult to convince the silly little girl to let him tie her up, but he'd managed it. And then he had his way with her. His fumblings had been over-eager and clumsy, and upon putting his hand between her legs he'd prematurely ejaculated in his underpants. But that hadn't bothered him. The real satisfaction had come from the fear he saw in Wendy's eyes. It had made him feel as if he could do anything he wanted in the world. Afterwards, he'd shown her his Polaroid collection of animals he'd tortured and killed, threatening to do the same to her if she told anyone what had happened. She'd promised to keep quiet, and for several weeks she kept that promise. But then it had all come out in a wave of anger and bitter accusations. His mother hadn't even asked him if the accusations were true. She'd simply paid whatever it had taken to buy the silence of Wendy's family.

That experience had taught Edward two valuable lessons. Firstly, that no one would ever know or love him as completely as his mother did. And secondly, and most importantly, that everything was for sale to those who could afford it

By the time they got to Southview, the hunger was on Edward like a hand pulling invisible strings. He tried to resist it, knowing he shouldn't risk going to the bunker. But it was no good. His appetite demanded satisfaction. 'I'm taking Conall for a walk,' he told his mother. 'I need some fresh air.'

'Don't go too far,' Mabel cautioned.

'Don't worry, Mother.' Edward patted the wolfhound. 'I've got my bodyguard here to take care of me.'

Mabel arched a dubious eyebrow. 'He's as soft as a puppy. Aren't you, boy?'

She ruffled Conall's shaggy grey coat, before puckering her lips at Edward. As he bent in to give her a quick peck, she caught hold of his cheeks and held his lips against hers. Several long seconds passed. His stomach was churning, but he didn't pull away. Finally, she released him. He forced a smile and turned to leave.

Once outside, Edward wiped away the sticky-sweet scum of his mother's lipstick. The bitch had paid her money and now, he knew, he was going to have to start making good on her investment. But even that nauseating prospect couldn't dent his mood. He felt strangely light on his feet. As the invisible strings carried him towards the woods, he held the image of Bryan Reynolds's final moments in his mind, savouring it like the memory of a lover's last embrace. He'd watched plenty of weak people die. But to watch such a powerful man die, and to know it was because of him... God, it made him feel as if he could walk on water. His mother had always drummed into him that he could achieve anything if he put his mind to it. He'd grown up believing he was destined for greatness. But as he'd been passed over time and again for Cabinet, his belief had curdled into doubt then bitterness. The false expectations his mother had instilled in him had become just one more reason to hate her. At that moment, though, he felt his self-belief returning like a tide.

I won't be passed over again, Edward swore silently. *Now is my time. Now is my turn to be the one with the real power.*

He'd encountered so much disappointment in the last few years – the ousting of his party from government, the stagnation of his career, and now all this recent nonsense. But as he hurried towards his destination, he was thirteen years old again. Everything was ahead of him. Everything was possible.

On his way out of the city, Jim stopped to stock up on supplies for the stakeout of Edward Forester's house. Instead of the usual caffeine- and sugar-loaded snacks, he filled a basket with bottled water, fruit and salad. He stared gloomily at the packets of cigarettes and Pro Plus behind the checkout counter, wondering how he was going to keep himself not only awake but alert during what might be long hours of surveillance. He'd only been up a few hours, but already tiredness was washing over him in great, dizzying waves. As he returned to his car, another wave hit him. He pinched his eyes shut, leaning against a lamp-post. Frank Geary's words echoed back to him. *Christ, look at us. Some of the nastiest bastards in South Yorkshire used to fill their pants at the sight of us. They'd laugh in our faces if they saw us now.* He opened his eyes, glancing around as if worried someone might have seen him. But there was nobody.

Following the satnav's instructions, Jim headed along Ringinglow Road. Large houses lined the leafy suburban street, which rose gently towards a brown hump of moorland with scraps of mist drifting across it. A mile or two beyond the edge of the city, he passed the turn to the house of secrets and horrors that had started him on this path – the Baxley house. A deep furrow appeared between his eyes. Had that really only been a matter of days ago? It felt more like a lifetime.

Jim flicked on his fog lights as mist enveloped his car. He hoped the conditions were clearer at Southview, otherwise there wasn't going to be much to see. When he passed through the other side of the mist, the landscape unfurled itself in front of him like a lush green carpet. A mile or so away, and far below, the stone houses of Hathersage nestled in a deep valley. The road descended towards them, snaking its way down steep hillsides of bracken and sheep-grazed grass. Still high above the bottom of the valley, he turned onto a road that ran parallel to the imposing gritstone escarpment of Stanage Edge. The mist moved in again, thicker than before. The satnav led him unerringly through a tangle of undulating, drystone-walled lanes to his destination.

To the left of the road, closely clustered trees overhung a two and a half metre high wire fence. To the right, a tall yew hedge sculpted into battlements presumably marked the boundary of Southview's garden, although it was impossible to be certain, since the house itself was lost in the mist. Jim pulled over and killed his lights. He didn't want to risk getting any closer before he'd had a chance to have a good look at the lie of the land. A couple of hundred metres back, where there was no fence, he'd noticed a gap in the trees. The lane was too narrow to turn, so he reversed along the road and into the gap. Muddy wheel-ruts led to a small clearing where several trees had been cut down and stacked. He parked behind a log pile that concealed him from the road, and settled in to wait for the weather to clear.

Tiredness pressed down on Jim like a heavy blanket. He lowered his window, partly to try and stave it off with fresh air, but also so that he could hear any comings and goings on the road. Even so, and even though he kept telling himself not to think about her, his mind soon drifted into daydreams of Margaret. He missed everything about her – her face, her conversation, her laugh, her smell, even her nagging. But most of all he missed the way she gave him perspective, the way she enabled him to compartmentalise the sordid mess that was the world he came into contact with daily. She hadn't even had to say anything. A simple touch from her had been enough to drive out the images that haunted his nights. He could still remember her hands against his skin, soft and warm. But the memory was fading, like a photograph left out in the sun. Soon there would be nothing left of it. And the idea of facing life without even that to cling to was almost as terrifying as the images themselves.

The sound of an approaching vehicle brought Jim's attention back to the present. Deadened by the mist, it reached him faintly from the opposite direction to where he'd come. He jumped out of the car, clambered up the log pile and peered over the top. But the mist was still too thick to see anything. The sound of the engine lessened. His straining ears caught a low metallic squeal – perhaps of ill-oiled gate hinges – followed by the unmistakable crunch of tyres on gravel. Was it Forester returning home? he wondered. And if so, where had he been? Jim was still turning the questions over in his mind when he heard a second vehicle. The engine's growl was deeper, suggestive of something larger. Maybe a van or a four-by-four. The noise suddenly died away. But this time there was no metallic squeal or crunch of gravel. Someone was sitting outside Southview, motionless in the mist. Were they keeping tabs on Forester? Were they watching out for anyone else who might be watching the house? Or was there some innocent reason for their being there? There was only one way to find out.

Jim descended the log pile and headed towards where he thought the second vehicle had stopped. He paused upon reaching the wire fence and eyed it uncertainly. In his younger days he would have scaled it with ease. Nowadays the prospect was as daunting as climbing a mountain. But if he remained outside the fence the risk of being spotted by someone coming along the road was too great, so he hooked his fingers into the wire. Sweat popped out on his body as he hauled himself upwards. With a grunt, he flopped over the fence, lost his grip and dropped heavily to the ground. A small explosion seemed to go off inside his left knee. He collapsed onto his back and lay gasping, clutching his knee and chest, not sure which hurt more. After several minutes, his breathing returned to something like normal and the pain eased off. Grabbing the fence again, he pulled himself upright. As he stepped away from it, more explosions lanced through his leg. He gritted his teeth, holding in a groan. The pain was intense, but he could walk.

'Just what I fucking need,' he muttered under his breath.

Keeping within sight of the road, Jim picked a path through the undergrowth of bracken and bramble. He passed a padlocked gate. He guessed it wasn't the gate he'd heard opening, as it led onto a dirt, not gravel, track. He flinched as a pheasant rocketed up into the leaf canopy. His hand went to his chest again, where his heart thudded a worrying staccato. He leant against a tree, waiting for it to calm down. His ears pricked at the crunch of gravel. The sound was closer than before and made by feet not tyres. Then came the metallic squeak. He pressed himself flat against the tree, peeking around it. Edward Forester materialised through the mist, walking as if in a rush to get somewhere. He was dressed like a country gent in green wellingtons, brown corduroys and a waxed jacket. In one hand he held a walking stick, in the other a lead attached to a grey wolfhound. Jim jerked back fully out of view as the dog suddenly pulled towards his hiding place.

'What is it, Conall? What's the matter, boy?' Forester asked in a voice full of a strange urgency. The dog barked and another pheasant burst from the undergrowth.

Jim expelled a small sound of relief as the pair continued on their way. But his relief was only fleeting. Forester was heading in the direction of the gap in the trees. If he saw the car, Jim would have to act fast. The most important thing was that Forester wasn't allowed to get warning to whoever else might be watching his house. Although just how the hell he was going to get back over the fence and tackle a grown man and a twelve-stone dog in his condition was another matter entirely. Grimacing, he limped after the politician with as much stealth as he could muster. Another little breath of relief left him when Forester stopped at the padlocked gate. He unlocked it, stepped through and snapped the padlock back into place, before letting the wolfhound off its lead. Conall bounded away into the trees on the opposite side of the track, barking and scattering more pheasants.

Forester followed the track, walking like a man on a mission. The mist didn't penetrate far into the woods. Even so, Jim struggled to hobble along fast enough to keep the politician in view. The sound of the wolfhound crashing through the undergrowth had faded away into the distance.

He flicked open his telescopic baton in case it returned and picked up on his scent. The baton's cylindrical shaft was slim and lightweight, but a whack from its solid steel tip would be enough to make the dog think twice about attacking him.

Jim arrived at a clearing, in which stood some kind of bunker. Forester was already closing its iron door behind himself. There was the sound of a heavy lock sliding into place. With uneasy eyes, Jim took in the squat concrete structure. The place looked like an old bomb shelter. But it obviously wasn't being used as such any more. So what was it being used for? A face came into his mind – an angular, scarred face. Bryan Reynolds. Was it possible? Was Reynolds being held in there? His instincts told him it was more than possible. It was probable.

Bent low like a soldier, Jim advanced towards the bunker. He checked to see if there were any windows at its rear. As he'd expected, there were none. The only apertures were several small air vents at ground level. He checked out the iron door. It was sealed as securely as a safe. It would take explosives to open it.

Another even more disturbing possibility occurred to Jim. What if Melinda, or some other missing prostitute, was in there? Maybe Forester was torturing them, even killing them, right this moment? If that was the case, he had to be stopped – now! Jim took out his phone, his features riven with uncertainty. What if he was wrong? If he called in reinforcements only to discover there was nothing incriminating in the bunker, the game would be up. He'd have no choice but to tell Garrett everything. Even worse, Forester would remain free. No, he had to be certain. But the thought of what that certainty might cost someone was enough to draw deep lines in his face.

Jim retreated to the cover of the trees and dropped to his haunches. There was no tiredness now. The pain in his knee and the tension in his mind warded it off more effectively than any amount of caffeine or sugar. From somewhere in the distance beyond the bunker came the deep, throaty bark of the wolfhound.

Chapter Twenty-Three

You're a copper. That means Melinda's your problem. And if you don't see that, you're in the wrong line of work. No matter how hard he tried, Reece couldn't stop Jim's words from going round in his head. His dad had once told him how he'd felt 'called' to be a cop. Reece had never felt that calling. He'd become a copper for two reasons: partly because he knew it would make his mum proud; but mainly to prove to his dad that he could do the job. He'd made detective inspector in half the time it had taken his dad. The day he got his DI's badge had been the most triumphant of his life. But looking back on it now, he wondered whether that was the moment the rot set in. He'd achieved what he wanted. He'd shown the old bastard that not only could he do the job, but he could do it better than him. After that, the daily grind of being a copper – the frustration, the danger, the sense of never quite being in control – had quickly started to get to him. Even so, he'd never seriously questioned whether he was cut out for the job. Until now.

Jim Monahan had shrugged off a heart attack to chase down a suspect. The guy was clearly obsessed. Possibly even a little unhinged. And yet in his presence Reece had felt a sting of shame sharper even than the first time he'd pocketed dirty money. Jim's words had brought home to him just how petty his triumph over his father had been. Even more distressingly, they made him realise how little he understood about what it really meant to be a copper. He understood one thing, though – to give up searching for Melinda was to prove beyond doubt that he wasn't fit to wear the same badge Jim did.

Reece took out his police ID. He stared at it a long moment, brows rutted, eyes seeming to search for something. Then he thrust it back into his pocket and stood up. 'I've got to go out for a while, Dad.'

Frank turned to his son. 'Do you have to?'

Reece looked back at him, speechless. His dad had never said such a thing to him before. He'd always made it plain he was glad to see the back of him. More surprising yet was the concern he saw in his dad's eyes. Silence and anger, those were the only ways the bastard ever usually expressed himself. Bitter experience had taught Reece how to deal with that side of him – either stay well out of his way, or if that wasn't possible, do whatever he said. His thoughts returned to the hospital. What had the doctor said that had exposed this new facet of his dad's personality? Once again, there was only one answer he could think of, and it was almost enough to make him sit back down. But if he did that he knew he'd never be able to get Jim's words out of his head – at least not until he handed his badge in.

Frank repeated his question, and this time Reece replied, 'Yes, I have to.'

'Then be careful.' Frank grinned as if to make light of his concern. 'And don't do anything I wouldn't do.'

That was too much for Reece. He left the house, tears pressing against the backs of his eyes. He didn't let them out. Tears were a sign of weakness. His dad had taught him that. When Reece had learnt his mum was dead, he'd felt like his insides were being put through a mangle. But no tears had come. So he was damned if he was going to cry for his drunken, wife-beating father. As he shoved the car into gear, an angry thought welled up inside him: *Even if the bastard is dying, he's got no right to suddenly start caring, to try and make me feel something more for him.* 'No fucking right at all,' he muttered, his voice a sharp rasp.

With a wrench, Reece turned his thoughts to the matter at hand. Like his father had said, he needed to be careful. The last thing he wanted was for word of what he was doing to get back to Doug or, God forbid, DCI Garrett. If he turned up any concrete evidence that Melinda's disappearance was connected to Freddie Harding – and given the limited investigative moves he could make that seemed unlikely – he'd have to bite the bullet and fess up to his partner. But otherwise, he would treat this simply as a run-of-the-mill missing person's case.

Reece traversed the city centre to Wicker, a busy thoroughfare of local shops, pubs and takeaways. He parked in the shadow of a railway bridge that arched over the road. Making his way around the back of a shop, he climbed a dingy flight of stairs and knocked on a door. After a long moment, Wayne opened it. The pimp's face looked as if it had been used as a football. There were butterfly stiches over his eyebrows. His right arm was in a sling. The bruised pouches of his eyes widened at Reece. He recoiled from the door, almost falling over as he grabbed for a baseball bat. Reece was on him in a heartbeat, wrenching the bat from his grasp. Wayne groaned as Reece pinned him against a wall.

'I don't want trouble,' said Reece.

Wayne glared doubtfully at him. 'So what do you want?'

'Just to take a look around.'

'Then you'll leave me alone?'

Reece nodded.

'Alright, look all you fucking want.'

Reece let go of Wayne. He kept hold of the bat, though. There was no sense putting temptation in front of such a vindictive bastard. The flat was a poky place with a shabbily furnished living room, a tiny kitchen, an even smaller bathroom and one bedroom. Reece checked out the bedroom first. There was an unmade double bed strewn with Wayne's clothes. A joint smouldered in an ashtray on a bedside table. One wall was fitted with a mirrored wardrobe. Reece slid the wardrobe open. A selection of barely there dresses hung on the rail above several pairs of high-heeled shoes.

'Are these Melinda's?' asked Reece.

'Well they're not fucking mine.' Wayne pointed at a bin liner in one corner. 'The rest of her crap is in there.'

Reece looked in the bin liner. It contained various bits of makeup and some skimpy underwear. Not much to show for a life. 'I'm taking this.'

'Go ahead. What do I give a fuck?' As Reece resumed his search, Wayne added, 'You're wasting your time. There's nothing else of Melinda's here.'

Reece's phone rang. 'Shit,' he muttered when he saw it was Doug calling. He briefly considered not answering, but he knew Doug wouldn't bother him unless it was urgent. He walked quickly from the flat, putting the phone to his ear. 'What's up?'

'I need your services,' said Doug.

'I'm looking after my dad.'

'He'll have to look after himself for a couple of hours.'

'I'm sorry, Doug, I can't leave him.'

'Bollocks you can't!' Doug shot back. 'This isn't a request, it's a fucking order. You get your arse here right now.'

Reece's forehead wrinkled. He'd heard Doug angry plenty of times before. But he detected something else in his partner's voice, something unfamiliar – a note of anxiety or warning? He couldn't be sure. 'Where's here?'

Doug gave Reece an address in Crosspool, an affluent suburb on the west side of the city, adding, 'I'll be waiting for you a few doors along.'

'I'll see you in ten or fifteen minutes.'

Reece hung up. He turned at a sniffing sound and saw that Wayne had followed him into the stairwell. 'What's that I can smell?' asked the pimp, his swollen eyes glimmering with sly amusement. 'Oh yeah, it's bullshit.'

'If a word of this gets back to Doug...' Reece trailed off, letting the implied warning hang in the air.

'He won't hear a word from me, I swear it. Of course, if

my payment's a little short next month, you'll understand, won't you?'

Reece eyeballed Wayne a moment longer. Then, with a sigh, he nodded. He turned his back on Wayne's smug face and headed for his car. He slung the bin liner into the boot, reflecting gloomily that its contents were going to cost him dear, most likely for no return. As he drove out to Crosspool, inner-city terraces and high-rise flats gave way to privet-hedged suburban semis and detached homes. Reece pulled in behind Doug's Subaru. He got out of his car and ducked into the Subaru's passenger seat.

Doug treated Reece to a broad grin. 'Good lad. I knew you wouldn't let me down.'

'So what's the deal?'

'You want in on the big money, right? Well this is your chance.' Doug pointed to a modest detached house. Like its neighbours, the house was well kept with a large garden. Unlike its neighbours, the house's windows were fitted with steel shutters that when closed would make the place practically impenetrable. It also had an alarm box and two security cameras under the eaves.

'Who lives there?'

'A family. Husband, wife, couple of kids. Just as you'd expect. Only this family is hiding a big secret.'

'Which is?'

Doug tapped his nose. 'It's a surprise. Don't worry, mate, you're going to fucking love it.'

Doug got out of the car. Reece followed him to the boot. Doug took out two bullet-proof vests with 'POLICE' stitched on them in white lettering. Reece's eyebrows drew together. 'I thought you said a family lived there.'

'It's just a precaution. Better safe than sorry.'

They pulled on the vests and zipped up their jackets over them. Doug strapped a Taser to his belt. Then he lifted a black metal battering ram with two handles and a flat circular head out of the boot and passed it to Reece. There was a metallic clatter as he slung a bag over his shoulder. 'You know the drill. You knock on the door with old faithful. Then we go in hard.'

'What's in the bag?' asked Reece as they approached the house.

Doug grinned again. 'You'll find out soon enough.'

There was a sign on the front gate that read 'THIS PROPERTY IS PROTECTED BY STEEL CITY SECURITY'. Reece sized up the front door. It was windowless with a heavy-duty lock and two deadbolts. Not easy to get through, but he'd taken down similar doors back when he was a PC. The trick was to strike the door as close to the main lock as possible, letting the weight and momentum of the ram do the work.

'Ready?' asked Doug, his eyes bright with adrenalin.

Reece nodded. His adrenalin was pumping too, but even so he felt calm. After the emotional tumult of the last few days, it was almost a relief to be doing something that required nothing more of him besides brute force.

Like a boxer about to get into the ring, Doug sucked in a breath and puffed it out in a couple of quick gusts. He unholstered his Taser. 'Let's do this.'

Reece swung the battering ram like a pendulum. The door buckled, but the locks held. He struck the door again and it burst open with a splintering crash.

'Police!' shouted Doug, charging into the hallway. 'Nobody move!'

Reece followed his partner into a living room furnished with a white leather three-piece suite, a sideboard cluttered with ceramic pigs and a large plasma-screen television. A heavily built, forty-something man sprang out of an armchair. Although it was early afternoon, the man was unshaven and wearing a vest and boxer shorts. Doug shot him with the Taser. The gun's two metal barbs sank into his chest. There was a crackle of electricity. The man took a couple of jerky steps towards Doug, before collapsing face first to the carpet. As Doug knelt on his back and cinched his wrists with plasticuffs, a busty, orange-faced blonde in a pink tracksuit dashed into the room through a door at its far end.

'Leave him alone, you bastards!' she yelled.

'Control that bitch,' said Doug.

His words were unnecessary. Reece was already advancing towards the woman, extendable baton in hand. 'Calm down, we're police.'

'Bollocks you are. Where's your ID?'

Reece flashed his badge too quickly for the woman to read his name. 'I need you to put your hands behind your head.'

'This is bullshit. You can't come in here without a warrant.'

Reece raised his baton. 'Hands behind your head. Do it!'

The woman's eyes flicked frantically towards the cuffed man. As if he'd given a signal, she spun and darted back towards the door. Reece gave chase and caught hold of her arm. But not before she managed to press a red button in a small black box attached to the wall. A piercing alarm began to blare. The woman tried to wrench away from Reece, but he twisted her arm up behind her back and forced her down to the carpet. She screamed, kicking like a crazed animal and twisting onto her back. Reece yanked her hands together and cuffed them in front of her. She spat a glob of phlegm at him. 'Fucking cunts! You'd better get the fuck out of here or—'

Doug inserted a key into the black box and twisted it, silencing the alarm and the woman. He flashed her a sneering smile. 'Or what?' She stared back of him with an expression of shocked realisation. 'That's right, bitch. No one's coming.'

'You're not police,' said the man, his voice tight with pain.

'As far as you're concerned right now, I'm God. So you might as well shut the fuck up and let us do what we're here to do.'

'Fucker!' hissed the man. 'Do you know who I am?'

'You're Graham Porter. Bryan Reynolds's money man.'

Reece darted a frowning glance at Doug upon hearing the gangster's name, but said nothing.

'Then you know you won't get away with this,' said Porter.

Snatching Reece's baton off him, Doug strode over to Porter. The handcuffed man cried out and curled into a ball as Doug rained down several ferocious blows on his back and arms. 'Now are you going to shut your gob or am I going to have to keep on beating the crap out of you?'

Porter nodded rapidly to indicate the former option. Doug turned to Reece and gestured with his chin. 'Put them on the sofa and keep an eye on them.'

As Reece did so, Doug spread a hand-drawn plan of the house's ground floor out on a coffee table. Two Xs were marked on the map – one where the sideboard stood and another in the adjacent room. Doug sent the ceramic pigs crashing to the floor with a sweep of his arm, then attempted to drag the sideboard away from the wall. 'Christ, this thing's heavy,' he grunted. 'Give me a hand here.'

The two men manoeuvred the sideboard into the centre of the room. Then Doug took a Stanley knife, a claw hammer and a chisel out of his bag. He cut the carpet close to the skirting board and pulled it away from the floorboards. He drove the chisel between the floorboards and started levering them up. When he'd removed several, sweat glistening on his broad tanned forehead, he reached down into the gap and lifted out a bulging holdall. He unzipped it, revealing bundles of used tens and twenties, each thick enough to choke a horse.

'Bloody hell,' breathed Reece.

Doug waggled his eyebrows at him. 'Told you you'd like it.' He zipped the bag back up and headed into the neighbouring room. There was the sound of more carpet and floorboards being pulled up. From upstairs, it was joined by the plaintive coughing wail of a baby.

'That's my daughter,' said the woman. 'I need to go see her.'

Reece shook his head.

'Please,' continued the woman. 'She's only eighteen months and she's got a bad cold. She could be choking on her snot.'

Reece glanced at the ceiling, his forehead furrowed. The coughing grew louder, more painful sounding. He thought of his dad being gradually suffocated by the tumours growing in his lungs. With a warning look at the woman and Porter, he poked his head into the back room. Doug was stooped over, straining to prise loose a floorboard. 'The woman wants to go see her baby,' said Reece.

'Sod the baby,' Doug retorted breathlessly, without looking up from his task.

'She says it's ill. I'm taking her upstairs.' There was a steely note in Reece's voice that suggested he'd made his mind up and nothing was going to change it.

Doug looked at him with a little shake of his head. 'Alright, but bring Porter in here first.'

Reece hauled Porter to his feet and shoved him to the floor in a corner of the back room. 'Don't you fucking move from that spot.'

Drawing the woman along behind him, Reece made his way upstairs to a nursery decorated in the same shade of pink as the woman's tracksuit. A chubby baby was standing at the bars to a cot, cheeks flushed apple-red, tears and snot streaming down its face. 'Shh, Mummy's here,' soothed the woman, stooping over the cot. She made as if to pick the baby up, but her hands went under the mattress and yanked something out. As she whirled to face Reece, he saw a handgun. He made a grab for it. The muzzle flashed. The retort of the gun filled the little room. Then it was like he'd been hit in the chest with a sledgehammer. He staggered backwards and fell to his knees, his mouth opening and closing like a fish out of water, his ears screaming like a hundred babies. The woman rushed past him onto the landing.

Doug's voice came up the stairs. 'Reece?'

Reece rose unsteadily and charged after the woman. She was standing on the top step, aiming down the stairs. The gun went off again as his shoulder connected with her back. There was a puff of plaster as a bullet thunked into the wall behind Doug's head. Reece and the woman tumbled head over heels, landing in a heap at the foot of the stairs. Still fighting for breath, he grabbed the gun and disentangled himself from the woman. Her eyes were closed. Blood was trickling from her scalp down her forehead. Doug stooped to check for a pulse in her throat.

'Is she dead?' croaked Reece.

'No. What happened?'

Reece held up the pistol – a Glock 9. 'It was in the cot.'

Doug gave another shake of his head. 'It's a sick fucking world we live in. You OK?'

Reece's fingers explored the spot where the bullet had hit his chest. The steel-plating was dented but intact. He nodded.

Doug helped him to his feet. 'We'd better get our shit together and get out of here.'

They carried the woman into the living room and dumped her on the floor. There was a second holdall next to the first one now. Doug quickly packed away the tools, while Reece retrieved the battering ram. Reece made to pick up one of the holdalls, but Doug shoved the toolbag into his hand, saying, 'I'll carry them.'

As they headed out the door, Porter shouted after them, 'Dead men walking! You're dead men walking!'

There was no one in the street. The gunshots didn't seem to have drawn any unwanted attention. Reece reflected that any neighbours who weren't out at work had probably taken them for a backfiring engine. After all, this was hardly the kind of area where gunshots in the middle of the day, or at any other time, were normal occurrences. They stowed their gear and the holdalls in Doug's boot, then jumped into their cars and accelerated away. They didn't drive fast. There was no need. Porter was scarcely likely to call the police to report the theft of his boss's drug money.

Doug led Reece back down towards the city centre and beyond into Hillsborough. As Reece drove, he kept tightening and untightening his hands on the steering wheel. He'd been stone cold calm during the raid – he mentally corrected himself, *No, not raid, robbery* – but now his heart was beating like it wanted to escape his chest. Porter's parting words kept echoing in his head. *Dead men walking! You're dead men walking!*

Doug pulled up outside a two-storey sooty brick building tucked down a quiet side street. The front door had a steel-reinforced frame. Steel shutters covered the windows. There was an alarm box and CCTV camera under the eaves. To one side of the building was a yard enclosed by a wire gate and a brick wall with razor wire on top. A sign on the gate read 'WARNING: GUARD DOGS PATROL THESE PREMISES'. There were no dogs to be seen in the yard. But there was a black Audi.

Doug opened the front door and punched a code into an alarm keypad. Glancing around warily, he removed the holdalls from the boot of his car and headed inside the building. Reece followed him into a room cluttered with cardboard boxes. As Doug locked the door behind them, Reece said, 'Porter's right. We are dead men. We've just as good as declared war on the number one scumbag in this city.'

Doug eyed Reece with a twinkle of secret amusement. 'You let me worry about that.'

'How the fuck am I not supposed to worry? Reynolds is going to be coming at us with everything he's got.'

Doug laughed his deep, throaty laugh. 'Trust me, Reece. Everything's going to be fine.'

'How can you be so certain?' Reece's eyes narrowed. 'Has something happened to Reynolds?'

'Maybe. Who knows? *Things* just happen to men like him all the time.'

Reece exhaled an irritated breath at his partner's cryptic response. 'Come on, Doug, haven't I earned a straight answer?'

'You did good back there. Apart from that fuck-up with the woman. How's your chest?'

Reece pulled up his t-shirt, exposing a cricket-ball-sized livid red mark on his left pec.

'You're gonna have one hell of a bruise.' Doug wagged an admonishing finger. 'You know, Reece, I've noticed something about you. You're too bloody soft. One of these days it's going to get you seriously hurt.'

'Look, all I want to know is why I shouldn't pack my bags and head for the nearest airport,' said Reece, refusing to be deflected from his line of inquiry.

Doug tapped his temple. 'Use your head. Do you really think I'd fuck with Reynolds if I didn't have some serious muscle to back me up?'

Reece's thoughts returned to the sign he'd seen on the gate of Porter's house. 'Steel City Security. Who are they?'

'They're me, along with some good friends of ours you'll be meeting soon.' Doug indicated the room around them. 'As you've probably gathered, this is our little headquarters. A few years ago we started providing security for people who need it more than, shall we say, your average citizens.' He illustrated his words by flipping open a box, revealing a CCTV camera cradled in polystyrene. 'And it's been a nice little earner. But we're ready to expand now and go on to the next step. If you keep playing your cards right, you can come along for the ride too.' He removed a couple of bundles of cash from one of the holdalls and proffered them to Reece. 'There's enough there to pay off your woman's debt and have some left over.'

Reece motioned at the holdalls. 'What about the rest of it? There's got to be close to a million quid there.'

'Don't worry, you'll get the rest of your cut once it's been divvied up. You're part of an outfit now, and just like with the police, everyone in the outfit gets paid their dues.'

Reece accepted the cash. He stared at it. This was his future. This was Staci and Amelia's future. And yet his eyes were troubled.

'What have you got that look on your face for?' said Doug. 'You should be celebrating. You're going to be a rich man. We both are.' He clapped Reece on the arm. 'I tell you, the way things are going for us, the people we've got in our pockets, we're going to end up running this fucking city.'

He moved aside several boxes, revealing a man-sized safe, and punched a code into an electronic lock. As Doug stowed the holdalls in the safe, Reece caught a glimpse of more cash, a small arsenal of handguns and ammunition, and maybe half a dozen plastic-wrapped blocks of some light brown substance. Reece's frown intensified. *Heroin!* His experienced eyes weighed up the blocks at around a kilo each. Depending on its purity, they had a wholesale value of around fifteen or twenty thousand pounds apiece. Of course, their street value was exponentially higher.

Reece's hand strayed to the Glock in his jacket as his mind replayed the events of the past hour: Doug beating

Porter; the screaming baby; the woman pulling out the gun. *You're part of an outfit now.* He heard Doug's words again, and with them came the thought, *You're not a copper any more, not really. You're a gangster.*

Chapter Twenty-Four

His hands trembling with excitement, Edward fired up a petrol-run generator. A bulb flickered into life, dimly illuminating a rectangular concrete-floored room. In the centre of the room there were two sealed steel drums, a stack of bags of lye, and a couple of shovels and pickaxes. On the rear wall, an assortment of power tools and numerous plastic containers marked with skulls and crossbones occupied shelves attached to a wooden backing board. Edward pulled at one of the shelves. There was a click and the backing board swung smoothly outwards, revealing a second room.

This room was roughly half the size of the first and lit by a seedy red bulb. To the right of the concealed door there was a metal-framed bed with a pillow and a sleeping bag, to the left a fold-down camping table with a gas stove on it. Against the rear wall was a second set of shelves. At a glance their contents might have belonged to a survivalist preparing for Armageddon. But a closer inspection would have quickly revealed otherwise. Most of the shelves were stocked with bottled water, tinned and vacuum-packed food, gas canisters, pots and pans, toilet paper, a first-aid box, a pair of night-vision goggles and a couple of gas masks. One, though, was entirely given over to video tapes and DVDs, each with a name and date on it, running in chronological order from left to right; the earliest was marked 'Roxanne Cole – 20/2/1980'. Two more shelves were crammed with almost every sex toy imaginable – dildos, whips, restraints, blindfolds, spanking paddles, nipple clamps, tubs of lube, leather gimp suits – as well as more sinister items like cattle prods, pliers and surgical knives. In front of the shelves stood a video camera on a tripod, and a wheeled TV stand with a video, a DVD player and a television on it.

But it was what was on the adjacent walls that identified the room as the lair of something monstrous. Thirty-seven photographs were stuck to the dirty-grey concrete. Like the videos and DVDs, each was marked with a name and date. The photos were mostly of young women. Several were of not yet, or just barely, pubescent girls. Those were Edward's favourites. All the photos' subjects were naked. And all of them appeared to be dead. Their eyes were open, but vacant. Their jaws were slack. As to the cause of their deaths, it didn't take an expert to work out it hadn't been natural. Their bodies were artworks of abuse, arranged to show off their cuts, bruises, ligature marks, burns, breaks, tears and missing body parts to maximum effect.

Any normal person would have been stopped dead in their tracks by this horrific installation. Edward barely afforded it a glance. He changed into a gimp suit and pulled on the night-vision goggles. As he'd done with the first set of shelves, he swung the backing board away from the wall, revealing a metal door with a horizontal glassed slit at head height. He peered through the slit into a third room about half the size again of the second. The only light inside the room seeped through the slit. A naked young woman was lying on a mattress. Her skin appeared a decayed green through the goggles. But she wasn't dead. The yellow cuts of her eyes stared back at Edward. She knew from the light that she was being watched. He smiled, relieved. It had been Freddie's turn with her the previous night. Freddie had promised not to finish her off, but sometimes he got carried away.

'Hello, Melinda,' Edward mouthed silently. He watched her for a while, enjoying the tremors of terrified anticipation that shook her skinny, battered body. Several times in the past he'd seen victims pass through their fear into a kind of numb hopelessness. When that happened, they were of no more use to him. Upon his last visit, it had seemed as if Melinda might be going that way. But now she appeared to have pulled back around.

Edward took off the goggles and drew back the bolts. A faint wrinkle of distaste crossed his face as he entered the tiny room. The stench of human waste hung heavy. But that wasn't what bothered him. What bothered him was the way the red light accentuated the slight womanly curve of Melinda's belly and breasts. Freddie knew what he liked. But what he liked wasn't easy to get hold of. More often than not, he had to make do with girls like this one – the kind of slutty late-teens who populated 'barely legal' porn sites. Wendy Atkins's timid, gullible face rose into his mind again. What he wouldn't have paid to have a girl like her here. Or even a boy, he reflected, his thoughts turning fondly to Mark Baxley. But those kinds of opportunities appeared about as often as a comet in the sky. Kids like them simply didn't exist on the streets his brother trawled for victims. Even when they were young enough to suit his tastes, someone else had always been there first, tainting their innocence, taking the edge off their vulnerability. As things stood, the only way to get hold of another Wendy Atkins or Mark Baxley – and not just for a few hours of fun, but for the rest of their short life – would be to snatch one from a garden, or a shopping centre, or some such thing. And the prisons were full of idiots who'd attempted that kind of nonsense.

Edward ground his teeth. For almost two years he'd been working on a project that, in the near future, would have provided the opportunities he desired. But this Grace Kirby business had thrown his plans into disarray. He sighed. He would just have to make the best of what he had. 'How's our guest doing today?'

Melinda made no reply. Even if she'd wanted to, she looked as though she barely had the strength to speak. Her face and body were a welter of bruises. Dried blood crusted her lips, abdomen and inner thighs. Her eyes were glazed and bloodshot with dehydration. Edward unscrewed a bottle of water and proffered it. She made no move to take it. 'I'd drink something, if I were you,' he said, setting it down at her side. 'The body can survive for weeks without food, but only a few days without water.'

His lips curled upwards again as Melinda reached for the

water. So she wasn't quite ready to die yet. That was good. As she drank, he removed the bucket from the room. It was almost brimful with a toxic stew of piss and shit. He made a mental note to reprimand his brother. It was Freddie's job to empty the bucket. Melinda stopped drinking when Edward moved the camera into position at the end of the mattress. Her tremors turned into body-racking shakes. 'Assume the position,' said Edward.

Melinda shook her head frantically. *Good*, thought Edward, *good!* He liked resistance. Not too much, but a little. He raised a cattle prod warningly. A sob filled Melinda's mouth. She clamped her teeth together and swallowed it with a grimace. Then she managed to say a word, just one word, but it was enough. 'No.'

Edward hit Melinda with the prod. She screamed, stiffening like some kind of macabre mannequin. He fastened leather restraints around her wrists and ankles, before straddling her waist. She briefly struggled to buck him off. Then she went limp and her eyes drifted away from his, seemingly staring at nothing. He whipped a hand across her cheek.

As if jerked out of a deep sleep, Melinda's eyes darted back to Edward's, wide with disorientated fear. That was all the encouragement he needed. He stooped and sank his teeth into her right nipple. He'd intended to take his time with her, but now that it came to it he couldn't hold back. She screamed again as he chewed and tore at her flesh like a ravenous animal. Blood gushed hotly into his mouth. His own blood pumped hotly too, filling his groin to bursting.

He groaned and twitched for a few seconds, then slowly drew himself back into a sitting position. He spat a bloody chunk of flesh into his palm. Her breath coming in strangled gasps, her eyes once again blank, beyond horror, Melinda stared at her severed nipple.

Edward displayed his prize to the camera. Then he rose and returned to the second room. Carefully, almost reverently, he removed a glass jar from the shelf. The jar was full of murky brownish liquid with numerous shrivelled scraps of skin floating in it like dead leaves. He unscrewed the lid and dropped the nipple into the liquid. He put the jar down and stepped back from it, head tilted and eyes narrowed, as if studying a piece of art. After a long moment, he picked up the first-aid box and turned his attention to Melinda. Her eyes were closed. She didn't appear to be breathing. He checked for a pulse in her wrist and found one. He pulled up her eyelid. The pupil was dilated and sightless. She wasn't playing dead. He took a wad of gauze out of the box and taped it over her mutilated breast. Not that he cared whether she bled to death, but there was no sense in letting the mattress get ruined. Besides, the actual killing part held limited interest for him. It was Freddie who had a thing about seeing the light go out in their eyes. It wouldn't be fair to deny him that pleasure.

When Edward was done staunching the wound, he uncuffed Melinda, opened a tin of peaches and left them in a plastic bowl by the mattress. He liked to give them something sweet for their last meal. He didn't intend to see her again. He'd taken all he wanted from her. The next time he visited the bunker, she would be sealed in a steel drum, marinating in Freddie's special cocktail of chemicals. And after several months her gelatinous remains would be disposed of in the external grave pit. He closed the door, shot the bolts and swung the shelves back into position. He heated up a pan of water and scrubbed his face and hands with a soapy cloth. Then he changed into his clothes and headed for the front door. His hands were perfectly steady now as he turned off the chugging generator. He felt full, sated and relaxed, ready to take on the world.

Chapter Twenty-Five

Every few minutes, Jim was forced to adjust his position to ease the throbbing in his knee. His face was fixed into a grimace, and not just because of the pain. He kept thinking and trying not to think about what Forester might be doing. Was someone being killed in the bunker? Were they breathing their last breath right that minute? It was gut-wrenching to crouch there doing nothing with such questions swirling in his head. But what else could he do, unless he was willing to risk letting Forester slip through his fingers? What he was going to do when Forester emerged from the bunker was another question he didn't have a satisfactory answer to. If he tackled Forester and found nothing incriminating, the result would ultimately be the same as if he'd called in Garrett. He needed to get a look inside the bunker without Forester's knowledge. *But how?* he wondered. *Perhaps I can distract him somehow and sneak inside. It would be risky but what other—*

Jim broke off from his line of thought as the wolfhound emerged from the trees at the far side of the clearing with a rabbit clamped between its jaws. It placed the rabbit on the ground and nuzzled it. The rabbit twitched and kicked out with its hind legs. The dog skittered away from it barking, then darted back in and snatched it up. It toyed with the rabbit for several minutes, then seemed to get bored with the game and started sniffing around the clearing. Jim adjusted his position again, ready to pop up and strike out should the dog catch his scent. The wolfhound nosed aside a patch of long brown grass, providing Jim with a glimpse of a low mound of ash. It pulled something out of the ash and began to chew on it. What the hell was it? A burnt chunk of wood? As the dog turned the object over in its paws, Jim's eyes gleamed with sudden interest. No, it wasn't burnt wood. It was a boot. A high-heeled boot.

Jim rose and advanced towards the wolfhound, brandishing his baton. The dog eyed him warily, letting out a deep rumbling growl. 'Get out of here,' hissed Jim, giving a warning slash through the air. 'Go on.'

The wolfhound retreated, but didn't run away. Keeping his eyes fixed on the dog, Jim stooped to pick up the boot. It had a metal-tipped stiletto heel and a sharply pointed toe. The upper was made of wet-look PVC, most of which had been melted into a congealed, sooty mass. A grim frown clouded his face. Melinda had been wearing identical boots in the photo Reece had shown him. He jerked around at the sound of the iron door grating open. At the same instant, the wolfhound barked and lurched at him. Instinctively, he flung the boot into the trees and the dog went tearing after it. As Edward Forester stepped into view, Jim bore down on him like a train. There was no more need for subterfuge. He was certain now – Melinda was in the bunker. Whether she was dead or alive was another matter.

Edward's eyes jerked wide. 'Who the hell—' he managed to gasp out before Jim lashed the baton across his shins. Letting out a shrill cry, he collapsed to the ground. He flung his hands up in front of his face as Jim stooped to grasp the collar of his coat.

Oblivious to the pain in his knee, Jim dragged Edward back into the bunker. 'Is there a light in this place?' he demanded to know.

Edward twitched a finger at the generator.

'Don't you fucking move,' warned Jim, reaching to fire it up. As the bulb blinked into life, he pulled the door shut. There were two heavy-duty internal bolts. He shot them and turned to Edward, his eyes as sharp as scalpels. 'Where is she?'

'Where's who?' whimpered Edward.

'Don't play games with me.' The threat of violence seethed just below the surface of Jim's voice. 'Where's Melinda?'

'I don't know who you're talking about. Please, you have to believe me! You've made some sort of mistake.'

There was no hint of a lie in Edward's expression. Like all his kind, he was a consummate actor. If Jim hadn't known better, he might have been taken in by the politician's frightened, sincere eyes. 'There's no mistake. I know exactly who and what you are. You're Edward Forester, Labour MP for Sheffield South-East. Your mother is Mabel Forester. Your father was Norman Harding. His son, Freddie Harding, is your half-brother. Like him you're a rapist.' Jim recited the date and time that had been tattooed onto his brain ever since the night of Stephen Baxley's murderous rampage, 'On the first of October, 1997, at ten forty-three p.m., Stephen Baxley, Marisa and Herbert Winstanley, Henry Reeve and yourself drugged and molested Mark Baxley and Grace Kirby in the basement of the Winstanleys' house.'

As Edward listened, his face grew waxy with the realisation that this was one situation he wasn't going to be able to talk himself out of. And yet, knowing no other way, he persisted to try. 'You're right about who I am. As for the other things you said, I don't know where you're getting your information from, but you're wrong.' He pressed his hands together as if in prayer. 'I swear to you on everything I hold sacred, I'd never hurt anybody, least of all a child.'

Jim's lips stretched into something that looked like but wasn't a smile. 'I didn't say Mark and Grace were children.'

Edward's eyes danced as if searching for something he'd lost. 'You didn't have to. I've read about them in the newspapers. That's how I knew how old—'

'Enough!' Jim barked. 'You wouldn't know how to tell the fucking truth if your life depended on it. Which is unfortunate for you because it does.'

Tears sprang into Edward's eyes. 'Oh God, please don't kill me. If it's money you want, I'll give you all I have.'

Jim's nose wrinkled as if he'd smelt something nasty. 'You can't buy your way out of this.'

'I... I...' Edward stammered, as if he couldn't compute what he'd heard. 'I wish I could help you, but I don't have the answer you want.'

There was an echoing metallic boom as Jim brought his baton down hard against one of the steel drums. Edward clutched his hands over his head, dissolving into a blubbering mass. Jim glared at him, blood pounding in his veins, urging him to smash his skull into a hundred pieces. The man was more rotten than any of the governments they'd lived under. The sooner he was crushed out of existence the better. But this wasn't just about Forester. There were others out there who had to be brought to justice – Freddie Harding; Amy and Grace's killer; everyone who'd ever been to one of Herbert and Marisa's 'special' parties. And besides, killing Forester would almost be an act of mercy compared to what he would suffer in prison. A warning thought came to him: *You still need to find the evidence to put the bastard in prison.*

Jim's eyes travelled the room. Power saws, corrosive chemicals, lye, digging tools – everything you'd need to dispose of a body. Along with the PVC boot, they were incriminating items. But they weren't enough. He needed more, much more if he was going to bury Forester for life. His gaze lingered on the steel drums, whose lids had been welded shut. 'What's in these?'

'Petrol for the generator,' Edward managed to say, his voice shaking badly.

Jim looked at the shelves again, contemplating whether to use the tools to cut open the drums. His forehead wrinkled as something occurred to him. He measured the room with his eyes. It was seven or so metres long by about three metres wide. From outside the bunker was ten, maybe even fifteen metres long. Surely that meant there was another room. But where was the door to it? He scanned the floor, thinking that maybe the bunker had an underground level. There was no visible trapdoor. He pushed aside one of the steel drums. It was heavy. The effort made his head reel. There was nothing under the drum but concrete.

'Move the rest of them and the bags of lye,' he told Edward, struggling not to let his wooziness show through in his voice. The politician was a coward. That was obvious. But even cowards were capable of attack when cornered – especially if they sensed weakness.

Edward obeyed. Again, no trapdoor. 'There's nothing here but what you see.'

Jim made a doubtful noise in his throat. 'Give me the door key.'

Edward tossed Jim a bunch of keys. He locked the door. 'Now lie flat on your face, hands behind your head.'

Jim stamped on the floor in a couple of places, producing a dull, solid sound. He approached the shelves, removed a plastic container and rapped his knuckles against the backing board. It echoed hollowly. He pulled at a shelf tentatively, then more forcefully. There was a click. The board swung outwards a few centimetres. Jim flashed Edward a triumphant glance. The politician wasn't looking at him. His eyes were closed and he was grinding his face into the floor as if trying to dig a hole with his nose.

'On your feet,' said Jim.

Edward didn't seem to hear. There was blood on his forehead where he'd rubbed the skin away. He was making a small whining sound in his throat, like a dog in pain. Jim grabbed his collar and hauled him upright. He twisted one of Edward's arms up behind his back, warning, 'Any sudden movements and I'll break it.'

He guided Edward towards the shelves. 'Open it.'

Edward fully opened the door and they entered the second room. The first thing Jim saw was the shelves with their array of supplies, video tapes, DVDs and sex toys. Then he saw the photos, and in that instant, he knew Vernon Tisdale had got it right and everyone else had got it horribly, horribly wrong.

Jim forced Edward down to the floor again. Edward made no attempt to resist as Jim snatched a pair of handcuffs off a shelf and snapped them around his wrists. The politician squeezed his eyes shut, trembling uncontrollably, mumbling to himself.

'What's that?' growled Jim, pushing his face close to Edward's. He caught the word *mummy*. 'Mummy can't save you now, you sick, sick, sick bastard!'

Jim stood over Edward, the baton quivering in his hand as if electrified. He didn't merely want to beat Edward's brains to a pulp any more. He wanted to damn him to the same hell of cruelty and agony as he'd damned his victims. But he couldn't do it. His gaze returned to the photos. Roxanne Cole, Carole Stewart, Jennifer Barns, Cheryl Wright, and all the others, they deserved better than that kind of justice.

Drawing in a slow breath, Jim stepped away from Edward. His gaze traversed the tapes and DVDs to the year 1997. He pulled out DVDs until he found what he suspected he would. 'Mark and Grace – 1/9/97' was written on the cover. His features tightened at the memory of what the film contained. There was enough here to make sure Edward Forester never again breathed free air. It was more than Jim had expected, but still less than he'd hoped for. Even so, now was the time to call in Garrett. Jim took out his phone. Whether because of the thick concrete walls, the isolated location, or a combination of both, there was no signal.

'Shit,' muttered Jim. His eyes measured the walls again. This room was maybe three or five metres long. That meant there was perhaps another three metres unaccounted for. He pulled at the shelves. They came away easily from the wall, revealing the bolted door. He didn't even bother to look through the slit in the door. He simply threw back the bolts and opened it. Stomach knotting at the stench, he entered the room. His heart gave a heavy beat when he saw the girl. She looked worse than a lot of corpses he'd seen. But then she lifted her head and her pretty blue eyes peered at him through their raw, swollen lids. Her body stiffened as he dropped to his haunches at her side.

'It's OK, Melinda,' Jim said gently. Seeing her staring at the baton, he put it away. 'My name's Jim Monahan. I'm a policeman. You're safe now.'

Melinda's fear-paralysed limbs didn't relax. But a tiny glimmer of hope mingled with the terror in her eyes. The glimmer grew as Jim took out Edward's keys, found the one that fitted the padlock at her neck and removed the collar.

'Can you move?' asked Jim.

'Yes,' Melinda replied in a dry-throated whisper. Quivering with the effort, she raised herself into a sitting position, then to her feet. She swayed as if she might fall over. Jim reached out to steady her, but she shrank away from him against the rear wall, eyes darting about like those of a trapped animal searching for an escape route.

Jim spread his hands, palms outwards. With one hand, he reached slowly to take out his police ID and displayed it to Melinda. 'I'm not going to hurt you, Melinda. I'm going to take you away from this place.'

Melinda's gaze flickered between the ID and Jim's face. Jim had the same coloured eyes as the man – or men – behind the gimp mask. But that was where the similarities started and ended. Jim's eyes weren't mean little piggish things, they were wide-spaced and wide open, and even in his ID photo, a sort of weary, sad compassion shone through.

Jim motioned for Melinda to follow him into the second room. She warily moved away from the wall. Even with the ID, she wasn't ready to believe. Was this just another game? Another way to give her false hope in order to wring every last drop of perverse pleasure from her? A man was lying on the floor outside the door. He looked respectable, like someone's father. But she'd learned a long time ago not to trust appearances. Was he the one who'd done this to her? She couldn't tell without seeing his eyes. And his eyes were tightly closed. Her breath snagged in her throat as she caught sight of the photos. It was like standing in a room of mirrors and seeing your death reflected back at you over and over again.

Jim yanked off Edward's wellington boots and trousers. With a knee across the back of his neck, he unlocked the cuffs and removed his wax jacket. He re-secured the cuffs and proffered the clothes to Melinda. 'Put these on.'

She hesitated, repulsed by the thought of wearing her abuser's – if that's what this man was – clothes. But also suddenly wondering at the absence of other police officers. Surely any policeman would have called in back-up before tackling someone so dangerous. 'How did you find me?'

'There's no time to explain now.' Jim was thinking about the second vehicle he'd heard pull over outside Southview. If someone was keeping an eye on Forester, how long would have to pass before they came to check on him? 'Please. We've got to move quickly.'

Still, Melinda made no move to take the clothes. It was clear to Jim that he wasn't going to gain her trust with words alone. Christ knew what sort of games Forester had played with her head. He took a spray can out of his pocket. 'This is pepper-spray. Take it, and if I make one move you don't like feel free to use it on me.'

Melinda reached out tentatively, then quickly took the can. She examined it as though trying to work out whether it was genuine. She noticed the man on the floor watching her. His eyes were only open a slit, but it was enough. She thrust the can towards them and pressed the nozzle, shooting a stream of spray. He jerked his face away. A second or two passed. Then he began to writhe and cry out, 'It burns!'

'Good!' Melinda's voice burst out of her in a surge of shuddering rage. 'I hope it burns your fucking eyes out.'

She made to hit Edward with another blast of spray, but Jim caught hold of her arm. 'That's enough,' he said, his voice as gentle but firm as his grip.

Melinda jerked free. 'It's not fucking enough. It'll never be enough to repay that fucker for what he's done.'

I know, said Jim's eyes. But he didn't move out of Melinda's way. She glared at him for a moment. Then the rage seeped away, leaving only pain and exhaustion behind. Tears trembled in her eyes. Swiping them savagely away, she reached for Edward's clothes. The trousers were far too big for her, but they stayed up after she knotted their belt. She tried the boots on, then kicked them off. If she needed to run, there was no way she would be able to do so with any great speed in those clumping things.

As Melinda dressed, Jim dragged Edward into the cell and secured the collar around his neck. He took a couple more sets of restraints from the shelves and cuffed Edward's feet to his hands. Even though he doubted Edward had the balls to do it, he didn't want to give him the chance to rig up some way to hang himself. After closing and bolting the door, Jim headed for the outer room. He didn't like leaving Edward in the bunker, but if something happened on the way back to the car, he was going to need both hands free. Besides, he doubted anyone else had a key, except perhaps Freddie Harding. And it seemed unlikely to him that Harding would risk coming here during daylight hours.

Edward's clothes hung on Melinda like sacks, giving her the appearance of an ill-used rag doll. Jim shot her a cautioning look. 'Stay close to me and stay quiet.'

Jim opened the door, watching his phone to see if there was a signal. Stepping into the fresh air, he had the feeling that he was returning from the twilight zone of someone else's diseased dream to the real world. Melinda emerged blinking into the pale day. She sucked in a deep, shuddering breath. Tears came into her eyes again. This time she let them roll silently down her cheeks. The scent of wet earth and leaves, the shrill ring of birdsong, these were things she'd never paid much attention to before. But she noticed them now. It was intoxicating. She wanted to close her eyes and drink them in with every fibre of her being.

'Drop the phone and get on the fucking ground!'

Melinda heard the voice before she saw the speaker. A man stepped into the clearing. He was short and stocky with crew-cut greying hair and a goatee. He advanced a couple of paces, aiming a handgun at Jim.

Jim's eyes grew wide with recognition. 'Stan... Stan Lockwood. Easy, easy, don't you recognise me? It's Jim Monahan.'

'I know who the fuck you are. Now do as I say or I swear to Christ I'll shoot!'

Such a response, Jim knew, could only mean one thing – Stan was working for Forester. Upon seeing his ex-colleague, he'd hoped for an instant that Stan was back on the force.

Even as the thought flashed through his head, he'd realised it couldn't possibly be true. A couple of years ago, Stan and a young DC he was mentoring – Liam something-or-other – had been dishonourably discharged after a brutality complaint was made against them. They'd been seen by several witnesses beating up a suspected drug dealer. There were whispers it was because the dealer refused to cough up protection money. Both men had been lucky to avoid prison.

As Jim dropped his phone and lowered himself to the ground, Stan switched his aim to Melinda. 'You too. On your face.'

Melinda hesitated to obey, her gaze darting towards the trees that suddenly seemed so near yet so far away.

'Don't even think about it,' said Stan, reading the intention in her eyes. 'You'd be dead before you got three paces.'

Melinda dropped down beside Jim, whispering frantically, 'Who is he?'

'Someone I used to work with,' replied Jim.

'A cop?'

'No, not any more.'

'No fucking talking!' snarled Stan, striding forwards to snatch up the phone. He pressed the gun against the back of Jim's head, quickly frisking him. He took out Jim's extendable baton and wallet. Keeping the gun on Jim, he patted down Melinda. 'You could hurt someone with this stuff, little girl,' he said, upon finding the PAVA spray.

'Just give me the chance,' hissed Melinda.

Stan's mouth twitched with amusement. Flinging the can

into the undergrowth, he stepped back from the face-down figures. 'Now, where's Forester?'

Jim jerked his chin at the bunker. 'In there.'

'Is he alive?'

'Yes.' Jim glowered up at his ex-colleague. 'You do realise what kind of man you're working for, don't you?'

Stan made no reply, but the scowl of distaste that passed over his grizzled face left his thoughts in no doubt.

'And you can live with that?' went on Jim.

'Better than I can live with working my guts out for sod all.'

Jim shook his head with sad disgust.

Stan's scowl grew fiercer. 'Don't you fucking look at me like that, Jim. You think you're so much better than me, but you're not. The only difference between you and me is I don't need anyone to do my dirty work for me.'

Jim's gaze fell away from Stan. The meaning behind his words was obvious – Bryan Reynolds had talked. And if he'd talked, he was dead. Jim wasn't sure how the knowledge made him feel. Not that it really mattered any more. Soon he would no doubt be meeting the same fate as Reynolds.

'Yeah, that's right, I know what you did,' continued Stan, grinning in satisfaction at the effect of his words. 'Not so fucking high and mighty now, are you?'

'I'm not proud of what I did, but I didn't do it for myself.' Jim glanced at Melinda. 'I did it for her and everyone else Edward Forester's ever hurt.'

'Well, more fool you. Only an idiot would take a risk like that for anything other than money.'

'Is that why you joined the force? For money?'

The muscles of Stan's jaw contracted, as though Jim had touched a nerve. 'You know something, Jim, I'm going to really enjoy feeding you to—' His words changed into an, 'Oomph,' as a grey flash of fur hurtled into him. He went over like a felled tree under the impact of the wolfhound, crying out as Conall's teeth sank into his thigh. The sharp crack of a gunshot echoed through the trees, sending a flock of startled rooks into the air. Conall fell down instantly dead, his skull a ragged mess of bloody fur and shattered bone.

Jim had seen the dog burst from the undergrowth and guessed its intent. He scrambled to his feet as Stan pitched sideways. He barely had time to wonder whether it would be best to make a run for it or try to tackle Stan, before he realised there wasn't time for either course of action. Melinda was still struggling upright when Stan swung his gun away from the dead dog towards Jim and her. Jim grabbed her arm and tried to pull her back into the bunker. Her eyes swelled with a horror that made it clear she would rather be shot than return to that black hole. She wrenched herself free, screaming, 'No!'

Her hysterical strength threw Jim off balance. He staggered and tripped over the bunker's threshold. His breath whistled between his teeth as he landed on his back on the concrete floor. Through tear-misted eyes, he saw Melinda run for the trees, her arms flailing like a puppet with broken strings. Standing unsteadily on his injured leg, Stan took aim at her. Another shot rent the air. She staggered, but Jim couldn't tell whether she'd been hit or if it was an instinctive reaction to the noise. He willed her desperately to stay on her feet, and somehow she managed to. Then she was in amongst the trees.

Straining to suck air into his winded lungs, Jim clambered to his feet and made to yank the door shut. Stan jerked towards him and the gun's muzzle flashed again. Sparks flayed Jim's face as the bullet ricocheted off the door. His vision punctuated by a galaxy of dancing lights, he groped frantically for the bolts. Once he'd shot them and turned the key in the lock, he slid back down to the floor. The winded sensation wasn't fading, it was intensifying, squeezing the strength out of his body, radiating in tingling waves down his left arm.

Not now, he thought, clenching and unclenching his hand with difficulty, *please not now*.

Chapter Twenty-Six

Stan's gaze jerked between the bunker and the fleeing girl. What the hell was he supposed to do? He couldn't let the girl get away. But neither could he leave the bunker unwatched. He glanced at his leg. Adrenalin was overriding the pain, but it was obvious the dog's teeth had gone deep. Blood had already soaked down to the knee of his jeans. 'Shit! Fuck!' he exclaimed, snatching out his phone. Tyler was going to tear him a new arsehole for this. 'We've got big problems,' he said, when Tyler came on the line. He rapidly recounted what had happened.

'Are you certain you hit the girl?' asked Tyler, his voice as coldly calm as ever.

A little shudder ran through Stan. He was an ex-cop. He was used to reading people. But he couldn't read Tyler. And that made him nervous. The fucker was as emotionless as a machine. If he'd cut him open, he wouldn't have been surprised to find wires. 'Yeah... well, ninety-nine per cent certain.'

'Then stay at the bunker. Monahan's far more dangerous to us than the girl. If you hit her, she probably won't get far anyway.'

'What are you going to do?'

'I think it's time we put our back-up plan into action.'

'What back-up plan?'

'I'll explain when I get there. You say you've got Monahan's phone. Are there any numbers programmed into it?'

Stan opened the phone's contact list. 'Only two. One for someone called Margaret. And one for... Fucking hell, the other number's Reece Geary's. What's his number doing in Jim Monahan's phone? You don't think Reece is helping him, do you?'

Tyler was silent a moment as though mulling the possibility over, then he said, 'Give me Margaret's number.'

Stan did so and asked, 'What about Reece? What are we going to do about him?'

'Let me worry about that. You just concentrate on making sure Monahan doesn't hurt Forester.'

'And just how the hell am I supposed to stop him from doing that?'

'Talk to him. Feed him some bullshit. Say you've got the girl and you'll kill her if he touches Forester.'

'But what if—'

'Fuck what if. Just do it.'

The line went dead. Stan scrunched up his face, muttering, 'Do this, Stan. Do that, Stan. Do fucking everything.' He limped to the iron door, rapped on it with his gun and shouted, 'Jim.'

'What do you want?' Jim's voice was eerily muffled by the thick door.

'Just to talk.'

'We've got nothing to—' Jim faltered briefly, then continued, 'to talk about. And don't try to get in here or I'll kill Forester.'

A wrinkle of thought gathered between Stan's eyes. The snap shot he'd fired off at Jim hadn't found its mark, as evidenced by the bullet pockmark on the door. So what was the breathless, pained edge in Jim's voice about? Was the prick having another heart attack? 'You don't want to do that. Not if you want the girl to live.'

'She got away. I saw her.'

'She didn't get far. I winged her good and proper.'

'Let me hear her voice.'

'She's passed out. I reckon she'll bleed to death unless I do something. Look, Jim, why don't you open this door so we can talk properly. I know you're not interested in money, but maybe we can come to some other arrangement.'

'Fuck you, Stan. You were a lying piece of shit copper. And now you're a lying piece of shit murderer.'

A flush of angry colour climbed Stan's thick throat. He hammered the gun against the door again. 'You're going to die in there, Jim. Do you hear me? You're going to fucking die.'

There was another pause, then Jim's voice came again, steely with resolve, 'If I die, it won't be alone.'

Doug's gaze lingered on the contents of the safe. It gave him a buzz of satisfaction to see the holdalls nestled amongst the neatly stacked cash and heroin. Another two or three years of this shit, then it would be goodbye Sheffield, hello Bangkok. He shut the safe and turned to Reece. 'Well I'd say that's been a very successful—' He broke off as his phone vibrated. He pulled it out. It was Tyler. He put the phone to his ear, relishing the thought of telling him how well the job had gone. The bastard seemed to think his judgement was infallible. But this time he was wrong. Reece had proved himself more than worthy of their trust. 'It's done. Everything went—'

'Are you alone?'

'No.'

'Then go somewhere where you are.'

Holding up a finger for Reece to stay where he was, Doug opened a door and climbed some stairs to an attic room that was empty except for cobwebs and dust. 'We can talk now.'

'I want you to do that other thing we discussed.'

Doug's face creased. 'What changed your mind?'

'Monahan's not in hospital. He's in Forester's bunker.'

'What! How did he get in there?'

'I assume he forced Forester to let him in.'

'Forester's in there with him!' Doug shook his head as though he couldn't believe what he was hearing. 'Jesus fucking Christ, Tyler—'

'The situation's not as bad as it sounds,' Tyler cut in again. 'But we need to move fast if we're going to keep it under control. Is Monahan's ex-wife called Margaret?'

'Yes. How did you know that?'

'Stan's got Monahan's phone. Don't ask how. There's no

time to explain. Her mobile number's on there. You need to get her to meet up with you.'

Doug pursed his lips in thought. 'I could tell her Jim's in trouble.'

'That's what I was thinking.'

'What if she doesn't go for it?'

'Then you'll just have to do things the hard way. But there's no point taking that risk if you can get her to come to the bunker of her own free will.'

Doug heaved a breath. 'Christ, just when I thought my luck had changed for the better, another load of shit drops on my head.'

'We've got another problem. Your boy Reece's number is in Monahan's phone.'

'So what? They work together. My number's probably on there as well.'

'No, it's not. There are only two numbers on Monahan's list of contacts.'

Doug shook his head again, his eyes deeply troubled. 'No way. I know what you're thinking but there's no way fucking way Reece is helping Jim Monahan.'

'Then why has Monahan got his number?'

'Maybe Jim got wind of Reece's search for the missing whore. He could've spoken to Vernon Tisdale. The two of them used to know each other.'

'That's possible. But I don't want to stake my life on a possibility. Do you?'

Doug's fingers tightened on the phone as though he wished it was Tyler's throat. The bastard was right. He was always fucking right! And yet Doug couldn't bring himself to accept his words. Not with the memory of Reece flinging himself at the gun-wielding woman still fresh in his mind. 'I'm telling you, Tyler, Reece is with us one hundred per cent. You should have seen him today. I'd be dead now if it wasn't for him. So fucking forgive me if I'm not willing to put a bullet in his head on the strength of a phone number. In an hour or two we'll have Jim Monahan in our hands, and you can ask him what the deal is with Reece. And if it turns out I'm wrong, I'll personally make Reece wish he'd never been born.'

The line was silent a few seconds. Then Tyler said, 'If it turns out you're wrong, I'll make you both wish you'd never been born,' and hung up.

'I'd like to see you fucking try it,' Doug hissed at the dead phone, but there was a fear in his eyes that didn't match his words. He peered through a shuttered window. The street was deserted. There would never be a better time for putting a bullet in Reece. He shoved the thought away. A few hours were all it would take to be certain. He owed Reece that much. Didn't he? His lips compressed into a twitching line, he headed back downstairs.

'Was that one of our friends?' asked Reece.

Doug didn't reply. He stepped closer to Reece.

'What's wrong, Doug? You look worried sick.'

'You tell me.' Doug's voice was low, almost threatening. '*Is* there something I should be worried about?'

'You mean apart from Bryan Reynolds?'

'Fuck Bryan Reynolds!' Doug's hands shot out and

gripped Reece's wrists. 'We're locked together now. If one of us goes down, both of us go down. You know that, don't you?'

Reece nodded. He'd known that from the first moment he took dirty money. 'Have I done something to piss you off?'

Doug continued to stare searchingly at his partner. Was that a guilty flicker in Reece's eyes? Or was the big man simply worried about possible reprisals from Reynolds? If the latter was true, surely it stood to reason that Jim hadn't taken him into his confidence. If the former... Doug's stomach gave a twist. He'd never killed anyone before. Not directly. Could he really do it to someone, especially someone he liked? He silently scorned the question. *Like* had nothing to do with it. This was about survival. And he would do whatever it took to survive.

He suddenly jerked into motion, releasing Reece's wrists and hurrying to open the front door. He ushered Reece outside, then set the alarm and locked the door. He jumped into his car and lowered the window. 'Go back to your dad's house and stay there. I don't want to hear you've been anywhere else between the time it takes you to get there and when you next hear from me. Is that clear?'

'Yes.'

'I fucking hope so, Reece. For both our sakes.'

The Subaru's wheels kicked up loose gravel as Doug accelerated away. He punched Margaret's number into his phone. She came on the line after a couple of rings. 'Hello, Margaret,' he said, his voice friendly but grave, 'my name's Doug Brody. I work with your ex-husband, Jim.'

'What's happened? Is Jim alright?'

The concern in Margaret's tone was palpable. Doug's lips curled into a smile. This was going to be easy. 'No, I'm afraid he's not.'

'He's not had another heart attack, has he?'

'No, but he will do if he carries on like he's doing now. And it's not only him I'm worried about.'

'What do you mean?'

'Jim's not been himself recently. Not since he started working on this one particular case.' Doug had learnt long ago to always use half truths to make his lies believable. 'Has he spoken to you about it?'

'No. The last time we spoke he said he thought he was in trouble, but that the situation had changed.'

'Oh, the situation has definitely changed. But not for the better. I don't really want to say much more on the phone. Would you be able to meet up with me this afternoon?'

'I'm working. I'm not sure I can get away.'

'Please, Margaret. I wouldn't ask if I didn't think you could help.'

There was a pause, then Margaret said, 'Do you know Bailey Street?'

'Of course. It's not far from police headquarters. I can be there in five minutes.'

'I'll be waiting at its top end.'

'I'll see you soon. I'm driving a silver Subaru.'

Doug put on an extra burst of speed, but not so much as to attract unwanted attention. He scanned his surroundings uneasily as he neared Bailey Street. He was a little too close to headquarters and the law courts for comfort. The last thing he wanted was to be seen by a colleague. He climbed past apartment and office buildings towards the upper end of Bailey Street. A middle-aged woman with bobbed brown hair signalled to him. He recognised her vaguely from work parties. She was exactly the type of woman he would have put with Jim – not bad-looking, but not particularly good-looking either; modestly made-up; modestly dressed. Not his type at all. He liked them short-skirted and big-titted.

Doug pulled over, lowered the passenger window and with an easy friendliness that suggested he knew her well, motioned for Margaret to get in. She peered into the car with a faint, uncertain frown. 'You probably don't remember me,' he said, 'but we've met a couple of times before, five or six years ago.'

'Yes, I remember you,' said Margaret. 'I don't remember Jim and you being particularly good friends, though.'

'We weren't back then. We only really became mates after you two got divorced.'

Margaret looked at Doug a moment longer, then ducked into the car. 'So what was it you didn't want to say on the phone?'

Doug heaved a sigh as though what he had to say weighed heavily upon him. 'Like I said, there's this case we're working. A murder case. I can't go into too many details, but it's one of the worst I've been on. Really horrific. And the thing is, we know who did it, but we can't nail him. The evidence just isn't there. It happens like that sometimes. You've just got to accept it. But Jim refuses to. He's determined to nail this guy, no matter what it takes.'

'So what are you saying? That Jim might end up losing his job?'

'I'm saying he might end up in jail himself if someone doesn't talk some sense into him. I've tried but he won't listen to me.'

'And what makes you think he'll listen to me? I phoned him after talking to you, but he didn't answer my call.'

'Jim loves you, Margaret. You're the only one he'll listen to. I know it's asking a hell of a lot, but will you come with me and talk to him?'

'What? Right now?'

Doug nodded. 'He's with another colleague out in the Peak District, near Bamford.'

'What's he doing there?'

'That's where the man he's after lives.'

Margaret sat in frowning thought for moment. Then she said, 'Wait here. I'll have to let my boss know I need the rest of the day off.'

'It would be best if you don't tell your boss why or where you're going.'

'I wasn't about to.' Margaret got out of the car and entered an office building.

Doug phoned Tyler. 'She went for it.'

'Call me when you get to Southview,' said Tyler, and hung up.

A scowl pulled at Doug's face. Would it kill the fucker to show a bit of appreciation? He lit a cigarette and smoked tensely. He flicked it out the window when Margaret reappeared and got into the passenger seat. They headed out of Sheffield along the green floor of the Rivelin Valley. Mist clung to the wooded slopes that rose steeply to either side of the road, but it was fast being burnt away by the pale afternoon sun. They crossed the broad stone arches of the Ladybower Reservoir Bridge and turned onto a narrow lane that climbed high above the cottages of Bamford.

'Is that where the man Jim's after lives?' asked Margaret, when Southview's mock battlements and sprawling gardens came into view.

'Yes.'

'Bloody hell. Who is he?'

'He's nobody special. Just someone with money.'

Doug drove past the house and pulled over at the padlocked gate to the woods. He phoned Tyler again and said, 'We're here.'

After a couple of minutes, Tyler jogged into view and unlocked the padlock with a pick. He opened the gate and waved Doug through. After snapping the padlock back in place, he got into the back of the Subaru.

Margaret held out her hand to him. 'I'm Margaret, Jim's ex-wife.'

Tyler made no reply, but he shook her hand, noting its palm was slightly clammy, suggestive of nervousness. His own was dry as a snake's skin. Margaret's eyes narrowed a fraction, as though she wasn't quite sure what to make of him.

'This is going to knacker my suspension,' grumbled Doug as the Subaru bumped over the dirt track. He braked again at the entrance to the clearing. The wolfhound was still lying where it had been shot. A mud-spattered black Golf GTI was backed up against the door of the bunker. 'Where's Stan?'

'He's looking for the girl.'

'What girl?'

'I'm not sure, but I'd guess it's the missing prostitute your boy Reece was searching for.'

Doug's face screwed into an agitated knot. 'Are you saying this girl's on the loose somewhere around—'

'Excuse me,' cut in Margaret, looking from Doug to Tyler with pinched brows. 'But what exactly is going on here? Where's Jim?'

Tyler pointed at the bunker. 'We've got him in there for his own safety.'

Margaret's frown intensified. 'His own safety?'

'We didn't want it to come to this, but Jim forced our hand.'

Tyler got out of the Subaru, motioning for Margaret to follow. She pulled up abruptly, putting a hand to her mouth at the sight of the dead dog. Tyler beckoned her again, but this time she remained motionless. She'd lived with a cop long enough to know when something didn't smell right. And this whole situation suddenly smelled worse than the dog's evacuated bowels. She tensed as Doug's hand curled around her upper arm. His grip was gentle, almost reassuring. But she sensed that if she tried to resist, it would turn steely hard. She allowed herself to be guided towards the bunker.

'Call to Jim,' said Tyler.

Margaret passed her tongue nervously over her lips and remained silent.

Doug's grip tightened a little. 'Do as he says, Margaret.'

She shot him a sharp glance. 'Let go of my arm and I will do.'

Doug released Margaret's arm, smiling and spreading his palms as if to say, *Your wish is my command.* She hadn't thought he was a bad-looking bloke upon first seeing him. But it suddenly struck her how smarmy and cheap he looked with his expensive suit and orange tan. Wrinkling her nose in distaste, she turned to place her hand on the door. Its surface was pitted and corroded by rust. Was Jim really on its other side? Imprisoned for his own good? There was only one way to find out. 'Jim,' she called tentatively.

'Louder,' said Tyler. 'That door's five centimetres thick.'

'Jim!'

Several seconds passed. Then, as if from a long way off, Margaret heard Jim's voice. 'Margaret, is that you?'

He was in pain, Margaret could tell that instantly. But there was a note of something else in his voice too. Panic? 'Yes, Jim, it's me. Doug Brody brought me—'

'Doug's with you?'

'That's right, Jimmy boy,' shouted Doug. 'Your old pal Doug's here.'

The door shuddered as if from a blow. 'You lay one fucking finger on her, Doug, and I swear to Christ I'll tear your heart out with my bare hands!'

'How can you even think I'd do something like that?' Doug said in a tone of mock hurt.

'You've got five minutes to open this door, Monahan,' said Tyler, his voice so cold that Margaret looked at him with a shudder. He was holding a black-handled Bowie knife. 'After that, I start cutting pieces off her. Understood?'

Chapter Twenty-Seven

As Jim's pulse had eased off, so too had the pain in his chest. But at the sound of Margaret's voice it flared up again, like petrol poured over flames. She was as good as dead. He knew that the instant he heard her. Regardless of what he did, they couldn't allow her to live. He clenched his fists and eyes against the knowledge. He wanted to tear his own heart out almost as much as Doug's. How could he have been so blind? How could he not have seen that once he'd crossed the line this was the only way it could ever end? The genie was out and there was no way of controlling it. There was only more violence, more death.

Time. He had to play for time. It was the only thing he could do. If Doug was on Forester's payroll, it meant Garrett didn't know about Amber. Which also meant there was no chance of Freddie Harding leading the DCI to Forester. That left one hope – Melinda. If she made it to a phone...

'I know what you're thinking,' said the voice Jim didn't recognise; the voice that turned his guts to ice. 'You're thinking the girl might get to a phone and call for help. And who knows, maybe she will. But I doubt it. Not with the amount of blood she's losing. Either way, it makes no difference to Margaret, because in...' There was a pause as if the man was checking his watch, 'exactly three minutes and forty-two seconds, I'm going to start cutting her fingers and toes off, then her ears, nose and tongue, then maybe her nipples. After that, I might start removing her internal organs. I know how to do it in such a way that it'll take her hours to die.'

'You bastard, you fucking bastard,' Jim breathed in an agonised whisper. Tears burning in his eyes, he hurried towards the rear of the bunker. He snatched up a scalpel from the shelves and opened the door to the tiny, stinking cell.

Edward's bloodshot, swollen eyes bulged like saucers at the sight of the scalpel. 'Oh Christ, don't kill me,' he cried. 'I'm begging you, please don't kill me.'

'Shut your mouth,' snapped Jim, stooping to remove the restraints from Edward's ankles. He used them to bind one of his own wrists to Edward's. Then he hauled Edward to his feet and shoved him towards the outer room.

'One minute thirty seconds,' came the shout from outside.

Edward's head jerked up at the sound of the voice, fresh hope flaring in his eyes. It was all Jim could do to stop himself from driving the scalpel into Edward's eyeballs. The bastard deserved a lot of things, but not hope. He pressed the blade's diamond-sharp edge against Edward's windpipe. 'Who is he?'

'His name's Tyler – or at least that's what he calls himself. He's a killer. That's all I know.'

'Tyler,' Jim murmured, his forehead creasing. He'd never known anyone by that name on the South Yorkshire Police force, or, for that matter, any other force. He began counting down the remaining time in his head. Every second was a grain of sand running out of the hourglass of Margaret's life. Every second was a chance for Melinda to get help.

'Ten seconds,' said Tyler. 'Five, four, three...'

'OK,' Jim shouted. 'I'm coming out.'

As he drew back the bolts, there came the sound of a car engine starting up outside. He twisted the key and opened the door. He pushed Edward forwards, the scalpel at his throat. The politician's pale, hairy legs trembled like twigs in a breeze. Margaret was standing about ten metres away from the bunker. The pain screwed deeper into Jim's chest at the sight of her fear-swollen eyes. There was a knife at her throat too. The man holding it was maybe a couple of inches taller than Jim and well built. He had short dark hair and several days' worth of stubble on his face. Jim guessed him to be in his late thirties or early forties. As soon as he saw the dressing taped over the man's eye, Jim knew he was standing face to face with Amy and Grace's killer. A VW Golf was pulling away from the bunker with Doug behind its wheel. Doug stopped at the edge of the clearing and got out of the car, wearing his trademark idiot grin and pointing a handgun at Jim.

'Let Forester go,' said Tyler.

'Sure, as soon as you let Margaret go,' replied Jim, his voice as tight as his chest.

'That's not going to happen.'

'Then Forester stays right where he is.'

'Well, well,' said Doug. 'I think this is what they call a Mexican stand-off.'

Tyler shook his head. 'In a Mexican stand-off no one has the upper hand. That's not what we have here. You see, Jim, I really don't give a toss about Forester. Yeah sure, he's worth a lot of money to me. But what's money, if you don't have your freedom? You, on the other hand, love Margaret. Don't bother denying it. It's written all over your face. So here's the deal. You let Forester go and I give you my word Margaret will die fast and painless. If you don't let him go, Doug's going to put a bullet in him. And then I'm going to go to work on Margaret while you watch. So what's it going to be? I'll give you another ten seconds to decide.'

There was a matter-of-factness about Tyler's voice that left Jim in no doubt he meant every word. Jim looked at Margaret, his eyes full of desperate uncertainty. Staring tearfully back at him, she gave a shake of her head. 'Don't do it, Jim,' she said, gulping her words out.

He had to do it, though. The thought of dying held little fear for him. But the thought of Margaret being tortured to death was more than he could endure. Slowly, like a terminally ill man holding on to his final seconds of life, he dropped the scalpel and uncuffed Edward.

Edward turned towards Jim, his beady eyes shining with triumph.

'Move away from him please, Mr Forester,' said Tyler.

As Edward approached Tyler, his gaze fell to the dead dog. The shine left his eyes. His nose twitched with displeasure.

'It attacked Stan,' explained Tyler. 'He had no choice but to kill it.'

'Well you can bloody well deduct fifteen hundred quid from the idiot's fee. Conall was a top pedigree.'

Doug edged towards Jim. 'On your face, Jimmy boy.'

Holding Margaret's gaze, afraid that if he looked away it would be the last time he saw her alive, Jim got down on the ground. What little breath he had gasped out of him as Doug rammed a heel into his spine and zipped his wrists and ankles together with plasticuffs. The tingling was back in his left arm. His vision was growing grey. With every ounce of will he possessed, he held onto consciousness and Margaret's eyes.

'Is this his wife?' asked Edward, eyeing Margaret with the same look of mild disgust he usually reserved for his own wife.

'Ex-wife,' corrected Tyler.

'So go on then. Keep your word. Kill her.'

'All in good time. For now she's of more use to us alive.'

Edward's mouth puckered in disappointment. 'Why?'

'We need to know how Monahan found his way to you and if he's been working with anyone else on this private investigation of his.'

'You mean there might be others out there like him?'

'It's just a precaution.' Tyler saw no profit in telling Edward about Reece. The shrill edge in the politician's voice and the way his eyes darted around as though he expected to see enemies lurking behind every tree, told of nerves stretched close to breaking. The last thing he needed was Edward flipping out on him. 'Most likely there's no one. But if there is, we may need some form of leverage to persuade the good detective to give them up.'

'You lying bastard,' hissed Margaret, reading the intent of Tyler's words.

'Hush now.' Tyler tightened his arm against her throat, choking off her oxygen. She struggled briefly, eyes bulging, mouth working silently, then went limp.

'Margaret!' Her name tore out of Jim's throat. He fought frantically to writhe out from under Doug's boot. As Tyler lowered Margaret to the ground, Doug whipped the pistol across the back of Jim's head once, then again and again until blackness took over.

Pulling on plastic gloves, Tyler approached the steel door and made to close it. He didn't even glance at what was inside the bunker. That was none of his business. 'Wait,' said Edward, 'my wellies are in there.'

He quickly retrieved them. Tyler locked the door and returned the key to him, saying, 'Go home and get yourself cleaned up. Don't leave the house or phone anyone. I'll call you as soon as we find the girl.'

Edward blinked as though he'd been slapped. The girl! How could he have forgotten about her? 'Are you saying she got away?'

'Stan's on her trail.'

'What if he doesn't catch her?' The note of hysteria in Edward's voice grew more pronounced. 'Oh God, Oh Christ—'

'She's weak and badly injured,' cut in Tyler, pointing at

a sprinkling of dark spatters on the grass to illustrate his words. 'My guess is she won't make it out of the woods.'

'But what if she does? It'll be the end of everything.' Edward jabbed a trembling finger at Tyler. 'You stupid bastard! How could you let this happen?'

'I didn't let this happen. You did. And it's going to cost you another couple of hundred thousand at least. But we can discuss payment later. For now, go home.'

Tyler's voice was as deadpan as his face. But there was something underneath his words, some quality of unspoken warning that made Edward glance nervously at the knife in his hand. Hugging his arms across his shivering chest, Edward turned and started towards Southview. He'd only taken a couple of steps when the echoing sound of a gunshot rang out.

Tyler and Doug exchanged a glance. 'How far away do you reckon that is?' asked Doug.

'Maybe half a mile.' Tyler turned to Edward. 'From the sounds of it, I'd say your problem just got solved.'

'It could be someone out shooting pheasants,' Edward said doubtfully.

'No. That wasn't a shotgun blast.' Tyler took out a phone and dialled Stan. The line rang. One ring, two, three, four...

Melinda had taken more than a few punches in her life. And that was what it felt like to be shot – like the hardest punch she'd ever taken. There was no pain. Not at first. Only the feel of all the air being knocked out of her lungs. She staggered. But somehow, through some mixture of desperate strength and sheer force of will, she managed to stay on her feet. Her momentum carried her in amongst the trees. She could have wept with relief as they closed ranks around her like a protecting wall. But she didn't have the breath for it. She felt as if she was straining to suck air through a straw. The mulchy leaf-littered ground seemed to cling to her feet like glue. Her body screamed at her to stop, to give up, but her mind refused to listen. Another gunshot reverberated through the woods. She tensed in anticipation of being hit, but the ping of a bullet striking metal told her the shot hadn't been fired at her. She didn't glance back, she just drove her legs with all the strength she had.

Thorns pierced the soles of her feet, branches whipped her face, roots tripped her over. And every time she fell it seemed as if she wouldn't be able to get back up. But somehow, clawing at earth and bark, she managed to. The initial numbness of shock was wearing off. An itching, burning sensation was rapidly building where the bullet had passed through her right shoulder. There was an inconspicuous-looking little hole in the wax jacket. But when she touched her hand to it, blood instantly pooled in her palm. *I'm bleeding to death! I'm bleeding to death!* The panicked thought threatened to overwhelm her. She fought to drag her mind back to the one certainty – if she didn't keep moving, she would die. Putting one foot in front of the other. That was all that mattered. *One foot in front of the other, one foot in front of the other.* She repeated the words over and over in her mind like a prayer.

When Melinda reached the fence, her eyes filled with

tears of shattered hope. Beyond the wire, a patchwork of fields strung with tatters of mist sloped towards the grey rooftops of a village. The houses were only a mile or two away, but she may as well have been looking through a telescope at the moon. Her legs felt rubbery. She could barely move her right arm. She would have struggled to climb some stairs, never mind a fence. She staggered along the fence, searching in vain for some gap she might squeeze through or crawl under. Body quaking, eyes closed, she leant her face against the wire. It was over. All that was left for her to do was wait for death, whether it be from loss of blood, or at the hands of the ex-cop who'd shot her, or maybe at the hands of the man he worked for. What was his name? Forester. Yes, that was it. She gave a frantic, determined shake of her head. No, she would rather push her hand into the bullet wound and tear out her own insides than give that fucker the pleasure of killing her.

Melinda stripped off the heavy wax jacket and flung it over the fence. She removed the belt, before chucking the trousers over too. Trying not to look at the blood-swathed right side of her body, she slipped the end of the belt through the buckle to make a loop. She tied the same end of the belt tightly to her right wrist. Then she reached up with her left hand as high as possible and grasped the fence close to a post. She hooked the toes of her left foot through the wire at knee height and pushed off the ground with her right foot. Pulling herself upwards, she swung her right arm in an agonising arc and attempted to hook the belt loop over the top of the post. She missed and dropped to the ground.

Her knees threatened to give way. She clung to the fence like it was a life buoy, drawing up her strength for a final effort. She propelled herself off the ground again. This time the loop dropped over the top of the post. It pulled tight as she put all her weight on her right arm. Then it was like someone was pouring boiling fat over her shoulder. For a second, she thought she was going to pass out. But she didn't. She caught hold of the top of the fence with her left hand, brought her feet up higher and jerked herself upwards. She managed to get her armpits over the fence, then her belly. The wire drew deep gouges in her skin as she squirmed forwards. Then she was falling. For a second she hung suspended by the belt. She let out a strangled scream. Then the knot came loose and she fell in a gasping, groaning heap to the ground.

Melinda wasn't sure how long she lay there for. Ten, fifteen, twenty minutes, maybe longer passed, before she found it within herself to get to her feet. She put the jacket back on, but left the trousers where they were. She didn't have the strength to retrieve the belt. Moving like someone in a dream, she staggered onwards. A band of mist swallowed her up, turned her around and spat her out to the left of where she'd just come from. The realisation tore a sob from her. It was only a matter of retracing her path forty or fifty metres, but each step felt like a mile. More mist rolled in, cold and clammy. She clambered over a low drystone wall and slithered down a steep grassy bank. She took several more faltering steps, before stopping abruptly as the ground fell away in a sheer drop. The crag was as tall as a two-storey house. Bundles of angular boulders and broken stone millwheels clustered at its base.

Melinda jerked her gaze from side to side, frantically looking for a way down. There wasn't one that she could see. She rolled her eyes bitterly skyward, thinking, *Why are you doing this to me?* She flinched at the sound of a stone rolling down the bank behind her. Someone was climbing over the wall! She couldn't see them in the mist, but she could hear them grunting with effort. As she flung herself to the ground behind a hump of grass, a figure lurched into view. It was the ex-cop. In one hand he held the gun, the other clutched his injured thigh.

'Fucking bastard dog,' Stan muttered, limping unwittingly towards the quarried edge. As Melinda had done, he pulled up sharply, swaying on the lip of the cliff. In that instant, she knew what she had to do. There was no space for hesitation. A second or two from now he would regain his balance and the chance would be gone. Adrenalin pumping fresh strength into her limbs, she scrambled to her feet and ran at him. She hit him without even sufficient force to leave a bruise, but it was enough. He toppled forwards. He didn't utter a cry, but his finger twitched on the trigger, sending a bullet into the void. He hit the boulders below with a dull crunching sound and tumbled away out of sight down the slope.

Melinda stared after him for a moment, her chest heaving. Then she resumed her search for a way down. After a short distance, she came to a narrow gulley with a trickle of water in it that descended between two quarried faces. She clambered down the gulley and over the jumble of boulders at the foot of the crag. She flinched to a halt at a sound – a gurgling that wasn't made by the water. She was about to hurry away from it, but the ring of a mobile phone stopped her in her tracks. She stood briefly frozen with indecision. Then she warily made her way towards the ringing.

Stan was lying on his back in a patch of bracken. There was no visible sign of injury, but it was clear he wasn't going to be getting back up. His face was pale and bluish around the lips; his fingers were curled into paralysed, shaking claws. As Melinda stooped over him, his eyes bulged up at her without seeming to see her. The gun was nowhere to be seen. She felt broken bones moving and grating beneath her hands as she searched for the phone and found it in an inner pocket of his jacket. She cut off the call and dialled 999. It only occurred to her as the operator picked up that she didn't have a clue where she was.

Tyler dialled Stan again and went straight through to an answering service. A frown traced itself upon his forehead, barely visible, but there. 'He's on the phone,' he said in response to Doug's questioning look.

'He's probably trying to call you back.'

All three men stared expectantly at the phone. It didn't ring.

'What does that mean?' asked Edward, his voice twanging with anxiety.

'Go home,' repeated Tyler.

'Something's wrong. I know it. That little bitch has done something to—'

Tyler twisted towards Edward, and what the politician saw in his eye made him break off and retreat a step. Doug quickly ushered Edward on his way. 'Please, Mr Forester, do as he says. Stan probably just can't get a signal. You know how poor the coverage can be out here.'

Shooting panicky glances at Tyler, Edward reluctantly resumed heading towards the gate.

'He's starting to get on my nerves,' said Tyler. His declaration drew a surprised glance from Doug. It was the first time he had known Tyler to express his feelings about anyone or pretty much anything.

'I thought you had no nerves.'

Others had said that before. And like Doug, they'd been wrong. Tyler had feelings, but showing them was a luxury he hardly ever allowed himself. He'd regretted his words the instant they were out of his mouth. The world was a shark pool. And the sharks were constantly watching for an opening to move in for the kill. No doubt, at that moment they circled a fraction closer. Lowering his inscrutable mask back into place, Tyler fastened Margaret's wrists and ankles together with plasticuffs. 'Help me lift her.'

'Where to?'

'The boot of your car.'

'Why my car? Why can't we put her in the Range Rover?'

'Because you're a cop. You're less likely to be stopped.'

Doug popped the Subaru's boot and they lowered Margaret into it. Tyler jerked his chin at Jim. 'Now him.'

'It'll be a tight squeeze. What if they suffocate?'

Tyler shrugged. 'Quickly. We don't have much time.'

They packed Jim into the boot back to back with Margaret. Doug had to lean heavily on the lid to get it shut. Tyler tried Stan again. This time his phone rang, but he still didn't answer. 'What the fuck's he playing at?' wondered Doug.

Tyler took out his knife. 'Let's go find out.'

Chapter Twenty-Eight

As Edward trudged back to Southview, he hugged his arms across his shoulders, his bald head bobbing like a cork on a rough sea. Everything was falling apart. All his plans, all his years of hard work, all of it was falling apart. There would be no Cabinet position, no moment of greatness. But worst of all, there would be no respect. He would be held up for the public to revile, ridicule and spit at like some sort of Victorian grotesque. The thought made the ground seem to tremble as if it was giving way beneath his feet.

Mabel Forester was waiting in the hallway, glass of sherry in hand. 'My God,' she breathed as he stepped into view in his shirt, socks and underpants, blood smeared over his forehead, his eyes swollen and bleary. 'What happened?'

Edward made no reply. He kept his gaze on the floor, suddenly afraid of what he might do if he looked into his mother's eyes.

'I asked you a question,' Mabel continued more sharply, catching hold of Edward's arm as he stepped past her.

'Please, Mother, just leave me alone. Please...' Edward trailed off as though he didn't have the energy to continue.

'No, I won't leave you alone. I want to know what's going on. And I want to know now.'

His voice faint, almost unintelligible, Edward said, 'She's gone.'

'Speak up, boy. And look at me when I'm talking to you.'

Slowly, but inexorably, Edward raised his eyes to meet his mother's gaze. 'You lied to me.'

'What are you talking about? Lied about what?'

Edward's voice suddenly burst from his throat. 'Everything!'

He yanked his arm free, sending his mother staggering into the coat stand. She lost her grip on the sherry glass and it fell with a crash to the floor. For a moment, they stared at each other as if both too shocked to react. Then Mabel's piercing blue eyes flashed with a terrible light. Flinching from it, Edward turned and started upstairs.

Mabel's voice rose in a shriek of rage. 'How dare you turn your back on me! Get back down here.'

Edward's footsteps faltered, but didn't stop. His mother's anger terrified him, although not as much as what he felt building inside him. It wasn't the hunger, but it was something born of the same frenzy. With every word she hurled after him, it welled up further, like rising floodwaters, threatening to engulf him. He clutched the banister, heart pounding, head reeling.

'Look at you,' shouted Mabel, pursuing her son. 'Sometimes I have to ask myself how I ever gave birth to something so pathetic.'

'I've wondered the same thing too,' said Edward, his voice half choked. 'I even thought about trying to find out if I was adopted. Then I realised it makes no difference whether or not you're my real mother, either way you created me. You made me what I am today. Everything that's happening is your fault.'

Mabel caught hold of Edward's arm again at the top of the stairs and wrenched him around to face her. 'You know who you sound like? Your father. He was incapable of taking responsibility for his own actions too.'

'Lies. Lies. All of it lies! I... I...' Edward stammered off into silence, unable to bring himself to say the words in his head, knowing his mother would consider them the ultimate betrayal.

'Go on, say what you're thinking.' Mabel's voice was goading. 'For once in your life, have the courage to speak your mind.'

Swallowing the words even as he spoke them, Edward said, 'I went to see my father, and he told me the truth. He didn't walk out on you. You walked out on him.'

Edward tensed, expecting to feel the sharp sting of a slap. But his mother didn't raise her hand. Her face showed no trace of surprise, only contempt. A swell of realisation broke over him. 'You knew.'

'Of course I knew you'd been going to see the *bastard*.' Mabel hissed the word with pure venom. 'I know everything about you, Edward. You're my beautiful baby boy. I wasn't about to let him poison your mind against me.'

Edward shook his head as if trying to throw off a bad

dream. His voice came distant and dazed. 'It was you. You killed him. You took him from me.'

'I've never taken a thing from you, Edward. All I've ever done is give, give, give. Without me you'd be a nothing, a nobody. Just like your father was. And what thanks do I get for it? You sneak off behind my back to see him.' Mabel's ranting voice gathered momentum like a boulder bouncing down a hillside. 'And what makes it even worse is, you chose to believe him over me. Mind you, I don't suppose I should have expected any different. You've always been more like him than me. A weak-minded fool. That's what he was. And that's what you are. Do you hear me?'

But Edward didn't hear her any more. He only heard the floodwaters whooshing and roaring in his ears, urging him, compelling him to shut the old bitch up once and for all. Suddenly, without thought, he wrapped his hands around the loose, turkey-like flesh of her throat and began to squeeze. Her mouth opened and closed spasmodically. Her eyes swelled as if they might pop out of their sockets. She tried to twist free of his grip, clawing at his hands. But he was too strong. Gradually, a bluish-purple tinge seeped into her face. Then her eyes glazed over and her arms dropped to her sides. He kept on squeezing. He knew from experience that a victim's lungs and blood stored enough oxygen to keep them alive for several minutes even after unconsciousness set in. When he finally released her, she tumbled like a cloth doll to the bottom of the stairs. Like someone in a trance, he descended towards her, took hold of her arms and dragged her into the kitchen. He opened a drawer and lifted out the heavy cleaver the housekeeper used for dismembering the chicken carcasses.

He pulled his mother's tongue out of her mouth and sliced it off. He flung the pink worm of flesh away, turned her onto her face and positioned her arms at her sides. He tore off her wig, exposing short wispy grey hair and a liver-spotted scalp. Then he began to hack at her neck. He'd watched Freddie dismember enough corpses to know it was crucial to start the beheading from the back of the neck. If you started from the front, the windpipe and surrounding flesh, arteries, muscles and ligaments slowed the blade's momentum, making it difficult to sever the spine. His blows were inaccurate. The first few failed to break anything more than skin. But finally the blade lodged between the vertebrae. He jerked it free. It took him several more whacks to find the same spot. His mother's spine separated with an audible pop. After that, it was like carving a tough joint of beef.

A slick of blood spread from Mabel's corpse as Edward cut through the final scraps of skin. Clutching her head in both hands, he went to the living room. He placed the head in the centre of the mantelpiece, sightless eyes facing him. It took a moment to get it to balance upright. Then he opened his mouth and all the words that had been pent up in him for so many years came pouring out.

'I've tried, Mother. All my life I've tried to be what you wanted me to be. But it was never enough. Nothing I did was enough. Was it? You poisonous old bitch. I hate you.

Do *you* hear *me*? I hate everything about you. I hate your mouth, I hate your hands, I hate your breasts, I hate your stinking cunt, but most of all I hate your voice.' He clamped his hands over his ears, as if even now he could hear his mother yelling at him. His own voice took on a childish tone. 'Yes, Mother. No, Mother. Three bags full, Mother.'

Edward jerked his gaze towards the empty space at his side. 'What was that? OK, I'll ask her.' He looked at the decapitated head again. 'It's Wendy Atkins. You remember her, don't you, Mother? She wants to know why you didn't try to find out if she was telling the truth. Nothing to say? Well, it doesn't matter because I know the answer.' He turned back to the empty space. 'I used to think she was protecting me. But I was wrong. She wasn't protecting me, she was protecting herself. You see, Wendy, she was terrified that if the truth came out about what I did to you, then the truth about what she was doing to me would follow it. Isn't that right, Mother? I said, isn't that right, Mother? What's the matter? Cat got your tongue?'

Edward put a hand to his mouth as if to contain a laugh. But there was no laugh in his small brown eyes. There were only tears. Suddenly, he shook his head so hard he almost lost his balance. 'No, Mother. I won't accept responsibility. I won't. I won't. Why should I? You did this to me. Yes, you did. Yes! You! You!'

The undergrowth was flattened where first Melinda then Stan had trampled through it. Here and there, spots of dried blood were visible. Tyler and Doug followed the trail to the fence. 'Resourceful girl,' remarked Tyler, eyeing the belt. He effortlessly scaled the fence. Doug followed somewhat more slowly. The trail was less obvious on the short grass of the field, but despite this their pace quickened. They no longer needed to see signs of Melinda's passing to know where she was headed. The distant rooftops made that obvious.

When they reached the crag, Tyler stood scanning the landscape. Once again, he phoned Doug. But instead of putting the phone to his ear, he listened intently to his surroundings. The only sounds to be heard were the calls of birds and the sighing of the wind through the crag. They descended the gully.

Doug stopped suddenly. 'Do you hear that?'

Tyler nodded. Putting his finger to his lips, he hunched low and crept towards the guttural gasping sound.

Stan was still alive, but his eyes were no longer open and his gasps were rapid and shallow. 'He must have fallen,' murmured Doug, grimacing.

'Or been pushed.' Tyler dropped to his haunches and searched Stan's pockets. 'His phone's gone. His gun too.'

Doug cast an uneasy eye over their surroundings, as if expecting to see the missing gun trained on him from behind a nearby bush or rock. 'We need to get him to a doctor.'

'He's beyond that.'

'You can't know that for sure.'

'Do you hear that bubbling sound? His lungs are

punctured and filling with fluid. He'll be dead before we can get him back to the car.' Tyler's words were a flat, emotionless statement of fact.

'Fuck! So what do we do? We can't just leave him here like this.'

'No, we can't.' Tyler reached into Stan's jacket again and took out his wallet and the Range Rover's keys. Sheathing his knife, he moved to pick up a heavy stone.

Doug's eyes widened with horror. 'What the fuck do you think you're doing?'

'Making it as difficult as possible for your lot to identify him.'

'You're crazy!'

Ignoring Doug, Tyler hoisted the stone high over Stan's head. 'Don't,' warned Doug, jerking his pistol towards Tyler. 'We're going to carry Stan to my car. I worked with him for over ten years. He showed me the ropes when I was a rookie. That might not mean anything to someone like you, but it damned well does to me.'

Tyler stared at Doug, no trace of fear in his eyes. 'You do realise your colleagues are probably already on their way here? And we've got to deal with Forester and his mother. Think about it, Doug. We can't let them live. Not now. We can still make it through this, but we've got to move fast.'

A spasm jerked at Doug's face as he turned Tyler's words over in his mind. Tyler subtly adjusted his grip on the stone, readying himself to hurl it at Doug should his words not have the desired effect. Releasing a heavy breath, Doug lowered his gun and nodded to say, *Go on, do it*. He turned away as Tyler brought the stone down on Stan's head. There was a crunch of bone. Stan's limbs twitched, and twitched again as Tyler heaved the stone back upwards and downwards. When Stan's face had been reduced to a shapeless pulp, Tyler tossed the stone aside and began to climb the gulley.

Doug looked at Stan. 'Goodbye, mate,' he said, swallowing a nauseous lump. Then he hurried after Tyler.

They sprinted back across the fields and through the woods. Doug jumped into his Subaru and accelerated fast towards the gate, no longer caring about the suspension. Tyler followed in the GTI. When they got to the gate he hopped out and picked the padlock. He took a petrol canister from the GTI's boot and handed it to Doug, along with the keys to the Range Rover. He told Doug where the Range Rover was, adding, 'Burn it out then head for the farm.'

'What about you?'

'I'll see you there. Don't wait for me.'

As Doug pulled away, Tyler removed a Beretta pistol from the GTI's glove compartment. His phone vibrated in his pocket. He took it out, half expecting it to be Edward Forester phoning for an update. But it wasn't Forester. He put the phone to his ear and waited for the caller to speak.

'I thought you had this fucking situation under control.' The voice that came down the line was deep and commanding and very angry.

'I do, sir.'

'Then why the fuck has a call just come in from a girl

claiming to have been abducted by someone called Forester? I assume she was referring to Edward Forester.'

'Yes, sir. But don't worry, I'm about to silence Forester for good.'

'No. The bastard's got Herbert Winstanley's book. He claims he's destroyed it, but I don't believe him. I *want* that fucking book.'

'It's going to take time to find out where it is.'

'You've got about ten minutes. And that's only because the dispatcher had to ping the girl's call and triangulate her location.'

'Ten minutes won't be enough.'

'Then take him to the farm and do what you do best.'

'Yes, sir.'

There was a click and the line went dead. Tyler drove to Southview's gates. He climbed over them and darted towards the house, not bothering to conceal his approach. It went against his natural instincts, but there was no time for stealth. The front door stood open. Gun at the ready, he entered the hallway. He glanced down, feeling the crunch of broken glass underfoot. A smashed glass lay in a puddle of its former contents on the tiled floor. Tyler caught a whiff of sherry.

His gaze jerked towards a closed door at the sound of Edward Forester's voice. It was as shrill as before, but now there was an added intensity to it – a shrieking, babbling intensity that went beyond the realm of simple hysteria. It rose even higher, as if he was frenziedly trying to scream down another voice. But there was no other voice.

Tyler nudged the door open. Edward was facing a fireplace. When Tyler saw what he was talking to, for the first time in as long as he could remember, he couldn't keep the shock from his face. 'Forester!'

Edward jerked around at the sound of his name, blinking like he'd been dragged out of some dark, deep hole. A man was standing in the doorway. His features seemed hazy to Edward, as if he was looking at him through a net curtain. It took him a moment to work out who the man was and why he was aiming a gun at him.

'The girl,' murmured Edward. 'You haven't found her.'

Tyler shook his head.

'Then you're here to...' Edward trailed off into a strangled sob.

Tyler nodded. 'Where's Herbert Winstanley's book?'

'It's gone, it's gone, gone.' Repeating himself in a voice as hollow as a coffin lid, Edward turned back towards the mantelpiece. His mother's bloodless face was sunken and shrivelled. She didn't look like herself any more. Nothing was itself any more. His world was gone. He spread his quivering arms like a crucifix. 'I'm coming, Mother. I'm coming.'

'Not quite yet you're not.' Tyler grabbed one of Edward's arms, twisted it and thrust him towards the door.

Edward craned his head over his shoulder, keeping his eyes on his mother for as long as possible. He didn't resist as Tyler pressed the gate button and guided him rapidly along the driveway to the GTI. Tyler opened the boot, shoved him into it and slammed it shut. In the darkness that enfolded him, Edward saw their faces – the ugly-beautiful, dead faces of all the girls he and Freddie had killed. And in his head he heard their bitter, accusing voices. 'It wasn't me,' he screamed at them. 'It was her.' But they didn't listen. They never listened.

Chapter Twenty-Nine

Jim regained consciousness with a gasp. His first thought was, *Margaret! Where's Margaret?* He opened his eyes and saw only darkness. His chest pain had subsided to a dull, constricting ache. But his skull felt ready to split open. He gulped down air, struggling to get enough into his lungs. It wasn't only the pain that made it difficult to breathe. He was wedged into a space smaller than a coffin. The juddering engine noise told him he was in the boot of a moving vehicle. His arms and legs tingled with pins and needles, but not enough to stop him from feeling another pair of hands against his. They were soft, slender hands, and as cold as clay. He knew their touch as intimately as he knew the scent of their owner.

'Margaret!' The word came in an anguished whisper. Squeezing her hands, Jim repeated her name. He closed his eyes with relief when first her fingers, then her body twitched against him. But that relief was tempered by the knowledge that her death had only been postponed for however long it took to get wherever they were going. She began to jerk around like a landed fish, her breathing even more strained than Jim's. 'Easy, Margaret, easy,' he soothed.

'Jim?' she gasped.

'I'm here. Try to breathe slowly. Follow me. In... out... in... out.' Margaret followed Jim's lead and her breathing gradually eased off. 'That's it. Now listen to me. Have you got anything in your pockets we could use to break the cuffs? A nail file perhaps?' There was little hope in Jim's voice. Even if she had a nail file, it would take hours to saw through the tough plasticuffs. Time they almost certainly didn't have. But anything was better than simply lying there, passively awaiting their fate.

'No.'

'Can you roll onto your other side?'

'I'll try.' Margaret squirmed and twisted, until Jim felt her breath hot against the nape of his neck.

He gave an involuntary little shudder. 'What can you feel behind you? Any sharp edges or latches?'

'No.'

'OK. Now I'm going to turn.' Sweat popped out on Jim's forehead with the effort of rotating his body. His face pressed against Margaret's. His lips unintentionally brushed hers. He shuddered again, more deeply. His half-numb hands groped around behind his back. There was nothing much to feel there. Just the underside of the boot's lid and the rough felt of the boot's lining. He twisted onto his back, telling Margaret to do the same. Her body partially overlapped his as she manoeuvred herself into position. 'When I say "now" hit the boot's lid as hard as you can... Now.'

With what little force they could generate in the cramped space, they drove their knees against the underside of the boot's lid. Pain flared in Jim's injured knee at the impact.

The lid barely quivered. They hit it again and again with the same results. Every time he exerted himself, the vice in Jim's chest turned one twist tighter. 'It's useless,' he conceded reluctantly, his breath coming in a rattling wheeze.

'What's going on, Jim? Why are they doing this to us?' Margaret shot the questions at him in a rapid, trembling voice.

The answers caught in Jim's throat like shards of glass. He freed them with a hard swallow. The least Margaret deserved was the truth. 'There's a man.'

'The one who was in the bunker with you?'

'Yes. I did something...' Jim paused a breath, then corrected himself. 'I tried to do something to him. I... I...' He fell silent again, his voice cracking with the effort of saying what he felt must be said.

'What did you do, Jim?' Margaret urged.

'I tried to have him killed.' The words came out in a shudder that was part shame, part relief.

Margaret was silent a moment. Then, her voice tinged with incredulous shock, she asked, 'Why?'

'All the things that man's done. All the women and children he's raped and murdered. He was going to get away with it. I couldn't let that happen. Something inside me, it... it just snapped.'

'So you went to those woods to kill him.'

'No. I was looking for...' Jim trailed off into a leaden breath. 'Ah, what does it matter now what I was looking for?'

'It matters to me.'

There was a note in Margaret's voice that sent a rush of blood through Jim's contracting arteries. 'I wanted to find the evidence to arrest him. I wanted to do things right.'

'What changed your mind?'

Names passed through Jim's thoughts and out of his mouth. 'Amy Sheridan, Grace Kirby, Bryan Reynolds. Enough people have already died because of me.'

'Are you saying you killed those people?'

'Not directly I didn't. But if I hadn't lost control, if I hadn't lost sight of everything I once believed in—' Jim's voice hitched on a sob. 'Oh Christ, I'm sorry. I'm so, so sorry.' He slammed his head back against the base of the boot. 'It's all my fault. It's all my fucking fault!'

'That's your problem, Jim.' Margaret's voice was sad but gentle. 'You think everything's your fault. But it's not.' She nuzzled her face against Jim's neck, the way she used to when they were in bed. He drew in a trembling breath, his heart a boiling soup of sweet-and-sour emotions. He'd dreamed about feeling her body against his again for so long. But not like this.

They lay in silence for a while. Then they felt the vehicle turning, followed by the tremor of tyres bouncing over a rough surface. 'I just want you to know,' murmured Margaret, pressing closer. 'If I'm going to die, I'm glad it's with you.'

You're not going to die! Jim wanted to yell at her. But he knew it wasn't true. They were both going to die, slowly, agonisingly. He ground his teeth in impotent rage at the thought. The vehicle stopped, but the engine remained running. There was the muffled sound of a door closing. He felt Margaret's body stiffen in anticipation of the boot opening, but the vehicle pulled forward. After maybe a minute, they came to a stop again. The engine died.

'Give me as much space as you can,' said Jim.

Margaret flattened herself against the rear of the boot. Jim drew his knees towards his chest, coiling himself up like a spring. Several breathless seconds passed. The boot clicked open. Doug's face loomed into view. Jim kicked out with his tingling, cramped legs. Doug swayed backwards, easily avoiding the kick. 'Whoa,' he laughed. 'I thought I heard you two lovebirds moving about in there.' He grabbed Jim's legs and hauled him out of the boot. Jim's breath whistled between his teeth as he hit the ground face first with a splat.

'Help!' screamed Margaret. 'Help us!'

'Shout as loud as you want,' grinned Doug. He jerked his thumb at Jim. 'There's no one to hear you but him and me.'

Jim rolled onto his back. A quick scan of their surrounds confirmed Doug's words. They were in a muddy farmyard. A collection of ramshackle barns huddled around a stone farmhouse in the shadow of a bleak, heather-blanketed hill. A dirt track stretched away from the yard towards a line of trees. The sight extinguished Jim's last spark of hope. Even if Melinda somehow managed to avoid capture, there was no help coming, not out here.

Doug closed the boot, took hold of Jim's ankles and

dragged him towards the house. He opened the front door. 'On your feet, Jim.'

His injured leg trembling as if it might give out at any moment, Jim struggled to his feet. 'I always knew you were an arsehole, Doug,' he said, glaring at his colleague. 'But I didn't think you were a fucking scumbag.'

'You should be careful not to piss me off any more than I already am. It could prove very painful for you.'

'Take these cuffs off me and I'll show you what pain is.'

Doug's grin broadened. 'You'd like to kill me, wouldn't you, Jim?'

'I'd like to see you where you belong – rotting in prison.'

'Maybe we could keep each other company in there,' Doug said with a meaningful gleam in his eyes. 'Get to know each other better. Who knows, we might find we've got a lot in common.'

'I have nothing in fucking common with you.'

'Oh, I wouldn't say that. For starters, we're both willing to kill for what we believe in. For me it's money, for you it's whatever fucked-up idea of justice you have.'

'You must know you're not going to get away with this, Doug.'

Doug regarded Jim with amused contempt. 'You've been in the job too long to be so naive. I already have been getting away with it for years.'

'You're the naive one. Edward Forester might get away with it. People like him usually do. But not people like you or me. We're the ones who always get fucked over.'

'No one's fucking me over. Especially not that prick

Forester.' Doug took out a handgun and motioned Jim forward with it. Struggling to keep his balance, Jim hopped up the steps and shuffled along the hallway. Doug shoved him into a room with a chair bolted to its floor, sending him sprawling. When Jim hit the floorboards, a bomb seemed to go off inside his chest. Blackness threatened to overwhelm him again, as Doug hoisted him into the chair and bound him to it with a leather strap.

'How do you like our interrogation room?' Doug asked.

Jim made no reply. His head rolled onto his shoulder. His breath came shallow and uneven.

'What's the matter, Jimmy boy?' Doug's voice was full of mock concern. 'You don't look too good. Is your heart playing up again?' He slapped Jim's face. 'Don't go passing out on me. We need you conscious so you can talk.'

Jim hoped his heart did finally give out. He knew what was coming, and he knew it would be better for both him and Margaret if he died right then. But his heart kept on beating. The damn thing was as stubborn as its owner, he reflected with a grim smile.

'That's it, you keep smiling while you can,' said Doug. 'Soon Tyler will get here and the real fun will begin.'

Doug left the room. Jim writhed weakly against the strap, but there was no give in it. Doug returned with Margaret slung over his shoulder. He dumped her down by the door. Jim's vision swam towards her. Pale and shaking, she clung to his gaze. 'I'll leave you two alone to say your goodbyes,' said Doug, closing the door. A lock clicked into place.

As quickly as she could, Margaret shuffled on her bum

over to Jim. 'Are you having another heart attack?' she asked, her voice ragged with anxiety.

'I'm just winded.' Jim glanced at the chest of drawers that were the room's only other furniture. 'See if you can open those.'

Margaret pushed herself to the drawers and pulled at their handles. 'They're locked.'

'Can you move the whole thing?'

'No. I think it's attached to the wall.'

Jim wasn't surprised. Doug was an arsehole and a scumbag, but he wasn't a careless man. Margaret returned to Jim. She knelt before him, gazing silently into his face. Then she lowered her head to his knees, and sobs began build in her chest.

'I need you to do something else, Margaret.' Jim's voice was hoarse, but calm and imploring. 'I need you to kill me.'

She jerked up to look at him, her eyes horrified and uncertain, as though wondering if she'd heard correctly.

'We don't have much time,' continued Jim. 'They're going to torture you to try and make me talk. And they'll succeed and others will suffer.'

Margaret shook her head frantically. 'I can't.'

'You've got to.'

'But someone might come and rescue us.'

'No one's coming.'

Still shaking her head, Margaret pressed her head against Jim's legs again.

'Please, Margaret. Don't you see, this is the only way we can beat them.'

'You bastard,' came Margaret's muffled, sobbing voice. She raised her head, her eyes flooded with tears, her face stretched with anguish. 'You fucking, fucking...' She trailed off into grief-racked silence.

'I know,' Jim said softly.

'No, you don't know!' Margaret cried in a whisper. 'I love you. I still love you.'

Her words were a pain to him so sweet and sad it brought tears to his eyes. 'Then do this for me.'

Margaret's mouth opened and closed, but only incoherent sounds came out. She squeezed her eyes shut as if trying to block out an image too terrible to bear. Hauling in a breath that shook her whole body, she visibly took hold of herself. 'How?'

'Loosen the leather strap, loop it around my neck and put all your weight on it.'

With a dazed, stricken expression, Margaret stood and turned her back to Jim. She fumbled at the strap's buckle to no avail. 'It's too tight. I can't undo it.'

'Yes, you can. Take a breath and try again.'

Margaret sucked in a slow, shuddering breath and attempted once more to work the belt loose from the buckle. Her heart gave a sickening lurch when the strap suddenly slackened in her fingers. Awkwardly, she manoeuvred it up around Jim's neck and pulled it into a loose loop. She turned to him. He urged her with sad, resolute eyes to do what needed to be done. There were so many things he wanted to say. But there was no time. She stooped to kiss him. He drew in her taste, her tenderness, everything about her that he'd yearned for through all the long, lonely years. And in that room of pain and fear, he felt, if not happiness, then at least a kind of peace.

Tears streaming down her face, Margaret moved behind Jim and leaned all her weight on the strap. He pushed forward against it, as if in a tug of war. He felt the buckle biting into his neck. He felt his airway being choked off. He felt pressure building behind his face, pushing at his eyeballs, bloating his veins. He felt the agony of knowing he was leaving Margaret behind. Then he felt nothing more and knew nothing more.

The door opened. Doug stepped into the room, followed by Tyler and Edward. For an instant all three stood as if paralysed by what they saw. Then Doug leapt forward and drove his knee into Margaret's midriff, crumpling her into a heap. Tyler tore the strap from Jim's throat and felt for a pulse. He didn't find one. Hooking his arms under Jim's, he lowered him to the floor. He tilted his head back and checked to make sure his airway was clear, before pinching his nose and breathing into his mouth. Then he planted his hands in the centre of Jim's chest, one locked over the other, and gave several quick hard thrusts. As he methodically repeated this process, a sound filled the room – a high-pitched sound like a chattering monkey. Edward was laughing. He was laughing so hard tears were streaming down his cheeks.

'Shut the fuck up!' yelled Doug

Edward's laughter grew louder. Doug lunged at him, landing a hard jab to his gut. Doubling over, Edward staggered forwards and fell on top of Margaret. She tried to shove him off, but he clung on. Her face wrinkled with revulsion as his tongue slid out and licked her ear. Doug prised him loose with a couple of well-aimed kicks to the ribs.

'One more sound out of you and I'll break every fucking bone in your body,' warned Doug.

Tyler delivered several hammer-fist strikes to Jim's chest. Jolting as if he'd been hit by a cattle prod, Jim gasped in a breath. His eyes snapped open and filled with despair at the sight of Tyler. As his gaze sought out Margaret, his despair was replaced by surprise and then a spark – the faintest glimmer – of hope at the sight of Edward curled up in agony. Surely Edward's presence could only mean one thing – Melinda had managed to evade capture. If she'd put the police onto Edward, his protectors would have to become his destroyers to save their own hides. Jim knew that Margaret and he would almost certainly be long beyond help by the time his colleagues tracked Edward to the farm – if indeed they managed it at all. But even so, he drew a little cold satisfaction from the thought that Edward would be joining them in the grave.

'I'm afraid you don't get off that easily,' said Tyler, a trace of something in his voice that might have been admiration.

'Fuck me, Jim, you're one crazy bastard,' Doug said, as Tyler rolled Jim into the recovery position.

Tyler motioned to Edward. 'Strip him and put him in the chair.'

As Doug did so, Tyler set about cutting the cuffs off

Jim and Margaret's ankles. 'What are you doing?' asked Doug.

'Putting them in the basement.'

Doug indicated Edward. 'Don't you think they should see what happens to our friend here? It might give them something to think about.'

'They'll have plenty to think about soon enough.'

Tyler helped Margaret to her feet. Jim struggled to rise, then fell heavily back. Tyler steered Margaret out of the room into the kitchen. Doug followed, dragging Jim by the feet. The basement exhaled a dank breath as Tyler opened its door. He flicked a light switch and prodded Margaret down the stone stairs. Then he and Doug carried Jim to a gloomy, low-ceilinged room. The basement ran the length of the house. Its brick walls had once been painted white, but were now mottled with damp and dirt. In one corner there was a metal bucket that gave off a tang of human waste. Jim found himself hoping that Forester got to spend a little time down here before his end came. Not that it would make him think about what he'd done to his victims. Bastards like him were incapable of that kind of remorse. But it would be fitting nonetheless.

They dumped Jim down beside a chain dangling from an eyebolt in the wall. Tyler looped the chain through Jim's cuffs, doubled it over so there was no slack and padlocked it. Doug chained Margaret to another eyebolt in the opposite wall.

'I know how to secure a prisoner,' grumbled Doug as Tyler checked Margaret's chain.

'Yeah, I saw that upstairs,' Tyler said in his bone-dry voice.

'How was I supposed to know they'd try something like that?'

Without affording Doug a glance, Tyler headed back upstairs. Doug scowled after him. With a hoarse chuckle, Jim said, 'The pay might be better, but the management's the same.'

Doug turned his glare on him. 'Fuck you. He's not my boss.'

'He acts like he is.'

'Yeah, well, our friend the politician acted like he was my boss too. Look at him now, tied to a chair about to have his insides rearranged.' Doug's perma-tanned face split into a grin. 'How's about that for getting away with it?' He turned to follow Tyler. The light went out and the door banged shut, engulfing the basement in absolute darkness.

Margaret's voice reached Jim in a trembling whisper. 'I'm sorry, Jim. I tried.'

'No, Margaret, I'm sorry. I was wrong to give up hope.'

'What are you saying? That you think there's a chance we might be rescued?'

'No. I'm just saying never give up hope.' *Never give up hope!* The words echoed in Jim's head like a truth long forgotten. He'd said them dozens of times to the families of missing persons. And he'd kept on saying them even when he stopped believing in them himself, because he knew that if you gave up hope, there was nothing else left.

'When that man fell on me, he whispered something.

He said, "The book's under the attic floor by the window."
Does that mean anything to you?'

'Yes.' There was surely only one book Forester could have meant – Herbert Winstanley's little black book. A crooked smile tugged at Jim's mouth in the darkness. Forester wanted to take his fellow sickos down with him. And Jim would have liked nothing better than to oblige the bastard. But barring a miracle the secret of the book's location was going to die with Margaret and him. And he didn't believe in miracles.

Chapter Thirty

Reece watched Doug speed away from the headquarters of Steel City Security, wondering what the hell had got him so riled up. He'd seen that look in his eyes before when his partner was about to beat the crap out of someone. It occurred to him that maybe word had got back from Wayne Carson that he'd resumed searching for Melinda. Wayne had sworn to keep quiet, but that meant nothing if he thought he could profit more by opening his gob. He nodded to himself. That had to be it. He got into his car and headed towards the city centre. As Doug had suggested, or rather demanded, he intended to go home and stay there, but not before he'd paid Wayne a visit.

Pulling over on Wicker, Reece stashed the bundles of cash in one pocket and the Glock in another, then headed up to Wayne's flat. He hammered on the door until the pimp's voice came through it. 'You'd better pack that in or the next thing that'll be hitting my door is your fucking head.'

'Open up.'

Wariness replaced Wayne's irritation. 'Aw, fuck. Not you again. What do you want now?'

'I've got something for you. Open up and I'll give it to you.'

The door remained firmly shut. 'Look, just piss off, will you? I'm trying to get some sleep.'

'I know what you did, Wayne.'

'I dunno what the fuck you're talking about. I've not done anything.'

Reece greeted the assertion with no surprise. He would have been amazed if the devious little prick had said otherwise. 'Listen, I'm not here to lay a finger on you.' His voice was suddenly weary, drained of aggression. He'd driven over there intending to confront Wayne, but now that it came to it all he wanted to do was give him the money. His memory kept replaying the images of what had happened in the short space between this and his previous visit to the pimp's flat. *That* was his world now – a world where a mother kept a gun in her baby's cot. There was no going back. He knew that. But if everything went to hell, if he lost his job, even if he ended up in prison, it would be worth it so long as Staci got out of this life and into one worth living. 'Right now, I don't care what you have or haven't done. I've got fourteen thousand, three hundred and fifty quid for you here. Do you want it or not?'

A moment passed. The door opened on a security chain and Wayne's shifty eyes peered out. 'Let's see it.'

Reece took out the money. Wayne eyed it uncertainly but hungrily. 'Sixteen thousand and the bitch is yours.'

'What's the other sixteen hundred odd quid for?'

'Let's call it a matchmaker's fee.'

Wearing an expression of intense distaste, Reece peeled off the required amount. The thought of haggling over

Staci like she was a piece of meat was as repulsive to him as the pimp's face. He passed the wad of cash through the door and repocketed the little that was left over. 'Congratulations,' said Wayne. 'Staci's all yours. Tell her she's got until tomorrow morning to get herself and her shit out of my house.'

'You're a generous man.' Reece's voice was thick with sarcasm.

Wayne bared his yellowed and chipped teeth in a grin. 'So I've been told. Now can I get back to my beauty sleep?'

Reece wedged his foot against the door as Wayne started to close it. 'One more thing. If I ever so much as see you talking to Staci again, I'll kill you.' It wasn't so much a threat as a simple statement of fact. 'Do we understand each other?'

Wayne's smile wavered, but only for a second. 'You don't need to worry about that. The bitch is your problem now.'

'I'll be seeing you soon. And your payment had better not be a penny short.'

This time the pimp's smile vanished. 'What about our deal?'

'Forget our deal.'

'Why?'

'You know why.'

As Reece turned and headed down the stairs, Wayne shouted after him. 'Fucked if I do. I told you, I've not done anything. I've not spoken to anyone.'

A trace of doubt clouded Reece's face. Wayne sounded genuinely indignant. Was it possible he was telling the truth?

Reece dismissed the idea. What other reason could Doug have for being so pissed at him? 'Who smells of bullshit now?' he shot back, taking out his phone.

Wayne shouted something else, but Reece wasn't listening any more. He was thinking about what he was going to say to Staci. He didn't want to tell her over the phone. He wanted to see the look in her eyes when she realised she was free – free from the street, free from fear, free to live and love. But if Doug got wind that they'd met up, the shit really would hit the fan. Reece placated himself with the thought that when this business with the Winstanley case had died down a little, Staci and he would be able to spend some time together. And not an hour here or a few hours there, but real time, the kind of time it took to truly get to know each other. For now, though, hearing her voice would have to be enough. As he dialled her, the phone vibrated in his hand. Smiling, he put it to his ear. 'I was just about to call you. I've got something to tell—'

'I need to see you,' broke in Staci. Reece frowned at the anxiety in her voice.

'We can't risk meeting up right now. You know that.'

'Please, Reece. I'm worried about Amber. I think something might have happened to her.'

'Like what?'

'I don't know. After you left this morning, a red BMW parked up outside her house. I went out to buy some cigs a while ago. When I got back the BMW was gone. I knocked on Amber's door—'

'Fucking hell, Staci. I thought we agreed you were going to stay away from her.'

A note of hurt joined the worry in Staci's voice. 'I was worried about her. She's my friend.'

Reece heaved a sigh. 'I'm sorry. I didn't mean to snap. It's just you do realise what it'll mean for us if you get dragged into the Winstanley case, right?'

'Amber knows better than to mention my name.'

'Even so, if any of my colleagues were to see you talking to her it could ruin everything for us.'

'No one saw me talking to her. She wasn't in. Or if she was, she didn't come to the door.'

'Have you tried phoning her?'

'About a dozen times. But she's not answering. That's why I'm so worried.'

'There's no need to be. She's probably just been taken to the station to be interviewed.'

'Yeah, that's what I thought, but...' Staci tailed off uneasily.

'But what?'

'I don't know. I just didn't like the look of that car. If it was coppers, why did they sit outside the house so long before taking her in?'

'Did you get a look at the driver?'

'No. The windows were tinted. But I took down the reg. It's PK38 LMG.'

Reece thought for a moment. Staci's instincts told her something was wrong. That was one thing prostitutes and cops had in common – they knew better than to ignore their instincts. On the street, that was often the difference between living and dying. 'OK, I tell you what. I'll phone someone and check that Amber's where I think she is.'

'Thanks, Reece.'

'I'll speak to you in a minute.' Reece hung up and dialled Scott Greenwood. When his colleague picked up, he said, 'Hi, Scott, it's Reece, how's things?'

'Could be better. Mind you, I'm not complaining. How's your dad doing?'

'Not too good.'

'I'm sorry to hear that.'

'Any developments in the Winstanley investigation?'

'No.'

'What? None at all?'

'No, not a bloody one. We've been hitting the brick wall for days now. The DCI's convinced Bryan Reynolds could give us the answers we want, but he seems to have disappeared off the face of the planet.'

Reece's head was suddenly reeling. Doug hadn't told Garrett about Amber! Jesus fucking Christ, why hadn't he told him? Was he somehow involved in what had gone on at the Winstanley house? He had to be. What other explanation could there be? But involved how? His mind raced over the possibilities. Doug must have realised Vernon Tisdale would put him on to Freddie Harding. So he obviously hadn't known Freddie was connected to the Winstanleys until Amber came forward. That meant there had to be someone else, someone who didn't want the police going anywhere near Freddie, someone with the money and influence to arrange for witnesses to disappear. Reece put his hand to his eyes as if trying to block out a painfully bright light. Was it really possible? Doug was a crooked bastard, but was he crooked enough to protect a rapist, maybe even to commit murder? If he was, no one who knew about Freddie was safe.

'Listen, Scott,' said Reece, struggling to keep his tone casual, 'I need a favour. Some arsehole backed into me and drove off this morning. Can you run a plate for me?'

'Sure. What's the reg?'

'PK38 LMG.'

The muffled sound of typing came over the line. Then Scott said, 'Black Golf GTI?'

'No, a red BMW.'

'O-Oh, here we go. The Golf was reported stolen six months ago in Liverpool. The plates must have been swapped. Sorry, Reece, you're not having much luck at the moment, are you?'

'No,' Reece agreed grimly. The fact that the BMW had dodgy plates gave yet more credence to Staci's feeling that something was badly amiss. It also meant the lead was a dead end. 'Thanks, Scott.'

'No problem. And good luck with your dad. Tell him we're all thinking about him.'

'I will.'

Reece ducked into his car and drove fast to Staci's house. Her eyes widened when she saw him. 'What are you doing here? I thought—'

'Don't worry about that now,' broke in Reece, scanning

the street uneasily. So far as he could see, there was no one in any of the parked cars. He stepped into the hallway, closing and locking the door behind himself.

Staci put her hand to her mouth. 'Oh my God, it's Amber, isn't it? Something *has* happened to her.'

'I don't know. Not for sure. All I know right now is she's not at the station.'

'I knew it! I fucking knew it. Oh God, oh God, what are we going to do?'

'I'm going to find out where Amber is. You're going to pack a bag and go stay in a hotel for a few nights.'

Staci shook her head. 'I can't leave here. What if she comes back? She might need me.'

I don't think she's coming back. Reece kept the thought to himself. He didn't want to panic Staci any more than she already was. 'She's got your number, hasn't she?'

'Yes, but—'

'There's no point arguing, Staci. You can't stay here anyway. Wayne wants you out.'

Staci's eyebrows pinched together. 'Why?'

Reece sighed. 'I wanted to do this differently. I wanted it to be a... I don't know, a celebration.'

'Just tell me, Reece.'

'I paid off your debt.'

'What? All fourteen-odd thousand?'

Reece nodded. In his mind, he'd pictured Staci's eyes lighting up with joy at the news. But instead, they became narrow, almost suspicious. 'Where did you get that kind of money from?' she asked.

'What does it matter where it came from? All that matters is we can be together. We can live together.'

Reece reached out to put his hands on Staci's shoulders, but she took a step backwards. 'Who did you tell about Amber?'

'Only Doug.'

'No one else?'

Reece felt a sharp pang of hurt. Staci was staring at him as though trying to work out if he was who she'd thought he was. 'No. I swear to you, Staci, I'd never knowingly do anything to hurt you or anyone you care about.'

Staci continued to look narrowly at Reece. 'I'll get my things together,' she said after a moment, as if she'd accepted his words. But a certain distance remained in her eyes.

As she hurried upstairs, Reece stared dejectedly after her. This was supposed to be the moment when their life together really started. But instead, it felt as if a new wedge had been driven between them. Staci reappeared with a suitcase. Reece took it off her and carried it to his car. As she got into the passenger seat, he said, 'Lock the doors and wait here.'

Reece crossed the street and hammered on Amber's door. He shouted her name through the letter box. No response. He hadn't expected one. He just needed to be sure. There was so much hanging in the balance. So many futures. So many lives.

'Have you any idea where Amber might be?' asked Staci as they drove towards the city centre.

'Yes.'

'I could come with you.'

Reece shook his head. 'I need you to get a room and stay there until you hear from me.'

He pulled over in front of a tall, wedge-shaped building of tinted glass with 'Novotel' above its entrance. He proffered what remained of the money Doug had given him. She hesitated to take it. 'What if I don't want to stay in this city any more? What if I was to go to the station and get on the next train out of here?'

The thought of it was like a physical pain in Reece's chest. Part of him wanted to possess Staci, to own her, but it was a part of him he would never give in to. He'd seen what possessiveness could do, the way it ate you up and turned you into everything you hated. 'I'd try to stop you, but I wouldn't force you to stay. I'd never force you to do anything.'

The distance left Staci's eyes. She leaned in and kissed Reece on the cheek. 'Thank you,' she murmured in his ear. 'Be careful,' she added, taking the money and getting out of the car.

Reece watched her until she was inside the hotel's lobby. He turned the car and headed back to Hillsborough. As he passed through the shadow of the football stadium, he glanced at the street where Grace Kirby's parents lived. If he continued along the road he was on it would, he knew, eventually bring him to the house where Grace Kirby, Mark Baxley and Amber had been raped and abused, and where God knows how many others had suffered similarly, perhaps even been murdered. *Is Doug really part of that?*

he asked himself again. *And what the fuck are you going to do if he is?* His hands clenched on the steering wheel as Doug's words echoed back to him like a bitter prophecy. *We're locked together now. If one of us goes down, both of us go down.*

Reece cruised past the headquarters of Steel City Security. In the yard, a man built like a heavyweight boxer was bending over the Audi's boot. The man closed the boot and headed around the back of the building. A baseball cap shadowed his face, but even so Reece recognised him. His name was Liam Collins. They'd gone through police training and risen through the ranks together. *They're me, along with some good friends of ours*, Doug had said about his business partners. But Reece had never counted Liam a friend. There was a mean streak a mile wide in the guy. He liked to pick fights. And once he got going with his fists, it was hard to make him stop. Reece was only too aware that he himself wasn't exactly a saint. But unlike Liam, he took no pleasure out of hurting others. When Liam had been brought up on a brutality charge, the only surprise was that it had taken five years for it to happen.

Reece parked up further along the street. He got out of the car and, watching out for CCTV cameras, skirted the wall that enclosed the yard. He jumped and caught hold of the top of the wall. His face twisted into a grimace as shards of glass cemented in amongst the razor-wire cut into his fingers. But he didn't let go. He pulled himself up and peered over the top. Behind the building there was a garage, its door open, revealing the front end of a red

BMW. He squeezed his eyes shut briefly, as if hoping that when he opened them he would discover the BMW was a hallucination produced by his troubled brain. But there was no denying the truth of his eyes. Surely this confirmed it. Surely there could be no more doubt. Doug was behind, or at least involved in, Amber's disappearance.

It gave Reece a tight, almost queasy feeling in his stomach to see Liam polishing the BMW's passenger door with a cloth and spray bottle.

Reece lowered himself back to the ground, indecision raking at his face. Grace Kirby was dead. Amy Sheridan – one of their own, for Christ's sake – was dead. Amber was surely dead, or soon to be so. Who was next? Jim Monahan? Himself? Staci? He gave a sharp shake of his head. The thought of anyone hurting Staci was too much to bear. He took out his phone and found John Garrett's number. His finger hovered over the dial button. If he pressed it, his career was over, his dreams of a life with Staci were over. What if he was wrong? What if Liam wasn't cleaning away forensic traces of Amber? What if Doug's purpose wasn't to kill her, but to protect her? They were desperate, self-deceiving thoughts. He knew that in his gut. Just as Staci had known something was amiss. But he couldn't bring himself to make the call, not while even the faintest flicker of doubt remained. He had to be absolutely one hundred per cent fucking sure.

Chapter Thirty-One

Tyler slapped Edward's face, not particularly hard, but hard enough to get his attention. Edward's eyes focused on him briefly and vaguely, then faded back off to whatever other place they'd been lost in. His head lolled like a broken stem as Tyler hit him again. Tyler wrenched Edward's chin towards him. 'There's no point pretending, Edward. I know you can hear me. I can see it in your eyes. I'm going to say the same to you as I said to Monahan. You're going to die today. That's not in question. The only question is, how? You can die slow or fast. It makes no difference to me. The choice is yours. All you have to do is tell me where the book is.'

Edward remained silent, his eyes seeming to stare through Tyler.

His face expressing neither disappointment nor annoyance, Tyler approached the drawers. He unlocked the uppermost and took out a leather roll tied up with string. He unfurled the roll on the floorboards, revealing an assortment of knives. There were long and short knives, knives with smooth and serrated blades, kitchen, combat and surgical knives. 'Some people – people like yourself, perhaps – like to use all sorts of instruments for torturing prisoners. But all you really need are a few good knives.'

He plucked out a scalpel. A swift slash of it opened a short but deep cut in Edward's soft, hairy paunch. Edward writhed and let out a small gasping scream.

'Imagine if I did that a hundred times,' said Tyler. 'Do you really want to find out how that feels? And these are only love bites. What about when we get into the really messy stuff?'

Still Edward said nothing, although the tremors that vibrated through his body spoke as loudly as any words.

Tyler pressed the blade against Edward's flesh again. Once, twice, ten, twenty times he repeated the procedure, until Edward's stomach and chest were a patchwork of bloody, winking wounds. Edward shook his head frantically, his face glistening with tears, sweat, mucus and saliva. 'No, Mummy,' he sobbed, 'I won't! I won't! You can't make me.'

Doug entered the room. He looked at Edward with a mixture of curiosity and revulsion. 'Who's he talking to?'

'His mother.'

Doug shook his head. 'The guy's mad as a bag of frogs.'

'Seemingly.'

'There's no seeming about it. Look at him, for fuck's sake. You might as well put a bullet in his brain right now for all the sense you'll get out of him.'

'No. We've got a long way to go yet. Haven't we, Edward?' Tyler stooped to look into Edward's pain-blurred eyes. 'We can go on like this for days. But then you know that, don't you? You've been where I'm standing. The Chinese have a word. *Lingchi*. It translates as *the lingering death*.

You'll know it better as the death by a thousand cuts. This punishment was reserved for the worst criminals, people like you and me. A really skilled executioner was said to be able to make the procedure last two or even three days.' He glanced at Doug. 'Hold his head steady.'

Doug moved behind Edward and grabbed the sides of his head. With an expert aim, Tyler darted the scalpel into one of Edward's eyes, then the other, careful not to go deep enough to pierce the brain. A scream tearing from his throat, Edward wrenched his head sideways. Doug reeled away, his face specked with blood. He rubbed anxiously at his own eyes. 'Jesus, Tyler, you could have warned me what you were going to do. Who knows what I could catch off the bastard.'

'The executioner often started by putting out the condemned's eyes,' continued Tyler, ignoring Doug. 'The idea being that the loss of one sense amplifies the others, and thus increases the pain.'

'Mummy!' howled Edward. 'Mummy!'

Staying close to the wall, Doug approached the door. There was a slight paleness under his tan. 'I'm going to wash my face. Do you...' He swallowed, then went on, 'Do you want a cup of tea or anything?'

Again, Tyler showed no sign of having heard. His gaze travelled Edward's body as if weighing up which part to slice off first. Closing the door behind himself, Doug went into the kitchen and splashed water on his face at the sink. His shoulders stiffened as another scream ripped through the house. He moved quickly to close the kitchen door. Then he filled the kettle. There was no tea or milk, so he made a black coffee. As he sat sipping it, more screams pounded on his brain. On and on they went, until he felt like plugging his ears. He didn't consider himself a squeamish person. He'd seen plenty of blood over the years, much of it spilled by his own hands. But this... you had to be a soulless fucker to do something like this.

Pressing a tissue against his bleeding fingers, Reece headed back to his car. With a deep breath, he forced himself to settle down and wait and watch. Minutes ticked by. An hour. Two hours. The cindery sun dipped behind the hills of Sheffield. The gate swung open and the Audi rolled into view. Liam got out and locked the gate, then accelerated away. Reece waited until he reached the end of the street, before pulling after him.

He followed the Audi through Hillsborough to Rivelin Valley Road. Houses gave way to trees and fields, and beyond them, steep hills dissolving into the darkening sky. Feeling more conspicuous away from the city, Reece dropped as far back as he dared. He put on a burst of speed when a patch of mist obscured the Audi from view. Beyond the mist, the first fingers of moonlight were touching Ladybower Reservoir, and Liam was heading into the coils of the Snake Pass. Several miles away to the east, a helicopter searchlight was sweeping over the high ridge of Stanage Edge. Reece reflected that it was probably searching for a missing hiker or climber. His dad had often used to take him hiking on Stanage as a child. The Mountain Rescue helicopter was a common sight up there.

Reece wondered grimly what purpose Liam had for driving out into the middle of nowhere. There was an obvious one he could think of – finding a body dump site. There were plenty of lonely places out here where a body could lie undiscovered for months, years, maybe even forever.

Reece kept losing sight of Liam as the road wound its way across the dark spine of the Pennines. He resisted the temptation to draw closer, knowing the Audi's taillights would come back into view beyond each bend. But then he rounded a corner and they weren't there. Glancing rapidly from side to side, he spotted the lights heading along a dirt track that branched off the main road. With a mixture of relief and foreboding, he cut his lights and turned onto the track. He drove slowly, almost at a walking pace. When Liam stopped, Reece did likewise and turned off the engine. The Audi's headlights illuminated a farm gate. Liam opened it, pulled the car forwards, then reclosed it and continued on his way.

Reece pulled up by the gate. There were two signs on it, but it was too dark to read them. It wasn't too dark to see the chain that secured the gate. He was going to have to continue on foot. He climbed over and broke into a jog. His pace faltered as a scuffling, scratching sound came from beneath the trees that were clustered to either side of the track. He pulled out the Glock, squinting into the darkness. There was nothing to be seen. His nostrils quivered at a musky animal smell. Was this place some kind of farm? he wondered. Or was it a wild animal he'd heard? He started after the Audi again. It was several hundred metres away now, but he wasn't overly afraid of losing it. An impassable mass of hills loomed in the near distance.

Beyond the edge of the woods was a grassy field with a small collection of buildings at its far side. The Audi's bobbing headlights revealed a farmhouse and several barns. Reece hopped over a drystone wall and scurried across the field. In many places the grass had been worn away to muddy earth that sucked at his trainers. The animal smell was much stronger here, rancid rather than musky. At the edge of the farmyard, he dropped down behind a rusty bath that served as a water trough.

Liam was bending over the boot of the Audi again. He lifted out a long, sausage-shaped object wrapped in black plastic and duct tape. As he hoisted it over his shoulder, an arm decorated with a familiar Celtic band tattoo flopped into view.

Amber! Reece pressed his forehead against the bath, eyes closed. He'd come so close, so fucking close to the life he longed for. But it had slipped from his grasp, even as he'd taken hold of it. There was no more doubt. No indecision. No choice. He knew what he had to do.

Outside the kitchen window, a thickening veil of darkness drew down. And still the agonised cacophony continued. It swelled to a shrieking, sobbing crescendo, then suddenly stopped. Tyler came into the kitchen, sweat glistening on his face, his hands lathered in blood. He approached the sink.

There was a kind of hidden wariness in Doug's eyes as they followed Tyler. 'Is he dead?'

'No. Passed out.' Tyler washed his hands, then stooped to drink from the tap.

'I take it he's not told you anything.'

'I'm not sure he's got anything *to* tell.'

'So why don't we just kill him?'

Wiping his wrist across his mouth, Tyler regarded Doug steadily with his dark, unreadable eye. Doug blinked away from his gaze. Tyler had a way of making him feel exposed, vulnerable, even weak, as if he could look into his mind and see his doubts, his insecurities. It was a feeling he wasn't used to.

The sound of an approaching vehicle attracted their attention. 'That'll be Liam,' said Doug, rising to his feet, relieved for the excuse to leave Tyler's presence. He headed outside, his cocky grin back in place. But there was a kind of forced rictus about his expression that made it seem more like a scowl. 'You made it,' he said to Liam.

'Yeah, although I thought I was going to have a fucking heart attack when I saw that helicopter. Where's Tyler?'

His grin slipping a little, Doug jerked his chin at the house. He pointed to the bundle of plastic and duct tape. 'Do you want a hand carrying that?'

Liam shook his head. 'Nah, she doesn't weigh more than a feather.'

As Liam carried Amber's corpse into one of the barns, Reece

took out his phone and dialled. Garrett came on the line sounding stressed. 'DI Geary, is this urgent? I'm—'

'Yes, sir,' broke in Reece in an intense whisper. 'There's been a murder.'

'What was that? You'll have to speak up. There's a lot of noise where I am.'

'A murder,' hissed Reece. 'Someone's been murdered. Doug Brody's involved.' The line was silent a moment. Garrett had heard him that time alright.

When the DCI next spoke, his voice was slow and grave. 'Let me make sure I understand you perfectly, Detective Inspector Geary. You're accusing a fellow officer of murder.'

'Yes, sir.'

'And you have proof of this?'

'I'm looking at a dead body right now.'

There was another pause, then, 'Where are you?'

'I'm not sure exactly.' Reece described the farm's location as best he could, adding, 'Doug's here, along with at least two accomplices. I have reason to believe they're armed and extremely dangerous.'

'Listen carefully. I want you to stay put and keep your head down. We're on our way to you. In the meantime, I'm going to put you on to Scott Greenwood, and you're going to give him as much info as you can on your situation. Is that clear?'

'Yes, sir.' Reece's voice was like lead. 'That's clear.'

As Reece fed Scott Greenwood tactical information, he watched Doug puffing agitatedly on a cigarette. When

Liam reappeared, Doug dragged open the doors of a second barn. Liam backed the Audi inside it, the rear headlights illuminating a Golf GTI – undoubtedly the stolen GTI whose plates were on the BMW – Doug's silver Subaru, and a red Subaru. Reece's brows angled further down over his troubled eyes. Bryan Reynolds had last been seen driving a red Subaru. Was that why Doug had been so unconcerned about reprisals from the gangster? Was Reynolds's body somewhere out here as well?

Doug and Liam went into the farmhouse. Reece relayed their movements to Scott, adding, 'Do you want me to try and get a look through a window?'

'No. Just hold tight,' said Scott. 'The AFOs will be with you soon.'

Hold tight. The words made Reece want to grind his face into the mud. He was about to lose his job, his freedom and Staci. His mum was dead, his dad was dying. What the hell was there for him to hold tight to?

'I don't suppose you've got any idea where Jim Monahan is?' went on Scott.

A dart of anxiety pierced Reece's self-pity. 'No. Why?'

'We've found his car abandoned.'

'Where?'

Scott hesitated a moment, before replying vaguely, 'At a crime scene.'

It's already starting. I'm already under suspicion. Swearing inwardly at himself, Reece thrust the distressing thought away. He needed to stay focused. This wasn't just about him. A fellow officer's life might be at stake.

Tyler picked up a bucket and returned to the interrogation room. Edward's head was slumped against his chest. He looked like a corpse in the process of being dissected. His nipples had been sliced off. There was a bloody hole where his right ear had been. His fingers and toes had been removed to the first knuckle. Two matching strips of flesh were missing from his thighs. Tyler scooped the severed bits and pieces into the bucket. Then he checked for a pulse in Edward's wrist. There wasn't one. He retrieved a stethoscope from the chest of drawers and listened at Edward's chest. Silence.

Tyler took out his phone and dialled. When the call was answered, he said, 'Forester's dead.'

'Did you find out what I need to know?' enquired the voice on the other end of the line.

'No.'

'Then why is he dead?'

'He must have had a weak heart. I don't think you've got anything to worry about, sir. He lived long enough for me to be almost certain that if he had anything to say, he would have said it.'

'Almost certain isn't fucking certain at all! Christ, why am I surrounded by idiots?' An infuriated sigh filled the line. Then the voice continued in a more controlled tone, 'What about our other problem? Have you spoken to him yet?'

'I'm just about to.'

'Then get to it. And try not to fuck it up this time.'

'I didn't fuck—' Tyler stopped as the line went dead. He stared at the phone with a shade of something that might have been irritation in his eye. Whatever it was, it disappeared as Liam and Doug entered the room.

Liam puckered his lips into a mock wince at the sight of Edward. 'That must have hurt.'

'He's dead.'

'Did he talk?' asked Doug.

'No. But Monahan will.'

The three men headed for the basement. Jim and Margaret blinked up into the faces of their captors. 'Hello there, Jim,' said Liam. 'Long time no see.'

'Liam Collins. Why aren't I surprised to see you here, you piece of shit?' Jim's voice was weak, but thick with contempt.

'Best watch your fucking mouth,' scowled Liam. He made as if to punch Jim, but Tyler caught his wrist.

'No one touches him but me.' Tyler squatted down by Jim, studying his face intently. 'How are you feeling?'

Jim made no reply. The pain in his chest was coming and going. He felt faint and tingly, and seemed to have no strength in his right arm. But a little life had seeped back into his legs. He wasn't about to tell Tyler that, though.

Tyler unlocked Jim's chain, then handed the keys to Liam. 'Bring the woman.'

Tyler hooked his forearms under Jim's armpits and hauled him up the stairs. Jim made no attempt to use his legs. Every second he could buy would give a little more time for something to happen, for someone to come. Liam prodded Margaret along with a handgun. A flicker of surprise crossed Jim's face as Tyler lugged him past the interrogation room. His surprise turned to revulsion at the sight of Edward Forester. If anyone deserved such a death, it was Forester. But still, it twisted something deep inside him to see the politician's mutilated body.

A horrified cry escaped Margaret as she saw Forester. 'Take a good look at him, bitch,' sneered Liam. 'You're about to find out how that feels.'

The farmhouse's front door opened. A dark-haired man in a bomber jacket and military-style black trousers emerged, walking backwards, dragging something. Reece glimpsed an arm dangling limply, followed by the rest of a body. He recognised Jim's brown leather jacket and faded blue jeans. *Oh Christ, don't let him be dead*, he thought. A tiny spark of relief flared through him as Tyler – assuming that's who the man was – turned so that his and Jim's face were visible. Jim was deathly pale, but his eyes were open and alive. Tyler had a broad, expressionless face and a boxer's flat nose. When Reece saw the gauze pad taped over his left eye, he knew he was looking at Amy Sheridan and Grace Kirby's killer. Doug came out of the house next. Then a woman Reece had never seen before, her features taut with fear, her hands cuffed. Liam was close behind her, a handgun jammed against her spine.

The grim little procession made its way to the barn Liam had taken Amber's body into. Reece waited until they were all inside, before rising and darting across the yard. As he peered around the barn door, a putrid smell of animal faeces filled his nostrils, causing his already churning innards to clench even tighter.

Tyler flicked a switch and a single strip light flickered dully into life. 'Fucking hell,' muttered Doug as his shoes sank into the thick green-brown slime that coated the floor. 'These shoes are Italian leather. Handmade. They cost five hundred quid.'

'Lower the harness,' Tyler said.

Still muttering to himself, Doug ascended to the hayloft and cranked the winch handle. Tyler caught hold of the harness, secured it around Jim's waist and motioned for Doug to take him up. Jim groaned as he was hoisted into the air and the harness bit into his groin. Taking out his knife, Tyler turned to Margaret and cut off her plasticuffs. He gestured at the ladder. 'Up you go.'

Margaret started to climb, followed by Tyler and Liam. As she pulled herself over the top of the ladder, the first thing she saw was an arm trailing out of a bundle of plastic and duct tape. Then she saw the blood-spattered workbench and the tools and raincoats hanging on the wall beside it. She stood stooped over, holding her stomach as if she might vomit. 'You people are monsters,' she said, her words coming in quick pants.

'No,' said Tyler. 'We're just businessmen.'

As Liam jabbed his gun into Margaret's ribs again, Tyler grabbed Jim's arms and pulled him onto the floorboards.

Jim lay on his back, dragging in raspy breaths. The harness had squeezed out what little air was in his lungs.

'Give him some slack,' said Tyler. As Doug did so, Tyler propped Jim up against a couple of bags of feed close to the lip of the loft and loosened the harness off. 'There you go. Now breathe. Breathe.'

Jim lifted his gaze to Margaret's. And in her eyes he saw reflected back at him all the hope and longing, all the sorrow and love he'd ever felt.

'That's right, Jim,' continued Tyler. 'Look at her. You have the power. It's up to you how she dies. All you have to do is answer one simple question. Other than Bryan Reynolds, who have you told about Edward Forester?'

'What does that matter now?' Jim asked hoarsely. 'Forester's dead.'

'You don't need to worry about why it matters. You just need to think about whether you want to watch Margaret watching bits of herself be fed to Kong.'

'Who's Kong?'

'Answer my question and you needn't ever find out.'

'No one. The answer's no one.'

'Why do I find that hard to believe?'

'I don't know. I tried to have Forester murdered. That's not exactly the kind of thing you want to broadcast.'

'Enough of this bollocks!' put in Doug. 'Why is Reece Geary's number on your phone?'

Jim's eyes narrowed a fraction. So Reece was in on this too. But he obviously didn't know the whole truth. Otherwise why would he have been searching for Melinda? 'I heard Reece was trying to track down a missing prostitute,' he said, choosing his words with care, aware that Reece's life hung on them. 'So I went to speak to him. But I didn't tell him anything.'

Doug shot Tyler a triumphant look. 'You see,' he said, half laughing with relief. 'I told you.'

Tyler stared at Jim like he was reading the lines that the long years had etched into his face. As if satisfied by what he saw, he gave a nod. He approached the wall of tools and took down a knife with a long, narrow blade. He turned to Margaret. 'Tilt your head back.'

She hesitated to do so, her panicked eyes darting between Tyler and Jim.

'Relax.' Tyler's voice was uncharacteristically soft, almost tender. 'In medieval times knives like this one were used to euthanise the seriously wounded and sick.' Margaret trembled as he touched a finger to the hollow where her breastbone met her neck. 'The blade is thrust down behind the ribcage into the heart. It's over in an instant. I promise you, you won't feel a thing.' He glanced at Liam. 'Hold her steady.'

Liam wrapped his arms around Margaret. Her tear-filled eyes locked with Jim's. Her trembling lips forming a silent prayer, she slowly tilted her head.

'Wait!' cried Jim as Tyler raised the knife. 'I... I...' His voice cracked as he fought to hold back tears. It flashed through his mind to mention the book, to use it to buy Margaret a few more moments of life. But he couldn't do it.

Forester's name wasn't the only one in the book. There were other abusers, other rapists, maybe even other murderers. If the book fell into the wrong hands, they would escape justice. He couldn't allow that to happen. Not at any price.

'Do it,' said Liam. 'The prick's just stalling.'

'Shut your mouth,' said Tyler. He regarded Jim with his impassive eye. 'Go on. Say what you want to say.'

I love you, Margaret. That was all there was left to say. Jim gulped at the air, desperately trying to get enough into his constricted lungs to speak. But he couldn't. All he could do was mouth the words silently, tears spilling down his cheeks. Margaret made a movement of her chin as if to say, *I know.* Tyler turned back towards her, and gripping the knife's handle with both hands, gently placed its point against her neck.

Oh Christ, oh fuck, thought Reece. There was no more time to wait for back-up. The woman was going to die unless he did something. He raised the Glock and advanced into the barn. 'Police! Step away from the woman and toss your weapons down here!'

Every eye in the hayloft jerked towards Reece. Jim's lungs swelled with relief, yet his eyes remained cautious, almost disbelieving. Was it possible? Were they going to be saved?

'Whoa, Reece,' said Doug, stepping forwards. 'It's me, it's me.'

'Don't you fucking move, Doug,' warned Reece, keeping his eyes and the gun trained on Tyler and Liam. 'You two, do as I say or I'll shoot.'

Neither man moved. A thin line of blood ran from beneath the point of the knife. 'Go on, do as he says,' urged Doug. 'This is just a misunderstanding. I'll handle it.'

Tyler's eye swung uncertainly between Doug and Reece. He retreated a couple of steps from Margaret. 'Not that way,' said Reece, suddenly aware that if Tyler ducked down at the rear of the loft he would be out of his line of sight. 'Step towards me.' Tyler obeyed, but didn't put the knife down. Liam did likewise.

'I won't tell you again to toss your weapons!' barked Reece.

'Easy, Reece,' said Doug, spreading his hands. 'I'm going to reach into my jacket and get something. Don't shoot.'

'Slowly,' cautioned Reece.

Doug took out a pistol, holding it by the barrel. He threw it into the mud behind Reece. 'You see, like I said, this is just a misunderstanding. We're all friends here. You know Liam. And this is Tyler. They're our business partners.'

'They're no partners of mine. Neither are you, you murdering piece of shit.'

'We didn't want to kill anyone, Reece, but you forced us to. I warned you, didn't I? I warned you not to waste your time looking for that whore.'

'And what about Grace Kirby? What about Amy Sheridan?' Reece jerked his chin at Jim and Margaret. 'What about them?'

Doug's face twitched into a grimace. 'OK, so things got a bit out of control.'

'A bit out of control?' Reece repeated incredulously.

'Amy's dead, Doug. Her children have got to grow up without a mother because of you.'

'I know, and believe me, I feel like shit about it. It wasn't meant to happen, but it did, and there's nothing we can do about that now.'

'Yeah there is. You can spend the rest of your life in prison.'

'Fuck you, Reece,' snarled Liam. 'If we go down, you go down.'

Doug held up a placating hand. 'No one's going down. Reece is upset because a friend of ours was killed. That's understandable. But I think I know how to make him feel better about it.' He pointed towards the farmhouse. 'There's a suitcase in there with two million quid in it. We took another million or so off Bryan Reynolds. That's three million to divide between us. You can take your share and walk away. Or you can come in on this with us. And we can get rich together. It's up to you, Reece.'

Reece shook his head. 'It's too late for that.'

'What do you mean?'

'He means your colleagues are already on their way here,' Tyler stated calmly.

'You fucker!' exploded Liam, eyes bulging at Reece as if they were about to burst out of their sockets.

'Drop the gun, Liam.' Reece's tone was forceful, but with a note of pleading. 'Don't make me shoot!'

'No, wait, wait,' Doug said desperately. 'It's still not too—'

His voice died as Liam jerked his gun towards Reece.

A shot echoed through the barn and surrounding hills. Liam staggered backwards a couple of steps, staring at Reece with a sort of dumb disbelief. The gun dropped from his fingers. As if feeling for a heartbeat, he put his hand to his chest where the bullet had entered. His mouth opened and closed, but all that came out was a wheezing, ticking sound. His knees buckled and he collapsed to the floorboards. The ticking rapidly wound down into silence.

'Oh Jesus, Reece,' gasped Doug. 'Oh Jesus Christ, what have you done?'

Ignoring him, Reece trained his gun on Tyler. 'You've got ten seconds to drop that knife or I'll put a bullet in you too.'

Tyler dropped the knife, cupped his hands to his mouth and let out a high-pitched, 'Sooee!'

'Pack that in,' demanded Reece.

But Tyler called out again, 'Sooee!'

'This is your last warning—' Reece broke off upon hearing a distant squeal. He shot an uneasy glance at the barn's doorway. The squeal came again, louder. Others joined it.

'If I were you, I'd put your gun down and climb up here,' said Tyler.

Reece looked at him incredulously. 'You're the one who's going to climb down here.'

'That's not going to happen.'

'Look, either you do as I say or I'm going to put one in your leg.'

'You do what you've got to do.'

Tyler's voice was as coolly calm as if he was exchanging the time of day with someone in the street. *Who the fuck is this guy?* wondered Reece. His gaze was drawn towards the yard again by the rising cacophony of squeals and grunts. Something was heading towards the barn. Fast. It sounded like a herd of pigs. But why should he be concerned about pigs? Then he saw them, and he realised why. They rushed into the barn in a rolling mass, headed by the biggest pig he'd ever seen. Locking its beady red eyes on Reece, the monstrous animal lowered its head and charged. Reece swung the Glock towards it and squeezed off a shot. As the bullet bit into its hairy flank, the pig let out a bellow that revealed a set of huge, curling brown tusks. But it didn't slow its advance. Reece sprinted towards the ladder and leapt on to it. There was a splintering sound as the pig's head connected with the lower rungs. Reece's legs were swept from beneath him. He managed to cling to the ladder, but the Glock fell from his grip into the seething herd. He drew his feet up out of reach as the pig barged into the ladder again, breaking the legs, leaving it dangling by the bolts that attached it to the hayloft.

As Reece lunged for the top of the ladder, Tyler loomed into view, holding a handgun. In that instant, Reece knew he was dead. There was no time to think, no time to feel. There was only time to close his eyes.

Margaret and Doug stared at the pigs, her gaze transfixed with horror, his with leering triumph. Jim barely afforded the pigs a glance. He knew this was Tyler's chance to make a decisive move. His gaze sought out Tyler in time to see him draw a gun and stride towards the ladder. Jim had nothing to draw but his breath. He hauled it in, sucking up all the strength, all the anger that remained in him. As Tyler neared the ladder, Jim pushed himself to his feet. His legs trembled, but held. Teeth clenched, he drove himself towards Tyler's blind side. Tyler was taking aim at Reece. *I'm not going to make it*, thought Jim. But then his shoulder hit home, and without even a grunt, Tyler toppled over the edge of the loft.

There was a crack, audible even above the clamour of the pigs, as Tyler hit the ground head first. A numb paralysis seized him from the neck down, and he knew his spine was broken. The pigs scattered, momentarily startled. Then they turned their glistening snouts curiously towards him. Kong was the first to move in closer. Tyler hammered his head against the mud, vainly trying to knock himself unconscious as Kong loomed over him. Kong opened his jaws, exhaling a rotten warmth. Tyler closed his eye as the jaws snapped shut around his face. He felt the tusks piercing his flesh. He felt his bones breaking. He let out a single, muffled scream, then was silent.

Shock wiped the grin from Doug's mouth. He lurched forwards and punched Jim in the face, sending him sprawling. As Reece came into view at the top of the ladder, Doug kicked him. Reece's head snapped back, blood bursting from his nose.

'We could have had it all!' Doug spat, aiming another kick at Reece. 'But you had to go and fuck it up!'

Reece flung up an arm, partially deflecting Doug's foot.

Dots of light were dancing in front of his eyes. He was losing his grip on the ladder. Another blow would surely send him toppling to the same grisly fate as Tyler. Doug drew his foot back to deliver it, but then stiffened as if he'd touched a live wire. Eyes bulging, mouth agape, he turned around, revealing the knife that Margaret had buried in his back.

'Fucking bitch.' Doug's voice came in a strangled rasp. His hands shot out to grasp Margaret's throat. She pulled away, but he clung to her with grim determination. Like drunken dancers, they staggered backwards.

'No,' panted Jim, struggling to stand. He collapsed back against the bags of feed, tears of frustration springing into his eyes as he realised his final strength had been spent on Tyler.

Margaret's breath whistled out of her as she collided with the workbench. Doug thrust her onto its blood-encrusted surface. His fingers pushed deeper into her flesh. She fought desperately to prise them off, but they were clamped onto her like a steel trap, crushing her breath away. Reece hauled himself into the loft and reeled towards Doug. He wrenched his partner's hands off Margaret and thrust him away from her. Doug stumbled and fell backwards. The breath heaved from his lungs as the knife was driven so deeply into him that its tip protruded through his chest, tenting his jacket.

Reece helped Margaret upright. 'Are you alright?'

She nodded, hauling in ragged gasps.

Doug coughed up blood as he vainly tried to find his breath. His eyes wet with fear, he stretched a hand towards

Reece, not in hostility but in appeal. Squatting down, Reece took it and silently watched his partner dying.

Margaret rushed to Jim, dropping to her knees at his side. They stared into each other's tear-filled eyes. There was blood on Jim's cheek. Margaret reached out to dab it away. Then she lowered her head against his chest. Her shoulders quaked as sobs pushed up from deep inside her. Jim stroked her hair and held her weakly to him.

It didn't take long for Doug's last breath to leave his lungs. Reece straightened and approached the edge of the loft. The pigs were still feasting on Tyler, fighting between themselves over his entrails. A throbbing, vertigo-like nausea filling his head, Reece turned to Jim and Margaret. 'They'll be here soon.'

'Thank you, Reece,' said Jim.

Reece shook his head. 'I don't deserve your thanks. Doug was right, I've fucked it all up.'

'How? Tell me how?'

Reece hesitated to reply, unsure whether he had the will to tell him. What difference would it make? The whole sorry tale was going to come out soon enough anyway.

'Quickly,' urged Jim. 'They're going to be here soon and then it'll be too late.'

Reece's forehead drew into creases of uncertainty. Too late for what? Was Jim offering to cover up for him? 'For about six months now I've been helping Doug run protection for pimps and small-time pushers.'

'And that's all, is it?' Jim's gaze flicked around the barn. 'You didn't know about any of this?'

'I knew Doug was into something bigger, but I didn't find out what it was until today.' Reece's eyes moved to Amber's plastic-wrapped corpse. His forehead pinched tighter. 'I could never be a part of this... sickness.'

'But you are a part of it. What I need to know is why.'

Sadness shadowed Reece's features as his thoughts turned to Staci. 'There's a woman. Someone I care deeply about. She was in trouble. I needed money to help her out.'

Jim looked at Reece as if trying to make his mind up about something. Then he said, 'How much have you told Garrett?'

'Only that Doug was involved in a murder.'

'And who else knows you were searching for Melinda?'

'The woman I mentioned, Melinda's pimp and Vernon Tisdale.'

'Can you rely on this woman to keep a secret?'

'Yes,' Reece said with absolute conviction. 'And it's safe to assume the pimp isn't going to be speaking to the police anytime soon. Which just leaves Vernon.'

'I don't think we need worry about him either. He'll be more than happy to keep our names to himself if he thinks it'll help bring justice for the damned.'

'So this is connected to those missing prostitutes.'

'Yes. But the less you know about that for now, the better. We need to keep this as simple as possible. Here's how we're going to play it.' Jim paused to gather his breath. 'You suspected Doug was crooked, but wanted to make absolutely certain you were right before you reported him. Keep the details of why you became suspicious limited.

Doug was associating with former bent coppers. That's enough. You don't want to have to give up the name of anyone who could implicate you. How did you find your way out here?'

Reece told Jim about how he'd followed Liam.

'That's good. Stick to that story. But leave out the part about Amber. You know absolutely nothing about the dead person's identity or why they were killed. And most importantly of all, you don't know anything about any missing prostitutes.'

'But what about Melinda? She's still missing—'

'No, she's not.'

Reece's eyes widened. 'You found her.'

'Yes.'

'How? Where?'

'She's safe. That's all you need know for now. I want you to clear your head of all that and concentrate on getting your story straight. Can you do that?'

'Yes.' Reece's voice was dazed, and not just because of the blows he'd received to his head. In the space of a few sentences, everything he thought had slipped from reach had been brought back within touching distance. And yet his eyes were more curious than grateful. 'Why are you doing this?'

'Because I'm part of this sickness too.'

'What do you mean?'

'I mean we've both made mistakes that have led to people's deaths.'

Jim and Reece stared at each other silently for a moment.

Then both gave a slight nod, as if exchanging an unspoken agreement.

'Just tell me one more thing,' said Jim. 'You're finished taking dirty money, right?'

'Fuck yes,' Reece stated vehemently. 'I'm not even sure I want to be a copper any more.'

'Then, for Christ's sake, find another line of work while you're still young.' Jim closed his eyes as he tried to think of anything he might have missed. They snapped back open. 'The gun! Where did you get the gun?'

'Off a dealer Doug and me were shaking down.'

'No you didn't. You found it in Doug's car. That was one of the things that led you to become suspicious about him. Has Doug handled it?'

'No.'

'Then you need to make sure his prints are on it.'

Blood dripping from his nostrils, Reece peered hesitantly towards the foot of the ladder. The gun had sunk from sight into the sheet of slime.

'Quickly,' hissed Jim. 'Get the gun, or it all falls apart.'

Reece descended the swaying, shattered ladder. Eyeing the pigs warily, he jumped down the last half a metre or so. The pigs paid him little attention. They were still hard at work on Tyler. Pulling up his sleeves, Reece plunged his hands into the mud. His fingers located the Glock. He swirled the mud off it in a water trough, then climbed back up to the loft and approached Doug. As he pressed Doug's fingers against the gun's grip, the pigs suddenly lifted their eyes to the barn's entrance, snuffling at the air.

'Throw the gun back into the mud,' Jim said urgently.

Reece tossed the gun over the edge of the loft. Jim beckoned him close again. 'Remember, you simply suspected Doug was up to something dodgy. The rest is a coincidence.'

'It's a pretty big coincidence, don't you think?'

'Yeah, well, that's just the way it plays out sometimes.' Jim's gaze was drawn by the sound of the pigs scuttling from the barn. 'You'd better get out there too.'

Reece held Jim's gaze a moment longer, only gratitude in his eyes now. He descended the ladder again and approached the barn's entrance, holding his police ID high. 'This is Detective Inspector Reece Geary!' he shouted. 'I'm coming out.'

The farmyard was empty. Nor could Reece see anyone in the deep pools of darkness enclosing it. But he knew he wasn't alone. 'This is Detective Inspector Reece Geary,' he repeated. 'There's an injured officer in the barn who urgently needs medical attention.'

A shadowy figure rose from behind the bath Reece had used for cover and motioned him over. Keeping his ID visible, Reece did as signalled. It was an AFO dressed all in black with a sub-machine gun slung across their chest. Glancing about, Reece spotted more armed officers hunkered down against the drystone wall and behind a pile of tyres. Several of them had their weapons trained on him.

'Stop right there,' ordered the AFO when Reece was a few metres away. 'Don't you move another fucking muscle.' He cautiously approached Reece, pulled his hands down behind his back and cuffed them. 'Is there anyone else besides the injured officer in the barn?'

'A woman. She's a friendly too.'

'What about the suspects?'

'They're all dead.'

'Are you certain of that?'

'Yes.'

The AFO handed Reece off to one of his colleagues. The rest of the team moved in on the barns and farmhouse. They quickly secured the area. Then the dirt track was illuminated by the lights of approaching police vehicles and ambulances, and the night sky was filled with the whoomp-whoomp of a helicopter. Reece's mind returned to the helicopter he'd seen over Stanage. Surely it had been searching for Jim. But what had Jim been doing out there? Had he been trailing Doug or Tyler? Or was there someone else involved? Maybe someone under the protection of Steel City Security. Or someone connected to Freddie Harding. Reece pushed the questions from his mind. None of that was his concern right now. Like Jim had said, he needed to concentrate on getting his story straight.

DCI Garrett got out of the lead car and hurried across to Reece. 'Take those cuffs off him,' he ordered the AFO.

'Doug Brody's dead, sir,' said Reece, struggling to maintain eye contact with his superior's probing gaze.

'I know.'

'Jim Mona—'

'I know that too,' Garrett cut him off. 'What I don't

know is how you and Detective Inspector Brody came to be involved in... in whatever the bloody hell this is.'

'A few days ago I made a discovery that led me—'

'Save your story.' Garrett indicated Reece's bloodied nose. 'Right now, you need to get that looked at.'

'Yes, sir. Thank you, sir.'

'Don't be too quick to thank me. Later there will be questions. Lots of them. And you'd better hope I like the answers you give me.'

Relieved to have a little more time to get his head together, Reece made his way to an ambulance. As a paramedic staunched the bleeding, Reece watched Jim being stretchered from the barn. He raised a hand to wave. Jim didn't wave back. The paramedic guided Reece to a seat in the back of the ambulance and closed the doors. The vehicle set off, followed by a police car. Reece took out his phone and dialled Staci. She picked up on the first ring and asked anxiously, 'Reece, are you alright?'

'I'm fine, baby.' Glancing at the paramedic, Reece lowered his voice. 'She's alive.'

'Who's ali—' Staci started to ask. Then realisation laced with trembling hope filled her voice. 'Amber!'

Reece winced, and not at the pain in his nose. 'No. Melinda.'

'You found her.'

'No, but someone did. I've got to go now. I'll tell you everything when I see you.'

'Wait. What about Amber? Have you found her too?'

'Yes.'

'And is she alive?'

In a voice as heavy as his heart, Reece said, 'No.'

Tears clogged Staci's voice. 'Oh my God! I knew it. I knew it.'

'I'm sorry, Staci. I tried.'

Staci quickly got hold of her tears. She'd worked the streets long enough to know how to handle grief. 'I know you did, Reece. And I want you to know that I...' Her voice grew hesitant, as if she was stretching for something she found difficult to say. 'Well that I... you know.'

A flicker of a smile lightened Reece's features. Staci hadn't said the words in her mind. But she'd said enough. 'I know, babe. I love you too. I'll see you soon.'

Chapter Thirty-Two

Jim held Margaret's hand as the paramedics wheeled him out of the barn. An AFO tried to guide her towards a police car, but Jim didn't release his grip until they reached the ambulance. Even then, his eyes followed her, reluctant to let go. He wasn't worried about what she would say to his colleagues. She knew better than to repeat what she'd heard him discuss with Reece. He just didn't want to be apart from her. Not now. Not ever again.

Garrett's bespectacled, harried face blocked Jim's view. 'How is he?' the DCI asked the paramedics.

'His heartbeat's irregular and he's having difficulty breathing,' replied one of them. 'We need to get him to hospital right away.'

'I'm not going to hospital,' said Jim, his voice muffled by an oxygen mask.

'Don't be foolish, Jim,' said Garrett. 'You could be having another heart attack.'

'I have to go to Edward Forester's house.'

'Can you give us a moment, please,' Garrett said to the paramedics. As they moved away, he regarded Jim with furrow-browed curiosity. 'What's at Forester's house that's so important?'

Jim remained silent.

'OK, so you're not willing to trust me,' continued Garrett. 'After the way I've treated you, I understand that. But regardless of your health, I can't allow you on to that crime scene until I've got some answers.'

'Oh, I've got answers,' said Jim. 'Enough to put your name on the map. How you want to be known is up to you. You can be the man who cracked a thirty-year-old case involving serial murder, paedophilia and police corruption. Or I can tell the newspapers how if I'd listened to you a young woman would be dead now, and Edward Forester and his accomplices would be free to continue their crimes.'

An angry, mottled flush rose up Garrett's neck. He stood in frowning indecision for a moment. Then he called to the paramedics, 'OK, let's go. I'll be riding in the back of the ambulance. We're going to be making a brief detour on our way to the hospital.'

'Before we go anywhere, you need to put out an alert on Forester's half-brother, Freddie Harding. The two of them were in this together.'

As the paramedics loaded Jim into the ambulance and set him up on an IV drip and heart monitor, Garrett relayed the information about Harding to several of his detectives. The DCI climbed into the back of the ambulance, the doors closed and the vehicle followed a police car away from the farm.

'How's Melinda doing?' asked Jim.

'She's lost a lot of blood,' Garrett said gravely. 'And that's just from the gunshot wound.' He gave a shake of his head. 'When I saw what had been done to her, it was difficult to believe she was still alive.'

'She'll pull through. She's strong.'

'Let's hope you're right. Look, Jim, no matter what I say, no matter what happens from here on, you did a good thing there.'

A trace of a surprised smile showed on Jim's lips. Was that humility he'd heard in Garrett's tone? The sadness quickly returned to his features as he thought about Amy. 'Do you think if someone does something good, it balances out the bad they do?'

'I don't know.'

Jim knew he shouldn't have expected any other answer. Such questions meant nothing to men like Garrett, men who played the percentages. He drew in a deep breath. The combination of oxygen and the IV drip were easing the pain in his chest. He felt the blood flowing back into his limbs.

'Let me ask you something,' said Garrett. 'Why do you make everything so difficult for yourself? And I'm not just talking about the job.'

Now it was Jim's turn to stretch for an answer. 'Margaret used to say I see too much. That I need to learn to see only the things that matter and let the rest slip by. Maybe that's what it is. Or maybe I'm just a natural-born pain in the arse.'

'Well you won't find any disagreement here. You're definitely a pain in the arse.'

Garrett spoke with conviction, but no malice, and maybe even a hint of affection. Jim gave him another look of surprise. The guy was a careerist and an opportunist. That was why Jim had known he would take him to Southview. But maybe he wasn't quite the prick Jim had thought.

The car leading the ambulance slowed as it approached a cordon of police tape at the end of the steep lane that led to Forester's house. A constable moved the tape aside to let them through. 'Get as close to the house as you can,' Garrett said to the driver. The ambulance weaved around the police vehicles clogging Southview's driveway. It pulled up in front of the steps and a paramedic opened the rear doors.

Jim removed his oxygen mask and indicated the IV needle. 'Take this out of me.'

'You really shouldn't be moving around in your condition,' cautioned the paramedic.

'I shouldn't do a lot of things, but I do them anyway,' said Jim with a meaningful glance at Garrett.

He rose from the stretcher and stood swaying. Garrett caught hold of him and helped him from the ambulance. Jim raised a hand to shield his eyes. Southview's grounds were lit by halogen spotlights that seemed painfully bright after the murkiness of the farm. The place was a buzz of familiar activity. Officers with corpse dogs were sweeping the grounds. Forensic bods carrying bagged and tagged evidence were coming and going between the house and a white tent on the lawn.

'We found Mabel Forester dead in the house,' explained

Garrett. 'She'd been decapitated. Her head was on the mantelpiece.'

Jim guessed at once that Tyler wasn't behind Mabel Forester's murder. The decapitation and display of her head would have served no purpose to him. No, her death was about humiliation, it was about her son getting back at her for any abuses, real or imagined, that she'd perpetrated against him.

Drawing looks that ranged from curiosity and concern to respect and admiration, Jim climbed the doorsteps. Garrett took two pairs of latex gloves from a box on the top step. As they pulled them on, the broad-shouldered, black-suited figure of DCS Knight stepped out the door. The Chief Superintendent's rugged strong features were set into a grim expression beneath his cap. Deep lines were etched around his pale-grey eyes. They grew deeper as he saw Jim. 'DI Monahan, I was led to believe you were on your way to hospital.'

'He is, sir,' said Garrett.

'Then what's he doing here?'

'Helping with inquiries.'

DCS Knight's voice took on a tone of rebuke. 'I must say I'm surprised at you, John. Not only is this man clearly not in any fit state to be here, but he's suspected of engaging in an illegal investigation. What makes you think—'

The DCS broke off as Jim stepped past him into the house. At the far end of the hallway, forensic officers were photographing blood spatters. They glanced around as

DCS Knight shouted, 'Inspector Monahan, what the hell do you think you're doing?'

Ignoring him, Jim started up the stairs.

'Get back here,' thundered DCS Knight. 'That's an order!'

Fuck your orders, thought Jim. But he didn't say the words. He wanted to keep every bit of breath he had for the climb.

'Jim, this isn't the way to go about this,' put in Garrett.

Jim concentrated on hauling the leaden weights of his feet up the stairs as fast as possible. He glanced over his shoulder at the sound of following footsteps. DCS Knight was hurrying after him, closely followed by Garrett. There was a chair at the top of the stairs. Jim's body pleaded with him to rest on it. Instead, he picked it up and threw it at his pursuers. DCS Knight caught it, but fell backwards against Garrett, who struggled in turn to hold him upright.

Jim quickly took his bearings. Straight ahead an open door led onto a bedroom. To his left, more doors led onto more rooms, lining a long, high-ceilinged landing. To his right, at the far end of the landing, there was another flight of stairs, narrower and steeper than the one he'd just ascended. He hastened towards it. At the foot of the stairs, there was a door with a key in it. He closed and locked the door behind himself. Groping around in darkness, he found a light switch. As he climbed the stairs, a hammering started up on the door and DCS Knight's voice rang out. 'I'll have you up on charges for this, Monahan!'

At the top of the stairs was a large attic, illuminated by the pale glow of a floodlight bleeding through a round window. Breathlessly picking his way around jumbles of dusty boxes and sheeted furniture, Jim approached the window. Sweat rolling down his face, he dropped to his knees and began to examine the floorboards. A loud bang from below told him that someone was attempting to break the door down. The door was old and heavy with a solid lock. It would withstand a good few shoulder charges. Still, he didn't have much time. His fingers ran over the head of a nail on one floorboard, before coming to a halt on the hole where a nail was missing from its neighbour. There was another bang, this time accompanied by the sharp sound of splintering wood. With his fingernails, he prised up the floorboard. And there it was. Herbert's book. It was only a little thing. But what it contained was big enough to kill for.

Jim snatched it up. His gaze skimmed over the names listed on its pages. Some he didn't recognise – *Thomas Villiers. Rupert Hartwell.* And some he recognised only too well – *Stephen Baxley, Henry Reeve, Charles Knight...*

Jim's eyes pinched into glinting bullets. There were names he wouldn't have been all that surprised to find in the book, but DCS Knight's wasn't one of them. He'd never particularly liked the guy, but he'd respected him. Other officers – Doug Brody and Stan Lockwood included – had been fiercely loyal to him back when he had Garrett's job. Knight had never hidden the fact that his ambitions stretched beyond CID. But he also genuinely seemed to care about the officers serving under him. And that drove the needle of betrayal in deep.

Jim twisted towards the sound of footsteps on the stairs. Scott Greenwood was first into the attic, followed by Garrett. 'This is exactly what I was talking about, Jim,' snapped Garrett. 'You always have to make everything so bloody—' He broke off as Jim held up the book.

'You need to take a look at this.'

Jim handed the book to Garrett. The DCI's anger swiftly drained away, leaving shock and astonishment in its wake. 'Is this what I think it is?'

'Yes. Where's DCS Knight?'

'He left me to deal with you.' Garrett turned to Scott Greenwood. 'Find the DCS. Let me know the instant you locate him. And this is very important. Do not, under any circumstances, allow him to leave without seeing me. Even if you have to physically restrain him. Do I make myself clear?'

Scott's eyebrows drew together. 'But, sir—'

'Don't question me,' snapped Garrett. 'Just do it. Fast.'

'Yes, sir.'

As Scott hurried from the room, Jim lowered himself onto a box. Garrett's eyes returned to the book as if double-checking that they'd read correctly. 'Fucking hell,' he murmured. 'This is... it's a...' He trailed off, unable to find the words to describe what it was. He turned a sharp gaze on Jim. 'Did you suspect him?'

'No... Well, maybe the thought passed through my mind. But that's all it was, a passing thought.'

'Do you think he knew what Forester was doing in those woods?'

'I don't know.' Jim hoped not, because if Knight knew about Forester, surely he also knew about Bryan Reynolds. Not that anyone would believe him now if he told them. But he could still do more than enough damage to derail the plan Jim had in mind.

Garrett's phone rang. He had it against his ear in the space of a breath. His features jerked into a frown. 'What do you mean, his car's gone?' There was the briefest of pauses, then, 'In that case, I want every officer we can spare out there searching for him.'

'They should be advised that he's to be considered armed and extremely dangerous,' put in Jim.

Garrett eyed him doubtfully, as if he couldn't get his brain around the idea. With a nervous lick of his lips, he repeated into the phone what Jim had said. He hung up, pressing his fingers to his forehead. 'Well that's it... It's out there now.'

Jim indicated the book. 'He must have known, or at least guessed, Forester had that.'

'And if he knew about that, who knows what else he was aware of.' Garrett heaved a breath. 'I need to call the Chief Constable.'

'What are you going to say to him?'

'I don't know, exactly.'

'You should do. Remember, what happens now, what you do right this moment, could define your whole career.'

Garrett gave Jim a narrow look. 'Alright then, let's hear it.'

Jim laid it all out. How he came to suspect Edward Forester was involved in the sexual abuse of Mark Baxley and Grace Kirby. How he tricked him into confirming those suspicions. How he tracked him down to Southview. And how he came to learn the true, and truly awful, extent of Forester's crimes. He was careful to make no mention of Bryan Reynolds.

'And how does this help me?' asked Garrett. 'After all, I knew nothing about your investigation.'

'Yes you did. You were fully aware of it. In fact, it was your idea. You kept it secret because of your suspicions about Forester's connections to officers within the police department.'

'And how did these suspicions arise?'

'Well, for starters DCS Knight vouched for Doctor Henry Reeve. Then there's Reece Geary.'

'Ah yes, DI Geary, how does he fit into this scenario?'

'That's up to you. From the little he's told me, Reece became suspicious of Doug Brody after learning he was involved with Liam Collins. We can use his story to give more weight to ours.'

'Did he know about Inspector Brody's involvement with Edward Forester?'

'Not as far as I know.'

Garrett's gaze dropped in thought. After a moment, he looked at Jim, uncertainty still glimmering in his eyes.

'You're playing me, I can tell. And I don't like to be played.'

'I'm handing you your career on a plate. Think about it, they're going to need someone to replace Knight. And who better than the man who exposed him for what he is?'

'And what do you want out of this?'

'I want out. Early release.' A sardonic smile traced Jim's lips. 'You promoted and me gone. That's two prizes for the price of one.'

Garrett's eyes remained narrow, but the uncertainty left them. 'I know there's a lot you haven't told me.'

Jim made no attempt to deny it. Garrett might not have been much of a detective, but he was no fool.

'And frankly, I think it'd be best for both of us if it stays that way,' continued Garrett. With a shake of his head, as if he couldn't quite believe what he was doing, he held out his hand. Jim shook it. Both men's palms were clammy with the thought of what the future held.

Garrett's phone rang again. He put it to his ear, and his features grew tense. 'They've located Knight's car,' he said to Jim. 'The helicopter's tracking it. He's heading towards Ashford in the Water.'

'Doesn't he live out that way?'

'Yes.'

'Then someone should contact his wife. We don't want another Stephen Baxley type situation on our hands.'

Garrett winced at the possibility of finding himself faced with yet another murder. 'Have you got your phone?'

Jim shook his head. 'Stan Lockwood took it.'

'I'm putting you on to Jim Monahan,' Garrett said into

his phone. He handed it to Jim and rushed off in search of another phone.

The familiar voice of Scott Greenwood came down the line. 'DCS Knight's turned onto Ashford Lane.'

Jim knew Ashford Lane from days spent in the Peak District with Margaret. It was a narrow road that climbed between grassy fields to Monsal Head, a popular beauty spot with sweeping views of the Monsal Dale. 'How far away from him are you?'

'A couple of miles.'

Scott gave a continuous commentary on Knight's progress. His voice jumped suddenly. 'He's pulled over at Monsal Head. He's out of his car. He's running towards the viaduct.'

Jim tried to summon up a mental picture of the viaduct. He hadn't been there in nearly twenty years, but he could still remember its stone arches that towered at least twenty metres above a gentle bend in the River Wye.

'What the hell's he doing?' wondered Scott.

Jim made no reply, though he knew the answer in the pit of his stomach.

Scott's voice spiked again. 'He's climbing the bridge's railings. Oh Christ, he's jumped! He's jumped!'

Lowering the phone, Jim rose and made his way downstairs. His body felt like waterlogged wood, but his heart felt light. Lighter than it had done in years. An air of shock hung over the crime scene. People were standing around looking at each other as if unsure what to do.

'Did you hear?' exclaimed Garret, rushing towards Jim.

'Yes.' Jim climbed into the ambulance, motioning for the paramedics to get going.

'I'll keep you updated on what happens with Knight,' said Garrett.

Jim nodded, but it came to him suddenly that he wasn't interested what happened with Knight. It was enough for him to know that the bastard was finished. Along with all the other bastards in Herbert Winstanley's little black book. Lying down on the stretcher, he closed his eyes and released a breath that seemed to come from the core of his being.

Chapter Thirty-Three

One by one the speakers made their way to the lectern at the front of the cathedral and delivered their eulogies to the packed pews. To one side of the lectern, facing down the central isle, was a coffin draped with a black cloth embroidered with the South Yorkshire Police insignia. Half the cathedral was given over to police in full regalia. The other half was filled with the deceased's family and friends. Midway down this side at the end of a pew sat Mark Baxley. The cuts and bruises on his face had almost completely faded. But his right arm was still in a sling. And his eyes were still shadowed with the pain of his own loss. At the front, flanked by their father and grandparents, sat two young children, a boy and a girl. Soft little sobs shook the girl's body. The boy was silent and blank-faced, too young to fully grasp what was happening.

Jim's gaze kept straying to the children. Noah and Lilly. He hadn't been able to remember their names when Amy was alive. But now that she was dead, he would never forget them. Once again, the question he'd asked Garrett echoed in his thoughts. *Do you think if someone does something good, it balances out the bad they do?* He knew the answer now. There was no balancing out good and bad. There was only living with your mistakes. His head dropped, weighed down by the knowledge. He closed his eyes, listening to the words coming from the lectern. He'd been asked to give one of the eulogies. But he'd declined. It was hard enough to hear his colleagues talk about Amy – about her gentle but strong character, her dedication to her job, her compassion, her willingness to make the ultimate sacrifice. It was almost more than he could bear to hear Amy's widowed husband talk about the loving wife and mother she'd been.

Margaret's hand sought out Jim's and gave it a squeeze. He lifted his head, drawing strength from her touch. If it hadn't been for her presence, he doubted he would have been able to bring himself to attend the funeral.

After the service, six of Amy's colleagues carried her coffin from the cathedral. A guard of honour formed an avenue to a waiting hearse. Beyond the cathedral square, the streets were thronged with people who'd come to pay their respects. The damp grey sky seemed to reflect their solemn mood. Some threw flowers into the hearse's path as the cortège crept by. Others wiped tears from their eyes or broke out into quiet applause.

Jim turned at a touch on his elbow and found himself looking into Mark Baxley's face. There were no tears in the man's eyes. He'd already done all his crying. 'Hello, Mark,' said Jim. 'It's good to see you up and around. How are you feeling?'

'Much better.'

'And how's your sister?'

'The doctors say she's making a good recovery.' A slight awkwardness came into Mark's voice. 'I just wanted to thank you for everything you've done.'

'You don't need to thank me.'

'Yes I do,' Mark insisted. 'I want you to know what it meant to me. What it will always mean.'

Jim gave a little nod, reluctantly accepting the words.

'When Charlotte gets out of hospital, she's going to live with me,' continued Mark. 'Will you come and see us?'

'I don't think I'll be around to. I'm going away soon, and I'm not sure when or if I'll ever be back.'

Disappointment came into Mark's eyes, but he managed a smile. 'I hope you'll be happy, wherever it is you're going.' He held out his hand. 'Goodbye, Detective Monahan.'

'It's not detective any more,' said Jim, shaking Mark's hand.

Jim watched Mark head off into the crowd of mourners. His gaze sought out Margaret. She was talking to Reece. Jim approached them. 'Reece was just showing me a photo of his fiancé and her daughter,' said Margaret.

Reece held out his phone to Jim. There was a photo of a slim, strawberry-blonde woman. Her face was too sharp-featured to be pretty, but possessed a kind of hardened beauty. She was crouched down with her arms around the shoulders of a chubby-faced, cheekily smiling young girl.

'That's the woman I told you about,' said Reece. 'Her name's Staci. The little girl's her daughter, Amelia.'

'They look happy,' said Jim.

'They are because of you.'

Jim shifted as though he had a stone in his shoe. 'You're not going to start thanking me as well, are you?'

A gleam of amusement entered Reece's eyes. 'I might. Why?'

'Jim's never been comfortable with gratitude,' said Margaret, hooking her arm though his.

'Well he'd better start getting used to it because Staci's dying to meet him. And Melinda's been pestering her to ask him—'

'Staci's not been to see Melinda, has she?' broke in Jim. 'Because if Garrett cottons on that they're friends...' He trailed off, letting silence fill in the missing words.

'Relax. They've spoken on the phone. That's all.'

'I hear Melinda's making good progress.'

'Physically, yes. Psychologically, I'm not so sure. She told Staci she's having nightmares every night. It would probably do her a lot of good to see you.'

Jim shook his head. 'I'd only be a further reminder of what she went through.'

The crowds of mourners were moving away from the cathedral – Amy's family to her local church where a private service was to be held before the coffin reached its final resting place; her colleagues to a nearby hotel to share a post-funeral drink. 'Are you coming?' Reece asked Jim. He hesitated to reply, glancing at Margaret.

'I'm going to head home. I feel tired,' she said. 'But you go and have a drink. I'll get a taxi.'

'No need for that,' said Reece. 'I'll give him a lift.'

Jim handed his car keys to Margaret. 'I'll show my face, have a quick drink, then slip away.'

She touched a hand meaningfully to his chest. 'I'll see you soon then.'

Jim leant in to kiss Margaret. His lips lingered on hers until she pulled back. He was determined never to take her kisses for granted again. She said goodbye to Reece and headed away. Somewhat reluctantly, Jim turned to follow the long line of his fellow officers. They passed a newspaper stand for the South Yorkshire *Chronicle*. The paper's front page carried a picture of DCI Garrett and the enticement of an exclusive interview with a man they branded as, 'the finest policeman in Yorkshire'.

'Have you read that?' asked Reece, his lips curling.

Jim spared the newspaper a disinterested glance. 'No.'

'I wouldn't bother. It makes it sound as though he solved the whole case single-handedly.'

'Garrett tells me he's confident you're going to be cleared for return to duty.'

'Apparently.'

'You don't sound too excited at the prospect.'

'No, it's not that. I've decided to stick with the job. I've made a lot of mistakes. Now I want to do things right.' A heaviness came into Reece's voice. 'The thing is, my dad's going downhill fast. I don't know how much time he's got left.'

'Your dad's a good man.'

'No he's not. But he's my dad, and I want to be there with him.'

They walked on in silence to the hotel. The bar was thronged with police, forgetting their grief in talk and drink. Many familiar faces greeted Jim as he approached the bar counter. Hands reached out to pat his shoulders and back. Suddenly, he found himself thinking back to when he'd joined up, recalling the warmth of realising he was part of something greater than himself, something that would never die.

Each friendly touch sent a shaft of guilt through Jim, strengthening the feeling that he was crashing a party he had no right to be at. He fought an urge to turn around and head straight back out the door. Maybe he had no right to be there, but he knew he had even less right to leave without first raising a glass to Amy.

'What are you drinking?' asked Reece.

'Whisky.'

'I thought alcohol was a no-no with your heart.'

'I think I can risk one drink.'

Reece ordered two whiskies. The barman filled their glasses and Jim raised his. 'To Amy.'

They clinked glasses and sipped their drinks. Jim resisted the impulse to throw his back in one at the sight of Garrett homing in on him. The way he was feeling, Garrett was just about the last person he wanted to speak to. Without affording Reece a glance, Garrett said to Jim, 'Can I speak to you a moment?' When Jim motioned for him to say what he wanted, the DCI added, 'Somewhere private.'

Frowning, Jim followed Garrett from the bar. In the days following their little chat in Edward Forester's attic, they'd gone over their story until it was as tight as a ball of yarn. But one loose thread remained. Freddie Harding. A nationwide manhunt was under way for him. There'd been apparent sightings of him in places as far apart as the Lake District and Cornwall. But so far he'd managed to evade capture. There was speculation in the press that he'd fled abroad. Jim doubted it, though. His guess was that Harding was hunkered down in some hidey-hole his late brother's money had paid for. Whatever the case, it was only a matter of time before he was tracked down. Jim awaited the day with a mixture of eagerness and dread. Eagerness because Harding was a danger to every woman he came into contact with. And dread because if Harding knew about Jim and Bryan Reynolds, then the whole ball of yarn could yet unravel.

'Don't look so worried,' said Garrett, turning to Jim in the lobby. 'It's good news. You're looking at the next head of South Yorkshire Police CID. I wanted to tell you before the official announcement is made.'

'Congratulations.'

'Thank you.' Looking as pleased with himself as he dared on such a sombre day, Garrett continued, 'I have a proposal for you. I'm going to set up a task force to investigate Herbert Winstanley's book. I'm looking for a DCI to run it. How would you like it to be you?'

Jim frowned again, this time in surprise. 'I thought you couldn't wait to see the back of me.'

'So did I, but... well, you know what they say about friends and enemies.'

Jim smiled thinly. 'I appreciate the offer, but I've done my time. I'm ready for something else now.'

Garrett nodded as if that was what he'd expected Jim to say. 'If you change your mind, the offer's open until I find someone else for the position.'

'I won't change my mind.'

'Good luck, Jim.' Garrett offered his hand and they shook briefly. He made to head back into the bar, but hesitated. 'Oh, I almost forgot. I thought you might want this back.' He pulled out the phone Stan Lockwood had taken from Jim and handed it to him. 'It was recovered from the clothing of the one-eyed man.'

'Tyler.'

'If that was his real name. As you know, we've been unable to find a match for his fingerprints.' Garrett gave Jim a sidelong look. 'It's funny. If I didn't know better, the contents of that phone might have led me to believe you and Reece were working together on the investigation of Edward Forester. But of course, I do know better.'

They held each other's gaze for several seconds, then Garrett turned to go into the bar. Jim looked at the phone. It was speckled with something that might have been dried blood. He approached a bin and dropped the phone into it. The one he'd bought as a replacement rang in his pocket. It was Margaret. But when he put the receiver to his ear, the line was dead. He dialled her back and got through to an answering service. Figuring Margaret was trying to call him at the same time, he went in search of Reece. He found him chatting with several colleagues. Jim finished his drink and said, 'I'm going to head off, Reece. Don't worry about that lift.'

'No, it's no problem,' said Reece. 'It's not far and this lot will be here until last orders.'

Jim said a few quick goodbyes, then they headed for Reece's car. As they left the city centre behind, Jim kept glancing at his phone. 'Are you expecting a call?' asked Reece.

Jim told him about Margaret's call.

'She'll have been phoning to make sure you're OK,' said Reece. 'You know how she worries about you.'

'Then why hasn't she called again?'

'She probably got side-tracked or maybe she's taking a nap. She said she was feeling tired.'

'Yeah, maybe,' agreed Jim, but he drummed his fingers impatiently on his thigh as they negotiated the system of roundabouts and one-way streets that separated the city centre from the encircling suburbs.

They pulled up outside the modest semi-detached house where Jim and Margaret had lived most of their married life. Although not for much longer, according to the for-sale sign planted in the front lawn. Jim's car was parked in the drive. The house's front door was slightly ajar. Jim felt a thump of unease in his chest. Margaret knew better than to leave the door open. He exchanged a glance with Reece, and both men got out of the car and hurried towards the house. Margaret's coat was hanging on the hook in the hallway. Her handbag lay on the carpet next to her shoes. Nothing unusual in that.

'Margaret,' called Jim. No reply. He shoved his head into the living room. The telly was on, but no one was watching it. The kitchen was empty too. Both men climbed the stairs. All the doors were open, except the one to the master bedroom.

'Margaret,' Jim said again. Still no reply. He reached for the door handle. Slowly opening the door, he saw Margaret's feet on the bed, still in their sheer black tights. *Reece was right*, he thought. *She's just taking a nap*. Then he saw something that made fear claw at his insides. The tights were torn at the knees. He flung the door the rest of the way open. 'Oh no!' he gasped, his eyes swelling out of their sockets. 'Oh no, no, please no!'

Margaret was lying on her back. She was fully clothed, but her blouse had been ripped open. A knife handle protruded like an exclamation mark from her chest. A bloody moat surrounded it. More blood flowed from defensive wounds on her arms. Her lips were drawn back in an agonised rictus. Where her eyes – her beautiful, soft hazel-green eyes – should have been there was nothing but gory black cavities.

'Now you know how it feels to lose someone you love.' The voice was male with a thick Yorkshire accent, and full of sneering triumph.

Jim's gaze jerked towards the speaker. He was a dishevelled balding man of about fifty with heavily stubbled, pinched cheeks and bitter little eyes. A pearly-white scar ran diagonally across his face from left to right. Freddie Harding!

A smile playing around his thin-lipped mouth, Freddie held up his hands in a *you got me* way.

'Don't—' Reece started to say to Jim. But even as he said it, Jim was launching himself at Freddie. Tears streaming down his face, his eyes burning like an out of control forest fire, he locked his hands on Freddie's throat. Freddie tried to wrench himself free, but Jim's fingers were vices tightening inescapably. Both men fell heavily to the floor, Jim straddling Freddie. Strings of saliva dropped from Jim's mouth as he gouged his thumbs into Freddie's windpipe.

'Don't,' Reece exclaimed again, grabbing Jim's shoulders to pull him off Freddie.

Jim drove an elbow into Reece's groin, doubling him over. Then his hand homed back in on Freddie's throat.

'This isn't the way,' Reece gasped hoarsely. 'It isn't the way.'

Jim showed no sign of having heard. Freddie's eyes were bulging and rolling. His breath was coming in shorter and shorter snatches.

'Think of Margaret,' continued Reece, his voice thick with desperation. 'She wouldn't have wanted this. And Amy. This isn't the kind of justice she died for.'

Jim's grip loosened. Not much, but enough to allow Freddie to wheeze in a lungful of air. Squeezing his eyes shut, Jim exhaled an anguish too deep to be heard. Then he released Freddie and his head sank into his hands. Reece gently lifted him to his feet and guided him to the landing.

Returning to the bedroom, Reece rolled Freddie over, knelt on his back and cuffed him.

'He deserved it,' croaked Freddie. 'He fucking deserved it.'

'One more word and I'll kill you myself,' growled Reece, grinding his knee against Freddie's spine. He pulled out his phone and called dispatch. Leaving Freddie on the floor, he headed out of the room again. Jim was no longer on the landing. Anxiety flaring through him, Reece rushed downstairs. He breathed with relief upon finding Jim in an armchair in the lounge. 'I've called it in,' said Reece. 'They're on their way.'

Jim made no reply. He just stared at the floor, his eyes swimming with tears, but strangely devoid of expression.

Reece searched for something to say that might offer some comfort. But what could he say? What could he do? Nothing.

Outside, a crowd of curious onlookers had gathered at a perimeter of police tape. Inside, SOCO officers moved methodically about their business. Jim seemed unaware of it all. The tears had dried up. All that remained was blankness. No one approached him. No one spoke to him. Several had tried without success. It was as if he'd withdrawn to some inaccessible place inside himself. Reece and Garrett watched him from the doorway.

'Stay with him,' Garrett said. 'Don't let him go anywhere alone.'

'I won't,' said Reece.

They continued looking at Jim. After a moment, as if Garrett's voice had reached him from a long way off, Jim said, 'Where would I go?' He turned towards them and, like an echo of himself, repeated hollowly, 'Where would I go?'

A letter from the publisher

We hope you enjoyed this book. We are an independent publisher dedicated to discovering brilliant books, new authors and great storytelling. Please join us at www.headofzeus.com and become part of our community of book-lovers.

We will keep you up to date with our latest books, author blogs, special previews, tempting offers, chances to win signed editions and much more.

If you have any questions, feedback or just want to say hi, please drop us a line on hello@headofzeus.com

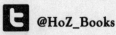 @HoZ_Books

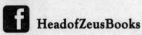 HeadofZeusBooks

www.headofzeus.com

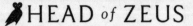 HEAD *of* ZEUS

The story starts here